for

Mary Moore Cathcart

and

Francis Dwight Cathcart

As Adam Early in the Morning

As Adam early in the morning
Walking forth from the bower refresh'd with sleep,
Behold me where I pass, hear my voice, approach,
Touch me, touch the palm of your hand to my body as I
pass,
Be not afraid of my body.

Walt Whitman
Leaves of Grass, 1891-1892, p. 267
Walt Whitman: Complete Poetry and Collected Prose
New York: The Library of America, 1982

Adam in the Morning

Adam in the Morning

by

Dwight Cathcart

Adriana Books
Boston, Massachusetts
2018

First print edition, Calamus Books, Boston, 2003

Printed from:
Adam in the Morning to Lulu 20180211.pdf
21910295_cover.pdf

David Carter's book, *Stonewall*, published in 2004 by St Martins Griffin, is now the standard work of historical scholarship establishing the facts about the series of events called "the Stonewall riots." The presentation of the riots in *Adam in the Morning* is based on the facts established in David Carter's book.

Quotations from *The Tempest* are from *The Tempest,* ed. by Virginia Mason Vaughan and Adam T. Vaughan, first published 1999, a volume from *The Arden Shakespeare,* an imprint of Thompson Learning, London. In *Adam in the Morning,* the initial use of a quotation from *The Tempest* provides act, scene and line numbers within brackets in the text: [1.2.362].

The small triangular-shaped park in Greenwich Village, in New York City, bounded by Christopher Street, Grove Street, and West Fourth Street, and situated directly across Christopher Street from the Stonewall Tavern, is officially named "Christopher Park." However, this small park has always universally been called "Sheridan Square" for most of the twentieth century and was so called during the period of this novel, the five days between June 28, 1969 and July 2, 1969 inclusive. This novel will continue the habit of almost all Village residents and will call the small park in question, "Sheridan Square." Any reference in this novel to "Sheridan Square," will be to the triangular-shaped park bounded by Christopher Street, Grove Street, and West Fourth Street. Howard Smith and Lucien K. Truscott IV, in their initial accounts of the riots published in the *Village Voice* on July 2, 1969, both unmistakably refer to Christopher Park as "Sheridan Square."

In *Adam in the Morning*, on Monday, June 30, 1969, Bo, Andrew, Billy, and Joseph have lunch in a restaurant at Perry and W. 4th St. During their conversation, Bo recounts what he has known of Mitzi's life, particularly how she conceives of herself and her body. The two sentences immediately preceding the sentence, "The restaurant is almost empty," have their inspiration in *Transparent: Love, Family, and Living the T with Transgender Teenagers* by Chris Beam, Harcourt, Inc. New Oak, 2007, pages 57-58.

"Cover photograph: Christopher Street, at Gay Street, Greenwich Village, New York, September 20, 2010, 8:46 pm
Photography: Dwight Cathcart

Author photograph:
Bill Chisholm

Adam in the Morning

Saturday, June 28, 1969
Early in the Morning

My name is Bo Ravich, and this is New York. I am a carpenter. I am thirty years old. It's two in the morning, Saturday, June 28, 1969, and I am sitting on these steps resting after work. I am preparing to build Caliban's cave in The Olympic, the theatre behind me—at Sixth and Washington Place—for a production of *The Tempest*, opening the first week after Labor Day. The director and the artistic designer have been here all day. What is taking so long is working out the design for the cave where Caliban lives, which has to contain the monster's energy and at the same time somehow to express it. The actor playing Caliban is a big sexy guy—he's six two or three, dark, Afro—and during the performance he's going to be mostly naked. The director—his name is Sergei Bachinsky—asked the actor to come by and talk to us. He asked him to take off his clothes and lie down and slither across the stage. Then we talked about what Caliban needed. It would be cool to have Caliban lying naked on my stage the whole time I work. I have worked with the director and the designer on three other productions—*Lysistrata, Comedy of Errors*, and *Measure for Measure*—so I know how they operate. The director works his way from a cloud of ideas in his head down to the reality of the stage floor. He talks his way through, talking mainly to the designer, and while this monologue is going on, the rest of us stand around and look interested. After they left this evening, I blocked it in by drawing pictures on the floor—made a possible shape for the cave so I could see it in my mind with this naked dude slithering out of it—before I shut things down and came out here to the steps of the

1

theatre to smoke a joint before I go home. I think we're at least a week away from any decisions on what the set is going to look like. Their problem—and I suppose it is mine also—is, *How do you build something that contains all that sex, and expresses it too?*

My brother Billy likes to do this, lie on the steps and watch the people go by. He's younger than me by twenty-two months, and it may be that he's smarter. We used to do this when we were in high school, in the afternoon, at the Cullen Building on the campus of the University of Houston, and we'd make up stories about people walking by. *This one is going to be picked up later today for murdering his wife. That one has just inherited 82 million dollars.* That kind of thing. Of course the people were interesting enough as it was without our making up anything about them. Why would they get themselves up so carefully to look the way they do, and choose that way to look? The building the theatre occupies is enclosed by a high cast-iron railing with a gate in the front at the foot of the steps. Through the cast-iron railing, I see the men and women passing by.

Up to the left, the next intersection is Waverly Place. After that, at the next intersection, Greenwich Avenue comes into Sixth from the left. Fifty paces into Greenwich, Christopher Street intersects from the left. The intersection of Greenwich and Christopher is called The Corner and is known as the finest cruising area in New York for men seeking men. Those men're going to want to cruise our play, once it opens and news of Caliban gets around. And it will. *Have you seen The Tempest? Go. Check out the actor playing Caliban. The hottest thing in the West Village. Big cock.* Men cruise me, too, right here on Sixth Avenue. They think I'm hot, which is gratifying. I'm Caliban's size—same height, a little skinnier—long blond curly hair, a mustache. The men on the sidewalk in front of me, some of them, are going to the bars in the district between Sixth and the river. Some are street kids—homeless—and some of those turn tricks. The biggest bar is the Stonewall Inn, on Christopher Street. All the gay bars are owned by the Mafia. The cops raided the Stonewall earlier this week. They did it on Tuesday, three nights ago. We go and give the Mafia our money, and we get back watered drinks, a ride in a paddy wagon to the precinct station, a night in jail paid for by the city—and two or three hours dancing on one of the only dance floors for us in New York. Bad deal, but that's the way it is in a city where legitimate bars have a sign in the front window saying, "If You're Gay, Go Away."

Adam in the Morning

Or "Homosexuals Are Not Served Here." We have the State Liquor Authority—we call it the SLA—to thank for that. They judge gay people to be "lewd and dissolute," and our presence in a bar is justification enough for the SLA to close the bar down.

I think it is worse than in Houston. My parents live in Houston. Houston has most of the problems, and the advantages, of twentieth century big American cities. I grew up there. My parents teach at Texas Southern University, which has always been a black school. They, and I, are white. He's in the history department, and she's in sociology. I went to public school—my parents were committed to supporting the public schools—and then I went to Oberlin. I don't know whether New York City is more dangerous than Houston, but my parents feel it is, and when we talk on the phone, my father asks me, "Are you OK? Are you safe?" Then my mother says, "We worry so about you."

What I don't like about New York—and what I think is worse than Houston—is the corruption, the police in league with the Mafia, graft and payoffs, learning that the Stonewall pays the police $1000 a week. It's the system. It's not gay people who are dissolute, it's the city and the way it is run. And New York is big enough to mean that the politics are like national politics, but they're here so you can see 'em up close. The expressways around New York were all built by Robert Moses, the head of all infrastructure construction in New York and environs, apparently since right after the Civil War. Highways can be beautiful, but Robert Moses builds nothing but crap. Ugly concrete, built right through city neighborhoods. He doesn't care about the people who live here or the way things look. Moses is illustrative of an American type. Nixon is another example. He never saw a demonstration by the people that he didn't want to ignore. On the other hand, I like the museums, the architecture, Central Park, the Seagram's Building, whole long stretches of Fifth Avenue, Broadway on the Upper West Side, and, of course, down here. Washington Square. Christopher Street and the Village, all of it. I like the people on the streets, the continuous flow of them, and I like the men. Tall, well-built, golden-colored skin with long curly dark-brown or black hair.

About dissolute New York: I shouldn't complain, because now we have the Republicans and Richard Nixon in Washington—since January—and we've known for a while that the whole country is dissolute. Why do we have a war still going on when the people have made it so clear that they hate this war? They thought, when they voted last year, that they were electing someone who was going to end the war. Nixon said he had a secret plan for ending the war. So people voted, he was elected, and now the war still goes on. And on. This week *Life* published photographs of all 242 Americans killed in Vietnam last week, including 42 killed on Hamburger Hill. Last month, the *Times* broke the news of the secret bombing of Cambodia. A week ago, the SDS held its national convention in Chicago and split into the Progressive Labor Party and the Revolutionary Youth Movement, which everybody calls the RYM, unsure of how to respond to a government that was so lawless, so brutal, and so indifferent to the people. Someone is making money off this. It's the system again. The people demonstrate and demonstrate and sing, "All we are saying, is 'Stop this damned war.'" And though that is all they are saying, the leadership of the country is deaf to them. There are many, including parts of the SDS meeting in Chicago, who are turning to violence.

We used to ask why Negroes were still being prevented from voting, and we got the same answer—the system. The Students for a Democratic Society, which is universally called SDS, back when it was concerned about racism and the voter rolls, was a place to go for a fairly searching inquiry into the power issues behind racism. When I was in Mississippi doing voter registration, that was what we talked about. That is, we talked about the power issues behind racism, when we weren't talking about how to overcome the fact that we were white kids from the middle-class so that we would have some credibility and be able to convince local Negroes to brave death and dismemberment to go to the polls where they could register to vote. Voter registration was my first big commitment after I left the University of Chicago, and it may have been my first big adult realization about the way the world operates. There's a reason Negroes in America are poor and badly educated and have been for hundreds of years. There's a reason that even Negroes in the North all live in ghettos. A class of people—that is, white men—benefits from keeping Negroes off the voter rolls and poor and down trodden. It is not merely that white men get rich off the backs of poor Negroes, although that's true of some of them. It is that keeping Negroes down and keeping poor people down enable rich white men to decide how

our cities are going to look and what countries we are going to attack
and what ones are going to be our allies and to set up the tax laws
and the welfare laws the way they find most beneficial to them, and
enable white men to decide what books are going to be published on
what subjects and enable white men to write the history books with
the great narrative of the last 350 years in America and to apportion
responsibility and blame in a way that is beneficial to them. One of
the things the system accomplishes is that it enables those in power
to escape responsibility and to blame others for their crimes and
failures. The 101st Airborne spent two months capturing Hamburger
Hill, and then the leadership abandoned the Hill to the Vietnamese,
who retook it without firing a shot. Nobody was courtmartialed for
this disaster. These things enable white straight men even to decide
what kinds of poems are going to be published and what kind of
novels telling what kinds of stories are going to be published. The
end result of this arrangement is that there is only one culture, and
this system has gone a long way toward destroying every other
culture that has arisen between the ocean on our right and the ocean
on our left. And of course, nobody has ever talked about the power
issues behind the oppression of queers.

I was twenty-two or so when I put all this together, when I
graduated from Oberlin with a BA in Government, and then from
Chicago, this time with an MA in History. My thesis was on
Alexander Berkman, an anarchist at the end of the nineteenth century
and beginning of the twentieth who was also a writer. It had been
coming on me during high school when I was on picket lines in
Houston and all during college—and of course every night of my life
sitting at the supper table in my parents' house—but once it came, it
settled in, and I have never seen anything that caused me to question
it. I read C. Wright Mills in high school—my parents gave me my
first one—and he introduced me to the idea that power is exercised in
our culture unseen, and that things are not what they seem. When I
got to college, I read Herbert Marcuse's *Eros and Civilization*, on the
effect on our sexual instincts of our drive toward higher civilization.
Marcuse says, "intensified progress seems to be bound up with
intensified unfreedom," which seems to be succinct enough. I read
the *Port Huron Statement* when it started being circulated in 1962,
which focused my mind pretty much. People are saying now that the
little bit of freedom we got in the last eight years is being met by the

5

conservative backlash we witnessed last year, when Gene McCarthy was beaten over and over again, by Robert Kennedy, by Hubert Humphrey, by Nixon, and by the insurmountable undefeatable power of the system to defend itself against the wishes of the people. Nixon. Cambodia. RYM. People say that it is impossible to overturn the steps we've taken toward liberty in this decade, but I doubt that. Nixon may be onto something, and we may not know what it is. He is out of control.

I lean back resting on my arms, my elbows on a step behind me, and watch through the iron railing the men walk by. My legs are stuck out in front of me, crossed at the ankles. I am a tall, lanky guy, and my jeans hang on my hips. I'm wearing a workshirt and a Levi's jacket. It was in late 1964, when I had been out of school for two years, that I discovered sex. I had been having sex, occasionally, since the tenth grade, and my brother and I talked about it some. It wasn't easy to talk about because I was beginning to have sex with guys and my brother was beginning to have sex with girls, and neither of us knew much about what we were doing.

"Guys!" my brother Billy said. But then he was cool about it. "Wait, you just took me by surprise. I just wasn't thinking of that. Sure, man. It's OK. I think it's cool."

But it was in 1964 that I really discovered sex. I was going to all these CORE meetings—that's the Congress of Racial Equality—in Houston and in Mississippi, and we were all working close together. Sometimes you saw a guy start hanging out with this girl. He'd bring her back to where we were living, and you'd realize he was in the bed next to you, humping. I put up with this long enough to know that it was going on and on. The guy who was humping the woman at night was talking during the daytime about freedom for Negroes and freedom for poor whites, and freedom for all of us from the iron control of the system, but he was never going to get around to talking about freedom for a man who wanted to suck cock. That just wasn't going to happen in CORE or in Mississippi.

Yet I saw it happen—that is, I saw men pair up with other men and go away somewhere private, and I caught on that it was OK. It was possible to do, if you wanted it. What happened was I found I was more interested in sex than in stopping the war. I found I was interested more in freedom for me than freedom for them, so my focus began to shift. I ended up dropping out just about the time SDS stopped caring so much about Negroes in the South and started caring more about the Vietnam war. I still go to SDS meetings—or did until recently—even here in New York, and I go to all the big demonstrations, but I can feel the shift in my attention. Men. And what makes me free.

Andrew is a year younger than me, and we first connected at Alternate U—it was in a class on *What is a man?*—when he walked in and sat down a few rows ahead of me and then turned to the side so he could see me and see the facilitator at the same time. I was aware of him looking at me. I could see him, even though I wasn't looking at him, and I liked what I was seeing. He's as tall as me and thin. He's one of those racial mixes from around the Mediterranean—or from New York City—tan skin, very long and very dark brown curly hair, large liquid brown eyes, thick eyelashes and eyebrows, thick mustache and beard trimmed fairly close, hair on his forearms. About half way through the discussion of the question of what factors are in play in creating a man's masculinity, it became clear that both of us knew we were checking each other out, so he got up from where he was sitting and came back to the seat next to me. He brushed against me a few more times than a person would who was doing it accidentally. So when he let his hand fall down in the space between us, I let my hand fall down to occupy the same space, except that I opened my hand and closed on his, so that we were holding hands. He said to the group, "What is a man? But the reason we are here, I think, is that we don't have any idea. For my father, it was easy. A husband was head of the household. Men looked after women and supported them. He was the breadwinner. His gender was clearly defined. Of course, there was a huge downside to all that—a man's gender limited the ways he could have sex, and it limited how intimate he was able to be with his partner and his children. There was no sense of equality between the man and his partner—he was one way and his partner was another way. It is hard for men right now because we don't know what the roles are, the guidelines. Most of us don't know how to conduct an equal relationship. We don't know how to act on our feelings, and we don't know how to act spontaneously. The gender roles most of us have been taught enslave us to ways of thinking and acting that aren't native to us. We want to be free. I want to be free, but I am not free, and that is why I am here at this class. I want to be in a room with other men, and I want to talk about how it feels, not to be free."

While he talked, he continued to allow me to hold his hand, which called the attention of all the men in the room. Men didn't do that in public. He squeezed my hand—his was moist from the heat—and we have been together ever since. It was good, meeting during that discussion, because while we think often about the gender roles we have been given by our system, we don't worry about being men. I don't think either of us is insecure about that one. It's an interesting subject, though.

I am tired. It is hard, working with someone like the director who is not really thinking in the terms I think in, so I have to translate everything he says into terms that can be useful to me. He talks about the "sense" the audience must have when they see Caliban coming up out of his cave—the sense of his confinement—and I am thinking in terms of one-by-threes and three-quarter inch plywood and how many people are going to be standing on top of Caliban's cave at its most heavily populated moment. We are talking two different languages here, and I came to understand a few years ago that it was part of my job as a carpenter and a stage hand to be the one who does the translating. I come up with possibilities, and the director says, *yes* or *no*. Of course, sometimes he comes up with possibilities, and I say *yes* or *no*.

I lie here on the steps, my right arm behind my head, watching the cars on Sixth and the men on the sidewalk, all going uptown. I first started doing carpentry at Oberlin when I wanted a break from studying and volunteered at a student theatre production. I didn't have any desire to be an actor, but I thought it might be fun to build the set, so I became a stagehand for a student production of *The Glass Menagerie*. After that, I was a stagehand—assistant stagehand helping out the people really doing the work—for two more productions before I got my BA, in 1961. Then I worked in another production while I got my MA at Chicago, but I was just a weekend carpenter, and it wasn't until I was in Mississippi in 1964 with CORE, when a gentleman in the hill country taught me how to use a hammer properly and how to use a handsaw, and how to measure properly and to get straight lines and to get everything square, that I became a decent carpenter. He taught me how to be a carpenter, and I taught him how to register to vote. I didn't mean to be a carpenter, but it happened and gradually it felt right. Since then, carpentry has been part of whatever job I have been doing. For the last four years, it has been the whole thing. I haven't yet started the process of joining the union. I'm in no hurry.

I watch the street. Some of the men on the street—more than on other nights—are running up to the corner where the Women's House of Detention is located. I hear police sirens. The House of Detention is a big brick building on Greenwich, on the south side of the triangle formed by Sixth and West 10th and Greenwich. On the other side of the triangle, on Sixth, is the Jefferson Market Branch of the Library, a nineteenth century building in heavy red-brick Romanesque. Andrew likes me being a carpenter. He likes my rough hands. He likes the way my hands feel on his tits. I'd like to lie here on these steps and have another joint, but something, some urgency—why are they running?—intrudes. I have to stand up. The level of energy in New York streets is so high that it's sometimes difficult to tell at any particular moment whether it's normally high or abnormally high.

I move down the steps and through the gates to the sidewalk and enter the stream of men going uptown. With the men around me, I am aware of the city, of its sounds and smells. Exhaust fumes, hot tar, the river, the salt air, the restaurant odors. My parents wanted me to be an academic. History would have been a good choice, following my father, studying the failures of the American experiment. But when I told them I was learning to be a carpenter, they seemed to understand. They really do understand the difficulties of being male in our culture. My mother wears her hair like a pillow on the top of her head, with long chandelier style earrings. She sat at the kitchen table when I told her, and she said, "Oh, Bo, do something that matters." And that was all she said about it. It had to do with dropping out of the American system, which I feel all around me. It corrupts everything it touches. In their way, they had dropped out of the American system, because they might have become distinguished academics in their fields if they hadn't dropped out of that particular rat race. Instead they chose a place that needed more good teachers than Texas Southern could get through the normal hiring process, and then they went there and settled in and made their contribution. Their biggest contribution may have been to me and Billy, because they taught us that most of what we are told in this country about the importance of money, the importance of position, the importance of power, the importance of God, the importance of respect for authority wasn't really true. My parents were teaching me to think for myself on these matters when I was in junior high school. When I was in college, in 1960, my parents gave me a copy of *Growing Up Absurd,* a book by Paul Goodman. He was saying the same things my parents had been saying since I could remember—about the system, the rat race, the corrupting effects of our culture, and about dropping out. His first sentence is "It is hard to grow up when there's not enough man's work," which I've never forgotten. And now I look around me, and I see the culture is only just now catching up to him and to my parents. He would have thought that carpentry was man's work.

The Women's House of Detention—it's where the city puts women convicted of minor crimes—is on the other side of Greenwich Avenue when I turn left off Sixth Avenue. Fifty paces ahead of me, at the corner of Christopher Street and Greenwich, men block the sidewalk. They are talking more than usual. This is "the Corner" where men gather to cruise, and talking is not part of the usual activity here. There are a lot of street kids out tonight. Andrew and I know one, named Mitzi, who we check up on occasionally. We buy her food, and give her money, and sometimes she sleeps on our sofa.

I move fast, looking around, and then I move around and through the groups of them until I can see clearly into Christopher Street. Last week, straight men went into Kew Gardens in Queens and cut down the trees that made the protected spot that gay men had used for cruising. We called the police, but when they came, they stood by talking to the men who were cutting down the trees and refused to stop them. Earlier this month the police raided five gay bars. The Snake Pit, the Checkerboard, and the Sewer never reopened. The trucks, parked in lots along the river and on the docks, another place men go for sex, have been dangerous this summer—you go in to blow a guy and you find your trick is a cop and you get arrested. Several nights ago, the Stonewall was raided. The city is making a concerted effort to limit our freedom. The whole street seems to be crowded with men, as far down as I can see. I see police lights—the flashing blue lights and the steady, larger, red lights and white lights on top of the police vehicles—down at the other end, near Seventh Avenue. It's the Stonewall again. I start to jog down toward the lights, moving around the little groups of men.

"Bo! Hey, Bo!"

Adam in the Morning

I don't stop, but I look around. I see no one who might know my name. I turn on my heels and run backward a few steps, looking for the man who called. I feel the warm air on my neck. Judy Garland's funeral was today. Thousands lined up yesterday to view her body.

"Bo! Over here!"

I see him. On the other side of the street. He is waving to me.

"Are you going? It's a riot! It's here!"

"What's here?" His name is Bobby. I know him from the bars. "What's happening?"

"The cops raided the Stonewall again, about an hour ago. Twice in one week. And the queens are fighting mad."

Jesus. "I'm going."

The queens are fighting mad. The queens get mad all the time. But they don't get fighting mad, ever. That's not what we do. The SLA, which controls the sale of alcohol in the state, has arranged it so that liquor licenses are not distributed to establishments that serve gay people. There is nowhere in the city that a gay person can be legally served a drink. That means that criminal elements are going to serve gay people their drinks. Specifically the Mafia. Now, for the Mafia to run a bar for gay people without a license and to keep it open, the Mafia pay off the police. The police, to keep the Mafia paying them off, regularly raid the gay bars. The cops have to raid the bars regularly, and the Mafia have to pay them off, because that is the way the system is set up by the SLA. And gay people, seeking a place where they can socialize and have a drink, are trapped between the cops and the Mafia. And at times like this one, they are extremely angry, because they are the ones that go to jail, when the cops bust a bar.

I run on, weaving in and out of the crowd in the street, loping, running toward the light. I have been a runner since junior high school. The crowd is no longer on the sidewalks. It spills over into the middle of the street. It becomes denser, harder to run through. There is more noise. Ahead, there is shouting. Men yell. I hear sirens. This noise is unusual at this hour in this stretch of Christopher Street, which is less commercial than it is on the other side of Seventh Avenue. The Northern Dispensary, a medical building built in the early nineteenth century, is on my left. I can't run any more, the crowds are too dense. I see people I know. All of Christopher Street from here to Seventh is packed, and Grove Street from Waverly to

Adam in the Morning

West 4th. This is much bigger than I thought. I stop and try to see over the men standing in front of me. The tension is familiar from Mississippi and from sit-ins in Houston and from all the demonstrations here in New York. I have been in crowds like this when I watched the police trying to control demonstrators. Their attempts always turn violent. The questions are, *Who is going to be hurt? What should we do?* We may be hurt ourselves. But we don't fight.

I ask the man standing next to me, "What's happening?"

He shrugs. "You can see for yourself. There are the cops—" He points at them. They are in blue, and they are moving through the crowds, strutting, being men. "—and there is the Stonewall. They've closed down the bar. They're arresting the customers and the staff members. We think they are letting the Mafia guys go because they pay them off. They're bringing out the people they've arrested and are putting them in the cars and taking them to the precinct headquarters. They seem to be concentrating on the drag queens and the flame queens." They would be. They want the managers and the staff because they are probably breaking federal law by not having a liquor license. They would also be breaking state law and local ordinance. They're arresting customers who don't have valid ID, and they're arresting men and women who are not wearing at least three items of clothing appropriate to their gender, which is state law. They would be performing examinations inside the bar to determine if the ones who claim to be transsexuals have had the surgery or not. If not, and if they're not wearing sufficient male clothing, they get arrested. The man's voice suggests that there is nothing to be done. "The cops are inside breaking up all the bar equipment. You can hear them using sledge hammers on the cash registers." He's right. I can hear the crash of sledge hammers breaking up the glass and the cash registers and pinball machines. It goes on and on and on.

There is a breathlessness—a hush—in the crowd around me as everybody listens.

Finally I hear one kid yell, "Fucking pigs!"

The cops look as if they are having to do some particularly nasty business. They come out of the Stonewall, some of them with a gay person in each hand, and try to move fast across the open space to the cop cars. They try not to look at us. They give off the sense that they are disgusted by having to touch us.

Another kid yells, "That's our place!" A cop looks up at us but doesn't answer. The crowd watches the assault on our place in a suspended moment of time, while the police, in a spasm of destruction, drag men and women out to the cop cars.

Somebody screams, "Gay Power!

There are squad cars parked in Christopher Street in front of the Stonewall. A patrol wagon is parked across the street. And what's happening is that the cops are bringing out people from the Stonewall and walking them to one of the squad cars or across the street to the paddy wagon. What seems so strange is that the scene is quiet except for the crashing sounds of glass breaking inside the bar and the occasional scream from the gay people looking on. What's happening at this moment is that the cops are trying to wrestle a big woman from the door of the Stonewall into one of the squad cars, and she's fighting back.

People are watching this, absorbed by her struggle. I doubt that any of us have ever seen anybody fight like she is doing. The crowd is quiet. The cops are using their clubs on her—they swing their arms, and their clubs make a thumping noise on the flesh of the woman's back and shoulders—and they get her as close to one of the squad cars as they can, and then she breaks loose. The crowd opens up to give her space—I think they open up out of respect for her, protectively—and then the cops have her again and are wrestling her back toward the squad car. They're hitting her with their clubs—the thud, thud again—and she has blood all over her face and head.

A cop says, "Cunt."

The men in the crowd wince. I've never seen anybody fight so hard. The crowd around me is tensed up, and people are muttering —"Shit! Jesus Christ! Look at that!"—and yelling and calling the cops pigs, and then they get her to the car. She slides through the car and comes out the other side. The crowd opens up for her—they're awed by her, I am awed by her willingness to take the beating—but the cops have her again.

One of them calls her *cunt* again, and then he says, grinning, "Do you like me forcing this on you?" The woman seems all arms and legs, breathless and kicking at the cops and pushing them off her. She is fighting, and she refuses to give in. A man near me says,
"Those bastards," then somebody in the crowd—it is one of the street

13

kids, in scare drag—cries out, "Help her!" A big cop picks her up from behind and throws her in the car. He turns to us and grins, and then he gives a thumbs-up signal.

Everything suddenly explodes. People in the crowd, the street kids, are now screaming at the police. It's become a mob. I look around me, and the faces of the people in the crowd are distorted with anger.

"Dirty copper!" One of the kids throws a handful of pennies. There is such a hail of pennies that the cops have to put up their hands to shield their eyes.

"Fascist pigs!" I yell loud enough for anybody from Seventh Avenue to the other side of the Northern Dispensary to hear.

"Give us back our place!"

"Let her go!" Men all around me are yelling and screaming.

"Pigs!"

The cop who threw her in the car—an overweight man with small eyes and a small mouth—looks at all of us and says, dismissively, "Faggots."

Somebody throws a can. It arcs above our heads, spinning slowly, the liquid inside circling out in a long string and breaking up into droplets before the whole thing falls on the bunch of cops.

Once they catch on, people around me look for things to throw —cans start arcing above our heads from all over the mob of men and women. Beer, soft drinks, whole, full, unopened cans that fall with a thump and clatter on the metal of the cop cars.

We throw pieces of concrete, paving stones, boards and iron, bricks from a construction site—and the air is filled with hard, heavy things that hit the cops and the roofs of the cop cars. When the first paving stones hit the top of the cop cars, they make a huge crashing noise, and the cops jump. A cop puts his hand to his eye, blood on his cheek, yelling, "Oh, fucking Christ!" The rocks and paving stones and concrete make them duck and hold up their arms and look around for protection. It is us who are on the offensive. This is satisfying. I'm looking for something to throw. The crowd moves toward the police, enraged. It's seeing the big woman being manhandled while she was fighting so hard, it's knowing that our place—the Stonewall —has been taken from us. It's remembering all the times in the Stonewall when they watered our drinks and insulted us and called us queers and faggots. It's remembering all the ways our culture treats gay people.

The crowd circles the car with the heavy woman. The cops are trying to drive it away, and somebody calls out, "Turn it over!" Suddenly we are a gang around the car, leaning against it, our arms straight against the sides. Somebody calls out, "One, two, three, now." We rock it, but they get away, their tires slashed.

There's more fighting. Now it's hand-to-hand fighting. The cops are enraged. They want to inflict as much damage on us as possible, flailing out all around them with their clubs, and all of us want to hurt them if we can. I get behind a cop and catch him in the crook of my arm, but somebody behind me hits me on my head with a club. I lose it for a second. I know I have blood. They are crazy with anger that we don't just give in to every fucking thing they want to do to us.

It is an unequal battle. The cops have clubs and firearms, and we don't have weapons, but we are fighting for ourselves, and the people on the other side are only fighting to oppress queers. It is like the fights I used to see during the sit-ins and marches in Houston between black teenagers and the cops. The cops in Houston had no idea what they were up against. A man I was standing beside a minute ago said, "I am so sick of this shit." He didn't say, but he meant, all of it. The watered drinks, the pay-offs, the raids, the police brutality, the SLA and their signs about refusing to sell alcohol to gay people, we only have a few dance floors in all of goddamned New York, they raided five of our bars this month—and left three of them closed— and the fact that they've arranged things so that the only bars for fags in all of New York are run by the Mafia. There are other things he was sick of too—we never acted together before this, when the police started beating up on us, and we didn't really think we could ever make them stop.

My head hurts. The crown of my skull. I touch it. I can't tell how bad the cut is. I don't know, there may be 300 men crowded in the little stretch of Christopher Street between the Northern Dispensary and Waverly Place at one end of Sheridan Square and Seventh Avenue at the other. It's a little space—small space with buildings mainly five or six stories high, so it's also an enclosed space—and the crowd is getting more and more dense. Men are still flooding down Christopher Street from the east and in from the west,

Adam in the Morning

from Seventh Avenue. They are running, and everybody seems to be going crazy. This is going to be big. This already is big. I have never felt such anger in the street when I was among gay people.

I want Andrew to be here. We live down Christopher Street at the west end. About a month ago, Andrew saw an ad in the *RAT*, the SDS paper, that invited all "young, radical, homosexuals" to a meeting to "develop a critique of heterosexual supremacy, both in society and within the Movement." He told me about it, and we went. It was at Alternate U. Andrew was disappointed that they didn't talk about police brutality, government oppression, the Mafia's invasion of our lives, cops using entrapment against gay men, the impossibility of finding a safe place for us in the city and the rest of the shit that's a part of our day-to-day lives. I liked it because we talked about the assumption that all men and women are heterosexuals, the failure of the institution of marriage, our culture's fear of sex, our civilization's failure to heal the split between the body and the mind. In the last eight years, we've had an intense discussion on the place of race in America, and we've been talking about women, and it is now time to have a similar debate on the place of sex in America. That's what they were doing at Alternate U.

Even though the police have weapons and their clubs, they are outnumbered, and something seems to be holding them back from using their firearms. It may be a side-effect of the disaster at Hamburger Hill. You don't bring out your biggest guns until you are sure that winning is worth the possibility that you will be blamed for the loss of life. I think half the police must have gone back to the precinct with the cars and the paddy wagon. They've not gotten any reinforcements since then, and the ones who stayed are in a tight little circle around the door of the Stonewall. Rocks and bricks rain down on them. They retreat into the Stonewall. I think they are afraid.

I see the battle in Christopher Street in front of the Stonewall. The cops have now barricaded themselves inside the bar, with us out in the street, assaulting the windows and doors. Four fairly big guys have pulled up a parking meter and, with great loud deep-throated battle cries, are running against the heavy wooden door. There is a crash, but the door doesn't give, and they pull back and go at it again. "OK, now. Again. One, Two, Three, Now!" They are sweaty and dirty and way out of control. They run toward the door, two on each side of the parking meter, throwing themselves against the door, driving the parking meter into the wood with a huge crash.

A guy, a smaller guy, wearing drag, a dress and makeup and a necklace—one of the street kids—runs up to the window next to the door and squirts lighter fluid inside, then runs back. He's afraid that the cops inside will shoot him, but he has friends, and they form a team, one running up and squirting the lighter fluid, and another coming after with a lighter. They are trying to burn the place down.

But it doesn't work, and they devise new strategies. Eventually, all the windows in the Stonewall get broken, upstairs and down, and then, if there is plywood barricading the window from the inside, men use a battering ram to break it. Men shout at one another across the mob, teaching each other how to do what they are trying to do. They start throwing Molotov cocktails.

But apparently, at least with the first ones, the cops on the inside are able to put out the flames.

Our side does not give up, and the bottles arc above our heads in the night air, the yellow flames spiraling against the night sky. I stare up at them, mesmerized by how beautiful they are. I think the whole scene is beautiful. And surreal. Gay men withdraw into the shadows. Gay men do not fight. Gay men suffer indignities. Yet here we are, fighting, making a spectacle in the street. We are seeing something bizarre in the extreme. It is a complete transformation of everything that gay means. I should look at *The Rebel* again. It is about rebellion. He said that rebellion means turning the world upside down. I must remember that.

Some man cries out in a voice that reverberates in the square, "We want our freedom!"

When the playgoer first meets Ariel, Prospero says to him, "What is't thou canst demand?" Ariel answers, "My liberty."

My liberty. Caliban wants his liberty too. "Freedom, high-day; high-day freedom; freedom high-day, freedom." *Freedom, high-day. High-day, freedom. Freedom.*

And Andrew also. I back up and go around the south side of Sheridan Square, along Grove Street, to Seventh Avenue, then back to Christopher Street again. I pass Village Cigar and run west to the river, the whole area quivering with energy. All of Christopher between Seventh Avenue and Bleecker is blocked with guys yelling.

"Hey, Bo!"

17

Adam in the Morning

"Bo!"

Men call to me, and I wave as I run.

"Hey Bo! Why are you running away, man!"

"I'm going to get Andrew! I'm coming back!"

They shout back, "Cool!"

It is after two-thirty. Andrew has probably already gone to bed. I run down Christopher, past Bleecker and Bedford and Hudson in long strides. The street opens up down here—it's wider, and the buildings seem newer and bigger—and then comes on another Greenwich Street. I have never known what that's about. We live on Weehawken, a little street one block in from West Street and the river, three or four blocks away from where I am now. Finally I get to Weehawken. The whole thing is only 100 paces long. Ours is the sixth building in from Christopher, on the right. It used to be a stable, apparently, because the ground floor has two large openings with round arches onto the street, suitable for horses and carriages going in and out. Our apartment is the second floor. I run up to the door. I have my keys. I am through the door without pausing and run up the stairs, skipping every other step. I insert the key and turn. I am in the kitchen—it's the first room a person enters from the stairwell, going past the bathroom door, in this familiar sequence of rooms—calling softly, "Andrew!" I am in the bedroom. I can see Andrew from the light from the kitchen. He lies on his back across the bed, nude, his dark curly hair falling forward across his temple and onto his forehead, his mustache hiding all of his mouth except his moist red lower lip, his angular body defined by his joints and bones, his feet tangled in the sheets. I sit down on the bed and put my palm on his chest.

"Andrew, wake up." Then, "I want you to wake up."

He moves, takes a deep sigh, and straightens out one of his legs. My hand on his pec, I feel him coming awake. I lean over and kiss him. "Hurry. Man. Wake up. Something big is happening."

He is waking up.

"Maybe the biggest thing ever."

He opens his eyes. "Bo?" His voice is low and growly.

"Yeah. There's something going on down the street. I want you to be there."

He's coming awake now, looking at me. "What?"

"A riot, down by the Stonewall."

"Riot. Why?" Then, "Was it Judy Garland?"

"No."

"What is it?" Then, "What time is it?"

"It's about two-forty-five. The cops raided the Stonewall, and everybody is pissed."

"Shit." He stares at me, hard. "A riot! Are they really fighting?"

"Yeah. They are."

"Like hurting each other?"

"Oh, yeah."

"You need me?"

"Yes, I need you. I want you."

He smiles. He's awake now. "It's nice to hear you say it." He looks at me. "Kiss me."

I do, and I stand up.

"You want me to get hurt too."

"Well," I punch his shoulder. "As much as possible."

He smiles and speaks slowly. "I don't know what I'd do without you. There's a riot, and you want me there so I can get hurt, so you come and get me." He disentangles his feet from the sheet and swings them over the side of the bed and stands up. "What time did you say it was? What day is it?" He rests his elbows on my shoulders, smiles, and we kiss again. "OK. Tell me about this." But before I can say anything, Andrew puts his hands on both sides of my face. "Jesus! You've got blood on your forehead. Let me see." He pushes me down on the bed again and looks at the cut on my skull. "Jesus. It's a real cut. It's bloody and dirty. And you've been hit in other places in your hair, I can see."

"It's nothing, Andrew. I think it's OK."

He pulls back, and puts his hands on his hips and looks at me. "So, we really are into something."

"Well, yeah." Now he is really waking up.

"OK. Tell me about it. From the beginning."

I do, while he pulls on his jeans and a t-shirt, and while he gets a handkerchief from his drawer and cleans the cut on my skull. I tell him about the raid, what I know, about the big woman fighting so heroically and the sudden explosion of anger in the crowd.

"They raided the Stonewall on Tuesday. Bastards."

We are running down the stairs and back out onto Weehawken and Christopher toward Seventh and Sheridan Square and the Stonewall. Andrew and I share an attitude. I don't ever have to argue him into any political position. I pay attention to what is happening on the street, and he reads political books, and we make a good pair. We run up Christopher toward Seventh. Side by side. "At last," he says, "the Revolution." Then, in a more casual tone, "How was work?"

"We're making progress. I am getting the director down from cloudy abstractions to something practical I can work with."

"Did you see Caliban?"

"Oh, yes. The director asked him to join us for several hours today so he could see what he looks like on stage—how big he is— and know how big his cave has to be. He asked him to take off his clothes for part of that."

"And you were thinking, *Finally, being a carpenter is paying off.*"

"I couldn't think of anything else, except how long can I drag this thing out—two weeks, a month, two months. How long does it take, anyway, to build a cave for one man out of one-by-threes and plywood, if it's supposed to look like a hill that at least two people can stand on?"

We can see the crowd up ahead. The cops have gotten reinforcements. The cop cars have come back, and now there are two paddy wagons. Whoever was barricaded inside the Stonewall has now come out. The fighting is making a lot of noise—men yelling at the other side, and calling to each other and the sounds of rocks landing on the cars. In the background are the sirens and the screaming of the tires of the cop cars when they throw on the brakes to stop on Seventh Avenue.

Andrew surveys the scene. "This is going to be close-quarter fighting."

"Are you prepared?"

"Oh, yeah." He drags out the OOOO sound. "This is going to be satisfying." The crowd is so big and so dense that it is hard to get through and to find the front. As we make our way through toward the action at the front, Andrew says, "I like it that there are so many on our side." There are maybe five hundred men and women here. Just before he turns to his work, he turns to me, "Thanks for coming to get me." If Andrew had been in Chicago, he would have gone with the RYM—the Revolutionary Youth Movement. He turns to the lines in front of him and wades into the fighting. I watch while he comes up behind a cop who is using his club on a kid. Holding his fists together and using them like a club, he brings them down hard on the cop's head and then his shoulders. The man staggers under the blow.

I feel hands on my shoulders. Two cops are trying to drag me toward the Stonewall.

"No, you shits." I throw out my arms, trying to grab onto something to prevent them from dragging me away. I am aware of not even being able to see what they look like. They get me on the head again. More blood. And on the shoulder.

I can't get footing. My feet slide on the paving stones. There isn't anything to hold on to.

"Faggot!"

"Faggot. You're under arrest."

"Oh, no. Not me, fascist pig." My torso spasms, and I break free of them.

By the time I am standing upright again, I turn around and see that the two cops are now at the center of six or eight men who are beating on them with their fists.

"Remember this, fucking prick."

"And this."

The guys—I know two of them—have gone berserk. They get one of them down and are kicking him. "Bigot."

"Bigot!wider view. The harshest fighting in the front is being done by little guys, the street kids. They swarm all over the cops. They jump on them from behind.

"They're incredible, aren't they?" It's Andrew, standing by my side. His head is bloodied, and he breathes heavily.

"How is your head?"

He shrugs. "OK. I'll live. At least through this. Are you OK?

"I'm still OK." Although I have a headache.

Andrew looks around. "Those kids are fearless." He is looking for someone. "Have you seen Mitzi?'

Mitzi's tough, amazingly beautiful when she gets herself together, and she's one of the gang of kids who float around the Village. I haven't seen her, yet, but in a crowd like this, she is likely to turn up. Everybody else seems to be turning up.

Adam in the Morning

Andrew and I go back into the fight. He yells back at me before he gets focused on the fighting. "Make sure she is OK, hear?"

The cops are trying to pick us off one by one. A couple of them try to take me again, but I run north on Seventh—Andrew is running too, south on Seventh—but they can't catch either one of us. Apparently it is not part of their battle plan to actually start shooting at anybody. In the Orangeburg Massacre, the police started shooting on less provocation than this. It may be that running away from them causes a distraction to the police. It is possible to learn the techniques of street fighting.

Riot police arrive—in two buses. They turn off Seventh into Christopher, toward the east, against the traffic, and park between Seventh and the Stonewall. They exit the bus in a run and take up a formation right there in the street, right in front of the Stonewall. They are in black uniforms and combat boots. They are more heavily armed than the other cops, and they carry more equipment. They wear helmets that have plastic shields that can be pulled down across their faces and body shields that they carry on their forearms. These body shields are tall and curved so as to cover almost all of their bodies, and wide enough to cover them from side to side, and in the night lights they shine with an oddly beautiful blue reflection. They apparently plan to clear the street of fags in front of the Stonewall. They position themselves to come toward us—we are near the corner of Christopher and Seventh—in a straight line across the street, one of them calling out orders to the rest of them, making it seem like a military operation. They carry their shields, edge-overlapping-edge, high enough so that the shields attached to their helmets become part of impenetrable armor.

Big men in black, completely armored, heavily armed, moving in unison down the street taking small steps. They seem irresistible, impenetrable, and easily the scariest thing on the street. What they look like, strong, completely armored, all in black, is matched by the harsh sound they make, moving in unison—*shu-shu-shu-shu*—and the effect is to baffle all of us watching them. They move down Christopher Street toward where we are, Seventh Avenue, forcing all of us to run away from them. Except we don't run. The kids who are at the front of our lines, nearest the TPF, are backing up a slow step at a time, matching the speed the TPF are advancing. I think what the TPF with all their power were expecting was a disorganized, terrorized rout. This is a tactical retreat. They mean to be sweeping the street clean of the rioters, but their muscular power was not designed for these small Village streets or for how courageous our guys are. Finally, our line dissolves, but we don't run away. We run around—Seventh to Grove and back to Christopher—behind the lines of the riot squad, who are surprised to find us behind them.

They reverse direction and come at us again in that stiff rigid way they have. This time, those in the front of our gang of rioters form a loose line and stand their ground as the TPF shuffle toward them. The kids shout taunts at the cops. "Hi, dirty copper!" The insult carries a sting because everybody knows the management of the Stonewall paid off the cops to prevent just the kind of raid that has started all this. "Dirty copper!" accompanied by a rain of copper pennies. The cops get closer and closer to the kids, who keep up their taunting. Then, suddenly, the line of them resolves itself into a kick line, where each man's arms rest on the shoulders of the men on either side of him, and they begin to kick, and sing.

> We are the Stonewall girls,
> We wear our hair in curls.
> We wear no underwear:
> We show our pubic hair.

This enrages the police, who break formation and chase the rioters, swinging their clubs in all directions, and yelling out to us, "Faggots!"

"Cock suckers!"

But, having no armor to encumber us, we run through streets we know better than the cops, who are only invaders in our town— Chairman Mao has something to say about this—and most of us are able to escape.

The riot police re-form and we re-form, and we play our game with them again, our arms across our brothers' shoulders, kicking our legs high in the air, singing.

> We are the Stonewall girls,
> We wear our hair in curls.
> We wear no underwear:
> We show our pubic hair.

Adam in the Morning

This happens again in Christopher, in Grove, in West 4th, in Waverly Place, in Greenwich Avenue, in Bleecker and Hudson. At one point, the fire engines, called when we were trying to set the Stonewall on fire, turn their hoses on us and scatter our kick line, a cool shower on a hot night.

I have lost Andrew. I go around Seventh to West 10th to Waverly Place. The police stand stunned and demoralized in front of the Stonewall, and I throw rocks. If one of my rocks should ever connect with a body, it would do real damage, but as far as I can tell, the cops are all completely hidden behind those clear blue plastic shields. I throw another rock.

"Give us back our bar!"

This is ironic, considering that it was never our bar. It has always belonged to the Mafia and to the police. The kids are still taunting the cops, and I see the cops take their clubs and go after the kids. I see the cops beating the kids for taunting them. I am tired of the running and fighting, but I search through the mob and find the fighting—it seems like all of the fighters are a foot shorter than I— and I lock my fists together like Andrew, and I wade in. The tactic is to try to land a blow without getting one yourself and to get away before they can arrest you or beat you or kill you or whatever cops do. So I look for a cop who is going after the kids. On the other side of Christopher, I find one, pink skin, flushed with exertion, sweat, who seems to want to cause permanent damage to a young woman. He takes his club and pulls it back across his chest, and just as he is about to bring it down on her, I am behind him and bring down my fists so hard on his shoulder my torso curves and my feet leave the pavement. I hope I have broken his collarbone. I don't think I actually do that, but I do surprise him. He turns to me—the kid gets away—and looks puzzled. I don't stay while he comes to his senses, I turn and run. I remember that these guys are the ones who are armed. I get away with clubbing another cop, and another one, and I laugh and think, Jesus, man, who needs guns! For a minute I feel invincible. I may even swagger a little around the periphery of the fighting, looking for my next target. In another kind of battle, it would be difficult to tell the good guys from the bad guys, but here, our virtue proclaims us. We are, every one of us, street kids in jeans and cutoffs and sandals, announcing our tribal loyalty. I swagger and

Adam in the Morning

I enjoy myself, and for a minute I feel like the biggest bully on the block. And since I have never been a bully before that I know of, I discover that I like the feeling—and savor it for a minute.

I retreat from the battle and find a high stoop on the building just west of the Stonewall, and I sit on the highest step, breathing heavy, watching the action. I watch while the riot police sweep Christopher Street, moving from Seventh toward Waverly Place and Sixth. I see a neighbor from Weehawken, and a man we know from Alternate U. I think what I am seeing is the gradual lessening of the intensity of the fighting. Our guys are leaving the battlefield. In the tangle of men and boys and women in front of the line of armed and armored cops, I catch a glimpse of Andrew, first—he's got blood all down one side of his face—and then I see Mitzi, who is in the place most exposed to the cops and whose short blond hair is matted with blood.

"Mitzi! Protect yourself!"

I see Andrew look up, find me, and look around for Mitzi. The riot police are moving in close to where Mitzi stands, and she seems mesmerized by their swinging clubs. In a minute, Andrew has moved over to a place near Mitzi and has caught her and dragged her to a more protected spot. Gutsy Mitzi resists being pulled from the action. From this distance, she seems half the size of the other men in the line. Andrew, holding her hand, comes through the crowd toward me.

Then, I see Caliban. He has heard me yell to Mitzi, and he looks up to find me. We see each other, and grin. We both raise our arms at the same time and shake clenched fists at the world. He, too, begins to move through the crowd toward me. I watch him move. Very sexy. Without his making any extra movement, I think a person would always be aware of his body. He's very smooth. Caliban gets to me a minute before the others do, and he grins again, and speaks. "All this —" he nods over his shoulder at the mayhem behind him. "—over sex!"

Mitzi has a low growly voice, and she glances at Caliban before she announces, "Well, we showed them, ain't we?" She sits down on the stoop next to me, and rests her arms on her knees. "We are never going to let'em run us out of our place again, ever, are we guys?"

All of us have been bloodied—you can't see where Caliban was hit until you see him from behind—and we're all tired.

"Guys, this is Caliban. And this is Mitzi, and this is Andrew." Mitzi is about to say something, so I say, "No, his name isn't

Caliban. He's an actor, and he plays Caliban. His name is Joseph Roche."

Caliban grins, and then he says, "My name is Joseph Roche. But you can call me Caliban if you want."

"Why don't we call you Joseph?"

"That would be fine with me."

"Are you a monster?" Andrew grins, and checks out Joseph from his head to his basket. Then he grins again.

"Absolutely."

Mitzi looks up at Joseph—he towers over her—and she says, "Well, you just remember I'm not afraid of a single fucking thing, and that includes you, Tootsie."

We four sit on the stoop and watch the crowd in front of us slowly dissipate, the people in the crowd floating away into the darkened streets around us, no longer taunting the cops, who now strut under the street lamps without much of an audience. Occasionally this cop or that one will connect with a gay person and threaten him or her with a club, but our people don't seem much interested in the conflict any more. It appears we won. That is, they could not drive us off the street until we chose to leave.

Andrew sits between my legs and leans back against my belly. He rests his head against my chest. He expresses intimacy, even in public. I can see, but I don't touch, a large spot of blood at the top of his head where the blood has soaked his hair and congealed there. Andrew comes from Brooklyn and went to Columbia for a BA and an MA. His last year there he was a member of the first gay student organization in America, called the Student Homophile League. His father is on the New York City Council, and when he came out to his parents, his father offered to send him to Europe for a year if he would give up "this thing you are so addicted to." But he refused, and now he and they don't have much to do with each other. The chill was caused by his parents, who stopped inviting him to family things. He has two brothers and a sister. His attempts to keep up with his family are painful and pointles.

Andrew has large dark eyes, long dark eyelashes, circles under his eyes, a great nose, and full lips. He has deep lines on his face—under his eyes and from his nose to the outer ends of his mouth—and therefore he has the kind of face that will be even more interesting when he is fifty than he is now, at 29. He majored in history and concentrated in modern history—the middle of the nineteenth century and afterward, Marx and later, including all the great twentieth century revolutions. Andrew writes for the local counter-culture rags and is a waiter right now at a restaurant on West 10th and Waverly Place. He writes from a radical leftist perspective. He is strong, tough, brilliant.

"Well," Andrew says, "that was an explosion."

I can feel his chest vibrating against my groin when he talks.

"I think I saw the most handsome man in the Village fighting right down there a few minutes ago, swinging his fists together and laying waste to the land. I think I even saw him swagger a stride or two. I think most people would agree that he had all the appearance of a conquering hero." Andrew loves me.

"Surely you didn't see such a man, here, on the streets of the Village. Swaggering?"

"Swaggering. Definitely swaggering." He looks around behind him. "Wasn't he swaggering, Joseph?"

"Oh, definitely. Swaggering. No question."

"Guys." Mitzi is getting impatient with these grown-up men around her acting so frivolous. "Come on, guys."

"Does anybody," I ask, "have a clean piece of cloth and something with alcohol in it? I think we ought to have a look at our heads. Mitzi, you first."

But nobody has anything. We should go home.

"I didn't expect this." Andrew turns around and looks up at me. "Did you?"

"No. Neither did I." The whole thing, I think, was a shock.

"Me neither," Mitzi says, "though I keep hoping."

I hear her, and I wonder where she gets her hope. I don't think she has had a place to live during the whole time we've known her.

"Well, yeah, I keep hoping too, Mitzi, but I haven't known what to hope for, if you know what I mean."

"Oh, big guy, I know what to hope for."

Andrew laughs. "What, Mitzi?"

"I want things to change, you big dumb shit." She hits him on his shoulder.

"Really, guys, what do we want?" I think it's an interesting question, considering it's us, sitting here, having just been through what we've been through.

"Is that it," Andrew asks, "or what is it?"

"Is what it?" Joseph tries to pin it down.

"Do we want change? Is that what we've wanted all along? Well, yeah, that's obvious, I think. What's not obvious is *what kind*." Andrew turns around and talks directly to Mitzi. "Your friends were leading the fighting. Every time, there they were, these kids, these slender beautiful kids, taking on New York cops. I loved seeing that. You all were leading it."

"Right. And where were you? All you butch faggots. Where were you? We're the only ones with balls."

"Mitzi, we were there. Not next to you, maybe, but we were there." Then I say, "We're on your side." Then, to Andrew, "I never thought we'd be fighting. That's what's so surprising about all this to me. I didn't know we had to fight." I don't fight much.

"What did you think we had to do, big guy?" Andrew asks.

"I don't know. I guess I thought we had to march to Selma or something. Have a big fucking march in Washington. Get somebody to make a speech, 'I have a dream—'"

The guys laugh at me.

"Did you?" Joseph smiles at me, disbelieving.

"Yes, I did." The conversation moves on without much forward momentum. We are all very tired. I think we are confused, too, by what happened tonight. None of us were hoping that suddenly the Village would explode in riots. We weren't thinking about fighting in the streets, I don't think. And now it has happened, and it is hard to fit it in with what we wanted. There are long pauses between people saying anything. We lie here on the steps, staring at the park in Sheridan Square, at the trash in the street, the broken glass and the rocks we were throwing a little bit ago, trying to make sense of it all. The parking meter lies on its side on the sidewalk in front of the Stonewall. What is this doing, here, in the middle of our lives? Actually, another way to put it is that the power of this riot has swept everything else before it. The Big Bang. None of us are going to be thinking of anything else but this. This riot and the unforgettable image of our kick line facing down the armed and armored cops in black combat boots now are the new reality, and any discussion of sex or even gender in America is going to have to begin here. We have ourselves declared a new reality.

Adam in the Morning

How much of where we are now in this country with respect to race is a result of Martin Luther King and non-violence, and how much of it is a result of the Watts Riots? And the riots last year in Chicago, in Washington, and in Baltimore? Was this that happened here tonight something that was necessary? And why? Have we shown them? Or is it that we have shown ourselves? Is this what we had to do before we could go on? Where are we going, that we had to start here? Mitzi says we are going to get change. I'll bet.

"I'm feeling fine, guys." Andrew twists around to look at me. He grins, and I kiss him. The others watch us. "How is everybody?"

I grin. A man's lips—big and muscular—are fine.

Mitzi says, "I'm doing a lot better than some cops in town, I bet."

"This is not over yet, is it?" Joseph asks. "I think this is just the beginning."

"Joseph, it is good to meet you, finally. I've heard about you from Bo. Tell me about yourself."

Mitzi slides over to be closer to me and Andrew. She puts her head on my shoulder. It is after four in the morning. I have to be back at work by ten. We need to get her head looked at.

"Well, what's to say, I'm an actor. I have been living here in New York for a year now. I moved to the Lower East Side a couple of months ago, and I've managed to stay employed the whole time I've been here in New York. I love New York." He laughs. "It's pretty exciting, too."

"And New York loves you."

"I hope. I was in Los Angeles before this, doing the same kind of theatre. I like this. Experimental theatre, small, loose companies, very political, with a new take on classical theatre. Something relevant. I've wanted to do this all my life. Besides," he said, "New York is such an erotic place."

"Welcome to New York."

"Yes, Welcome to New York," Andrew says.

"Did ya always wanna be an actor?" It's Mitzi.

Joseph gives a long, slow smile, looking at Mitzi. "It was after my sophomore year at UCLA, I went on a Freedom Ride—that was in the spring, late May, 1961—from Birmingham to New Orleans, and then in '63 and '64, I was in Mississippi doing voter registration. I was a volunteer first and then a field secretary with SNCC."

Adam in the Morning

"What's SNCC?" she says.

"Student Non-Violent Coordinating Committee."

"What's that?"

"A group of kids all around the country—but mainly in the South —who wanted to help black people in the South get their rights."

We're watching Mitzi grilling Joseph, and listening.

"Did you do it? Did you help 'em get their rights? Do they have their rights now?"

"Yeah, some of 'em."

"What happened? Why don't you still help 'em fight?"

"Things happened. I was in the Watts riot—it was a huge riot in Los Angeles that lasted a week in 1965. A lot of damage, about thirty people were killed."

"Was that as big as ours?"

"Oh, I guess. Probably bigger."

"Did that make things better?"

"I don't know. I'm not sure. After that, I got involved with a different group of black people."

"Who were they?"

"Non-violence was not working or had only limited use. This different group of black people were in favor of black people arming ourselves—carrying guns. They believed the only way to defend ourselves was to fight, using guns for self-defense. They were in favor of Black Power, of exploring what Black Power meant. They said it meant looking after our own—poor people, hungry people, and uneducated people—and it meant, when we were in the majority, going to the polls and voting and throwing the racists out of office. It meant fighting back when we were brutalized. That was justified. I was for Black Power. I *am* for Black Power. But now, I want to do something that is for me."

"What does that mean?"

"I'm a gay man, and everybody in this country shits on gay people, and I want to be with fags, and to see if that makes me feel any better."

"That's cool," Mitzi says. "I like that. I like being around people who are like me."

"I like hearing that," Andrew says. He reaches back and pats Joseph's thigh.

Adam in the Morning

Everybody goes silent, taken I think by the sounds of the city in the night—the traffic, the delicate clatter of some old cars coming down Seventh, distant sirens growing closer or growing more distant —and by the rich odors of the city. We're exhausted, and we hurt—I have a headache and clotted blood in my hair—and I am sore everywhere. But despite all that, we have a sense of warmth among us, of intimacy.

As people drift away, every now and then someone will see us and come over and speak, someone who recognizes me or Andrew.

One man stands below us on the pavement, looking up at us on the steps. He smiles. He is exhausted. "I never fought before, ever, in my whole life. Have you?"

"No." We are both speaking slowly. "Never. I thought you could get through without that."

"Apparently not." Then he seems to remember something. He looks up at all of us. "Are you guys OK? You're not bad hurt, are you?"

"Thanks. No. We're OK. How about you?"

He has blood in his hair, too. "Tired, beat-up, but I'm OK. Actually, I feel wonderful." He puts his hand to his head, touching the blood very carefully.

"Me too."

Andrew says he does too, and Joseph and Mitzi also.

"I'll call you, is that OK?"

"Sure. Do you have my number?"

"Yes. From the Alternate U class. You're Bo." He thinks about that for a minute. "And I think I've also got your number from an old SDS contact sheet."

"Ah, yes."

And then he goes.

It's time to bring this to a close. Everybody is OK. "I think I'd like to have something to eat. What about it, guys. Would you like to come back to our place for some breakfast? Eggs, grits, sausage, coffee? some grass? How about it?" I stand up. "And then maybe we can get everybody's head wounds looked at. I think we have enough vodka."

Our apartment is at the front of the building and has three rooms and a bathroom, big by New York standards. I have been in apartments where the bathroom and the kitchen were the same room,

31

which was a corner of the bedroom, and no living room. We have a kitchen, which you enter when you come up the stairs, and off that on one side is our bedroom, and on the other side is the living room. This means that the person standing at the stove can see everything going on in the bedroom and everything in the living room. There are no doors, except into the bathroom. Sometimes we have somebody spend the night on the big sofa bed in the living room—there's a small sofa bed in there too—and our apartment turns into something like a dormitory, where we are all in separate beds but carrying on conversations with each other. I expect before tonight is over Mitzi and Joseph will spend what's left of the night.

Andrew is at one side of the stove cooking the sausage and the grits, and I'm at the table with the vodka and some cotton. Joseph stands next to me, preparing the eggs.

"Mitzi?" I call her. "Come here. I want to look at your head."

She comes into the arch into the living room. "I don't want nobody to do nothing to my head. I like my head the way it is. You fuck around with somebody else's head if you want."

Andrew looks over at Mitzi and says, "Mitzi, get your ass over here and sit down on the chair and let Bo clean your cuts. Right now."

She comes, unwillingly, and plops down, and I am as careful as I can be with the cotton and the vodka. She winces and grimaces.

"You were wonderful tonight, Mitzi." I have my fingers in her hair, searching for cuts. I talk to her quietly. "You were a leader for our side."

Joseph, standing next to me, hears me talking. He speaks gently. "I saw you. I saw you climb up on the park bench and then turn to the kids behind you and wave your arm, waving them on. You were awesome."

She grumbles—she's not accustomed to compliments—and then she's gone, back into the living room.

It's a different experience having Joseph with his Afro on the chair in front of me. On him, they are harder to find.

"Are you always this gentle, big guy?"

"Not always. Sometimes, if the occasion seems to demand it, I can be very very rough. I try to match my manner to the moment. Right now, the moment seems to call for gentleness. I don't want to hurt you. Or mess up your 'fro."

"You're a very talented carpenter."

"I want you to like what I do."

Joseph has more cuts and bruises than I was aware of at first. In addition to the one on the back of his head, he has bruises around his forehead. This must hurt him, but he submits to it without flinching.

When I am done, Joseph stands up and says to me, "Now, why don't we swap places?" He looks at me and smiles.

So I sit in the chair and Joseph looks for cuts on me. He uses the vodka gently, cleaning my cuts and getting the blood out of my hair. I tend to lean back against him, but it is better if I remain sitting upright. It gives him more freedom of movement. I like feeling his fingers around my head.

"Is this OK?"

"Ah, yes. This is OK."

And then he kisses my head.

"Thanks."

He smiles.

Joseph turns to Andrew. "OK, I'll take over your duties, while you sit down and give your head to Bo. Your best head."

Andrew laughs and hands the spatula to Joseph and sits down. "Be rough, be very very rough, big guy, be brutal."

"Shit, I already was going to be rough, even without you telling me. I know what I'm supposed to be doing." I part his hair. He has dark hair in large curls or waves that fall all the way to his shoulders, and it is hard to find his scalp. I should spend more time on his scalp. I don't think I realized how erotic giving full attention to his scalp is. It may be that he is sitting between my legs.

"Take your time," Andrew says, his eyes closed, dreamily.

And so I do, Joseph occasionally checking us out while putting the food together. Andrew, I think, has the worst cuts and bruises of any of us.

Then I say, "I thought there was plenty of theatre on the West Coast."

"Not as much as is here. Nothing to match Broadway."

"But then television and the movies?"

"Yeah. But I wanted to be a stage actor first."

Andrew looks up and grins. "Do you find there are a lot of parts for an actor with your dimensions?"

Joseph frowns. "I'm limited to monsters, of course. But I do think I make an appealing monster, even a good-looking one. What do you say, Bo?"

"You're fine. I think if I were casting you, Caliban is about right for you, out of the parts in *The Tempest*. The only other part for a young man is Ferdinand, who is too young, too new. Besides, Ferdinand keeps his costume on throughout the play, and we couldn't have you keeping your costume on."

"Jesus, no. The more skin the better." Then, in a different tone, "How is the show shaping up?"

"The director is difficult to work with," I say, "because it takes him such a long time to talk out his ideas. I think he is brilliant, but while he is getting there, the rest of us are going crazy. Unfortunately, the set designer is flaky too. They feed off one another. Today was the first day, and they should have been ready to go. As it was, they brought you in to see if your presence would focus things for them. It did, but I am not sure if you did it in the right direction."

Andrew turns around. "Is that when Joseph was asked to take off his clothes?"

They laugh. Andrew leans back again in his chair between my legs. He is completely relaxed.

We talk theatre for a while, shows we've seen and liked, shows we've heard good things about but haven't seen, shows in which there are good parts for Joseph, that is, for a good-looking actor who is six two and very dark. We've all seen *Hair*, and we've all seen *Boys in the Band*.

Joseph says, "Did you see the play?"

"Oh, yeah," Andrew says. "It blew us away, man. It was the first time ever that I had seen us on the stage, a whole gang of us, not just somebody's friend or uncle, but a whole gang of men who were out to each other. When we went we didn't really know what we were going to see. Nothing we had heard about the play prepared us for the effect of seeing that on the stage, gay men out to each other."

"I hadn't realized how much we had been starved for just that —the image of ourselves on the stage. And when I saw it the first time, it took my breath away."

Adam in the Morning

"I wish I had seen it," Joseph says. "It was never brought to LA, but there's been so much publicity about it that we all knew what it was about and could say the famous lines to each other."

Andrew asks, "Where in LA are you from?"

"South Central."

"Watts?"

"Yeah. That was my neighborhood."

"How was that?"

"I learned a lot."

"Will you talk about it?"

"I learned that, as a gay man, I was going to have to look after myself. I learned that there are limits to non-violence. I've read most of the books. Malcolm X. Stokely Carmichael. Huey Newton. I had already done a lot of reading in what was behind the civil rights movement, and then, after Watts, I read a lot in Black Power and in Black Nationalism."

Mitzi goes to sleep on the sofa in the living room.

We talk about Judy Garland's death, and the extended funeral, which has been on the front pages of the newspapers all week.

I bring up the question of violence.

Andrew answers me. "Of course we had to riot. At some point, it was clear, we were going to take to the streets just like everybody else—just like blacks in the big urban riots and students everywhere —and start throwing rocks and setting fire to the city, and then keep on doing it until we begin to get a response from the system. We are not like the civil rights movement. They've had more than one hundred fifty years of the abolitionist movement—and the civil war— behind them establishing a right and wrong, and what the civil rights movement has had to do in the last ten or fifteen years is make the country live up to its promise. But there hasn't been any homosexual liberation movement in this country. There hasn't been a promise to us. There was one in Germany, I think, but not much of one, and that was destroyed by Hitler before the Second World War. Most people in this country don't know there are homosexuals here. They certainly don't know any personally. And if they do know about us, they think we are either sick or security risks. So, there's just us, nobody else for us to depend on, we don't have "friends," and we don't have more than one hundred fifty years to waste, catching up with the black folks. Talking, trying to achieve a moral advantage, doesn't work if the other side finds you repellant. Even making speeches doesn't help if nobody's listening. That's why we have to get out in the street and fight the cops. We have to earn respect. The other side has never given us a single indication that suggests that they would be receptive to an overture from us. So we have to get out on the street and try to hurt them."

He has taken over from Joseph the sausage and the grits. Now he turns around and looks at us. "There were times tonight when I thought the Revolution had come that we used to rap about. I thought, this was just the way it was supposed to happen. The pig police overstep their bounds one last time, and suddenly the people rise up —without prompting and without leadership—and, in their great might, smash the illegitimate and decadent power of the system. There were moments tonight when I marveled at there being no leadership, nobody out there saying, *Revolt!*, giving orders to the troops. And yet, look at the hundreds that came out of nowhere and faced down the cops. The cops could have fired their guns at us, but they didn't, because somebody on their side knew that they couldn't do it. There have been too many times in this country in the last ten years when the police have pulled their triggers and killed people in demonstrations and it has always made things worse for their side. Orangeburg, Watts, Chicago, and riots in New York almost every year during this decade. Summer in the city means rioting. And these cops know that history. There were moments when I thought, this is where the Revolution will start, here in Christopher Street, and it will spread from here to the Lower East Side and to Bed-Stuy and Harlem and then to Chicago and Detroit and to LA and Oakland and the rest of the West Coast, until the whole country—millions and millions and millions of men and woman across the country—is in revolt against the systemic oppression of the people. I thought, the Revolution that has been trying to happen for the past six or eight years has actually just been waiting for the right spark in the right place, and our Revolution is going to gather up all the powers and all the peoples who have been trying to revolt, and ours is going to go all the way to revolution, to a total cleansing of our civilization and result in a clean slate and an opportunity to devise a totally new way to govern ourselves. Nixon and his world are going to be wiped away—and all the repellant men he brought with him to oppress the people. His bombing of Cambodia. Then, at some point tonight I realized that this was not going to happen. I was disappointed tonight when I realized this is going to get only so big and no bigger. I was so ready for a thorough cleansing of the body politic, for something radical and clean."

"I know," I say. "It's infuriating that it didn't happen."

"Ah, man, worse than that. Worse than that. It's tragic. This may have been our moment."

"But, on the other hand, I know I am OK, and I know the system is lying about us."

"I don't think the Revolution is going to happen," Joseph says, speaking to Andrew. "The people who have the power are too entrenched, and I don't think we can shame them into giving up their power. I think we can *fight* them, like we did tonight, like you did tonight, but the fight has to be a much, much bigger thing than our battle around Sheridan Square. It's going to be much, much harder to bring down the power structure than most of us think."

"I know," Andrew says. "But I'm like Mitzi. I hope."

Nobody says anything for a few minutes.

I go into the living room. Mitzi is on the sofa, her face toward the back. I forget how young she is. I kneel in front of the sofa and lean over her. "Mitzi?" I wait a second. "Mitzi?" I see no point in waking her if she doesn't want to get up and eat. "Mitzi? Would you like breakfast?" But she doesn't wake up.

The night we met her—found her—it was 1967, and Andrew and I were on Christopher Street, walking along slowly, going east from down here by the river up toward Seventh Avenue. Andrew and I were talking about something—the war, Robert McNamara, *Marat/Sade*—and then I felt my wallet move. I feel it, and I grab behind me. The wrist I catch is this skinny thin thing, a kid's wrist, or a girl's wrist—I was expecting the beefy wrist of a grown man—and I almost let her go because that surprised me so. By the time I get turned around so I can see what I actually have gotten hold of, I realize it is one of the street kids, a girl! Andrew and I have talked about these kids since the first time we were together. These are our kids, we said. If they are lucky, they will grow up to be us. Of course if they aren't lucky, they will get killed on the street, living the way they do. Anyway, here I am, holding on to this kicking, screaming little monster, and I say, "You can kick all you want, missy, but I am not going to let go of you."

"You fucking faggot. Leggo of me!"

She tries to kick me in the balls.

Andrew stops laughing and starts helping me.

"Slow down, kid. Take it easy. We're not going to hurt you."

"But we're not going to let you get my wallet, either."

When she realizes we are not going to hurt her, she calms down a little, and her breathing begins to slow down.

"Now, kid, my name is Bo, and this is Andrew."

"Don't call me kid."

"Fine. What do you want us to call you?"

"Mitzi."

"OK, Mitzi. I got it," I say.

"Would you like some food, Mitzi?" Andrew asks.

I start walking toward the Silver Dollar, pulling her along a little. "I think you'd like some food, and Andrew and I were going in that direction, and we'd be happy to have you join us when we get something to eat."

She is sullen and angry, and she tries to get her wrist free from my grip, but she can't do it.

"What are you going to do with me?"

At that point, I stop walking and dragging her along, and I say, "Nothing." Then I let go of her wrist.

She steps back immediately, out of my range, and rubs her wrist.

I say, "We are going to get something to eat, and we're inviting you to come with us to get a hamburger. If you do that, we are going to give you some money—not much, but a little—and then we are going to go on about our business, to the place we were going before we ran into you and you do whatever you want to do."

"What do you want for your money?" The suspicion in her voice could cut through steel.

Andrew says, "Nothing. We don't want anything for our money."

And I say, "Yes, nothing. We don't want anything."

"Do you want to come?" Andrew asks.

She doesn't answer, but she doesn't run away either.

So I say, "We are going to walk on. If you'd like to come with us, you can follow us. That OK?"

She doesn't say anything, but she follows us, just out of our reach, behind.

At the Silver Dollar, we find a booth, but she doesn't join us. She stands a little bit away from us, just beyond the nearest table, and is positioned ready to run for the door if anything happens.

The waitress comes, and Andrew handles it: "We'd like two cheeseburgers with everything, and that young lady over there hasn't told us what she wants yet."

So the waitress asks her.

"Same thing those two are having."

The waitress shrugs and goes to get the food.

Mitzi won't talk to us while we wait. Mitzi is about five feet five or six, slender, dark blond hair cut short. It comes down just below her ears. She is wearing jeans and a frilly blouse, long earrings —slender chains with yellow glass beads at the bottom—and dark lipstick. She has plucked her eyebrows. She eats hers sitting alone at the table near us. It is hard for her to eat because she is trying to be ready to run if anything happens.

"Youse guys gonna pay for this like you said?"

"Yes, we are going to pay," Andrew says.

She still doesn't understand that, but she goes on. "You said you'd give me some money."

"Yes."

Andrew pulls out his wallet and gives her some money.

"Why're youse guys givin' away money?"

Andrew and I look at each other.

"Well, we know you're living on the street, and we know you probably need money—you tried to lift my wallet—and we're gay, so we feel a little responsibility for you. We'd like to help out a little."

"I don't need your fucking help."

Andrew takes a deep breath. "I know. We know you've been getting along without us, but we'd like to help, if you'd let us."

She checks him out, slowly, then speaks, slowly. "What do you want for it?"

"Nothing."

After several exchanges over that—she assumes we want to fuck her—she leaves as if she's running out of a bank she's just robbed.

Adam in the Morning

After that, we run across Mitzi pretty often. One of us would see her and call her name, and she would look around as if it was the cops after her, but then, before she could run away, we would call out, "Wanna get a cheeseburger?" And we'd go through the same routine, her following us into the Silver Dollar. We always give her money afterward.

Finally, she began to relax around us. She told us that, at first, she thought we were plainclothes cops. The first time we told her she could sleep on our sofa—it was November 1967—she asked us what we wanted for it, that is, she wanted to know if she had to put out for us, and when we said no, she said, "Well I want you to know I can chew your balls off, so don't try anything."

I go back into the kitchen. I see Joseph and Andrew, their heads bandaged, which surprises me at first. "She doesn't wake up. Let's eat."

I serve our plates and then sit down at the little table, Andrew and I facing each other and Joseph between us.

"So the fighting was for ourselves," Andrew says.

And I say, "Yeah. I think so. We proved we could do it—we proved to ourselves that we could do it, that we could fight back, and now we never have to take abuse again lying down. We had to prove to ourselves we can fight—"

Andrew smiles. "—even if we don't prove we can win."

"Yet. Right." It's Joseph. "We have to learn that, independent of them, we are OK. You know there has been a lot of organizing on the Coast, and I sense that it has gotten farther along than the organizing here."

We talk about the riots, how unreal it all seems. And yet there's the blood.

"Have either of you ever done this before?" Joseph asks us.

"Done what?"

"What we did tonight." He speaks to Andrew. "I saw you wade into the crowd, swinging your fists from side to side, using them like a club. It seemed like you have been trained to fight like this. Have you?"

Andrew laughs. "No. The movies. I think I have seen men fight like that in the movies. Maybe street fighting when I was growing up. I don't remember."

"You're a very impressive fighter." And then to me, "You were using the same technique, Bo. It really does look like you two went to the same school together."

"Thanks. I never thought about it. I saw the crowd and saw the cops and how they were using their clubs on people—on us, on American citizens—and it made me so angry I felt capable of doing anything. I wanted to inflict damage—hurt—on these men, and I wanted to keep them from hurting me and my friends any more."

I get up and start to wash the dishes. Andrew stands next to me. Joseph brings dishes from the table.

"How long have you two been together?"

"Since 1966, early summer. We met at a class at Alternate U." I grin. "The name of the class was *What is a man?*"

Joseph grins and shakes his head. "Important subject. Nothing we learned growing up is still true, and we need to work it all out ourselves."

It's done, and then I turn to the next item of business. It's late on a hot summer night in the city. "Would you like to crash here?"

Joseph smiles, then grins broadly. "Of course."

Andrew has his arms crossed over his chest. "There's our bed, and there's the floor."

"Do you mind? Is your bed big enough?"

I take his shoulder and pull him toward me. I kiss him. "It's big enough."

Andrew says, "Come with me, and I'll show you what there is in the bathroom." There's an extra toothbrush.

In the bedroom, Andrew and I strip. Joseph joins us. He takes off his clothes. He is aware we are watching him. We all have bandages and bruises, which show up more against our naked skin. I light a joint.

"I think, if none of us thrash around very much, we can all fit in this bed." Joseph's body I saw today. This is the first time that Joseph and Andrew have seen each other. "Are you a thrasher?"

He frowns and shakes his head. "No."

I don't think either of us cares anyway.

"You know, you can sleep on the floor in the living room with Mitzi—but don't touch her. That's the only rule."

"No, guys, I'd rather be here with you."

Adam in the Morning

We are interested in each other, so we get into bed, and without consciously touching, I can feel the cool of Joseph's body—his sweat —down the length of mine. Pretty much immediately, all three of us have erections. I'm circumcised, and Joseph and Andrew aren't.

"Can we touch?" Joseph asks. "What are your rules for this?"

Andrew takes a deep sigh. "No rules." Then, after a pause. "No rules." Then, "Yes, we can touch. You can do anything you want."

"Except the one. Leave Mitzi alone."

"Cool."

And so, after that, and before we go to sleep, we do what we want. Joseph has a fine cock, warm and firm, with beautiful-feeling ridges in it where the veins are, and for a few minutes I can feel his heart beating in his dick.

Saturday, June 28, 1969
10:30 a.m.

Joseph is six feet two or three, and his shoulders are very wide. I figure the entrance to Caliban's cave should be wide and low. He comes out of his cave as if he were a dog running out of his kennel, on his hands and knees, or maybe on his belly, pulling himself forward. Thirty inches by thirty inches, tight enough to be noticeable. Yesterday, when we discussed all this, the director said that the whole "tempest" scene in Act 1, scene 1 should be down front behind a scrim which can easily be removed, and the scenes that immediately follow—between Prospero and Miranda—should be in front on a bare stage. When Prospero decides to visit Caliban, he moves to a different part of the stage. Caliban will enter, first, on his belly, slithering across the stage. The odd thing about *The Tempest* is that there are only three places referred to in the text. The ship, Prospero's cell, Caliban's cave. The rest of it is somewhere on an island, but nowhere particular. In The Globe, the public theatre in Southwark, or Blackfriars, the smaller, more intimate enclosed theatre—wherever this was first produced—there would probably have been a trapdoor in the floor of the stage, or else, at the back of the stage, a "discovery" place, which was a kind of shallow recess in the rear wall of the stage used for Caliban's entrance in Act 1, scene 2.

Sergei Bachinsky wanted to come up with something more pointed than that. His idea was an imposing rock face rising maybe ten or fifteen feet above the stage. This rock face would remain in place all through the play. With the addition of various ropes and pulleys, it might serve as the setting for 1.1, on the ship. In the second scene, when Prospero enters with Miranda, they might enter on the top, with Miranda using her vantage point to see what was happening to the ship at sea. The largest part of this rock face could be a kind of balcony with a large opening that could be used for

Prospero's cell. Down at stage level and to the left could be a hole—like a drain hole in a curbing on a street. It would be low, maybe thirty inches high, wide, perhaps three feet wide, and with some practice it might be possible for Caliban to enter through this opening. At other points in the play, the main acting space would be the stage floor, but the rock face would provide a place for Prospero or Ariel when it was required for them to oversee the efforts of Ferdinand, or Caliban and Stephano and Trinculo, or the Neapolitan royalty. The designer—his name is Matt Kimball—seemed taken with this idea. It does give the sense of a Mayan ruin rising out of the jungle in Central America, a monument to ancient civilization in the midst of tropical abundance. It has other advantages. It is different from other productions of *The Tempest*. It emphasizes the ancient roots of the play, and it emphasizes the racial theme—white-and-red, white-and-black, slavery and freedom—and the anti-colonialism theme. The designer began to sketch out drawings, and when I saw them I told him I liked them.

I am working in a silent theatre. It is ten-thirty in the morning, and no one else is awake at this hour. The Olympic used to be a church—it seems to be fieldstone outside—and the basic architecture is Greek Revival or neo-Classical of some kind. It has columns across the front, with the gable end to the street. Inside, there is a stage area up front, flanked by columns, where there used to be a pulpit. Since it was a church, the auditorium has a level floor, and we use risers on all four sides for seating, with a decent-sized performance space in the center. Entrances are on the four corners. Directors and actors like our performance space because they are surrounded on all four sides by the audience. Everything inside the building is painted black, which means we usually don't have any "sets" to speak of. A chair. A rock. That's about it. Very minimalist and modern.

I hear the door open, and somebody walks into the auditorium. I can hear heels. It is a woman. It is Belle Underwood, our producer.

"You are here early. You should get a social life. Doing nothing but work in the theatre is a narrow way to live." She comes down to the stage—making a lot of noise—and sits in a seat in the front row and crosses her legs at the knees.

"Hello, Belle. Welcome." I stand up and turn to look at her. "I looked for you last night."

"Jesus, God! What happened to your head! Are you all right?"

"I'm all right, Belle. These are what is known of as superficial wounds. I got in a fight with the police."

"With the police? You're a mild-mannered type. What happened to make you change? Were you there at the riot, at the Stonewall? Of course you were. I wasn't. I was asleep, and none of my friends called me to wake me up and to tell me to get my ass over to Sheridan Square, because if I didn't go over there I was going to regret it all the rest of my whole fucking life. I can't believe you didn't call me. Why didn't you? I thought we were friends. I thought you cared about me. Oh, shit, of course we're not friends. You only care about yourself. I've known that all of my life, but I keep forgetting it. I keep forgetting that you only care about your own fucking self! Jesus!"

"Now, Belle." I sit down on a seat in the front row. "I didn't call anybody. I got Andrew. That's all. Only Andrew."

"Only Andrew!"

"Only Andrew. So what have you heard?"

"Holy Mother of God! This is what it was like on the streets of Thebes the morning after Ramesses II took his troops out to chase Moses and the Israelites to the Red Sea. Everybody thought there was only one option—the Pharaoh would chase them into the sea—but here the whole army of the Pharaoh's was now under the Red Sea, and nobody could think what to think. And on the other side of the Red Sea, the Israelites were stunned speechless at what had just happened. I mean, the Red Sea had parted for them, for Christ's sake! They felt like falling on their knees every moment and thanking Almighty God that they had been spared. Was this the first time this God of theirs had reached down into the flowing stream of history— entered Time—and altered events for thousands upon thousands upon thousands of people, and so people didn't know how to feel? Much less think? It wasn't as if they didn't like the outcome—they were glad they weren't under the water—but this was the first time that God had stirred up the flow of Time and made his presence felt in the created universe for so many people, and that was terrifying, awe- inspiring to the point that people didn't know what to say or do or think. And that's the way people are feeling on the streets of the Village this morning. Awed, bewildered, terrified, stunned, speechless. Very grateful. And, of course, very very proud. And it's worse, even, than their not knowing what to think. It's as if they've forgotten how. Or something happened last night, some blow to the

47

head, that left them unable to. What do you think about it all? How do you feel? Were you badly injured last night? I saw Andrew, and I see that you both were bloodied. Andrew was with the most gorgeous man I think I have ever seen in my entire life." She stops. "That is, aside from you and Andrew." Then she says, worried and concerned. "Has he left you? How are you, Bo? Are you all right? Do you still love me?"

I burst out laughing. "Oh Belle. This is the first time, since I've known you, when the times were in synch with your style. There's almost as much drama out there as you generate about yourself by yourself, just walking down the street. I'm fine. Of course I still love you. Andrew first, and then you. And Andrew still loves me."

"And who is that I saw Andrew with?"

"What did he look like?"

"Oh, I don't know—Apollo? Yes, he must look like Apollo. Or maybe Dionysus. Hyacinth? Narcissus? I don't know. He's very dark —he's Osiris. Wasn't he very dark?—and he has an Afro, and he's certainly beautiful. If he wore one of those Egyptian loincloths—gold lamé and hanging down to his knees in front—I'd certainly fall on my knees and worship him."

"I'm going to tell him you said that. He's another person who has come into my life. I think he may turn out to be a fuck buddy. You liked him?"

"Who knows? He is gorgeous, though. We only talked for a few minutes because I was on the way over here."

"What are people saying on the street?"

"Oh," she shrugs. "Everything has changed. The whole relationship between fags and the police has changed, between people in the Village and the police power of the state has changed. Everybody is threatening the police. If they do this or that— You know what it must be like. Do you want to have lunch?"

"Sure."

"Silver Dollar?"

"Noon? One?"

"One. What's the new one's name?"

"Caliban."

"Oh, right. Caliban is a monster. This one is a god, the one who was with Andrew."

"Belle. There is no such thing as gods. His name is Joseph Roche. He plays Caliban in *The Tempest*."

48

"This one?"

"Yes. This one. Ours."

"He spent the night with you guys?"

"Yes. What there was of it—four to ten or so, when I got up."

"Life is terribly unfair. I can't get any man, even a troll, to go to bed with me, and the three most beautiful men in all of the Village go to bed with each other! I think when you get ready to go to bed, you should make a rule that only two of you can sleep together. Then you should draw straws or something and tell the one who loses—or wins —that he has to go to bed with me. I could show him a good time. Isn't that a good idea? I would have what I want, your bed would have more space for the two of you. Life would be better all around, which is what we're going for, right?"

"What's the matter, Belle, why are you feeling lonely? This isn't like you."

"I don't know." She thinks for a minute. "I am aware of all of you having had this life-transforming event last night and everybody is feeling like comrades, and suddenly I feel left out."

"This is the Village, Belle. Most of the people you meet are going to be gay. You should spend time somewhere else."

"Thanks, guy."

I am drawing lines on the floor with chalk. After watching for a while, she gets up and comes out on the stage with me. "What's this?"

"It may end up being the set for *The Tempest*."

"I know, but what are you planning?"

"We need to make something that will do for the boatwreck. And we also need something that will function for Caliban's cave— something he can come out of—and later we need something that can be closed off with a curtain that Prospero can pull back—"

"—and discover Ferdinand and Miranda playing at chess."

"—and it would be nice if, when he pulls it back, the audience gets a glimpse of something that might be seen to be Prospero's cell. Something with his books, a globe, a telescope, a candelabrum, the things an astrologer and a Renaissance scientist and astronomer might have nearby."

"Ah!"

"And it would be nice if the style of each of these scenes didn't clash with the style of the other scenes, when the drunkards and

Caliban stagger across the island, or when the Neapolitan royalty and their nobles—"

"—that is, a plain black box—" Belle does not need much explanation.

"Well, yes, for us, that's the most economically feasible."

"And something tells me you are on a tight budget?"

"Ooo. Yes. Of course. Apparently, the largest expenditure is going to go for costumes."

She runs her fingers through her hair. "Doesn't it always?" She studies the floor again and then looks at me. "Why don't you—" She pauses. "—do it with a scrim lit to suggest Caliban's cave, and later to suggest Prospero's cell? Or—" She is thinking out loud and gesturing with her hands, her fingers with her very red fingernails outstretched. "—one scrim with Prospero's cell on one end of the stage and Caliban's cave on the other?"

I laugh. "You may be right. Caliban's cave and Prospero's cell are opposites, they represent the body and the mind, and it would be appropriate to put them on opposing sides of the back wall. In the Renaissance, there wasn't anybody to speak up for the nobility of the body, and nobody in this play. That explains our brief glimpse of Caliban's cave and our more extended view of Prospero's cell. Sergei has an idea."

"What?"

"He likes the idea of giving the stage some suggestion of an island civilization in ruin—Easter Island, with its immense statues of heads—or of a civilization created by native peoples also in ruins, in a jungle. Think of the stepped pyramids in the Yucatan. In both of these there would be the jungle and the ruined civilization, suggestive of Caliban's heritage despoiled by all these White Men with their books in foreign languages. It is a world defined by Frantz Fanon's *The Wretched of the Earth,* where people are divided into the colonized or the colonizers, and everything the colonizers do is characterized by the oppression and suffering of the colonized. We could do this in one construction, built behind the risers—a giant head or a step pyramid. The Neapolitans could tramp through the jungle on the island like Conquistadors."

"Is he committed to anti-colonialist themes?"

"We talked most of yesterday about this, pacing around the stage, marking things off, working through the text, Sergei and I and Matt, the set designer. He even got Joseph down here. He asked him to take his clothes off for us. He keeps thinking he has a way of doing it, but then he loses it again. The problem is that the text explicitly says Caliban was 'deservedly confined into this rock' [1.2.362]. 'This rock' means that there is a rock for Miranda to point to—or something that can be touched and seen. And whatever can be touched and seen is also a place of confinement for Caliban. He would like to come up with something that would be a place of confinement for Caliban but would also be suggestive of his island heritage. I wonder if that is possible. These goals seem contradictory."

"What is Sergei going for?"

"I don't think he is very clear on that yet. He's still working it out."

"Little late, isn't he?"

I smile. "Oh yeah. That's his way of working. You know that. But I don't complain."

"What do you think the play is about?"

"*The Tempest* is a tragedy. I think Caliban is the only character in the play who is at home in his environment, and it is not necessarily a bad thing when he attempts to have sex with Miranda—rape is Prospero's and Miranda's word—and to 'people' the isle with Calibans. Their children would inherit both the island that had belonged to Sycorax—and consequently Caliban's island—and the duchy of Milan and would be at home in both places. That is, their children would be at home in both their bodies and their minds, something that can't be said for the children of Ferdinand and Miranda, who will have a larger inheritance but a less important and less profound one. What happens at the end of the play—from late in Act 3, when Ariel says, 'You are three men of sin' [3.3.53], onward—is the imposition of the concepts of sin, and punishment for sin, and repentance for sin, and forgiveness for sin, on the world of the play, that is, the world of the island. Within the world of the play, it is Prospero we are concerned with, his being willing to forgive the sins of his former enemies, but if we have the play as an artifact in a larger argument that has been going on for thousands of years in our culture, the conflict between the body and the mind, or soul, it is a very sad play, because the last two and a half acts of the play show us the very best of our culture failing to achieve a synthesis of mind and body, apparently not even seeing that such a synthesis is necessary. And viewed from this perspective, Caliban suffers the fate of all dark-skinned people who confront the white race—he's turned into a clown. When that happens, we lose what he knows."

"What does he know?"

"The island and his body."

"Oh, Bo!" She has her hand in front of her mouth and seems stricken by what I have said. After a minute, as if remembering herself, she busies herself with her cigarette lighter, lights a cigarette, and smokes for a while, watching me. I draw pictures in chalk on the stage floor of men both clothed and unclothed.

"Is Joseph into men?"

I remember Joseph's energetic acrobatics last night. "I believe he is."

"Is that all he's in to?"

My parents believe that race—our culture's failure to deal with racial differences and distinctions and with responsibility for slavery and its consequences—is the principal issue before the nation. As a result, they left the career path they were on—graduate school leading to tenure-track positions in some major research university and a lifetime of scholarship and writing—and applied for and were offered teaching positions at Texas Southern University, a school in Houston that taught Negro undergraduates. They have spent most of their professional lives as teachers. They gave up prestige, salary differential, a certain kind of intellectual stimulation. This was a sacrifice they were willing to make for increased harmony between the races—for the future. I believe they were ahead of the culture in the nineteen-fifties, since they believed that there were no significant biological differences among the races and that what differences there appeared to be were mere socially- and culturally-induced phenomena, like the clown caricature that Caliban assumes in *The Tempest.* My parents accepted the racial stratification in TSU because they understood that at that historical moment, this was necessary—nothing else was possible—and that, since it was not grounded in a biological reality, it would eventually come to an end. They believed that their work at Texas Southern was hastening the day when people accepted as a fact that there were no significant biological differences among the races.

I grew up in the Houston suburb of Riverside which was predominantly black, because they were determined for us to live in an integrated neighborhood. I accepted what my parents taught me about race, but I saw all of these things on a more primitive level than my parents. All of my schools were segregated. My parents couldn't do anything about that. Grammar school was easy. At seven, we didn't know why any of us in the city park were the colors we were, and it didn't seem a very interesting thing to wonder about. "He's black" seemed true and obvious, and we could move on to "Can he play ball?" Junior high and high school were more treacherous and proved the validity of my parents' beliefs, for what had been a values-free fact about a person—his color—gradually became laden with meaning and values. Just as the black kids I knew on the playground were becoming "niggahs" as we grew up, I was becoming "a racist" or a "honky" or "white." I can remember the first time a kid on the basketball court at the park looked at me and said, "You're white." He wasn't just referring to the color of my skin. We were entering the adult world of race relations and were learning how to place ourselves in it. Since I was discovering that it was white people who had most of the power in our culture, it was difficult not to associate myself with that and even more difficult not to see the black kids I played ball with as weak or powerless or dumb. "Oh, that's just what people say about black people," my father said, "but it's not true. A person is black, and that doesn't mean anything. It doesn't mean that person is not as smart or less intelligent or powerless or weak or more prone to violence. It doesn't mean anything. And your being white doesn't mean anything either. Do you understand that, Bo?"

This was hard for me to understand, but I thought the issue was interesting. I had never thought before that grown-ups would take a characteristic of one of us and give it meaning that it didn't actually have. Like, I was discovering that I was turned on by boys. And at about the same time I discovered that boys who were turned on by boys were thought to be "queer." I didn't think I was queer or strange. I just thought I was me. It didn't mean anything—except to me personally—that I liked other boys. And people who thought it did mean something were wrong. I didn't talk to my parents about this at first. I just talked to my parents about the differences between being black and being white, and what all that meant. But later, when I was sixteen, I did talk to them and tell them I was turned on by boys. My parents had several friends who were homosexual, one of whom was Uncle Duncan. These men came to our house for supper and were members of the small group of their friends—academics and artists and musicians—who took part in the local scene and provided an extended family for my brother Billy and me. When I told them I was turned on by boys, my father said, "Well that is interesting. Maybe it would be good for you to talk to your Uncle Duncan. Would you like to do that?" I said, emphatically, no, and laughed, and then he and my mother laughed and told me they loved me, and they took a long time saying goodnight when I went up to bed. One thing my father said, before I went up, was, "Whether you are homosexual or not, you must not believe the things that people say about homosexuals. There is nothing, absolutely nothing, wrong with it, nothing even unusual about it, nothing 'queer,' and it does not mean that you are going to have any less fulfilling a life than your brother Billy—or than we have had." He held Mother's hand, and they smiled. "Don't you believe any of that. You have a wonderful life ahead of you."

I knew my parents were right, but that didn't make it easy to be their son or to be living in the situation we were living in, when I was in high school and what I wanted for a few years was to be anonymous and inconspicuous while I discovered what I was. My first boyfriend was a kid my age that I met on a basketball court on the campus of Texas Southern. His name was Tommy Sante. What happened was that one afternoon I was supposed to meet my parents at TSU for a ride home, and while I was waiting I went down to the basketball courts to shoot some hoops. I shot one, and then I ran down to the other end of the court, dribbling the ball, and shot again. I did this a bunch of times, running back and forth the length of the court with the ball. Then, there was this other kid on the court with me, playing defense. I didn't see him come up. He just appeared. He was very tall, like me, and had long arms, and he made it much harder for me to take my shots. But he was laughing at what was happening, and soon I was too, and when my parents pulled up in the parking lot and blew, I said, "See ya."

He said, "See ya," too.

Then I said, "Tomorrow this time?"

So it got to be a regular thing. These were our junior and senior years in high school—we were sixteen and seventeen—and we were so new to everything that we could say things like, "Last year, before I started shaving—" Tommy came from a big family. He had an older brother and four or five younger brothers and sisters. They all worshipped him. He was smart, talented, capable of working hard, and he was beautiful. He was very dark, skin the color of dark chocolate, large eyes, and white teeth, and even though he was dark, his hair was darker. We played at the TSU courts, and we played at the city park in Riverside—Tommy and I lived four or five blocks apart—and he spent the night at my house.

What made it rough was segregation. We didn't go to the same school, and we couldn't be on regular teams together, and there were things other than school and sports that we couldn't do together. We couldn't go to movies together, and it meant that we had to work harder to find ways to be together. We couldn't just be friends. That made me angry, but it also made us feel like we were putting something over on everybody else. They were all segregationist assholes, and we weren't, and we felt fine about that. I always stayed away from the other boys in my school—I didn't want to get into anything too intimate with any of them—and then one Friday afternoon we had been shooting hoops at TSU. Tommy and I were running back down the court, and he had the ball. I was close on him, but he kept coming, and then we were almost under the net. He jumped—I jumped too, but I couldn't stop him—and he made the goal. We came down together. My arms were still out, trying to prevent his making the goal. The ball fell through the net, and Tommy fell into my arms, his arms around me. He was laughing hard at what had just happened, laughing at having gotten past me and laughing at me for having stayed with him all the way down the court, at us being together. He put his head so far back on my shoulder that he was almost kissing the back of my neck. I thought, *Something just happened.*

When my parents came to pick me up, my mother invited Tommy to our house for supper. Mom asked, "How was practice, boys?" She always smiled when she talked to us.

Tommy said, "Yes ma'm. Hot. I'm tired out."

"Well, it's so good for you. It's such a good thing you boys are doing."

I asked him if he'd like to spend the night, and he said yeah, and then Mom asked him too and called his mother.

After supper, they left to go out to a meeting, and we washed dishes. Billy was out with his friends. "Your folks are cool."

I came up behind him—he was standing at the sink—and caught his traps in my hands. I massaged them a little.

He smiled, but he didn't turn around.

I ran my hands up under his t-shirt to his armpits. I squeezed his lats.

Then he turned around and faced me, holding out his arms. I walked into them.

He held me. "What're we doing?"

"We're holding each other. And I think we're going to kiss each other, if you'd like that."

I moved away a little from him. He was letting me take the lead here. So I took his head in my hands and, slowly, brought it to my lips. I kissed him lightly, once.

"Would you like to do that again?"

"Have you done this before?"

"No. But I know about it. My parents know. They have friends who know. You just act naturally."

"Is this OK?"

"This is fine. This is so OK."

And so, when we had cleaned up the kitchen, we went upstairs to my bedroom. I got undressed first. They were twin beds, one against each wall facing each other, and I sat on the bed and leaned back against the wall, facing his bed across the space between them.

He seemed to avoid looking at me while he was getting undressed, but when he turned around and faced me, he had an erection to match mine.

The next morning, when we were still in bed after sunup but before my mother called us for breakfast, we were in bed together. He had put his head on my chest and drew circles around my nipples, and sometimes licked me.

"Do you think I am handsome?"

"Oh, yes, Tom, oh, yes."

He smiled.

"What about me?"

"I think you are beautiful. I have always thought so."

We had sex again, and then Tommy asked me, "What do you think of two guys together? Is it really wrong? My parents say it is."

"No. It isn't wrong. My parents say it isn't wrong. That's just something people say. Stupid people. I don't mean your parents are stupid. I mean they don't know about this, about what can happen between men."

And that was the way it was, from then until we each graduated from high school about a year and a half year later. We had sex all the time, and we were best friends, and he felt torn between his parents' views and my parents' views. And we had to keep the whole thing—not just the sex, but even our friendship—secret from just about everybody but my parents. After we graduated, I went to Oberlin, where I lived in a student-run dorm called The Men's Co-op that was half gay male students and half straight male students. Tommy went to Texas Southern, which was more conservative than Oberlin, and there were fewer chances for us, and we drifted apart. He ended up getting married. I see him and his wife and children occasionally when I go back to Houston, but we never mention what happened when we were sixteen and seventeen.

Sergei Bachinsky, the director, comes in just before I leave for lunch with Belle—he ignores my bandages—and he gives me his ideas about the step pyramid in the Yucatan. "We can do the two openings. One on the left, small and low, is the opening for Caliban's dark cave, and one on the right, high enough for a man to walk into without stooping, and draped with a tapestry to close it, leads into Prospero's cell. These two would be over the two exits farthest from the door into the theatre. Beside these, backdrops along the wall behind the risers up behind the last row of seats present giant tropical ferns so large as to make the actors look as if they are walking through grass over their heads, and palm trees, and, above all this, the ruins of a step pyramid. Our perspective on the pyramid is similar to our perspective on the Empire State Building when we are standing on the sidewalk at its foot. The pyramid seems to tower over us and dwarf us and be about to fall on us and crush us."

"But I thought you were going to want me to actually build something that Caliban could crawl out of." He is not pleased with my intrusion.

"I want the audience to have a sense of the freedom theme that runs through this play. All of the characters, beginning with Caliban and Ariel, are in some way or other enslaved to something, and they all labor to free themselves. How do you think our actor would take to wearing a slave's collar?"

"Naked, with a slave's collar? He'd probably enjoy it. He might have difficulty playing it without an erection, however."

"That was not the answer I was expecting. We might use a leash, too."

We don't come to an understanding. That is, I have no idea what he wants me to do. Later, I leave and walk down Christopher Street.

The site of the riots is crowded with men and women looking at the debris and at the front of the Stonewall. One man is calling out, at regular intervals, in a voice that echoes off the buildings, POWER TO THE PEOPLE. Some of these men and women are bandaged about their heads like me, I guess from last night. I hear someone call out to me. I turn and see the caller and wave. There are signs posted in the broken windows of the Stonewall. One of them says, GAY POWER. Since I know BLACK POWER, I have an idea what *GAY POWER* means. *Those of us who were powerless in our system are now claiming power.* That's what a gay fist means—*We who were powerless are now strong, and we have taken our rightful place in our world, whether you allow it or not.* We've been hearing this talked about for the last year or more. I can see now that the people talking about it were radical visionaries of some sort, but we are no longer in a time of visionaries. What this sign speaks of is something that has arrived. The sign announcing GAY POWER is in the broken window of a Mafia-owned bar we have smashed. The sign announces the name of something that exists. It is a momentous shift.

I am reading about Cesar Chavez in *The New Yorker.* He is unionizing the Mexican-American farm workers in California, trying to make them a force equal to the power of vineyard owners. His work with the farm workers is inspiring, and it may be that what has happened during this decade is not so much the breakdown of communal values, the drugs and the sexual revolution, so much as it is the breakdown in the old way that power is distributed in our culture. Through organizing and through the grape boycott, Cesar Chavez is making the farm workers as powerful as the vineyard owners. Peter Matthiessen, who wrote the article in *The New Yorker,* ends the first installment by describing a visit he made to a small vineyard being picketed by the United Farm Workers. It is crucial to their success that at least a single farm worker for the vineyard leave the vineyard property and join the strikers. One young man, wearing a red and white bandanna tied around his head, finally leaves his place and walks toward the strikers, but, before getting to the property line, he hesitates. Matthiessen describes the intense moment, how the boy can't bring himself to quite leave the vineyard and join the strikers but also can't seem to return to his place. The owners of the vineyard, federal Department of Labor officials, the farm workers on the vineyard property, and the strikers with their red flags on the border road, all observe the drama of the young man all alone trying to make up his mind whether to remain on the vineyard property where he had no power and was ill-treated and ill-paid or to join the strikers and attempt to change his condition. In the end the boy gives in and returns to the crew of workers that he had left. Later, Matthiessen has an opportunity to talk with the young man. Why did he, at just the critical moment, turn around and return to his place among the workers? "The boy picked at the dust on his sandals. 'The whole world was awaiting me,' he murmured, 'and I became afraid.'" That was where the installment ended, with the boy's fear, and it has left me a whole week in which to meditate upon the question of fear.

There are cops patrolling the street in front of the Stonewall. They strut and swing their clubs, but not, I think, with the same bravado with which they walked this same beat yesterday. One of them seems agitated, as if he were apprehensive about turning his back on any group of us. I smile. So, last night is already having an effect. There are two other cops, one in the park in Sheridan Square, and one on Grove Street, all within sight of each other. There may be others. What are they guarding, after the damage has been done? After they destroyed our bar? Their bar? GAY POWER. It also announces us. GAY POWERFUL.

One of the things that has been widely noted about Caliban is the power of his poetry and the way he describes his island. He has a poetic sensibility that no one else on the island has, except, perhaps, Prospero himself. He reassures Stephano and Trinculo. "Be not afeard. The isle is full of noises,/Sounds and sweet airs that give delight and hurt not" [3.2.135-136]. We know that the great poet himself liked this ignorant—that is, untutored—native of the island because he gave him such powers of language and such a sensibility. All the others on the island, except perhaps for a few—Gonzalo, Prospero, Ariel, the sprites—blunder about in the jungle unknowing, have no feelings but fear, and are ambitious for the things that are not available on their island. Only Caliban is truly at home here, and only he is truly sensitive to the delights of his island.

Yet Stephano regularly calls him a "monster of the isle" [2.2.64]. He smells. Prospero calls him "a thing of darkness" [5.1.275]. Yet we are told repeatedly throughout the play that he is a monster. Miranda calls him a "villain" [1.2.310]. Prospero calls him, "Thou poisonous slave, got by the devil himself/Upon thy wicked dam" [1.2.321-322]. And a few minutes later, Miranda calls him "Abhorred slave,/Which any print of goodness wilt not take" [1.2.351-352]. In what way do any of these descriptions refer to anything real—that is, anything that the audience sees on the stage? Most scholars think when Trinculo says Caliban is "a fish: he smells like a fish" [2.2.25], he is referring only to his smell. In the same scene, when Trinculo and Stephano first come upon Caliban, he is said to have human legs and arms: He is not misshapen [2.2.33].

A number of separate justifications are given for the slavery in which Prospero and Miranda hold Caliban. He is accused of trying to "violate/The honour of my child" [1.2.349]. But Miranda herself does not mention this attempted crime. Prospero mentions it only once. Caliban responds only to express a hope: "Would't had been done;/ Thou didst prevent me, I had peopled else/This isle with Calibans" [1.2.352-353]. The charge of rape does not seem real. Miranda tells how she taught Caliban language, "But thy vile race/(Though thou didst learn) had that in't which good natures/Could not abide to be with; therefore wast thou/Deservedly confined into this rock" [1.2.359-362]. Apparently, Miranda's major charge against Caliban is that she didn't like him. It is a sleight-of-hand that Shakespeare foists upon his audience. On no good evidence, Shakespeare's audience is expected to see Caliban as a villain, as a savage, a "thing most brutish" [1.2.258], and therefore deserving of the most savage treatment.

The text of the play suggests that Shakespeare's first audience saw Caliban as an African. His mother, Sycorax, was a witch from Algiers, where he was conceived. The island of Setebos itself is close to the African coast. The reason the King of Naples was on a voyage was that he had taken his daughter to be married to the King of Tunis, who could have been a sub-Saharan African, or a Moor—that is, from the Barbary coast. The text also suggests that Caliban could be a West Indian or even a North American Indian. It seems, therefore, we don't need to look for the justifications for Caliban's enslavement. Prospero and Miranda enslave him because he is different from Prospero's race. He is dark. And the justifications for Caliban's enslavement function like the justifications for segregation in the American South before 1954: the text of the play implies that Caliban deserves harsh treatment because he is black. And the freeing of Caliban, in such a context, becomes a momentous act.

Christopher Street is full of noises that give delight and hurt not. Men and women on the sidewalks, in the summer air, talk to one another and call out to each other, full of joy and expectation. Happy as they are, the men of Christopher Street look as if they have been worked over with a bat, bruises, red lumps, the dark red that comes before scabbing. They look tired, too. The trees of the park in Sheridan Square are the full green of high summer, and make Christopher Street a woodland glade. The uniform today is cut-offs and flip-flops and tank tops, shades, and baseball caps sitting on top of head bandages. The Leatherman is on the left—the south side of the street—where Andrew and I buy our leather, vests and chaps. Both of us have biker's jackets from there, too. Fine stuff. It is almost one o'clock, and I am almost at the Silver Dollar. Belle will be there, and it is possible that she has found Andrew and Joseph.

The Silver Dollar occupies a double-wide storefront on the south side of Christopher between Bleecker and Hudson and is a sort of neighborhood café for the street. It's the place you go for hamburgers and fries. It's a place to meet friends for coffee and is always crowded. Belle is in a booth against the wall. She watches me walk toward her, moving around the tables between us, her eyes not leaving me, and not smiling. I slide into the booth opposite her.

"So. What's up?"

She checks out her cigarette, brushes off the ashes, and then looks back at me. "Well, everybody is talking about last night. I think people are exhilarated. I think they are astonished. And I think people are asking, 'What now?'"

"Do people have ideas?"

"Well, yes. You walk down the street and people are talking about everything under the sun. The Mafia owning bars. That has to stop. Police entrapment. That has to stop. Police brutality has to stop. The State Liquor Authority has to acknowledge that gay people are legitimate customers in bars throughout the city, and the SLA has to issue liquor licenses to gay-owned bars."

"That's good. We have to address those."

"You seem dubious."

"Well, we need to address those things, but even if we address all those things successfully, there're still things that have to be addressed that may be more serious than any of those."

"Like what?"

"The great characteristic that almost all gay people shared up to last night was fear, and what we saw on the street last night—people thought it was men fighting the cops, but it wasn't—was men shedding their fear right in front of our eyes. And our whole lives are going to be different, starting today, because we are going to start living our lives without fear. I don't know what it's going to be like."

"You've never been afraid."

"No. Well, yes, of course I have. It is the human condition to be afraid—afraid of being hurt. I have probably not had as much fear about this particular issue as many gay people, fear of exposure. I was not brought up in that kind of family. I was never afraid my parents wouldn't love me, like Andrew. I never felt vulnerable like that. But I have certainly felt the fear of scorn and derision that gay people are subject to. It is certainly true that as a community, our fear has characterized our dealings with the world."

"I don't believe that you have been afraid."

I have been afraid of not knowing what I was to do. Do I know what is the best way for me to live? And I have been afraid of being mocked.

She lights another cigarette. I hear the clatter of the restaurant.

"I worry about you looking like that."

"Like what?"

"The bruises and the cuts. Whatever you've got in your hair."

"I'm OK, Belle."

She stares at me for a long moment.

I met her even before I met Andrew. She is producing our play, and she was the one who hired me originally, in 1965. She and I wrote letters back and forth the summer before—the summer of 1964, Freedom Summer—when I was in Mississippi. I had hoped she'd hire me in the letters, but she didn't. She just said, "Come see me when you get to New York, and we can talk." So I did. She has a small office upstairs in The Olympic, and I visited her there. We talked for a little about my experience, about my education at Oberlin, about my being an apprentice stagehand on student productions, and about Freedom Summer and what I learned about carpentry. Then she asked me to join her for lunch across the street. I had never known a woman like her. Belle is self-dramatizing and tough as nails. She seemed very urban to me, and not at all given to the little gestures that soften even hard women in other places in the country, though I found out later that wasn't so. I like her. We became friends. I had to work a little at the difficulty of being friends while I was working for her. But she didn't have any difficulty with that. She let me know when she was the boss. She's about five years older than me, and good-looking in a florid way.

Andrew comes, bringing Joseph with him. They have bruises too. Brighter than last night, and, oddly, more of them.

"Hi, beautiful." Andrew slides his palm around the nape of my neck, his long fingers just touching my ear lobe. He leans over and kisses me.

Joseph sits next to me, and Andrew where I can see him, next to Belle. I can see Belle being aware of Joseph's presence, and I think it is interesting how Joseph apparently knows she is interested in him and seems to accept it, but ignores it. I don't know that I have ever seen a man so sexy and so accepting of his sexiness, and yet who is not a bully with it. It makes him a pleasure to watch.

Andrew speaks first. "My question is, 'What happened to Mitzi this morning?' Do you know? I got up, and she was gone."

None of us know.

"Do we all have our wallets?"

I shrug. "I've got mine." Joseph has his. I say to Joseph, "She's homeless, and she doesn't have a job, and sometimes she takes small things from us. We figure that's OK, as long as it stays small. We also give her money."

"The phone has rung pretty steadily all morning—your friends, my friends, our friends, all calling about last night. I made a list of names and numbers."

Belle tells them what we've been talking about.

Andrew considers the issues. "I don't know. I wonder. The way the SLA has treated us is not going away. When I first began to be aware—you know, I was fifteen—I saw the signs in the windows of bars, and I was amazed that a public authority like the SLA could get away with treating citizens of New York like that. Actually the first thing I was aware of was that I felt personally insulted, and that hasn't changed. Most of the issues that we faced yesterday are still with us. We can't get security clearances. We can't serve in the military. The way we have sex is criminalized in most of the states. The sodomy law in New York state makes us criminals right here. I think we learned something from the riots—we can work together, and we can fight, and we can force them to respond to us—but the issues we are going to be fighting over for the foreseeable future are the same issues we needed to address before last night. Our world hasn't changed. The larger issues we still have with us. Capitalism and its ruinous effects on the freedom of all of us in this country—"

Belle interjects. "That's what I said, Andrew."

"Well, I agree with you," I say. "What I was saying was that I think last night we lost our fear. There were men and women out there leaping on the backs of cops who, six or eight hours earlier, were afraid to acknowledge that they were gay. I don't think we have any idea what that means for us individually and also as a community. This is change of a different order from getting the cops to stop using entrapment on us. Without fear, or with less fear, almost everything we need to do now—our strategy and our tactics, even our goals—is going to be different. They have counted on us to be afraid. That head cop last night didn't bring many policemen, because he knew we'd be afraid and we wouldn't fight back. In his eyes, a raid on the Stonewall was a cheap win. Now, he's sitting there in the precinct thinking, *To raid the Stonewall means I have to bring a lot of cops.* It is going to cost a lot to raid the Stonewall. By losing our fear, we have raised the cost of everything they try to do to us. And then, for us personally, what does it mean to lose our fear? The fear of being hurt, being humiliated, being insulted, the fear of being exposed as a gay person. All those fears have kept us confined to our ghettos and our Mafia-owned bars. It is not just that now we can leap on cops. It's that all of those hundreds of actions and decisions and thoughts during the day that used to be determined by our fear, now are going to be determined by our courage. We are going to barely recognize ourselves, and that is true whether the Mayor gives in to any of our demands or not."

"Oh, yeah," Andrew says. "I like that. It's going to mean that when we do confront police entrapment, we're going to do it in an entirely different way—" He leans back in his seat. "We're going to be fierce warriors!"

At that moment, the door opens and two policemen walk in. The people in the café go quiet, and those who are facing the cops become watchful. The rest of us wait. The cops have their clubs out and are hitting them in the palms of their hand. They walk into the café and stop about ten feet in and survey the scene. Nobody does anything. Even the waiters are waiting with the food at the kitchen window. I can see the cops over to the left in the periphery of my vision, and mainly what I can see is Andrew's face, directly in front of me, and what is registering in his eyes. He is showing pure fury.

"Take it easy, Andrew," I say. I slide my hand across the table and let it rest on his wrist. "This isn't the time."

The cops leave.

Joseph is the first to speak. "They're asking for more."

"They are," I say, "except they probably are not thinking of it that way."

"Ignore them. Life is too short. Pick your battles."

We look at the door they went through.

"Tonight," Andrew says.

And I say, "Yes. Tonight."

We talk about fear and courage. A minute ago, when Andrew concentrated on the legal plight of gay people—the immediate legal predicament of gay people—and I was thinking of the emotional consequence of last night's battles, we were playing out a typical exchange between us. Andrew concentrates on injuries, psychic and physical, to individuals, caused by the authorities in the city—police brutality, police entrapment, sweeps of neighborhoods in which many many innocent people are charged with crimes they didn't commit. His mind and his feelings grasp tightly on the immediate hurt a person feels. I tend to see how all of us are being hurt. I don't know how many times we've had this conversation, where he is focussed on the needs of the individual and I am focussed on the needs of the group. This tension, between his way of looking at things and my way, is built into our relationship. But because we respect one another, we also have built into our relationship the way this tension is resolved. This is instinctive with us. On some particular issue, we stake out our respective turf at the beginning, repeat it several times, then gradually adopt the other's point of view as our discussions go on.

Joseph says, "Tell me more about Mitzi. She's part of your little group."

"We've known her for two or three years. We met her when she tried to lift my wallet one night in a crowd on Christopher Street. I grabbed her, and then we gave her some money and took her to get something to eat. We brought her here. There's a whole population of kids like her, gay kids just coming out and their parents are hostile to their being gay, or maybe they are cross dressers, drag queens or flame queens, or maybe they are transsexuals—most of them haven't had surgery because they don't have the money and I think a good many are not even thinking of surgery—and their families hate them and have kicked them out. Mitzi has been severely abused by her family. The city doesn't provide any services for them. The city even thinks they should be incarcerated. So there are these flocks of birds around the city, but more in the Village than anywhere else, these kids—children—stealing to stay alive, shoplifting, hustling, living on the street. They are way too young to be selling sex, but when you read about them, or when officials refer to them, they call them a disease, or a plague on the city, and they never seem to know that somebody owes these kids a childhood, at least, and a youth in a safe place. Some warmth and some caring and respect."

"It's a tragedy," Belle says. "I get so angry with this country, with the power structure that runs our country—"

"So we gave Mitzi our phone number," Andrew says. "She never used it, but it did get so that she knows where we are. She knows where Bo works, and she can usually find me here along Christopher Street somewhere, in the afternoon. She's pretty good. She doesn't come looking for us until she needs something pretty bad, and it's something we can give her—a little money, food, sometimes, in the winter a place to sleep. We told her that we would always give her a place to sleep and food."

The other two listen to us. "But I have a sense that she does pretty well without our help," I say. "She crashes with her friends. And we told her that if she ever got ready to come in off the street, she could come to us and we'd help her. But I doubt that ever happens."

"I don't know what we'd do, right now," Andrew says. "I have no idea how you bring a fifteen year-old kid in off the street."

"She must like you." Joseph speaks in a quiet voice.

"It is interesting," Andrew says, "what happened in the raid last night. The cops were roughest on the ones who don't fit their gender. The flame queens. They treated the Mafia people with some respect, the ones who've been involved in murder and in serious graft and major corruption, but they let their hostility for the queens become intensely personal. Why do you suppose they care whether or not a boy or a man wears women's clothes?" Andrew looks at Belle.

"It may have to do with how secure he is in his own maleness. But I have no idea. That's just pop psych. It is a tragedy, though, that these kids are driven to do the one thing that is going to enrage the men who have the most power over them. You know what I'm saying. Suppose they were driven to do the one thing that would most enrage, say, Unitarian-Universalist ministers, as a class. They could go ahead and do what they do for the rest of their lives, and still their paths would never cross the paths of any Unitarian-Universalist ministers. There aren't any down here, you know? They would never suffer for it. It's just bitter luck that made them need to do this one thing—wear women's clothes—that drives cops crazy. When cops are the ones who are around on the street with them, jostling for room and for power, carrying clubs and pistols—and not a Unitarian-Universalist minister in sight."

"Belle, what is this about Unitarian-Universalist ministers?" Andrew says. "Is this something I should know about?"

"Much of life," Belle says, "is just a question of how much bitter luck you have."

"I want to get to know you better, Belle," Joseph says.

"I've already told Bo to set you up with me one day real soon. We're thinking alike, big guy." Then she changes tone. "You know, you were talking earlier about now—" She is saying this to me. "—and what happened last night and where we are, and whether everything has changed or not, and what has changed, and I have been thinking about that while we've been talking. You said we have to decide where we're going now. Where are we going now?"

"I'll tell you," Andrew says. "We are going to form an organization."

"Something like SNCC," Belle says. "Or the Black Panthers. I think I'd like you to form an organization like the Black Panthers, if possible. They're tough. They're caring. And they are very photogenic." She checks us out. "How are you fixed for black berets? Could you help these guys with all this, Joseph?—Aren't you going to need guns?"

"Belle, be serious. Yes, I agree," I say. "But we have to get first things first. You guys saw the policemen come in here a few minutes ago. They're not finished with us, and we're not finished with them. We can't escape this, guys. We have to get through fighting on the street, and then, I think, we have to look at our situation and see what we have in front of us—which will be an organization."

Belle is the first to speak. "Well, if we really have a riot ahead of us, I want to be a part of it. Can I go with you guys? I've never been to a riot in the Village."

We laugh.

Andrew says, "Wear flat shoes, Belle. No platform heels." Then he repeats himself, "No wedgies."

She frowns.

I wonder if we could arrange some quick classes in street fighting. I wish Billy were here. He is a fighter in a way that I am not. In high school he ran with a tougher crowd. He played football, and he was the only white member of a gang the last two years in school. He was always getting cut up. I played basketball and wasn't in a gang, and fighting was foreign to my life, but he was good about getting in the right kinds of fights. He was always on the right side when the issue was race. Toward the end of our time in high school, I started getting challenged by players for other high schools—and sometimes from some of our own players—who didn't respect me for some reason. I think the reason was the obvious one—they had heard rumors or they suspected something. Billy was always there for me at times like that.

Billy stayed in Houston. He went to Oberlin also—he lived in the same student co-op, The Men's Co-op, that was half and half gay and straight that I lived in when I was there—and afterward he became a high school football coach in Houston. We are close. We talk on the phone about once a month, and our conversations are real ones. I told him right away when I met Andrew, and he tells me when he meets girls. He has been here and knows Andrew. Billy is comfortable with himself—who he is and what he is doing in his life—and he has a clear notion of right and wrong. If I called him, he'd come up for the riots tonight, but I didn't think about it soon enough. He's been brave since he was a kid. I'll call him this afternoon.

Mom and Dad are good parents. I am not sure I knew that, when we were growing up. I was too close to the action to be able to tell. Then I got some distance on it. Billy and I turned out all right—so far —and seem to have a grip on our lives that a lot of people I know don't. We're supporting ourselves, both of us seem to be trying to make a contribution, we think for ourselves, we stand up for ourselves. We seem to try not to hurt people, and, as Mom said, we try to do something that matters. I think they are pleased with us. Not that we are perfect—I don't mean to say that—but we're mainly OK for this phase of our lives.

One time recently, when my dad visited me here in New York, he went with me to The Olympic where I was building a set—it was for a show called *Riot* and was very topical. My Dad is like me—tall and thin and bony—with curly blond hair coming down over his forehead and ears. He sat on a folding chair and watched while I worked.

"Will you talk about what you're doing?"

I laugh. "Sure, Dad. What do you want me to say?"

"Well, what is it you're working on?"

Adam in the Morning

My dad usually likes me to start with the concrete facts. What is the name of the play?

"The play is called *Riot* and is a musical about a bunch of kids in some city. It takes place right now. The characters are all urban kids —big hair, beads, Indian jewelry, bib overalls—who look just like kids on the street outside. The show needs a set the actors can sing and dance on—various platforms at different angles and sloping at varying degrees. Right now, I am working on a long incline runway that goes from one side of the stage to another that actors can run up and down and that, in the big ensemble numbers, will have to hold a whole row of actors filling the whole runway from right to left. It has to be strong. And it has to hold thirty-five people averaging, say, one hundred and thirty pounds each."

I showed him the drawings the set designer gave me. There were three of them, sketches of the stage from above and from the front, showing the various platforms, and one side elevation.

"There are no numbers on these drawings."

"Right, I have to figure out how wide the runway is going to be, how strong it has to be, what size boards to buy, where to put it, what it's all going to cost—"

"And then it's your job to build it."

"Yes." I look at him. Why these questions? "I like the problem-solving aspect of all this, figuring out how to translate these drawings into a workable space on the stage that the actors can use, and then I really like the actual construction work, the measuring, sawing, hammering, screwing, putting it all together." At this moment, I am measuring off lengths of 1X3 pine that are going to make the basic framework of the runway, and I am talking to him whenever there's a break in my work. "I like making something that wasn't there before. Do you know what I mean?"

"I think so." He watches me for a few moments. "I try to see what you are doing and compare it to what I do in the classroom, and they are very different, I think. Basically what I do is give somebody something they didn't have before, some fact, some way of looking at a set of facts, some method of interpretation—"

I have been hearing him talk about his teaching all my life.

"One thing I like is the gradual accretion of the thing I am building. One day, it is a pile of lumber by the loading dock. Then, as the days go by, that pile gets smaller and smaller, and the organized construction on the stage gets bigger and bigger. I like that. Building.

I like the gradual accumulation of structure. It is perfect when there is nothing left of the pile of lumber at the moment I finish building the structure on stage."

"You know, Bo, I don't think I've ever made anything. I think that's astonishing. I've always been doing something else, teaching other people to make things."

"Dad, Dad—" In these conversations, he is always careful to keep from making himself look better than me. "Dad, you made me." I go over to where he sits, and I have my arms out, and so he has to stand up, and I hug him and kiss his cheek. "And you did a fine job of it, too." I kiss him again, and then I step back and look at him and have my arms out, and I grin. "Don't you think you did a fine job?"

He is flustered and doesn't know what to say.

"Fine job," I say, and smile.

The trouble with organizations—any of them, like the Black Panthers and SNCC and SDS, and CORE, and even organizations like the NAACP—is that the real enemy is not some misguided policy of the government's. The problem is not the government ignoring the common humanity of some of the people in favor of other people, and the solution is not to be found in forcing the government to realize the error its ways. The problem is also not our economic system—capitalism or communism—and the problem is not in industry, or the educational system, or in religion, or in our military. The problem is with civilization itself. To achieve a level of civilization, we have to give up a measure of our liberty. This is central to the thought of Sigmund Freud. The degree of individual liberty that has to be given up was much less a thousand, two thousand years ago. But for the past hundred years, in contemporary industrial society—society with a technological base—the degree of individual liberty that must be surrendered is enormous. Contemporary technological civilization requires citizens who are uniform and regimented. It is not merely that in our highly developed civilization, most of us have given up the right to carry guns, it is that we have given up the right to have sex in any but the few prescribed ways. Herbert Marcuse says that contemporary industrial society tends to be totalitarian. It is almost impossible to escape the power of contemporary industrial society. The power of technology is such that all of us have to give up much of our freedom in order to live in society at all, and what we give up the most of is sexual things. That's easy to understand. One of the major differences between primitive societies and advanced societies is the extent to which sexual things are repressed in advanced societies. Marcuse says, in *Eros and Civilization,* "The methodical sacrifice of the libido...is culture." Shakespeare knew this when he was writing *The Tempest.* Prospero's enslavement of Caliban is a symbol of an advanced society's domination over the libido. *We enslave it.*

"So what're people going to do this afternoon?" Joseph asks.

"I think I'm going back to the theatre for a little. I may be able to catch the designer there this afternoon. What're you guys going to do?"

"I'll walk back with you," Andrew says. "You going right now?"

"Yeah. No special hurry, but I thought it would be good to see Matt sometime today."

We all slide out of the booth.

Belle turns to Joseph. "So, want to take a walk over to the East Village? I'm going to get sandals."

Joseph grins, and then he steps back to let Belle walk in front of him. We make it to the door and out onto the street, into the hot summer city air. We stroll along, Joseph with me, and Belle with Andrew.

"Hey, big guy!" It's a man from the Silver Dollar, running after us. "Wait up!" He catches up with me, breathless from running, and he has a bandage on his head. "Excuse me. Can we talk for a minute?"

"Sure. What's up?"

"We've been thinking about last night. We're all a bunch of guys in SDS, and we've been talking about what next. I saw you last night, and I'd like to invite you to be a part of whatever happens now."

He hands me a small slip of paper with his name and phone number mimeographed on it. He grins. "My name is Heath. Call us and give us your name and number and address, and we can begin to put together a mailing list so that we can reach you to tell you about a meeting. OK? This way, you'll know when we've found a place to meet and about the meeting."

"Great." None of us have business cards except Belle, who gives him hers.

"If you reach me, I'll reach these guys."

"OK. But call me."

"OK."

And then he's gone.

Joseph speaks to me. "Am I going to see you later?"

"Oh, sure. I'll be at the theatre, then I expect I'll go home. Call me at home around six, and we can make plans for the evening." Then, in a more serious register, "You do know there's going to be another riot."

"Yes."

"I don't want you to get hurt."

"No. And I don't want you to get hurt." He turns his face to me and smiles. "I want to suck your dick again."

I laugh. We are at Seventh Avenue. Joseph and Belle go off to the right, on West 4th toward Washington Square. Andrew and I continue on Christopher into Sheridan Square. We stop at the Stonewall and the cops. In the broken window of the Stonewall is a piece of plywood. Someone from the Mattachine Society New York—it's a gay liberation organization that's been around for twenty years and has become stodgy and tradition bound—has written a plea in white paint. The plea is addressed to "our homosexual brothers and sisters" living in the Village to maintain order and decorum on the streets of the Village. It is a plea that is already out of date. Elsewhere on the plywood or pieces of broken glass in the window are other graffiti. "We're Open." "Support Gay Power." "They Want Us to Fight For Our Country, But They Invaded Our Rights." "Legalize Gay Bars." There are also anti-war signs. "STOP THE BOMBING OF CAMBODIA," and "NO MORE WAR," and "REMEMBER HAMBURGER HILL." While we stand in front of the windows reading the graffiti, other men come up and speak to us. We greet them, gripping the shoulders of some and hugging others.

We move on. Andrew puts his arm around my shoulders and leans over and whispers in my ear, "I had sex with Joseph this morning."

"Damn! And I wasn't there!"

"I begin to think you and I should go out west for a visit. If all the men out there are like Joseph, we should go out and explore."

"There couldn't be a lot like Joseph, his ease with himself, his confidence, his desire to please, his caring—"

He kisses me. "Did you enjoy last night?"

"Yes."

"Do you still love me?"

I laugh. "Yes, of course. Do you love me?"

"Yes." He whispers in my ear again. "So everything is OK?"

"Yes. Everything is OK."

We do this, assuring ourselves.

"Bo, this is about something else. I haven't been able to get it out of my mind all morning. Last night, in the middle of the riots, I started thinking that this is going to be big, and it's going to be important for us. I thought we ought to keep a full record of what is happening. Somebody ought to be saving everything, and not only saving all the stuff that gets generated around something like this, but also somebody ought to write a full history of what happened last night. Put down absolutely every single thing that he can remember. And somebody ought to start collecting the histories or memories of all the other people that he can be in touch with. We can't collect too much. So we're not organized yet, but until we are, I am going to appoint myself to be the historian of these riots. I'm going to get a box and start collecting stuff—like the flyers we saw in Sheridan Square earlier—and this afternoon, back at the apartment, I am going to start writing about last night. OK?"

The theatre is dark. We go in. "What Matt and Sergei need to do is decide on a basic interpretation of the play. They haven't done that yet, and that's why our discussions about the set and the rest of the design for the show are not going anywhere. I thought, when Belle first offered me this job, that they were settled on an anti-colonialist *Tempest*. Beautiful island. Beautiful natives—Caliban, Ariel, the other sprites—being corrupted by Europeans, who have their own subplots going on, infecting everything they come in contact with. Prospero's magic is the more advanced technology of the Europeans defeating the folk art of the innocent and free natives. But Sergei keeps getting distracted by the plots Prospero has set in motion. Is this what the play is about? What is it? You have to know and to hold onto what you believe—what's important—without allowing your focus to waver."

Andrew comes over to stand before me. I am sitting on a stool, randomly placed on the stage. He pushes my knees apart and stands between them. "They don't see what they're doing?"

"I think they have a dim notion. I think they think they have chosen an overall conception of the play, and now they are just discussing the details. But they don't seem to understand that they are entertaining fundamentally different—and conflicting—versions of the play."

He stands in front of me, between my legs. My hands are on his shoulders. I feel the thereness of his shoulders, the solid impenetrable mass of his body. With my hands on his shoulders—his deltoid muscles—I can sense his breathing and the vibrant motion of all his body. I see him in my mind with no clothes, drawn by a master artist —one unwavering line to make his outline, others to draw under his pectoral muscles, his navel, and the outline of his dick and his balls hanging against his thigh. A simple picture, powerfully erotic, Picasso's Minotaur. He looks down and to his right, his face drawn only by a line for his eyelashes and his full lips. Just enough in the drawing to suggest unmistakably who the drawing is of. Through his t-shirt, I touch his tits. He lifts his head and looks at me and smiles. Then he takes the hem of his t-shirt and pulls it away from his body —and up. He smiles more broadly now. My hands are open and flat against his skin, and I slide them up the sides of his torso. I run my thumbs across his nipples. I pull my rough thumbs across his nipples, and I pull gently on them between my thumbs and my index fingers. He throws his head back and closes his eyes and sighs deeply.

There is no one to speak about the needs of the body. We have experienced ourselves, each one of us, but I think we don't know how to think about the body. We don't know what words to use or what attitude to take. We are embarrassed by our sex, but it is unclear why, and we don't know how to be un-embarrassed. Powerful erotic images cause a kind of blindness. They are so disconcerting that, to deal with them, we turn them into crimes, as in Prospero on Caliban's proposing to have sex with Miranda, or into worship, as in Ferdinand and Miranda. We are living through the sexual revolution, but powerful forces are in reaction already, and it may be that this, right now, is as liberated as we are ever going to be. This moment, the high point. We can't waste this.

"Joseph wants to move in with us," Andrew says.

"I figured he would propose that. What did he say?"

Andrew shrugs. "We had sex when we first woke up, and afterwards he said something like, 'Have you guys ever thought about having another guy move in?'"

"And?"

"I said we'd never discussed it. He wanted to know why, and I said it'd never come up. Nobody had shown up who raised the question. Then he said he wished we'd think about it."

"What do you think?"

"I don't know. He's a powerful, erotic figure. He's great in bed. He's an interesting guy. I like his West Coast take on things. I love it that he comes to us with his history—the Freedom Rides, CORE, SNCC, Mississippi, the voter registration drives, Watts. He seems thoughtful and kind. He's very open. He's very smart. I love that."

"OK," I say, "let's think about it. Do you think something like that would work?"

Andrew laughs a little. "Oh, sure. It certainly worked last night. But work for how long?"

"Yes."

"Yes, what?"

"Yes, that is the question. How long?"

"For a night, a week—"

"You and I have been together for three years," I say. "Then he goes away and leaves us. Or, less comfortably, he and one of us go away and leave the other one of us here. Or even worse, some two of us kick the third one out."

"Any of those things could happen any time anyway," Andrew says. "Some dude walks down Christopher and before any of us know it, the whole configuration of our lives has changed."

"It is hard."

"What?"

"I can tell you I love you, and my impulse is to build on that, make a promise of some kind, or, worse, make several promises to you, right here, right now."

Andrew finds another stool and sits down next to me. He reaches for my hand. "Yes."

"Yes, what?"

"I know what you mean. What you are saying. I wonder why that is?"

"About being in love?"

"Yes," Andrew says. "Why does that make us want to promise something? Why isn't being in love enough for us?"

"I don't know. I don't know. I don't know. I think it is hard because I want to control the future, be together always, have this always. I want you to promise me that this will never change."

He squeezes my hand. "I have the same impulse. But let's try not to, OK? Hold off as long as we can. I think one of the things that makes what we have together what it is, is our sense of our freedom."

Neither of us wants to discover that we are together because a number of years ago we promised to be together. So I ask him, "Do you want Joseph to move in?"

"I don't know. I told him we'd probably think about it—we'd talk about it—and live with the idea for a while. I told him not to expect an answer anytime soon. I also told him he ought to speak to you directly."

"It is way too early to decide if we want to bring in somebody else, and then there is the separate question of whether Joseph is the one." The idea is disturbing—and at the same time exciting. What are we doing here?

The trouble with sexual freedom is, I think, the same problem with all kinds of freedom. It requires that we be adults and take responsibility for our actions and for the consequences of our choices. We will no more be in complete control of our lives if we are completely free than we are now when we are only partially free. But if we are free we cannot blame our lives on any other person. If we are free, people no longer control us, but the direction our lives take is controlled by events, by chance, by the wind and the weather, and by our nature, by our height and our appearance, and if we are free, it is necessary to know what is ours and what is not ours, to sort out the causes of effects from the merely incidental.

"By the way," Andrew says, "did you see that the Charleston strike has been settled? It was in the *Times* this morning. The Southern Christian Leadership Conference is now dangerous to oppose. That's very powerful."

"What did they get?"

"The hospital agrees to rehire all the striking workers, a minimum wage of $1.60 an hour, the right to unionize, and a grievance procedure. They had a complaint, they stuck together, they never gave in, and they were fearless. Imagine, black in the middle of the Old Confederacy, and they won!" He shakes his head.

Andrew leaves me, and neither Sergei the director nor Matt the designer show up at the theatre.

I call Billy in Houston, and I tell him about last night.

"Holy smoke! Are you all right? Were you in the fighting?"

"Oh, yeah! I was in the middle of it all right. I got banged up some—some, but nothing serious. I'm OK."

"No, exactly what happened to you. The head? The shoulders? Tell me exactly." This is like Billy.

"Several—four or five—blows to the head that drew blood. I never lost consciousness. When I was down, I got kicked a number of times. I don't think I broke any ribs, and the bruises I have are all small ones. I am in a little pain now, but not much. Billy?"

"Yes?"

"I'm telling you the truth."

"That's a relief. Tell me about the bruises."

I do.

"I guess the reason I am calling is that it didn't end last night. It's continuing tonight."

"How do you know?"

"The energy on the street. The cops are pissed, because there hasn't ever been a time since anybody can remember when the cops weren't able to control the street, and they couldn't last night. The cops got chased into the bar, and they had to barricade themselves inside to keep the mob from killing them. They were truly scared. And no matter how many of the riot cops they put out, they never were able to clear the street of rioters. I think that stunned them. There's going to be a second riot tonight."

"Are you going to be careful?"

"Yeah, I will. I am going to try not to get into any one-on-one challenges tonight."

"Bo?"

"Yeah?"

"Do you want me to come? It is too late to get up there tonight, I think, but I could check. In any case, I can be up there tomorrow." His voice is warm and loving and reassuring. "You know I can. You know I'll come. We can fight the cops together, like we used to do."

"Yes, yes, I know." I think it must be for this that I called him— the warmth and the love and the offer to come.

I didn't tell Billy about Tommy Sante at first, and then Billy guessed that something was up.

"Why are you and Tommy always in your room together with the door closed?"

I tried to get out of it. "We're studying."

"No, na-uh. I know what studying feels like. This is not studying. What're you two doing in there?"

I think what he was thinking of was drugs. In our neighborhood, in 1957, that was a possibility. So I invited him into my room, and I sat at the desk, and he lay on the bed, and we talked.

"OK. You've started dating girls, right?"

"Last year," he nodded. "Right."

"Well, sometime in the last three or four years, I've started getting interested in sex too—maybe when I was in the seventh grade—and do you know how you begin to notice that your relationship with girls is completely different from what it used to be?"

He nods. He doesn't know where this is going, but he loves me and he isn't suspicious of me, so he is willing to go wherever I lead.

"Well that's all happened with me, except with one difference."

He nods, again. He's waiting.

"I found that it was my relationship with boys."

There is a moment.

"Boys!" Then, "You're into boys?" Then, "Boys!"

I know Billy. He won't betray me. "I guess this is a shock, huh?"

He shrugs, speechless.

"Look, it was a shock to me too. But the things you know about me are still true. I love you. I love Mom and Dad. I'm still going to do something with my life that matters." I laugh. "I don't know what it is yet, but I'll please all of you."

"—Bo? Bo?" He stands up and comes over to me and holds me. "I love you. I'm OK with you. You don't have to please me."

"I know. I'll help you with this, Billy."

"Wait, you just took me by surprise. I just wasn't thinking of that. Sure, man. It's OK. I think it's cool." We're standing by the desk, and he is holding my elbows. Now he's grinning broadly. "Now, tell me what it's like to be turned on by a boy!" Then, "Are you turned on by me?"

I laugh. "No, kid. You're my brother, and you don't get turned on by your family members. It would be like getting turned on by Mom—or Dad."

So it was OK. My being gay is some awesome and potentially weird thing that has developed about me. It makes me more awesome, more interesting, a person he can be proud of—I am fighting battles alone—and that he can help.

"Do Mom and Dad know?"

"Yeah. Last month."

"How long have you known?"

"Oh, a couple of years."

"Oh, man—" He is seriously disturbed. "—and you didn't tell me! You shoulda told me, Bo!"

"I guess so. I was—I don't know, I don't think I was ready to tell anybody until just recently. It feels like yesterday."

Billy is in pain. He tries to sort out what I have told him, because it is possible that what I have told him means I have not trusted him on this.

"Is that what is happening between you and Tommy, when you go in your bedroom and shut the door?"

"Yeah." I am proud of that, because Tommy is a cool dude.

"Tommy!" Then, "Wow!" Then, his eyes round, "Do you and Tommy have sex?"

"Yes. Tommy and I have sex."

"Do Mom and Dad know?"

"Yes."

"Oh, sure, they'd be OK with it. Uncle Duncan and all." He closes his mouth and lifts his chin and smiles. "This is pretty cool."

Then he asks again about sex. He grins, and he says, "What do you do when you have sex?" Then, "Is it true what people say?"

I told him I didn't know what he had heard, but I sit down again at the desk, and he gets on the bed again, his head at the foot of the bed and his feet on the pillow, his hands behind his head, and then he looks at me intently, and I start telling him about sex between men. We talk about this for a long time. I think, if Billy is going to be my friend for all my life, he can't be turned off by the idea of sex between men. If he is, there will be this hard negative knot in his mind, preventing us from being close. So I try hard to make what Tommy and I do together sound OK to Billy. I think the truth is that Billy and I have always loved each other, since we were babies, I guess, and if I tell him I did something, that is enough for Billy to think it is a fine thing to do.

"Does anybody else know?"

"No. You, and Mom and Dad, and Tommy."

"So I guess nobody has tried to give you grief over this."

He's thinking of what goes on at school and on the playing fields, thinking about me and Tommy being subjected to all that.

"No. I have never gotten that from anybody. Nobody knows, man. Maybe when other people know—"

Then he took my hand in his and gripped it hard and would not let it go, and he said, "I promise you, if anybody ever gives you grief over this, I'll be there for you. I'll have your back. That's a promise. Any time, any place."

He was fifteen. Billy had always been a cocky little bastard, and after he found out he had a queer brother he became a little more cocky. *Don't fuck with me or my big brother.* Got that? I dare ya!

"Anyway," he says, talking to me from Houston about whether he should come up to New York for the riots, "I think I will call and get the schedules on the airlines so if I want to come in a hurry, I can do that. I won't do anything without talking to you first. OK?"

It is really fine to be in the middle of a riot fighting the police and to have your brother fighting next to you.

"Where're you going to be later?" Billy asks. "I want to talk to you again."

I have mixed feelings about Billy's coming. He is no longer the scrappy kid he was when we were sixteen and fifteen, smaller than me, with a foul mouth. He grew up, never got taller than me, but he did get heavier. He lifted, and he bulked up, and his size connected with his attitude made him imposing. Sometimes it made him even a bully, since he was so sure that he knew what was right and wasn't shy about telling everybody else. Things are pretty complicated right now, and I could go without his coming and complicating them further.

The theatre is quiet. I am the only person here since Andrew left. Belle stops by to say she will call about tonight, then she goes. People speak of the lull before the storm. It is the moment before the storm takes everything with it, including our air. It can be a kind of breathless quiet. It is this quiet that we notice now, on the street.

At five o'clock it is clear that the director and the set designer are not coming. The sun is still way above the buildings, and when I sit here on the steps of the theatre, it gives everything on the east side of Sixth Avenue a gold glow. The traffic on the Avenue has begun to decline—it is still as fast as it ever is, but there is less of it. Traffic on the sidewalks of New York doesn't subside until the early hours of the morning—so many people, the sidewalks crowded, going uptown, going downtown.

A man and a woman, middle forties. She's blond and has curly— frizzy—hair down to her shoulders. A white t-shirt, denim skirt, high heels. She's talking to the man she's walking with, gesturing, her fingers extended. They're walking downtown toward me from the intersection with Waverly Place. Her face is turned toward him. He wears a suit and looks uncomfortable in the heat. He keeps his eyes steady on the sidewalk ahead. I hear her sharp voice as they approach me.

"—that's what it's all about, isn't it, taking on responsibility? I told Pamela—"

They pass on, going downtown.

Most people are not talking, even if they are with someone. College kids going uptown who show a lot of skin. They wear shorts and tank tops and Keds. The group of them—four or five slender kids —know where they're going, and there doesn't seem to be a leader. They could be students at any of the colleges in Manhattan, and their clothes don't help identify them. The young people at City College look just like the young people at Columbia.

There are two boys—young men—who may be together. Each of them has large liquid brown eyes. Both of them have longish brown hair that blows forward, covering their ears, and sideburns. They wear shirts whose sleeves have been cut off across the shoulders, tucked into their jeans, large belts and big oval-shaped buckles, and Frye boots. It is a classic look. The shorter of the two is talking and laughing, while the taller one is about to burst out laughing.

"—I don't know what it was, but I couldn't stop laughing. There I was sitting with him, and she was looking at us and getting this worried look on her face. I thought, you'll never—"

They are gone. Sitting here, leaning forward, my legs spread apart a good bit, my elbows on my knees, my hands together, I am aware that I can count the persons who have passed me in the last two or three minutes. So many men and so many women. So many men and women forming couples, so many men forming couples, so many women forming couples. So many people alone of each gender. That is, I might be able to come up with the numbers of men and women who are gay. If I were better at math, I could produce percentages. So many races—white, black, brown, Southeast Asian, South Pacific, Asian, South Asian. But of course that can't be done. Or done accurately. The easiest to categorize and enumerate is gender—the number of men and the number of women who have passed in front of this theatre on this corner at Sixth and Washington Place around five o'clock in the afternoon on a hot, sunny Saturday, very late in June, 1969. But even that's tough. Their clothes are no good. Men and women wear the same. And their body shapes are only sometimes helpful. Their physiologic equipment? The identity they carry around with them in their heads? How do I know what gender a passerby on the street holds in his or her head—or between his or her legs? That person may look like one gender and yet think of herself or himself as another gender. You may get it wrong, not just because you glance at a person and read them one way when they are another way. You may get it wrong because the only way to get it right is to sit down with that person and start listening to what she has to say. And you may get it wrong because there is no way to make a category for that particular person. What about trying to sort people out by gay and straight? How do you do that? The way a person looks? The way he acts? What if he looks straight and acts straight in every way except that he has sex with men? All of us know men like that. What if he looks straight and does nothing with men but kiss them? Or suck their cocks? Or hold hands? What about men who say they are gay but do nothing of any kind with men? Categorizing people is difficult, maybe impossible.

We have friends who tend to think in terms of gay people, as in gay-people-as-opposed-to-straight-people. For those people, all of us are gay people. They are inclusive when they talk about gay people. They include Mitzi among the gay people they think about, which would be OK if Mitzi were a he and attracted to the same gender Andrew and I are attracted to. But Mitzi is really a woman, and the fact that our culture says she has genitals that indicate the other gender does not in any way affect the attraction she feels for men. Mitzi is not gay in any way but the merely biological. She is a woman attracted to men. There are scores of these kids—and grown men and women too—around us all the time whose psychic selves differ from what their bodies might tell us, and who are not gay in any way but the merely chromosomal. And we must ask them to tell us their gender as well as tell us whether they are gay or straight, because our ignorance about them is profound. Andrew and I know people who count them all as gay. They also count as gay, men who are only sometimes gay, or only partly gay. Then there are men who are straight and who have no difficulty with their gender, and whose most deeply felt sexual experience is with other men. The trouble with all this is that, after a person has counted the men and women who are always and totally into their own sex, and the men and women who are always and totally into the opposite sex, he begins to count people who are none of these things. And it may be that the people who are none of these things are more than the people already counted. And it is right here that the effort to divide the world into two fails. Because the way it works is that we start forcing Mitzi into Billy's or Andrew's mold.

In like manner, the categories we use to describe races are inadequate as well as absurd. Octoroon. Mulatto. Mixed race. Half breed. We are less pure than any of those would suggest, the mingling of various racial strains having been completed thousands of years before any history that we know anything about. Our attempts to categorize the persons that we meet into a few categories is a dream. What is "white"? An inadequate attempt to describe an appearance that is currently approved in this culture.

I walk up the avenue. The sun, the golden buildings, this glorious weather. In New York in the summer, you never forget how it was on this same street in February, and this memory makes the feeling of summer that much more intense. This afternoon I am carried along by a flood of men and women going in my direction. I turn onto Greenwich Avenue and then into Christopher. On the sidewalk, I have New Yorkers all around me—of every race and color, of every age and of every gender and intelligence, and of every beauty—and we seem, each in our private New York way, joyful. That can take my breath away. I wonder if it is possible to feel affection for every New Yorker? What we—all of us—drive toward is freedom. We want freedom. Freedom in our feelings. Freedom in our selves. Freedom in our bodies. The human race is too various to be anything but free, and we are not free.

At the Stonewall, the handmade signs change hourly. *Support Gay Power. Gay Power. Freedom now!*

There are men and women handing out flyers. I take copies from everybody. One headline says, *Equality!* Another says, *Freedom now!* Another, *Down with Sexism and Homophobia!* Passing the Stonewall, I am aware of a noticeable heightening of feeling. This ground— these few feet of concrete—has been marked by last night's courage and fearlessness. This spot is going to take its place alongside the other places in New York memorable for what happened there—that is, for an event that changed the life of the city. One nearby building is The Triangle Shirtwaist Factory at 29 Washington Place, just half a block off the east side of Washington Square, where, in 1911, one hundred forty-eight young women died when the factory where they worked caught fire and burned, there being no fire escape and no other way for the women to escape the flames. Of these, eighty-six burned to death in the building, and sixty-two died when they jumped from ninth-floor windows to escape the fire. It was found afterward that the owners of the factory had locked them in. The building still stands, and you can walk down the sidewalk and stand on the spot where they died.

I walk through the milling crowds, cross Seventh, and continue down Christopher. At first the buildings are low—two and three stories—but at Bleecker they are four and five stories high, mainly brick, and the street itself is no broader than Christopher between Seventh and Sixth, two parking lanes and one driving lane. Very intimate, very urban. At Greenwich, Christopher broadens out into four driving lines—two in each direction—plus the parking lanes.

Joseph is waiting at the corner of Christopher and Weehawken, sitting on the pavement, his back against the building. People look at him and step over him as they pass.

He smiles at me. "I was beginning to think you all weren't coming home."

"If I had known you were going to be waiting on the pavement, I'd a come sooner. Come upstairs." We walk up to the building and climb the stairs. "How did you and Belle do? Did you go to the sandal-maker's?"

"Oh, yes. I bought a pair myself. I get them in three weeks. Hers are cool. She is going to wear them tonight."

I let us in, and he turns around and lifts his arms and puts them around my shoulders so that I am in close to him. He opens his mouth and kisses me. I slide my hands up his arms over his triceps and delts and lock them behind his neck. Our erections play with each other between our legs. He kisses, very gently, the bruises on my forehead.

All the rooms in our apartment are painted dark maroon with black trim. There are big theatre and movie posters. Our books are all in the bedroom, on boards-and-brick bookcases, Andrew's books on the bookcases against the wall, and mine under the windows.

We end up lying on the bed facing each other, arms still holding the other close. "How do you like Belle?"

He laughs. "She's fine. She's wonderful. She wants to have sex with me."

"That's Belle. She doesn't waste time. Did you?"

"No, not this afternoon."

"But you think you will."

"Uhhhmmmm. I don't know. Maybe." He is not committed to the idea.

"I am thinking about it." I consider this before I say it.

"About what?"

"Sex with Belle." That is not exactly what I am thinking about.

"You? That's a surprise."

"Why?"

"I thought you were content with Andrew."

"I am content with Andrew. This is separate, different."

He doesn't say anything.

"It's an experience I've never had, and most of the men in the world have had it. I thought I'd like to have it too. I think Belle may be the right person. She's loving, over-the-top, protective. She's sexy. She'll be fine. It would be fun—and funny. I think both of us would enjoy it."

"Would you—I am so surprised I can't figure out what to say." His face is very close to my face. "Is this a whim? Or some long-term geologic shift?"

"No. Well, yes." I don't really know the answer to that question yet. "I don't know. It depends on whether she wants to, on how she feels about all this. And of course it depends on how I feel at the moment. I haven't talked to her about it yet. I know she likes me. I like her. And she knows I have always been gay."

"Have you ever had sex with a woman?"

I laugh. "No. Have you?"

"When I was a kid. We were all fooling around in high school, and that was part of it." He goes silent for a minute. "And then, since I grew up, I've had sex with women, you know, communes I've been in, the big marches, and demos. My work on voter registration in Mississippi. You get high, and all sorts of things happen. There are all these bodies around, and it's hot! And men too of course. A lot more men than women. I'm totally oriented toward men. But you know how it is." Then he says, smiling, "Look, I didn't know you had plans with her."

"I don't. I've never talked to her. I have no claims. Belle is free to do what she wants. Belle has always been free to do what she wants. So are you."

He kisses me again.

We lie on our sides, facing each other. "Can I ask you a question?"

His face is very close to mine. "Sure. What?"

"Why is a man with your background and history in Harlem interested in two white dudes in the West Village?"

He smiles. "I could ask, you know, why two white dudes in the West Village picked up a black dude from Harlem during the first gay riots ever."

"Yeah—" I'm composing my thoughts about this. "I know."

"But to get to the question you asked. Don't you think a black man from Harlem can be interested in a sexy white carpenter in the West Village?"

"I mean the politics of it all—"

"I know what you mean. You have a feeling that I should be uptown doing something for the betterment of my race, instead of downtown doing something for the betterment of other fags."

"I guess when you put it that way."

"That black men and white men don't belong together right now, that somehow race trumps everything else. I'm always going to be a black man, just like you are always going to be white. We are both always going to be fags. And sometimes both of us are going to be interested in racial issues, and sometimes we are going to be interested in sexual issues. I guess I do know that sometimes one of us is going to be interested in racial issues and the other is going to be interested in sexual issues. Life can be complicated. But now it is not complicated. Now is my time to be downtown with you." He stretches. "I should say I am enjoying it."

"I'm glad you're here. Is it temporary, your time here in the West Village with us?"

"I don't know. I'm here, and I'll stay here as long as it feels right. One of the reasons I left Harlem was I came to feel that it wasn't right any more. I was aware of wanting to be in a community of fags. A group of us, six or eight brothers and sisters, would be out going to clubs after some event, and I was aware that people were pairing off. But it didn't seem possible for me to pair off. That felt lonely. I wanted to suck more cock, and I wanted to be with other cocksuckers, so I left Harlem to see what I could find down here. I found a job, and I found the two of you. Now I have to see how long this will work. I think it would be cool to find a community of men who are fags that includes a good number of black men and a good number of white men, or where the black component is something significant and isn't seen to be *other*. There are other ways this ideal community we're talking about here could be composed. At other times in my life, I've wanted a community of black men, some of whom are straight and some of whom are fags. I've also wanted a community of black men, all of whom are fags. That's kind of what you and Andrew have here, with the races reversed. There are times when I just need to be around black men. However it is arranged, I want to feel at home in all parts of me. Do you understand that?"

"I understand that. Sure. I want to learn more."

"I can help you."

"We don't know many black gay men."

"No?"

"No. I'd like to know more. There've been other times in my life when I've had a lot more black friends than now."

"Well. Maybe I should seize this moment to tell you that I don't know many white gay men. Let's see how things work out. And if you guys are as cool as I think you are, there are some black dudes I could introduce you to."

"Is it OK for me to ask you these questions?"

"Oh, yeah. It makes us close." He kisses me. "And I have a lot of questions to ask you too, about being white." He smiles and kisses me again. "You don't seem like a devil."

"I'd like to do what I can to make sure you're OK."

"Hey. I want to make you and Andrew OK." He kisses me. "But it might be better if we let it be my responsibility to be sure I am OK, and I'll let it be your responsibility to be sure you're OK. Then if there is something you want me to do, you should tell me. And I'll tell you."

"That sounds good."

He kisses my forehead again.

"Joseph?"

He smiles at me.

I kiss him again, this time a deep-throated kiss that takes a minute.

"I want to say that I understand if what you have with us is temporary. Andrew and I don't make any promises to each other. We don't need to have you promise us anything either."

Afterward he goes to sleep. He's lying there on the bed, facing me, his face relaxed by sleep, his lips slightly parted. I wonder where my copy of *The Rebel* is? I ease my way out of the bed and slip into the kitchen. I light up a joint. The phone rings. It is Belle.

"I have thought about the plans we made this afternoon. I ran into Helena—" She is the business manager for the theatre. "—and we decided it would be best if we went together tonight. Is that OK? Are you sure I have to wear flat shoes?"

"Belle, Belle, you will be running from the cops, dear. You need flats. Wear your new sandals."

She grumbles and hangs up.

The phone rings again immediately. It's Billy.

"Look, guy. I have reservations for New York. I'll get in about five tomorrow, and I will call you from JFK. Can I stay with you?"

"Billy, you don't need to do this. We're OK here—"

"Oh, I think I do. I have to come see my brother and be sure he's OK."

"Well, I'm OK, and just knowing you are willing to come is great. Besides, I don't know if there is going to be more rioting after tonight. Are you sure you think you should come? It's a long way, and it costs a lot of money."

"Well, buddy, I already have my ticket, now, so I just think I will come on. You don't have to look after me. I can look after myself. You know that. Now, don't think about this any more until six o'clock tomorrow afternoon, when I'm going to show up on your doorstep."

Jesus, it's hard to focus when you're high. I look at the list of people who have called today—about twenty-five names—and wonder when I will have time to call them back. I am standing with my back to the counter, naked, my hands behind me on the counter edge on each side of me, when Andrew comes in.

"Where have you been? I thought you were coming here when you left me today."

"I was, and then I thought of how many people might be here— Joseph—so I went to the Silver Dollar and occupied a booth for the last two hours. I got a lot down on paper."

He sees Joseph in our bed and grins. "Our big friend is a busy guy." He puts his arms around me and kisses me. I see him check out my bandage and the bruises on my forehead, even while I am checking out his. "How are you?"

"I'm OK. Actually, I'm fine." I smile, tilt back my head, and look down my nose at him. I show him the joint. "This is fine stuff you bought. Heady."

"Yeah, that's another reason I went to the Silver Dollar instead of coming here."

"Billy called."

He has me in his arms again, his nose in the corner of my neck, and he kisses me there, his lips apart, so that I can feel the wet inside of his mouth.

"The times are heady. What did Billy want?"

"He's coming to New York tomorrow."

"Why?"

"To see us, to riot in the streets. You know Billy."

He laughs. "That's fine of him. Are you OK?"

"Oh, yeah. Things are getting a little complicated. But everything is fine. Whatever is going to happen at the theatre is going to be fine. Whatever it is. And I like Joseph. He worked for SNCC. He seems like a good man. He's a really good man to have around right now. And, my man, I am ready for whatever is going to happen tonight in the street." I pull back and look at him. "I feel like I am ready for the big job.

"What is the big job, big guy?"

"Oh, the Revolution. Isn't that what all this is about?" I hand him the joint. "Are you ready?"

"I think what's gonna surprise'em is how much we're gonna fight and how good we're gonna be."

Mitzi stands at our kitchen table under a large red and black poster of Che. She's emptying her pockets, reaching in and pulling out her change and a few bills and pieces of paper. She takes off her jewelry, her rings and a silver chain and leaves a little pile on the kitchen table.

"They never think we can fight."

"What're you doing, Mitzi?" Andrew asks.

"Y'see, if I get busted tonight, it's good not to have stuff in my pockets, which I can lose to the cops or to the other girls in the tank." She looks at us. "I thought you guys were a safe place to drop all this shit. And just keep it here until I come get it." She is wearing jeans, a pale thin frilly blouse, and sandals with jewels.

We nod.

"I'll come tonight, unless I get busted. I recommend you don't take anything with you, either. One piece of ID, and nothing else. Leave all your money except a little bit, and anything else like rings or necklaces. Anything valuable."

We watch her strip for battle. Joseph shrugs, grins, and starts emptying his pockets. Then we all do.

The phone rings. It is the man from last night, the exhausted, wounded one who stood in the street and wondered if we were OK.

"Hi, my name is Stephen. I spoke to you last night in Sheridan Square. You were sitting on the high stoop next to the Stonewall."

"Hi, Stephen. I remember you."

"Hi, I'd like to get together with you and get your take on what you think is happening. I think some of us who are in SDS might have a contribution to make to where we go from here. Would you be interested, if I can pull together a group of us?"

"Coming to your apartment? Sure—"

I get his name and number, and he says he will call when he can pull this together, sometime this week. Stephen and I talk about the story earlier in the week in the *Times,* about the SDS meeting in Chicago and the big split there. There's Stephen from last night, and there's Heath from the Silver Dollar. And there's the list of callers with twenty-five names. There's a lot of energy in the community.

The gang is still talking about what to take when going on a riot.

"What's a good piece of ID to have, Mitzi?" Andrew asks.

"Take your driver's license. Everybody is expected to have one, and they are easily replaced," Joseph says. "And a housekey with no identifier." This is what he learned in Mississippi.

I ask Mitzi if she has an ID. She does, but she doesn't tell me what it is.

"I'm going to count my bread when I come back, and it all better be here."

"We won't steal from you," I say.

She doesn't think we will. The four of us stand at the kitchen table, ready to leave for the Stonewall. It is a quarter after eight.

"OK, guys."

And then we go, rumbling down the stairs. I lock the deadbolt and get the locks on the street and then catch up with the guys. It's getting dark. When we turn onto Christopher, I can feel the tension in the neighborhood. The sidewalks of New York are often—are usually —very crowded, but tonight they are crowded with people all of whom have a single place to go. This feels strange.

"Look," Andrew says, "They're handing out flyers."

A boy on the other side of Christopher with a stack of paper over one arm is shouting, "It's ours! Take it back!" His voice easily carries to our side of the street, reverberating against the brick buildings. "It's ours! Take it back! It's ours! Take it back!"

Andrew drops back to walk beside me. He takes my hand. "They're talking about the flyers," he says, indicating the little groups of people on the sidewalk. Joseph and Mitzi are walking together. Our gang.

We pass another man with flyers. The headline says, "CHRISTOPHER STREET BELONGS TO THE QUEENS." He calls out. "Do you think queens are revolting?"

We all shout, almost in unison, "You bet your sweet ass we are!"

The man grins and holds up his thumb. Mitzi grins broadly.

Going east up toward Seventh Avenue, we cross Washington.

"This—" Andrew's arm takes in the whole scene, the large brick buildings, the traffic, the men giving out flyers. "—everyone on the street is engaged in the general unrest. Everybody's waiting for something to happen."

"This is the way revolutions start," I say. "The government is badly managed, and the people are oppressed, and one day—or night —somebody makes a mistake, some error of judgment, a trigger pulled in fear, a clumsy attempt to manipulate the Estates-Generale or to tax something that really really ought not to be taxed, a bar raided that ought not to be raided, and the result is rioting in the street, and the Revolution is on its way, after which the train of events can't be stopped. Very quickly revolutions get all the way down to basic questions. *How are we going to govern ourselves?"*

"What do you think?" Andrew asks. "Have we gotten there?"

"I don't think I know what you guys are talking about," Mitzi says.

"Where?"

"Mitzi, the point of no return, where, after this point, they can't go back and fix it all. There was a minute last night, when somebody really wise and smart—maybe from City Hall— could have come down here with a megaphone and said to all the guys rioting in the street, 'I'm really, really sorry about this. I'm really sorry this has happened. If you will give me and my staff just a few minutes, we're going to re-open the Stonewall Inn and invite all of you guys in, and tonight the drinks are on City Hall. The police have already been called off—they're loading up the buses now—and all those who have been taken for booking to the police stations are being brought back down here, where they belong. OK? We are very sorry about this terrible mistake. If anyone feels they have been treated badly by the police, I am going to designate a member of my staff to take your names so that you can be given medical care and so we can put you in touch with a Citizen-Ombudsman, who can put you in touch with legal counsel, if that is what you want.' And then, Mitzi, after somebody like the Mayor comes down here and says something like this, then maybe everybody will just go back in the bar and have drinks on the Mayor for the rest of the night and get drunk, and then everybody would go home, and there won't be any more rioting. But the trouble is, nobody came from City Hall to say those words, so the guys ended up staying on the street and rioting and attacking the cops and getting riled up, so that now what the Mayor faces is a major riot and major challenges to the way he governs the city, and, potentially, maybe even things that are more dire."

"None of us are going back to the way things used to be," Andrew says. "What is the question we are confronting?"

"That's part of what we have to work on. Something like How is our sex to be expressed? We know we aren't going back to the way it was yesterday. An even larger question is, '*How are we to be governed?*' And the police are pretty rapidly moving to fight on *those* grounds."

"I know how my sex is going to be expressed—loudly!"

We laugh. "Mitzi!"

Christopher Street is not very long, about four crosstown city blocks. It is one of the principal streets in Greenwich Village, and it runs northeast-to-southwest between Greenwich Avenue, just before Greenwich enters Sixth, down to West Street on the river. From Sixth Avenue, which runs down the middle of the island, Christopher passes the Northern Dispensary at Waverly Place, Sheridan Square, the Stonewall Inn, crosses Seventh Avenue and Bleecker, Bedford, and Hudson, before proceeding on to West Street on the river. Christopher is a kind of funnel—narrow at the Greenwich Avenue end in the center of the island and wide at the river end. From Greenwich all the way down to Hudson, Christopher is three lanes wide, a parking lane on each side and one for driving. Between Hudson and West Street on the river, the street is six lanes—one on each side for parking, and four in the middle for traffic, two in each direction. Between Hudson and Greenwich, there is a high brick wall on the south side, and on the other side of the wall is the churchyard of St Luke's Episcopal Church and its school. Traffic for the whole length of Christopher Street runs from Sixth Avenue to West Street. Between Greenwich and Washington there are a big red brick building on the south side of the street and residential buildings of three and four stories on the left. At the river end of the street, there are several big buildings, apparently apartment buildings.

Tonight, we are moving east on Christopher, toward Seventh and Sixth, climbing the slight incline from the river up toward the center of the island, moving against traffic, from the mouth of the funnel into its narrow part, where the pressure is. As we move east of Hudson, into the narrower part of Christopher, everything gets denser, the crowds and the anti-authority mood of the crowds.

"I've never done this before, gone to a demonstration or a riot over a gay issue," I say.

"I think few people have," Joseph says. "There have been very few demonstrations about gay issues for people to go to."

"Why have we been so slow?" Andrew asks. "Black people have been demonstrating for fifteen years, and the whole country has been demonstrating for five years against the war. The black hospital workers in Charleston—in *Charleston!*—have been on the street for almost a year. Why have gay people been so slow to get out into the street?"

"I think," Mitzi says, "every time I go on the street I'm giving the finger to everybody in power, and I know that, and I think they know that too."

"Yes. You are a model for all of us, Mitzi," Andrew says.

"Gay things have not been politicized," I say. "Things go on the way they have gone on in the past, and people don't question whether they should be that way, no matter how painful they are, until someone, some genius, says, 'Hey, guys, there are two sides to this issue.' And at that moment, the issue becomes politicized. We discover a new way to think."

"You were saying this afternoon that the big difference between yesterday and last night was fear." Andrew says. "You said at the Silver Dollar today at lunch that now that gay people have lost their fear, everything is going to be different."

"I never thought there was a gay question that was subject to politics—organizing, speeches, demonstrations, bills in Congress. The *gay thing* has always seemed to be about something like our freedom to suck cock, and I think I have been embarrassed to put that up for public discussion. It's odd. I didn't think there was any way to change the way things were. Now I do. In just twenty-four hours."

"There's something else, though," Joseph says. "I remember having a strong connection with the people in Mississippi. We were related, and everybody knew it. They were my brothers and my sisters in Mississippi, and I was going to help them. We were all black, but also we were all getting screwed by the system. The same thing is true here. We're brothers and sisters—we're all fags together —and we all get screwed by the system in just the same way."

"Speak for yourself, Tootsie."

"Well, most of us."

We laugh.

"Besides," Joseph says, "oppressed people always end up taking to the streets. Through violence. Fanon says that. 'The colonized man finds his freedom in and through violence.' That's what we're doing."

"I like that," Andrew says. "*I find my freedom through violence.* That's nice. Come on guys, let's see how much freedom we can find tonight."

We see cops. They patrol the street in pairs. They are breaking up any gathering of gay men of more than three persons. They come up to the men and say, "Move it along, move it along." They have their nightsticks out and gesture with them when they say, "Move it along." This is threatening and challenging. The men do move it along, and then, when the cops go on down the street, the men re-form into their little group and go on as before.

"OK, guys," Mitzi says. "I think I'll leave you here and take off by myself. I'll catch you later."

"Hey, Mitzi. You can't leave us." I yell at her, but she doesn't answer. "Mitzi! Be careful!" But she is gone, threading her way through the crowds until she disappears.

"She doesn't want her friends to see her with us," Andrew says.

"There's no reason for her to want to be with us," I say. "We are all fifteen years older than she is."

We hear a scream. We search the street around us. We are between Bleecker and Seventh. Two cops are beating a man and dragging him to the cop car. He has his hands up, trying to ward off the blows of the cops' nightsticks, screaming.

"What th'fuck!" Andrew, who has been holding my hand, drops it. He is searching for something to throw. We are stopped by a trash can, full of trash, and Andrew reaches into his pocket for his lighter.

In a second the trash can is on fire—it's paper and burns high instantly—and the cops, turning around to see the fire, let go of the man they had been beating.

He holds his lighter up for us to see. "This is going to be useful tonight."

The whole block is peopled by little groups of men and women, talking and checking out the action over their shoulders. I see Belle, in a group of four or five women. She's talking animatedly, waving her red fingernails, probably talking about Ramesses II.

A man with heavy dark eyebrows and a very thick mustache comes over to us. "That was cool, setting the trash on fire. There's not going to be any trash in any barrel on Christopher Street by the time this is over."

"Oh, much sooner than that, man, much sooner," Andrew says.

"I missed last night," the man with the eyebrows says. "Were you here last night? I wish I had been here last night."

"Yeah," Andrew says. "We were here last night." We were among the lucky few. "Hey look," he says, speaking to all of us. "We need to get things to throw. Help us."

So the four of us—including the man with the eyebrows—start looking for things to throw. Other people join.

The man says, "You know the Mattachine Action Committee—the MAC—is trying to pull together a meeting." The MAC was formed by some younger, activist members of the Mattachine Society New York. They wanted some organization that was more confrontational.

Men run back to a construction site on Bleecker to see what they can get. Joseph and I find a place where the paving stones have been taken up, and we collect a pile.

Somebody starts screaming from somewhere up ahead of us, near Seventh Avenue. The cops have another man, but it is too far away to see what's happening.

A man walks through the crowd passing out a leaflet. Its headline is WHAT TO DO IF ARRESTED.

"Great, I wish I had gotten this this afternoon, when I had a chance to read it." Joseph folds it up and sticks it in his jeans pocket. He looks at us and grimaces.

The man with the eyebrows is gone without telling us about the Mattachine meeting.

We leave our pile of rocks to someone else and make our way up to Seventh Avenue. It is completely dark now, the street lit only by the streetlights. At Seventh Avenue, we can see that Christopher Street on the other side is so crowded that the street is effectively closed to traffic.

A man walking with us begins to shout. "GIMME A G!"

And all of us answer, "G!"

And when we work our way all the way through the letters of "GAY POWER," somebody else starts yelling "WE WANT FREEDOM NOW!" Everyone joins in, and the chant reverberates off the walls of the buildings.

Somebody shouts, "CHISTOPHER STREET BELONGS TO THE QUEENS!" And people all over the street take it up, shouting in rough unison, CHRISTOPHER STREET BELONGS TO THE QUEENS!

A young man stands on the base of a street light and holds onto the lamppost and, leaning out into the street, is giving a speech.

"—time that brothers and sisters in the Village join the brothers and sisters all over the city rebelling against the system that is murdering our brothers and sisters in Vietnam and in the ghettos in this country, and imprisoning and murdering anybody who tries to expose the way it operates. It is a system created to enable rich folks to stay rich and to keep poor people poor. Corporations running this country own most of the wealth of the nation. And now, our new president is appealing to the racists among us, proposing to gut the Voting Rights Act of 1964 in exchange for votes—"

It is much easier to make that argument now, since Hamburger Hill and the bombing of Cambodia and this week's Life. I am walking between Joseph and Andrew. At first I hold Andrew's hand, and then I feel Joseph searching for my free hand, so I hold both of their hands.

On the other side of Seventh Avenue, just on the edge of the park in Sheridan Square, a makeshift podium has been erected—somebody has gotten a wooden box—and people are taking turns climbing up and haranguing the crowd. One young woman, who could be Mitzi's older sister except that she has a constant smile, big hair down to her shoulders, a very short skirt just covering her crotch, high, platform heels, seems to want to seduce us rather than harangue us. She stands so her audience gets a profile of her body, and she has a hand on the hip nearest to us. She tosses her head back and says, "Well, this has taken a long time!" The crowd laughs. Someone shouts out, "Hey, Linda, is that you?" Linda has a wise smile on her face and eyes that search the crowd. "What's left of me! But right now, what I want all of you to know is that—" It's an old Tallulah Bankhead joke. I am interested in her performance. She is playing to the gay people in the audience, but I am aware of all the others here who are not gay— older straight people in the crowd on both sides of us, and a significant number of kids who appear to be straight. I guess they've heard about the riots and have come down to see what's happening. Belle is standing over to my right, absorbed in the performance. Or maybe they have come down to take part. Here is a young woman playing her gay act on the street, before everybody here. We haven't seen that before. I speak to Joseph. "I find that moving. To see her putting on that act in public."

"Yes. She's out, isn't she? That's courage." Joseph glances at me and smiles, then gives his attention to the kid on the box.

I would say I have always been out, but I haven't always lived the way this young woman is living right now—where I was out to everybody who walked down the street. For someone who looks like me, it is easy enough to take advantage of the assumption in our culture that, unless you get evidence to the contrary, everybody you meet is straight. That is a kind of cover.

The young woman is gone, and another takes her place, playing to the same impulse in the audience to applaud the gay act being done in public.

Then it becomes overtly political. A very intense young man— long hair, thin flowered shirt, low bell bottoms slung on his hips—is talking about the cops. "—have to let them know, right now, that we aren't going to put up with them being brutal no more. This shit of them coming down our street with their billy clubs is going to stop. We're gonna meet violence with violence, man, and I predict blood is gonna to flow—"

The crowd gives a prolonged cheer.

"I want to be safe in my city."

Joseph and Andrew and I are holding hands. This afternoon Andrew and I kissed on the street. We are engaging in a whole range of behaviors, now, that we didn't engage in before early this morning —almost all of them are gay sexual behaviors. All around us, men are holding hands and kissing.

Conflicting with the speeches is the voice of a man who must be standing over near the door to the wreckage of the Stonewall. He's inviting everybody to come in. "Come in and see the damage the cops did to us!" He goes on and on with this, like a carnival barker, calling out "Free Soda!" I don't think anybody's going in.

The mood of the crowd gets more tense. The speaker is still talking about the cops. "This is gonna be known as the Battle for Christopher Street. We're gonna fight them man for man for every fucking inch of the street—" The crowd cheers.

There is another loud cheer, and Joseph asks somebody he is standing next to what's going on. The other man is grinning. "The queens up at the Corner have decided to close off Christopher Street. They're making a human chain across the street and are preventing any cars from entering."

"Let's go see what's happening." So we go east up Christopher. The crowds are filling all of the street now. They are alert, watchful, suspicious—and yet seem to have a holiday mood.

We hear chanting even before we get there. "CHRISTOPHER STREET IS OURS! CHRISTOPHER STREET IS OURS!" And when we get to the Corner, it is like what we were told. There are several hundred men blocking entrance into the street. A taxi that was trying to turn into Christopher Street is now backing away from the men and trying to back into traffic on Greenwich Avenue. "CHRISTOPHER STREET IS OURS!"

I wonder what the cops are doing, allowing all this to happen. They are not being very aggressive and aren't making any effort to keep the streets clear. There is a large group of them, maybe fifty of them, at the Corner, but they are merely standing around as if they are waiting for something.

Across Greenwich Avenue is the Women's House of Detention. It towers over this end of Christopher Street, a huge brick hulk out of scale with the other buildings in the neighborhood. I become aware of a rare beauty.

"Oh, guys, look. The House of Detention. Look up."

"Oh, yes," Joseph says. "Oh, *incredible.*"

Small flames are floating down from the cell windows of the House of Detention.

"Toilet paper set on fire," Andrew says. "It's beautiful."

The paper doesn't burn with a large flame. It seems to be just barely lit. The Women's House of Detention is twelve or fourteen stories tall, so the flaming tissue squares float down a long way before going out. Many men in the crowd around us stand and watch them come down.

A man next to me says the prisoners in the House of Detention are using the flaming toilet paper to indicate their solidarity with their queer brothers and sisters on the street—with us. I think of the French Revolution and the Bastille, and I wish there were enough of us to liberate the women in the House of Detention. Sade was in the Bastille when it fell to the Parisian mob. At what point does a very very angry crowd of gay men and women on Christopher Street in New York become a "mob"? I think of a mob as being out of control. I look around me at the men and women, and we seem very focused, very controlled.

"Oh, Bo, it's lovely. Like some benediction from Mount Olympus."

I turn around, and there is Belle.

"You know, they say most of the women in there are lesbians, women arrested for violations of sexual and gender regulations. They say that those pieces of paper floating down are directed at particular women, the lovers of the ones imprisoned in the House of Detention. Yet they seem like a benediction on all of us."

We hug each other, and smile—she kisses me—and then she goes back to her friends. She is wearing her new sandals.

A bus has been stopped at the entrance into Christopher Street, and it is now backing up, onto Greenwich Avenue. The crowd, it seems, is only allowing gay people to come onto Christopher Street, the crowd with its ethereal, heavenly flaming benediction from the prisoners in the House of Detention.

When we turn away from the flaming toilet paper, and look back down Christopher Street again, we see something else amazing.

"Jesus! Look at that!"

The trash cans down the sidewalk on Christopher Street are all on fire as far as we can see. The dimly lit street, the bonfires at regular intervals into the darkness. The image is celebratory, elegant, benign, very, very old, proclaiming our ownership of our street, reminding the world that we exist and are beautiful.

While the beautiful images suggest one thing, the crowd is experiencing something else. "I have never seen gay people on the street—" Joseph says, "—showing so much anger."

Some of this is directed at the cops, who are standing around uselessly on the street corner watching the packed street. I see a man take the lid from a garbage can and sail it, as if it were a Frisbee, toward a cop, across whose helmet it skids, spinning and without damage. I also see men and women throw heavy objects—rocks, bricks, boards—that land with great noise on the roofs of the cop cars and break windshields and dent hoods.

In response, the cops indiscriminately grab some person out of the crowd and take him away, beating him with their clubs. It seems to me that if anyone is out of control here, it is the cops. A year ago the TV images of the cops in Lincoln Park and Grant Park at the Democratic Convention in Chicago showed what everyone called a "police riot."

The tension on the street rises.

"This feels like it is going to be bigger than last night," Andrew says.

"It already is bigger than last night—" I say, "—more people on the street, more cops—but it hasn't come to a head yet."

I think this tension is partly the result of the cops feeling overwhelmed by the number of us surrounding them. They say there are two thousand of us and maybe one hundred of them. They are not going to let this get bigger and bigger and bigger. It is apparent that the police are going to call in the TPF, like last night.

When they come, there are about two hundred of them, and they get out of their buses in Greenwich Avenue, just under the House of Detention. Their plan is first to clear Greenwich Avenue, but they have difficulty because the TPF is set up to operate in phalanxes of fifty or a hundred men, in close formation, and that means they are not very flexible. The protesters can run ahead of them, without any formation, disappear down side streets, and then regroup behind the TPF, as they did last night. The protesters also operate with an intimate knowledge of the Village streets, which the TPF doesn't have.

We stay and watch these exercises. The TPF marches up and down Greenwich Avenue several times, clearing it of any clusters of protestors, before they turn into Christopher Street.

Joseph says, "Look at those guys."

"I know. They hardly seem human," Andrew says.

"It's all the armor—the visor and the shiny blue shield and all their weapons—and the way they are always in formation, taking orders. They are robotic."

"But they also seem very male. They're big guys, carrying a lot of equipment, wearing boots and helmets. When they're not in formation, they seem to swagger. You don't see that kind of man much nowadays. It's not in style."

"Our guys go for beauty," Joseph says, "instead of that kind of crushing masculinity. They're like tanks."

I'm thinking. "Think how many pictures you're seen in the last five years of a soldier with a rifle on one side of the picture, and some beautiful, but rather fragile man on the other side of the picture wearing beads and flowers in his hair, and offering the soldier a flower. No wonder our culture is in the middle of a nervous breakdown."

"That kind of masculinity—" Andrew says, nodding to the TPF in the street. "—is not very useful here. But—" And he laughed. "—it's great in bed, I would think."

We all laugh.

"I think they—" I nod toward the riot police. "—would see it the other way around."

"Those guys have become familiar sights on American streets in the last five years."

The TPF form their phalanx in the middle of Christopher Street and begin to move off down the street toward the Stonewall. Ahead of them is an almost solid mass of men and women who have been fighting the police of New York for two nights and who know that their home has been invaded and who feel pretty confident.

"Come on guys," I say, "we've got to be a part of this."

The TPF is moving slowly—their feet in a kind of shuffle—which makes them seem more robot-like and more threatening. Andrew, Joseph, and I are on the sidewalk next to them, moving slowly but keeping up with them.

Ahead of us the tangled mass of people is slowly sorting itself out. The people on the line from sidewalk to sidewalk—at the rear edge of the mass—are, it turns out, almost entirely the street people who did most of the fighting last night. Small guys and girls, slender, dressed not for a street fight but for—possibly—a dance in some club somewhere. They are pretty, in huge contrast with the TPF shuffling along beside us. It appears there is going to be a confrontation of two distinctly different conceptions of men and women.

The people on the rear edge of the mass ahead of us form a kick line from one side of the street to the other, facing the TPF, and they start their routine from last night.

We are the Stonewall girls, We wear our hair in curls We don't wear underwear We show our pubic hair.

The TPF is slowly advancing on them. We expect the kids to fall back, but they keep to their place, doing their routine, and the TPF advances.

"Oh, shit," Andrew says. "Can you see Mitzi? Jesus, she's going to get killed right in front of us."

I am searching the line. I don't see her anywhere.

"I haven't seen her since she left us at Bleecker Street."

Joseph puts his arm across my shoulders. "What do you want to do?"

"I'd like to get the kids out of harm's way. That's what I'd like, but I don't think those kids are going to do anything they don't want to do. But come with me, guys." They follow me into the middle of the mass of people in front of the TPF.

The TPF keeps shuffling forward, and the kids stay in place, sometimes doing their routine, and sometimes merely standing in place, their arms across each other's shoulders. There is, possibly, only fifteen feet between them and the TPF. Then thirteen feet, at which point the kids take up their dance routine again. The crowd around me is tense. There are the big men, armed with their pistols and covered with their armor, and then there are the kids and the rest of us. Then ten feet. The TPF can almost touch the kids just by reaching out their arms.

Then eight feet. Finally, at last, the kids break their line and turn and run, and the whole mass of men and women behind them turns and runs too. If they do get close enough to beat the kids, Andrew and Joseph and I are close enough to get into the fight.

"There isn't any dishonor," Andrew says, "in running from a confrontation with those guys. They are the most heavily armed policemen in the city, and they are trained to break skulls. The kids don't have any defenses or weapons. What they do have is incredible courage."

The TPF proceeds on toward Seventh Avenue and succeeds in closing off the set of streets around the park in Sheridan Square. All foot traffic is prevented from entering Sheridan Square. At this point, things get chaotic—several thousand protesters, about four hundred cops, a hot night in the city—and it is difficult to tell what is going on.

Someone on the other side of Seventh Avenue screams, and we hear people shouting at the cops.

Andrew, standing next to me, is angry. "They are walking through the crowd, looking for a fight."

"That's what cops do."

"Let's give them one."

"Suits me."

Andrew has a lower threshold of anger than I do. Watching cops in a situation like this is enough to outrage anyone. Armed with pistols and nightsticks, like Genghis Khan they stride through the crowd that is essentially peaceful. But Andrew carries around with him anger not related to the cops here at this intersection of Seventh Avenue and Christopher Street and their abuse on this night. Andrew and the cops go way back here in New York City, and he is generally enraged by their bullying, brutal, brutish behavior. He is aware of their graft-ridden ways, too, which adds to his anger at their swagger.

I think it is something else, also. I think the young woman at the podium, in all her self-mocking manner, showed a pretty high level of anger that almost all gay people have, at being treated the way gay people are treated in American culture. There is an element of hurt in it, which gives a resonance and edge to the anger. It's the low-level static of bigotry—the voice of the cop spitting out, "Faggot!" magnified a thousand times.

But I think what really drives Andrew's anger is his family. They don't like what he is, but they never bothered to go to any effort to learn anything about what he is. They never asked him any questions about it, about his discovering he was gay, about how all that felt to him, and then they never asked him how it is to live in America and to be gay. They know nothing about the history of gay people in America, and yet they feel they know enough to be judgmental, to vote against Andrew's interest in the polling booth and to join with others in condemning him and to exclude him from the family that he was born into. Andrew and Mitzi are the two most dispossessed of the four of us, and they feel driven into the front of the battle lines. I don't understand how anybody today can reject a member of his family over sex or gender, and yet it happens all the time.

When Andrew wades into the battle on Christopher Street, he carries all these things on his back, this anger and hurt, and the battle, the fighting, holding his fists together and swinging them from side to side, clearing the path in front of him, is one way of getting beyond the anger and the hurt. It is asserting himself, saying he is worthy of love, respect, and even of fear from those who know what he fights for. It is saying he loves himself, and it is saying he knows what is the truth.

I don't think we are different. He has more anger arising from this cause, and I have more anger arising from that cause, and the particular mix of anger and hurt differs from person to person. And, also—and this is important—the amount of resignation a person carries around with him, a kind of giving up, acceptance of defeat, differs from one person to another. But here around us, whatever the particulars, these people have enough anger to drive them to fight, and, I suspect, there are enough people here, men and women, to drive us to the Revolution.

I hear screams. The police on the other side of Seventh Avenue are forcing their way into a crowd of men and swinging their clubs indiscriminately, going for the head. All three of us are tall enough to be able to see over the heads of the crowd and to see what is happening. Men are screaming at the cops. Andrew strides forward, pushing men out of the way and moving toward the cops on the other side.

I hear him thunder, "This is our street!" He says it again. "This is our street!" And as he moves through the crowd, he says, over and over, "This is our street!" and "This street belongs to us!"

We go with him. I am concerned about what kind of mayhem Andrew may get into, but it appears that no matter how enraged he is at the cops, right now, he is not insane. He continues his thunderous shouting so much that it calls attention to himself and away from the street kids who are being beaten by the police. The cops drop the kids and turn to face Andrew. He keeps moving toward them—we see the kids disappear into the crowd—until the cops realize that Andrew is not alone. I put on my best strut, grasp my fists together, and bellow, "This is our street!" Joseph is beside me, shouting, "This is our street!" We move forward, Andrew in the lead, Joseph and me immediately behind, the crowd falling away on either side to give us space, toward the three cops who stand waiting, their billy clubs in their hands. I glimpse Belle in the crowd. Andrew gets there first. He is attacked by all three cops. They go for his head with their clubs. Somebody is saying, "Cocksucker!" at him. "Fucking cocksucker!" He's bloodied immediately. The blood is all over his skull and has soaked his hair and runs down his forehead and drips down into his eyes. But it doesn't stop Andrew, whose long arms give him an advantage. Two of the cops see Joseph and me and turn their attention to us, coming after us with their billy clubs, going after our heads. Mine gets in a good hard blow at my head before I get his club from him—my arms are long too—and stick it in my belt. I give him a good one on top of his head with my fists. I say, "Take that back and stick it to Nixon!" I've got blood all over me. I think we have the same idea at the same time—keep these three cops separated. Andrew is maneuvering his so that the guy's back is to me and Joseph, and he can't see what is happening. Joseph has his twisted around so that he is facing the rear, his head under Joseph's armpit, Joseph scrubbing his scalp with his knuckle and grinning. That Joseph. He knows what he is doing. And without even getting bloodied.

Andrew, whose head is very bloody, rises up to his full height just in front of his cop and brings his clenched fists down on the man's clavicle. The cop screams and drops his billy club.

Joseph leans over to me and whispers, "Disappear, guys." He moves past us and toward the crowd, toward all the other men fighting the cops, and, as he goes past Andrew, he says, "Disappear!" And then he is gone in the crowd. Andrew turns around and disappears also, into a different part of the crowd behind him. I turn around and go back the way I came and move into the crowd for cover.

Our goals are to harass the cops, keep them from driving us off the streets, keep them from seriously hurting any of us, and to hurt them. Everyone seems to know that anytime you see a cop whose back is exposed, *do him in.* The cops have more anger tonight than last night. They're angry they couldn't drive us off the streets last night and angry that we drove them into the Stonewall. Everybody says we humiliated them. Now they have come back to punish us. This feels more personal, and instead of their merely trying to clear the streets, their actions feel vindictive. And yet, they fail. It is as if they have not learned anything from ten years of fighting Americans in the street.

It is midnight. There are more than two thousand men on the streets around Sheridan Square, vastly more than there were last night. Standing near the center of things, we can't see the edge of the crowd. All over the crowd men are yelling.

Joseph, standing next to me, bellows, "This is our street!" Then he bellows again, "This is our street!" He stands with his legs apart and his arms held above his head, his fists held a little apart. "This is our street!" Men around us pick up his chant. "This is our street!" They have great, loud, male voices, and all around us men bellow, "This is our street!"

The cops come striding through the crowd, swinging their clubs from side to side, sometimes connecting with some man's head. They come toward one of the sources of the bellows, Joseph and me, but their problem is that, in coming toward us, they are in the middle of the crowd, and their backs are exposed. There are two cops coming toward us, in single file, and while I watch them, I see someone jump on the back of the second one. That person slides his arm around the policeman's throat and pulls his head back, and, using his fist, begins to hit the policeman's head. The cop tries to get free of this creature on his back, but he can't—the much smaller person has his legs around the cop's torso and his arms around his neck—and he can't escape. The cop cries out, the first cop turns around to help him, and suddenly Joseph moves very fast. As soon as the first cop turns his back on him, Joseph is on his back. He has his arm around the first cop's throat, and his legs around his torso—Joseph is entirely off the ground, riding the cop—and he throws back his head and bellows, "YOU. WILL. NOT. TAKE. THIS. STREET. FROM. US!" And then he brings down both his fists on the cop's skull. He slides down to the ground and disappears into the crowd. The cop is, I think, stunned that he has escaped without real injury, and for a minute, while he is checking himself out, he forgets to watch where Joseph is heading, and so he loses him in the crowd. There may be, maybe, forty cops at most in the vicinity of the park. But there are two thousand of us.

All over the crowd men are doing the same thing that Joseph and Andrew have done—taunting the cops, getting back at them in some way, then running away. It seems to be the accepted, generally understood, tactic.

Andrew is beside me, breathing heavily. "That was satisfying." He has a good bit of blood in his hair. In wiping it away from his eyes, he's smeared it across his face. Sometimes the men get away, and leave the cops searching through the crowd, and sometimes they don't get away, and they carry the wounds to prove it. "Christ, I hate those guys."

"How is your head?"

"I'll live. I don't think my head is broken. Just the skin is split. I will ask you to clean me up the way you did last night, when we get home, if you will."

I take his hand. "I'll do that."

"It feels great, giving these cops back some of what they've been dishing out for years."

It not only feels good to get back at them, but I suspect that it feels good to prove to himself that the message the cops—and his parents and family and most of the other people in our society—give that says *You're not worth shit* isn't so. I suspect that every time he can get in a lick at the cops, he's proving to himself just how much he is worth. *I am a man.*

"Where's Joseph?"

"I don't know. He was here a moment ago, and then he jumped a cop and ran away into the crowd, just the way you did. I haven't seen him since."

"Is he OK?"

"Yes. I think so. I am pretty sure he is." I am not much into vengeance, but I can understand what Andrew is going through. I don't see another way for him to recover from the damage his culture has inflicted on him. He has to go through a certain amount of this— fighting back, inflicting pain on our opponents—just so he can come out whole on the other side.

This is the only way we can get their attention and respect. The way things are set up, inflicting pain on them is the only way to make them stop treating us the way they are treating us—with such contempt and with such scorn. We must make it very, very expensive to treat gay people with contempt.

"Let's look for him."

"Yes."

"Go north on Seventh, and I'll go south. Go through the crowd, until there is no crowd on Seventh any more, and then come back here. If either of us finds him, we'll bring him back here."

The chaotic scene is difficult to search. Aside from the shouts of the crowd, I can hear the sirens of the cop cars as they arrive and leave, and I can hear the commands of police to one another. Every few minutes, I hear a scream of someone on the receiving end of a billy club. The satisfying part of all this is that we are still here. They haven't driven us away.

107

Joseph is an amazing guy. He has a strong sense of himself. He's not going to be driven away by anything. He has had experience in all this on the West Coast and in SNCC. Watts. I look for Mitzi at the same time I survey the crowd for Joseph. One big, one small, encompassing the range of our community. Where is she? She doesn't want to be found, for one thing. She comes to us when she needs something, but at other times she is self-sufficient in her little gang of street kids. She would not like it that I arrive out of the dark, tonight, and tell her to come home with us. On the other hand, if she wants to come to our apartment tonight, she knows where we are. I hope I don't stumble on her, here in the dark, hurt and bleeding.

She came to the theatre once and found me. She sat in a front row seat while I worked and she watched. I offered her money.

"No. You don't need to offer me money. If I need money, I'll tell you. I look after myself, and I been doing an OK job of that the last few years. I can feed myself and buy my clothes and whatever else it takes. I can look out for my needs." Then she stopped for a few minutes and watched me.

"Mitzi, that's OK. I know you can look out for yourself. But I wish you'd let Andrew and me offer sometimes. You don't have to take what we offer, if you don't want. But offering to help is what friends do, sometimes."

We were quiet for a while. I cut a couple of boards.

"Are we friends?"

"We're friends." Then I said, "Andrew and I are your friends, and I hope you are our friend."

She didn't say anything, but I think she understood what that meant. I think she was pleased.

But I don't find her anywhere in the crowd, and I don't know whether that is good news or bad news. Every glance I make, I am afraid of what I will find.

Then I am aware that we are being chased. There are some cops twenty or thirty yards just north of us on the avenue who are blowing their whistles and waving their billy clubs. All the people around me start to run south on the avenue. We are running hard, going south, into the traffic. There are probably one hundred of us. I glance behind me and realize that there are only two cops chasing us.

Somebody screams out. "Wait! There are only two of them! Turn around. Chase them. Catch them. Take off their clothes! Screw them!" The whole crowd of us running down Seventh Avenue slows down, turns around, and starts running up Seventh Avenue, this time running after the two cops who are just ahead of us, the crowd yelling, "Catch them! Fuck them!"

I am laughing. In a few minutes, I slow down and let the rest of them go on and catch the cops and do with them what they will. I look up as the crowd moves away from me, and I see Andrew and Joseph running past me screaming, "Catch them! Fuck them!"

"Hey, guys, over here. Come fuck me!"

They stop and turn and, seeing me, they laugh. They leave the chase to others—there are lots of others—and they come over to me.

We talk about what they have been doing, and I tell them my news, and we ask questions about Mitzi's whereabouts.

Then, in the raucous noise of the street, we hear a voice that is unmistakably Mitzi's.

"What, do you think you can get on your fucking bus and come down here to where I live and take my street from me?"

Andrew checks us out. "Let's go make sure she's not causing permanent physical damage."

We do. The cop is on the sidewalk, and Mitzi has been mocking him—but staying out of the reach of his billy club.

We walk up, and Andrew—particularly Andrew—swaggers.

"It looks like we're going to adjust the odds, here, officer," I say. "First there was you with your pistol and billy club against this young woman, here, but now the young woman has some friends. Us."

Joseph and Andrew and I arrange ourselves around the cop. He looks uneasily from one of us to another. "You can't get us all," Andrew says. "And whoever you don't get is going to get you. I mean, is going to fuck you. Do you understand? So why don't you just take all your weapons and trot on back to your friends?" The officer shrugs and turns and walks back to Christopher Street.

"Aw, what'd ya do that for? I coulda handled'im myself? I was kinda lookin' forward ta de-ballin' 'im, myself." Mitzi is pissed. She comes over and starts beating on me.

"I'm sorry, Mitzi. Next time you're having a one-on-one with a cop, I'll leave you alone."

She beats on my chest. "You fucking faggot!"

"Ah, Mitzi, we didn't mean to intrude," Andrew says. "I could see you had everything under control."

She looks at us and melts. "I know, guys."

"We're just standing with our friends."

"I guess you know I like to do it myself." She speaks under the roar of the crowd.

I put my arms around the necks of my guys. They're great to hold. "What time is it?" I ask.

"Two-thirty."

"What's happening?"

"I think people are going home."

I look around. People are leaving. Floating away into the side streets.

"Let's go home, guys."

"Mitzi?" Andrew asks. "You wanta come with us? You're welcome to spend the night with us if you want."

Mitzi thinks for a minute. Then she says, "Naw. I think I'll go find my gang, and then I might come over later. Is that OK?"

I say that's OK. "Come here."

She's close enough, so I pull her to me, and I hug her. "Be careful, now, hear?"

"Aw, Bo, why'd ya hafta do that?"

And then she is gone.

"Do you two want to go home?" I ask.

"Yeah," Joseph says, "whatever you suggest. I am done with this around here. I don't think I need to see the TPF for a while."

"OK. Let's go home."

We walk down Christopher Street, toward the river, toward home, the sounds of the riot receding into the background noise of the city.

When we get down near Weehawken, Joseph asks, "How about the docks, guys? Anybody here up for the docks?"

It's a fine idea. It's hot, and it will be cool down on the river. Besides, all the cops are up around Sheridan Square, so it will be safe on the docks. We cross West Street and walk up to the dock.

"Do we want to get the blood off?" All three of us are streaked and smeared with it.

"Naw." Andrew pulls himself to his full height, and he checks out me and Joseph. "It's our red badge of courage."

It is the last hour before dawn. We are aware of the river. We can hear it gurgling underneath the dock, and we hear the hiss of the wind coming across the waves. Intermittently, there is a light from buildings on the water's edge on the other shore. The sounds off the river give a sense of how big the river is, how wide it is, and how deep. There is a full moon above us.

We walk out to the end of the dock. Bodies take shape, lying on the surface of the dock. Andrew disappears, drawn by someone he sees, and, in a few moments, I am aware that Joseph has disappeared also. Then I see someone. He has a blanket—a sheet, a bedspread of some kind—and I lie down with him. The hot, impulsive, resistless coupling—like the powerful, resistless torrent underneath us. Later, I hear someone softly calling my name. It is Andrew. I answer, and he kneels on the sheet. I feel his hands. I become aware in the dark that there is another man lying down with us. Joseph. We three—and the unnamed fourth—drift off to sleep in the dark, the breeze cool for the first time since Saturday morning, the last of us asleep just as the first tentative pink and pale blue light of day shows itself over the Statue of Liberty in the harbor.

Sunday, June 9, 1969

"'Had I plantation of this isle, my lord—and were the King on't, what would I do?' Why does Gonzalo ask this question at this point in the play [2.1.144-145]? We haven't seen any of the Neapolitans since the first scene, when the ship foundered and, we thought, all were drowned. Now they come on the stage, at the beginning of the second act, remarking how fresh their clothes are. The King, Alonzo, is beside himself with grief because he thinks his son Ferdinand has drowned, but the others, his brother Sebastian, and Antonio, Prospero's brother, are rattling on, blaming everything on Alonzo and mocking Gonzalo. All of this seems aimless until Gonzalo pulls it all together with this pointed question, *Had I plantation of this isle, my Lord, and were the King on't, what would I do?* Is he pulling it together? or is his question one more attempt to distract us? Why does this happen here, now? What does it mean?'"

Sergei is pacing back and forth on the stage, talking to himself, and Matt Kimball and I sit in canvas chairs at angles to one another, listening.

"In a little bit, the play will be in train, that is, all the various plots of the play will have been set in motion, and after that the play runs with great speed down to the end, but that hasn't happened yet. These men enter and tell us they have just come from having almost lost their lives in the tempest, and they discuss the probable death of the King's son, Ferdinand, and then they bicker among themselves and tell a few bad jokes. The most senior courtier then asks, 'Had I plantation of this isle, my lord, and were the King on't, what would I do?' The question seems to be unprepared for. It is not a natural question to ask after the ship you were on sinks in a storm. What's going on here?"

Sergei lights a cigarette. "You see, the question is, how does this fit in with the rest of the play? Is this at the center of the play? Or is it merely a sideward glance, a momentary distraction? Is this speech part of the fumbling around that these characters engage in while they are marking time until Sebastian and Antonio mount their plot to kill the King, or is it something else? Ariel says, 'You are three men of sin,' and it could be that this line is the center of the play, that is, that the discovery of the sin in themselves is going to set in train the need for penitence, penance, forgiveness, and grace, which is the structure of the play, or it may be that individual sin has very little to do with what happens in The Tempest. It may be that Gonzalo, in his speech about the plantation of this isle, is closer to what the play is about—the problem the play discovers is a systemic failure of governance."

Matt smiles and interrupts, "I see what you're after. You're conceiving of a Tempest for our time, aren't you?" He looks away into the back of the theatre while he spins out a vision. "The Neapolitans enter in the second act, a bunch of wildly over-dressed urban types prancing through the jungle in their wedding costumes, a completely foreign environment to them, which is, to them, totally uninhabited, and they do what that kind of white man always does— he assumes it belongs to no one, and therefore it belongs to him. And he also assumes that if it does belong to anyone, those claims are insignificant and need not be honored. Consequently, he starts to colonize it. Gonzalo, looking about himself at the empty jungle—I see a backdrop with ferns bigger than the actors up behind the seats on all four sides—and says, 'If I were king on't, what would I do?' and then he proceeds to structure a government and an economy, a vision unlike the way the island is actually governed—the audience already knows how the island is governed and by whom—and also unlike the way England is governed at the time the play was written."

Matt furrows his brow. "What we experience on the stage is this small group of Neapolitan nobles in high court dress striding uncertainly into the jungle, dwarfed by the size of the ferns they are walking through, and one of these nobles is expatiating on a perfectly administered society. The society that he envisions is life in the golden age—no 'sovereignty,' by which he means no ruler, no monarch, no contracts, no private ownership of property, no inheritance, no classes, no occupations. Men and women both are to live in idleness, all things held in common, producing enough of what is necessary to, as he says, 'feed my innocent people.'"

Adam in the Morning

Matt, enjoying having the stage, which Sergei has given him, says, "So, if we pick up on this, if we ask the question, 'How are these lines to be played?' the answer would be, 'with grace and a certain seriousness.' Antonio and Sebastian may mock Gonzalo, and Gonzalo himself, the actor playing Gonzalo, can play it like a bumbling old fool. Or he can play the part like a wise and graceful old courtier, which he is. Prospero recognizes this at the end of the play. So we have Gonzalo play the speech as a wise and graceful old courtier, and his vision, once introduced into the play, remains a kind of target against which the actions of everybody on the stage are measured. The play may ask the question, 'How can we get to Gonzalo's vision from where we are?' Or, better, our production demonstrates how far from Gonzalo's vision is the world of the play, the human society on Prospero's island."

Sometimes I think Sergei and Matt haven't given this play a thought, and here they are, entrusted with the responsibility of directing it and of designing it for a significant production at one of the best off-Broadway houses in the Village. I think they should have been settled in their understanding of what the play is about at least a year ago, and they should have come to an agreement between the two of them before anyone else was hired. They should be clear about all this. It is amazing how often people are given responsibilities beyond their experience and abilities. I twist and turn in my canvas chair and don't see why I am here.

The Times this morning had a fifteen-inch story about the riots. We are called "homosexuals" by The Times. Of course, they missed the point. It is amazing that the newspaper of record, here in this city, in this decade, can't get right the mere facts about a riot involving this city's gay citizens. Their major error was in mistaking the point-of-view. They thought the riots resulted when the police, going about their lawful duties, were attacked by homosexuals. We know that the riots resulted when gay people, trying to exercise their rights as Americans to buy a drink on Friday night, were hindered and then beaten and arrested by out-of-control cops, who then spent the next three or four hours rampaging through the Village, beating up innocent bystanders. Why is that so hard to understand?

Belle called a while ago. She asked me not to leave until she gets here. She wants to talk to me and said it's about the riots, not about the play. I don't know if I will wait. If it were about the play, I would feel an obligation. It's not as hot today, so it's less oppressive to be

117

outside. I think I may find Andrew. We could take a walk through the Village, and then look for some place to go for brunch. On the other hand, we could find a bar that was cool and spend the afternoon getting drunk. Or, we could go to the dock for sex, or to the trucks for sex. Or go home for sex with or without Joseph. I am beginning to drift toward making a decision here—food and sex this summer afternoon in the city. And something cool to drink. And sleep.

I'm drifting toward an appreciation of Joseph, too. Andrew is fairly hot-tempered, and I tend to be analytic and cool about things. Joseph is somewhere between. He's been an activist for fourteen years. He's experienced in Martin-Luther-King-style non-violent street demonstrations, and he was also in the middle of the Watts Riot the whole week in which 34 people died. He has spent a year in Harlem at the New Lafayette Theatre, which is probably the best Black Arts theatre in America, which puts him on the cutting edge of black nationalism theatre in the East. He's read a lot. He seems to have read everything. This has given him experience that makes him an expert fighter, makes him cool, not excitable, reserved, and aware of other people. He's got presence. I like all that. I am drifting toward wanting him to want to be with us.

Billy will arrive at five this afternoon—he'll get into town at six or six-thirty—and we can talk then about what we are going to do. There may be more rioting tonight. And it may be that this is going to take a good many days to die down. Each day it gets bigger.

Sergei and Matt continue their analysis of abstractions. It is odd that they have not referred to the riots or commented on the bandages I have on my head or said anything about our production of The Tempest that would connect it to the rioting in the street the last two nights. Our audience is going to ask us to make such a connection, whether we do or not, and the popularity of our show is going to depend on whether we have connected with the spirit in the streets of the Village and how we do that. I think everything that happens in the Village from now on—for years—is going to be affected by these riots. It is going to change the way we see every single thing that we look at—a Rembrandt "Self-Portrait," a Kouros in the Greek collection, a Picasso of Maria-Therese, American eighteenth-century furniture.

I sit here, slouched down in my canvas chair, one foot on the floor, the other leg crossed at the ankle.

Sergei is speaking. "How much irony is there, in this play?"

Adam in the Morning

I presume that is a rhetorical question. The most famous piece of irony in the English language—many people say—is Miranda's line, "How beauteous mankind is! O brave new world, that hath such people in it!" The people she is looking at are robbers, drunkards, usurpers, in short, the dregs of the earth. Of course, she may be speaking only of their clothes.

"Sergei," I say finally. "I am going to have to make a phone call. And then I am going to have to visit the lumberyard down on West Street. Can you get along without me here?"

Sergei stumbles—I think it hasn't occurred to him that there are other things that need to be attended to—but then he catches himself. "Yes. Of course. Stop in this afternoon, or call me, and I will fill you in on what we have done."

"Right. I look forward to hearing all that."

These men don't think sequentially. I leave the stage and walk out through the risers to the front of the theatre. The front door opens, and someone walks in. It is—it is Joseph and Mitzi! They both have bandaged heads, and their faces are brilliantly bruised in different shades of pink and red.

The question that we confronted at Alternate U the night I met Andrew, What is a man?, is broader than the mere question, How is a man to act?, because it encompasses the notion that a person has a choice, that one is not limited by biology, that the whole conception of gender is more fluid than we have known.

"Hello! Welcome to The Olympic! You two look like the wounded in a Delacroix painting."

They grin.

"We thought we'd come over and see if you would come eat with us." Mitzi is, at times, appealingly shy.

"Hi, Bo." Joseph's sexiness shows on him. He has tied a strip of leather with tribal markings around his head. Thongs hang down his back. He looks like a native warrior. He smiles, then he kisses me.

"Sure, I can come with you. I was just leaving the theatre." I ask them to wait a minute, and I go upstairs and leave a note for Belle.

We walk out together and descend the steps and walk up to Waverly Place, where we turn left.

"How do you two feel? Mitzi?"

"I'm OK. Nothing wrong with me."

"Except for your head wounds. Did Joseph or Andrew look at your head this morning?"

119

"I did," Joseph says. "Everything appears to be fine."

"Did they let you take a bath this morning?"

Mitzi is a little impatient. "Yeah, sure. Lay off it Bo."

"Just asking. How about you? How is your head?"

"I think I am OK too. Andrew checked me out. I checked Andrew out. Our heads seem to be OK. Everything OK."

"Broken bones on anybody?"

"Andrew said the rest of him is OK. No broken bones. None on me."

"How would I know?" Mitzi looks at the street as if knowing about broken bones were too weak and cowardly for the likes of her.

"I think you'd know. Where is Andrew now? Is he at work?"

"Yes. He said he had the brunch shift today, and he left the apartment around ten-thirty."

"Did he say when he was coming home?"

"Around six, I think."

Andrew's restaurant is over on West 10th and Waverly Place. I can swing by there on the way back to The Olympic.

"So, good, everybody is OK. We got through that. Mitzi, it occurs to me that it might be good if you kept some clothes over at our place, just a change so if something like last night happens again, you could take a bath and get into some clean clothes. If you wanted, I could give you a little money and you could get some jeans and a t-shirt or a blouse. Something like that. Or a dress, if you'd prefer. One of us could go with you, or you could go by yourself. Or, if you want, you can just bring over some clothes you already have. What do you think of that?"

"Are you trying ta change the way I look?"

"No. I want—and Andrew wants—you to look any way you want to look. We will fix it so you have your own drawer to keep your clothes in."

She thinks about that for a while.

Joseph speaks. "Hey, Mitzi, the guy is offering you some free threads. Take 'em while he's offerin'. It doesn't matter what his motivation is as long as you get the clothes you want. And he's said you can have anything you want."

She thinks about that, and then she says, "OK. As long as it's free and I can get what I want."

"That's fine, then."

She's still thinking. "Can I have something else?"

"Anything. What?"

"I want a scarf. A soft scarf made out of thin material to tie around my neck. I'd like it to be lavender."

"You can have a scarf."

"My neck is real scrawny, and I'd like to cover it up."

"I can understand that." I have an idea. "Would you like to take Joseph with you when you go shopping? Carry your bags?"

She grins. She turns to Joseph. "How 'bout it big guy? You go shopping with me?"

"I'd like that. We could go after we get something to eat."

Andrew and I, when we first met, were in a time in our lives when we were sharply aware of how much gender affected the way a person navigates his life. We had learned from the women's movement that men get ahead quicker and make more while they are doing it. But we were also aware of how much for men and women— boys and girls—conforming to a gender is going to determine how much the culture accepts them and promotes them. Walking down the street and seeing the gang of street kids, I pointed them out, and Andrew said, "They are here on the street because there is nowhere else in our culture that gives them the freedom they need."

We head down to the Silver Dollar, passing all the men and women passing out leaflets and the little groups of cops strutting on the sidewalk. It is like a play or an opera. In a moment the leading lady is going to come on and sing an aria.

Even though it is Sunday, the Silver Dollar doesn't do brunch, but they do a fine breakfast and a decent lunch. In our booth, Joseph —he's sitting next to her—asks Mitzi, "Where do you spend most of your time in the city?"

She shrugs. "I don't know. Midtown, 42nd Street I guess. Work is better up there."

"Better than anywhere down here?"

"Yeah! You got all these johns, and they pay you better. I don't think they know much cause they aren't from the city."

"Tourists?"

"I guess."

"How long you been doing this kind of work?"

They seem to be having a private conversation. I am sitting opposite them, my back against the wall and my legs up on the seat. I have put my head against the wall. Mitzi seems willing to open up to

Joseph, and I want to give her space to do that, if that's what she needs.

She frowns. "I don't know. This is the summer, so I think it was the summer when I started. Two years ago, I guess."

"I bet you have stories to tell."

She laughs a small laugh. "Uh-huh."

"But you don't want to tell me any of 'em, do you?"

"Ya got that right, dude."

"Ya got friends?"

"Oh, yeah. My sisters. That's what we call ourselves. We're sisters. We tell each other everything." She looks him over. "I might introduce you sometime, if you watch yourself, big guy."

"—to your sisters?"

"Yeah. That's who we're talking about ain't it?"

"I lost you there for a minute."

"There're some beautiful women in our gang." She checks him out again. "Only you're a faggot, ain't ya?"

"Yeah, I'm a fag, but that doesn't mean you can't introduce me to your sisters. I like beautiful women. You're beautiful. Do you know that?"

"Watch it guy. When I first started growing up, I didn't know nothin, y'know? I thought I must be a fag, and I was pretty bummed out about that. I was about ten years old, and I was all into wearing frilly dresses and makeup and shit, and I thought the only guys who liked to wear frilly dresses were fags, and I was dreading growing up and becoming a fag. I used to spend a lot of time in front of a mirror, checking me out and seeing how I was looking, how I looked as a fag, and I didn't like what was happening to me. Then I began to get hold of it all. I realized I was going to grow up to be a woman, not a fag. And I was going to fall in love with a man who loved women. Cheez! That was a relief."

"You didn't want to be a fag."

"I don't mean no disrespect, but I didn't want to be no fag. There are a lot of different kinds of fags, and if I could have been one of the other kinds—I mean, you guys are pretty cool dudes, and you been good to me—but it seemed to me from pretty early on that I wasn't going to be the kind of fag you are. I was going to be the other kind of fag, wearing women's clothes all the time and makeup and saying darling every time I opened my mouth. That was not what I wanted. I didn't want to feel like I was faking it, you know? Shit. I wasn't going to fake it at all. But like I said I gradually began to understand that there are a lot of things going on, not just men and women and gay and straight. So I had more choices, and I began to feel better about things. I mean, me and the drag queens might look a lot alike, but we get there by coming from different directions, if you know what I mean. I'm not a man. I'm a woman. I'm OK where I am."

"You realized when you were real young that you weren't a boy."

"I never thought I was a boy."

"You don't see your parents."

"Naw. Not since I was real little. My daddy left us when I was about five or six. Then my mom got a boyfriend, and he moved in with us. When I was about thirteen I was wearing girls' clothes all the time, and my mom's boyfriend beat me regular, but I showed them they couldn't make me put on boy's clothes. My mom called me 'whore' and 'slut.' Her boyfriend kept on beating me—I think he did it just because he liked doing it, he used his leather belt—until finally I left. I put my clothes in a bag and when I was supposed to go to school, I walked out the front door and never came back. I came over here—all that stuff happened in Queens—and in a little bit I found a bunch of sisters on the street who took care of me and showed me how to do it."

"You don't go to school."

It is interesting what Joseph is doing. These are questions he is asking, but they come out like sentences, and they don't sound judgmental. It's like he's stating the mere truth. I think what I am hearing is what he may have learned how to do when he was working in voter registration in the South. On the other hand, this may be the kind of person he is. He is soothing and comforting and supportive.

"No. I guess I've gotten as much schooling as I'm going to get. I can't say I need it much, except that I would like to know more about some things."

"What things?"

"I'd like to know how you can get a lawyer when you get busted. I don't know that one yet."

"You haven't been in school for, what, three years."

"Ya got it. I had to spend all my time working."

"You're a girl."

"Yeah, I'm me. Mitzi." She turns her head so she is looking at me but giving Joseph a profile. "Check me out. Ain't I pretty?" She grins.

Joseph grins. "You're pretty. You're very, very pretty."

"You're cool." She thinks about it a few moments. "I tell ya what, guys. Would ya like to hear a story?"

We would.

"My sister is Violet. She and I look after each other. She's about like me, except that she's a little taller and a little heavier. We usually work together. I'm her mother. We help each other. We are on the north side of Forty-second, west of Eighth—it's about eleven o'clock—and suddenly I'm noticing this dude following us, and so I say to Violet, 'You or me?' and she checks him out and says, 'You?' So I slow down and let him catch up with me. He comes up even with me and says, 'Hello, beautiful. What's your name?' I tell him, and he says, 'That's a pretty name.' He smiles, and he says, 'A pretty name for such a pretty little girl.' He's tall and heavy. You could even call him fat—his waist is a lot wider than his chest—and he wears a suit even though it's hot. His hair is cut short and parted on one side and slicked down. I can see Violet up ahead of us laughing at him and at me and the mess I'm in, having to deal with him.

"I know what's up. I know what he wants, and I say, 'It'll cost ya.' He says, 'How much?' And I tell'im, and he says, 'That's too much.' So I say, 'Screw you, that's the price.' And then he says, 'Are you a real girl?' And he says he wants to see. I say, 'I'm as real as the balls you got hanging 'tween your legs.' And then I reach out and grab his balls, y'know, and just at that minute Violet, who has been kind of dropping back and is now behind the man, lifts his wallet, and all this happens at the same time, and just when he realizes his wallet is gone missing, I drop his balls—Jesus fuck! His ball sack was so loose and saggy!—and Violet and I take off in opposite directions. He didn't know which one of us had his wallet and which one he was supposed to chase. I went up Eighth, and Violet went down Eighth, and the funny thing is that he couldn't yell for the coppers 'cause it'd be clear what he was doing with us."

Mitzi is laughing so hard she's lost her breath and is gasping and hitting her chest. "And he had a lot of money in his wallet. We took the money and dropped the wallet in a trash can and took off through Port Authority to a subway down here to 14th Street. We knew once we were on the train, we'd gotten away. But ya know for a little bit there I wondered. Ya know he made me pretty mad when he said he wasn't going to pay the going price, like I wasn't worth it. And I am."

And when he said he wanted to see me, as if he has a right to see what I am and then pay me less money for it. Fuck that."

Things are quiet for a few seconds. Then Joseph speaks, very softly, very quietly. "And when you sleep at night, you do that somewhere outdoors."

It takes her a few seconds. She breathes in and out a few times. "There are places. We know about them. When I first started living on the street, when I first connected with my sisters, they told me about them. There are plenty of places under the roadways around the city—the elevated roadways—and in the drainpipes. And usually if they start to fill up with water, that happens slow enough so you can get out in time. Ya know how the whole city is built on an island, so there are a lot more drainpipes than you think there are. If you know how to do it, you can sleep in the subway, too. And the parks everywhere. Sleeping out is no problem now, in the summer. It only gets harsh in the winter, when it gets so cold outside." Her face shows none of the bravado it usually shows. She's just telling us the mere truth about her life. "Besides, I got my sisters, and I can stay with them if I want." What this means is that sometimes they can crash at the house of a girl who is still living at home, and sometimes at an apartment somewhere that they have access to.

"I guess you don't see your family."

"Naw. Well, sometimes. I know where they shop for groceries, and once I went over and stood across the street until they came, and I looked at them."

"You didn't say anything."

"Naw. I didn't want to say anything. I just looked at them and then when they had gone inside, I left and caught the subway back over here. It would have been too weird to say something to them. I've got my own life now, and it doesn't have anything to do with them."

We have finished eating. I pull out my wallet, and I pay for our food. Then I get money and slide it across the table to her. She sees what I am doing, and she watches it carefully. I think taking money from us is such a new thing that she still doesn't trust it. I look at her. "If that's not enough, I can give you some more."

"How 'bout this. If that's not enough," Joseph says, "Mitzi will tell me, and I will give her whatever she needs. Then you and I can talk. Is that OK?" The question is to me. It is, as he says, OK. He turns to her. "You still want me to go with you?"

125

She nods. Kind of gulps, and nods.

We all stand up and walk toward the door. On the street, I remember. "Look, folks. Billy is coming in this afternoon. Why don't you both come on back to Weehawken Street and have supper tonight, you two and us and Billy." I grin. "Anybody else we ought to invite? Mitzi you want to invite Violet?"

She frowns and says, "Naw. I don't guess so."

"Well you haven't met my brother, and I'd like you to meet him. He's cool. So be sure to come."

We're all walking toward Seventh Avenue, the narrow, leafy confines of Christopher Street.

"Come on, Mitzi," Joseph says. "I haven't been shopping with a lady since I left the West Coast. Let's make up for lost time!"

"Remember the point of your shopping trip. Mitzi needs an outfit she can leave at our house—a change of clothes—and then, if she can find another outfit for herself, that would be fine too."

So we split at Seventh, and I head over to West 10th to Andrew's restaurant, and then down to The Olympic where I can track down Belle and find out what Matt and maybe Sergei have done since I left. I dread that.

I can't get out of my head their discussion about Gonzalo and his plans for the local government. If he had been King over this isle, and King over what he calls "my innocent people," every person would have been equal, there would have been no religion, and Mitzi's stepfather wouldn't have beaten her, and she would never have had to leave her home.

Andrew is a waiter at Zanes, a new restaurant on West 10th. It's a beautiful street, it's a popular place, and you usually have to have a reservation. But it's two-thirty or so, so I ought to be able to get in and talk to Andrew. The host, who knows me, gets me a seat at the bar, and in a minute Andrew appears. He's in a black t-shirt and black jeans. He has a bandage on his forehead, held in place by a gauze tape wrapped around his head and tied in a bow in the back, which almost, but not quite, covers the abrasions and bruises on his forehead. Very South American jungle fighter.

He looks at me. "Hi, gorgeous. Everything OK?"

"Yeah. I won't stay. I just wanted to remind you that Billy is coming. Everybody is coming to our house for supper."

"Who is that?"

"Joseph and Mitzi and us and Billy."

"What is this about Joseph? He has been with us every minute since night before last."

"I don't know. Do you want me to tell him to go home tonight?"

"Can we?"

"Sure. We haven't made any commitment to him."

"Do you want to?"

"I don't mind him being around. I guess I like him being around."

"I do too. It's just that I thought we were going to have a conversation about all this before he moved in, and now it seems to have happened without us talking about it."

"Right. Look. We seem to be in a middle of a bunch of things, the riots, Billy's coming, Mitzi is around more than usual—I think that's a result of Joseph being here—and my sense of it is that we ought to let him hang out with us if that's what he wants. Then, when the riots die down, and Billy goes home, we can focus on Joseph. Ask him to stay, or ask him to go. In the meantime, think about this thing."

"OK, that's OK with me," Andrew says, "but I've been thinking. Should one of us speak to Joseph?"

"I guess so. I'll do it. Keep him up with what we're thinking."

"I think it's not that he's hang'n around, in the way. It's that he's here with us, and he's doing something positive—he's helping with Mitzi—making it possible for a lot of this to happen. I think we need to remember that."

Then Andrew gets to his real concern. "All this is very frustrating. I think what's happening is very important, and we need to be careful that we have a good record of it all, but I am so busy, I don't have time to take notes—I worked for about two hours this morning, but that is not enough. Two hours yesterday. I'd like to write—do some serious writing—but what with the riots and Mitzi and Joseph, and now Billy tonight—"

"I'm glad you reminded me. I'll try to ward off interruptions tonight until you're ready to deal with us—"

"I'd like time to get something down, if I can manage it." Then he looks at me. "Where are you headed?"

"The theatre. I am supposed to see Belle and Matt and Sergei. Then I'm going home so I can have things pulled together when Billy gets here. Otherwise, are you OK?"

"Yeah! Busy here—" He grins. "People are just throwing money at me. Love that. And Billy thinks there're going to be riots tonight! Coming all the way from Houston for 'em. I hope we can pull them off." He shakes his head. "You've got to go now. I've got to go now —back to work. Hey," Andrew turns back to me, "do you love me?"

"Yeah, dude." I'm outta there and head back to the theatre. The thing is that if all is held in common and if there are no magistrates and everybody is equal, then everybody's needs will be pretty much the same—there won't be rich people or poor people—and it certainly means that everybody's needs will be met. Even though he doesn't mention it, I think he also means there will be no distinction between men and women, and no distinction between gay and straight. Can it be that if all is held in common—Gonzalo's words are "all things in common Nature should produce/Without sweat or endeavor" [2.1.160-161]—that there can be plenty of variety but no difference? A whole range of genders—not just two, but as many genders as people want—and maybe a whole range of sexualities too? And whatever gender you are and whatever sexuality you are will be accepted and your needs met, just as there will always be food to feed my innocent people. "Nature should bring forth/Of its own kind all foison, all abundance./To feed my innocent people" [2.1.163-164]. I love that line to feed my innocent people. A vision of the Golden Age. But I suppose too paternalistic to work on Manhattan. If my needs are truly met by society or nature, I suppose I could stand a little paternalism. I don't think Sergei and Matt have a clue what to do with this play.

There are men on the street corners around Sheridan Square, handing out flyers and leaflets, even more than yesterday. Passing through, I take leaflets from the men near me. They say, WHAT HOMOSEXUALS WANT and WHERE DO WE GO FROM HERE? One flyer announces a meeting. Another flyer announces self-defense classes at the Alternate U, and the headline of another one reads simply THE HOMOSEXUAL REVOLUTION. And the most encompassing of all, POWER TO THE PEOPLE. Then there are the anti-war flyers. I start collecting flyers, with Andrew's box in mind. I make this a conscious effort to collect everything that is being passed out. On the back of each one, I have been putting the date and time and the location where I collected the flyer, so Andrew will know. There is nothing about any of this that leads me to believe that this is dying down. I take Waverly Place to Christopher, past the Northern Dispensary, and then east to Sixth Avenue. On the corner of Christopher and Waverly Place, a small, very thin man with long beautiful blond hair and piercing eyes, and a bandage around the crown of his head, is haranguing a crowd.

"—We are facing huge questions. And none of them have anything to do with the police or Mayor Lindsay or Governor Rockefeller or Richard Nixon. These questions have to do with us, who we are, who joins us on the street when we confront our enemies, why we have joined with our brothers and sisters to confront our enemies, and what we want to happen as a result of our confrontations. We are so new to all this, brothers and sisters, so brand new since we were born two nights ago, that we haven't learned yet what is us and what is them and we don't know yet what to call ourselves. We don't know yet what we want to be. Do we want to be the meanest son-of-a-bitch coming down the pike? Or do we want to be a follower of Gandhi and know that, even if we don't know which direction we are going in, it is non-violence that is going to take us there? What happened early Saturday morning was an explosion in our lives so profound—the Big Bang—that it seems to be the beginnings of all things. Life began for us on Saturday morning on Christopher Street, and now that it has begun, we must name ourselves, recognize our kind, determine our food, describe our sex, and observe the span of our years. Every single thing about us must be observed and noted—and done accurately, so succeeding generations won't have cause to say, 'they got it wrong, and now we have to do it over again'—"

Even if there are no more riots—no more large crowds in confrontations with the police—we have become politicized, and who we are and what we are, are now subject to debate among us. We are no longer interested in hearing what heterosexuals have to say on any of this. Who are we? And what does it mean that we define ourselves this way? We will talk to each other and listen to ourselves and determine the truth of our lives.

Belle is in her office when I get back to The Olympic. She has a very small, very chic bandage on her forehead, and she sees me take it in.

"Oh yes. I was struck last night by a particularly brutal officer of the law." She pushes her hair away from the bandage on her forehead, showing her brilliant red fingernails. Then she says, "Sit down. We have to talk."

I do. "What's up, Belle?"

"Can I trust you?"

I burst out laughing. "Belle! With what? The nation's plans for invading North Vietnam? New plans for bombing Cambodia? Of course you can't trust me. I will trot myself right uptown to the Times building and make sure they are in tomorrow's City Edition! But can you trust me with some piece of personal information about you? Of course you can. You know that. Now, which is it? The plans for invasion? Or your bit of personal information? What are you going to lower on me?"

She lights a cigarette and looks at me through the smoke. "Asshole." Belle wears more makeup than most women do nowadays.

I laugh. "Well?"

"Is it possible that Joseph could be interested in me?"

"I don't know." I am serious now. "I really don't know. Why?"

"I just wondered."

"He's a very sexy guy. And it's hard to tell what he's doing because he is so sexy, so attractive. Is he coming on to me? Or is it that he invites sexual responses even when he is not committing himself to anything? I don't know. My sense of him after knowing him for fully forty-eight hours is that he is not treacherous and he is not deceitful. He seems to be totally and fully honest. But admittedly that is not long to know a person. Why do you want to know?"

"Because I wondered. I wondered if there could be something between us. That's all."

"What has he said to you?"

"Nothing."

She is aware that she is not telling me the truth. Or the whole truth. "Belle. Tell me what's going on."

She lifts her chin and looks down her nose at the tips of her fingers. "I am trying to sort things out. I am five years older than you. I am thirty-five. For the last four or five years—for the whole time I have known you—I have been mulling over an idea. It is a plan. And to put this plan into effect takes another person. Can you see where I am going?"

"No, Belle. Tell me."

"I want to have a baby. I don't see anyone on the horizon that I want to marry, but I do want to have a baby, and I want to care for it myself. But I need a father. Getting me pregnant can be done in a number of ways. Some more intimate than others. So, over the past several years I have been looking for a potential donor. I think Joseph might be a possibility. But I don't want to present all this to him if he is going to look at me as if I've lost my fucking mind and then start laughing. You see my quandary."

"I see." I am wondering what to say.

"Has he ever had sex with a woman?"

"Belle, he has told me that he has."

"Was it an important relationship?"

"I don't know. You know Joseph. You can talk to him directly yourself, and it seems to me that it's less important how Joseph feels about sex with you than how he feels about becoming a father."

At that moment the phone on her desk rings. She picks it up. "Hello?"

A man's voice says something.

"Well, we were just speaking of you."

A man's voice.

She laughs. "Well, maybe we could have a drink later this afternoon."

She hands the receiver to me. "It's Joseph."

I hear Joseph, on the phone. "OK, I helped Mitzi get her clothes. She and I are going back to your house to leave an outfit there. We can talk later about all that. The reason I am calling is to ask you if I can help you with anything. I know you are at the theatre, and your brother is arriving at six-thirty—and Andrew is at the restaurant—and that you want to stock up on food for tonight and the next day or two. Would you like me to get the food? Tell me what I can do to help."

I can't think. "Jesus, thanks for offering. Joseph, look after Mitzi. Be sure she has what she wants and what she needs—and what she will take. I'll pay you back later. I am going to be here for another hour, so I will be home in about an hour and a half. Then you and I can talk about food. In the meantime, why don't you go through the refrigerator and look in the cabinet and see what we need. Except for tonight, I expect we will be eating out." I put my hand over the mouthpiece and speak to Belle. "Belle would you like to come to supper tonight?"

She shrugs. "Sure. I'd love that."

"Can you help Joseph get some food for us for tonight?"

She smiles. "Foxy critter, you."

I speak to Joseph again. "Joseph, Belle is here, and I have just invited her to supper. Can you coordinate things with her and the two of you arrange to get food? Just get it for tonight and for breakfast,

131

and I can worry about tomorrow, tomorrow." I check out these arrangements with Belle.

My head is beginning to hurt.

For all of my life, the sexuality of every person in our culture has had to fit itself inside the framework of heterosexual marriage. Every single sex act was in preparation for marriage or in fulfillment of marriage or outside of marriage or a rejection of marriage. Every single sex act was understood and received its moral value from its proximate relation to vaginal sex, which might lead to procreation. While there might have been individuals who said, I do this for the pleasure of it, and it receives its moral value from the intensity of the pleasure I feel, still all the people together understand that the central sexual relationship is formed with a cock and a cunt. Then, thirty-eight hours or so ago, for the first time in our culture, which is Western Christian culture some 2000 years old, men and women publicly rejected the whole set of values which had given sex its meaning. By picking up the paving stones and the bricks and heaving them at the cops, they destroyed the system of values by which their sex had been judged. They showed it was necessary, now, to construct another, different, system of values by which sex can be organized and understood.

On my way down to the stage, I pass a pay phone. I stop and call home. Joseph answers.

"Joseph. Get us some steaks for tonight, why don't you—unless you and Belle have other ideas. You can get good meat at the butchers on Bleecker, at Charles. And corn, and something to make a salad with. Do you have enough money? I'll give Belle money." And then I draw a breath and speak of another matter. "Look, Joseph. Belle wanted to speak to me of a desire she has concerning you. I told her that you had told me you have had sex with women before. Is this OK?"

Joseph says that what I have said is OK. He will take care of the food. I go back and give Belle money—she's already leaving, so anxious is she to have some time with Joseph—and then I head back down to the stage to meet with Sergei and Matt.

"Ah! I am so glad we waited! I think we are making progress. Come sit down and talk to us!" Sergei is English and has the abilities that come from good English schools, capped by RADA—the Royal Academy of Dramatic Arts. Sergei is standing in front of Matt, who

132

sits in one of the canvas chairs, his elbows on the arms of the chair, his fingers laced together to form a church. "Have a seat!"

"We were talking, Bo, of how conservative this romance is. By that I mean, we are accustomed, in the tragedies, to having our worldview shaken to its roots—there's very little surviving at the end of the play that we started the play with—and in the comedies, to a lesser or greater extent, we are subjected to Puck's view. 'What fools these mortals be!' But in The Tempest, the audience knows from the beginning that Prospero the Magician is pulling the strings that cause the storm at sea and that there will be no harm to any of the seafarers. There is hardly any suspense in wondering if Ferdinand is going to get Miranda or if the Neapolitans are going to get away with regicide or if Antonio is going to have to give up his dukedom. It seems that we end the play much as we began it, only with everyone restored to their rightful place or right senses, which includes Ariel and Caliban. So The Tempest takes a group of people who are in some way not in harmony with their world and, through the course of five acts, brings them into harmony with the sea and the sky and the island, and all the unseen forces on the island that blow and push and pinch and seem to endanger the human subjects of the island. In the end, though, our vision, our understanding of the world of the play has not been endangered. Even in such a lovely comedy as Midsummer Night's Dream, the audience leaves the theatre with the knowledge that even though we think we are at the top of the food chain in our world, still the world of the fairies sits atop our world, and when we go to sleep, the fairies are running free, with all our world in their power. In The Tempest, we get no such metaphysical revelation. Nothing about the nature of man. Nothing about life. Nothing about love. We end where we begun. A lot of serious, even profound, subjects touched on during the course of two hours traffic on the stage, but nothing really taken up and examined, nothing earth-shattering. Unless. Unless. Unless it is to be found in Ariel's request. Freedom."

He drops himself into one of the canvas chairs. "I'm exhausted. Look, Bo, Matt, let's call it a day. We've been working hard on this. Why don't we agree to meet tomorrow at, say, eleven. Monday at eleven. And why don't we give some thought to the idea of freedom in The Tempest. Freedom from what. Who doesn't have it. Why do they not have it. What do they have to do to get it. We can see what we come up with tomorrow."

Adam in the Morning

It is four o'clock, and we leave the theatre. It is hot, no clouds, the sun still harsh. Tonight we can cook on the roof. I leave the others and walk down Washington Place. The reason Ariel and Caliban are not free is that a man who is not native to their island has imposed his power on them and has defeated their native gods. Prospero justifies his enslavement of Caliban by condemning his sexual habits and calling him a "monster." But the real reason is that Prospero is a racist. He doesn't bother to justify his enslavement of Ariel. I get to Sheridan Square. A speaker stands on a box talking to a small group of men and to others walking by. "—join with our black brothers and sisters and with the women's liberation movement and with poor people everywhere and with all the dispossessed of our civilization and take up arms against our oppressors and overthrow them, and create a new civilization for free men and women who can each share equally in the natural benefits of this earth and can be truly free—" I pass on.

I weave in and out through the groups of people talking. More than most places in New York, the Village is a place for the exchange of ideas. Sheridan Square is one location, Washington Square is another. St Marks Place. I haven't been there in a long time. I will take Billy over to St Mark's Place. He would enjoy that. I will enjoy Billy's visit. I wish that my parents were here. Billy and I should arrange a time when we can all be together. I need my family around me, sharing this. I will talk to Billy about this tonight.

At the foot of Christopher Street, where I would turn into Weehawken, I go on to West Street and the river. The sounds off the Hudson, distinctly different from the sounds of the streets—the rustling of the water, and the winds whistling over the surface of the waves, what sounds like the throbbing of an engine of a boat I can't see somewhere on the water—are calming. I come down here—the same dock we come to for sex—and sit, my knees pulled up and my arms around them, one hand gripping the other wrist, and feel the power of the river. The sun comes from the southwest and is right in my eyes. In the Village, on the edge of the island, a guy is always aware of the river. I think of the power of the forces arrayed against us, and of the job that has to be done. It is like trying to hold back the tide. Who was that? Someone who shouted at it. Can we end all that and actually change things?

At our apartment, I find a note from Joseph. He and Belle have gone to the stores to buy food. Has Joseph moved in on us uninvited?

I don't know. I suspect we have invited him implicitly, and he has moved into the space we have made for him. Is he the kind of guy who would take advantage? I suppose so. We all would, given the chance. I don't feel like he's taking advantage. I lie down. I am very tired. It is a quarter of five. The phone rings.

It is Billy. "I'm here. All safe. I'll get my bags and then a cab and come directly to you. Is that OK?"

"Sure, that's OK. Thanks for coming. I love you.We've invited some people to come to supper tonight, so there are going to be people here."

I may have fallen asleep. Andrew arrives.

He smiles, and, without saying anything, he shucks off his clothes and gets on the bed with me. I get mine off too. Even though he has just come from a full shift at Zanes, he is not tired. His hands are all over me, and I respond. We kiss. I find his tongue and feel his cock jumping against my belly. Later, we fall asleep, deep, undisturbed sleep, contented and exhausted, his cock still leaping from time to time inside me.

We are waked when the front door opens and I hear Belle and Joseph come in.

"We're here! Your dinner guests are here with your dinner! Come out and welcome us! Joseph, go find them. Tell them to put some clothes on and come out here decent. I want a drink."

Our living room is not big. The front wall on the street has two windows. The other walls have no windows or doors, except for one large archway from the kitchen. On one dark, maroon wall, nearer the windows than the center, is a large movie poster for *Marat/Sade*, which is the short title for *The Persecution and Assassination of Jean-Paul Marat, as Performed by the Inmates at The Asylum at Charenton, Under the Direction of the Marquis de Sade.* The poster, like the play, is in black and white, with Marat at his bath, his head swathed in cloths and turned to face the viewer, and Charlotte Corday in profile, her arm holding her knife aloft. In the background are the bars of the asylum and, beyond them, a row of persons viewing the action of the drama. Like the play, the poster is disturbing. There are two sofas—a long one and a short one—a coffee table and an upholstered chair, bought second hand, a couple of small tables with lamps, and small bookcases. On the wall facing the windows are two more large posters, hanging next to each other. Reflections in a

Golden Eye and a Warhol film, I Am a Man. It's OK. It's comfortable. And it's the kind of place all our friends have.

I have put on shorts and a t-shirt. Belle and Joseph are in the kitchen when I come out, putting things away. They are a powerful couple to look at. Her colors are her white skin, her black hair, and her brilliant red lipstick and nail polish, while his colors are his rich dark brown skin, his black hair, the clear whites of his eyes, the red of his tongue, and the white of his teeth. I can understand a person inviting these two to his house, just because they are so arrestingly beautiful.

"Thanks for getting all this, folks. Who do I owe, and how much?"

"The receipt is here on the table, but that's just to let you know what we bought. Belle and I are paying for this."

The receipt is sitting on the same bills I gave Belle this afternoon. "Oh, folks, I wouldn't have asked you to do this favor if I had thought you were paying. Come on, let me pay." I scan the receipt. I leave the bills on the table.

Joseph takes me in his arms, kisses me, and says, "Nope."

Belle laughs. "We got everything for eight people, which is what you asked for—and then we got enough for four more in case any of us bring other people."

"Who are the eight?"

Joseph answers. "You and Andrew, me and Billy, Belle, Mitzi, and then that leaves enough for five or six more. Belle and I figured that you can just eat off this for several days while Billy is here."

"Thanks guys. I didn't mean for you to do this."

"We know," Belle says. She puts her arms around my neck and hugs me. "You're so good to all of us, that we thought we'd do you a favor."

She's good. "Well thanks. Belle, you remember Billy, don't you?"

"Oh, yes! Big handsome fella. Sweet kind of Texan."

We laugh at her. "Well, he's going to be here for several days, so you will have a chance at him, if you want."

Andrew, who took longer to get dressed than I did, comes in wearing shorts and a t-shirt. That guy. He still has an erection. He fixes a drink, then he makes an announcement. "Guys, I have some work to do before I can relax with you. I am taking notes on Friday night and last night. Give me an hour, OK? We need to be writing all this down so that we'll have a history of these riots."

Belle and Joseph look at him. "Sure. That's important," Belle says. "We'll entertain ourselves until you can join us. I'll think of something. It will be hard, of course, but I will try."

"It would be great if you could write down everything you can remember, too." Then he is gone back to the bedroom to the table there.

"Do you think he's right? I think he's right. I'm going to start writing all this down. Belle Underwood's Life, I think I'll call it. I think I want it to have a kind of eighteenth-century flavor. Maybe Moll Flanders. I think I need to be having more sex, however, don't you all agree?"

"Yeah, he's right," I say. "We should all write down everything. And I do agree, Belle, you should be having more sex."

"Thank you, so much, Bo. You always agree with me when it's important." Belle is at the refrigerator. "Now, who wants a drink? We have vodka, gin, bourbon, and Scotch, and we have Heinekens. I also brought my Acapulco Gold, here—" She takes the baggie out of her purse and places it carefully on the table, as if it were a surprise gift. "—and papers here. I figure you can roll your own. Now then. Who's for something with ice in it?"

I am.

Belle gets us what we want.

I get Andrew's box and the bunch of flyers I collected today.

"Help me, Joseph. This is for Andrew's work." I give him a pen. "Put today's date, the time—put 2:40 pm—and Sheridan Square on the back of each one of these. Put my initials too, so he will know later who collected these and when."

He grins. "In the coming Revolution, I want you on my side."

Belle observes our work. "Bo, thank you for having a brother in Texas who visits you from time to time so we can have a party! Jesus! How long has it been since we all were together? Two weeks? A month? I feel like it's been forever. I feel old and withered. Kiss me Joseph."

I ask, "Do we have ice, folks?"

They didn't buy any. For these drinks, there are the ice trays, but we need bags. We sort out duties, and it falls to me to go down and get a couple of bags of ice at the corner. Belle accompanies me.

On the street, she has much to say.

"Thanks," Belle says, "for arranging the time this afternoon when Joseph and I could be together."

"Glad to help. Did you get things straightened out?"

"Well, yes. I laid out what I am thinking, but I didn't ask him to participate. At least he didn't get up and run screaming down the street. He listened seriously—respectfully—and I asked him if we could talk some more about it. I told him I was looking for a man, and I asked him what he was thinking about—had he ever wanted to father a child, did he want to have a part in raising a child—and we talked about all that. I think we'll do a lot more talking, getting to know each other—"

"Then you're not thinking merely in terms of an anonymous sperm donor?"

"I can get that, I think, and I think I can raise a child by myself, but there are other options in addition to that. One is for me to have a personal connection with whoever becomes the donor, more than merely a contractual relationship. Another is finding someone who wants to have a part in the child's life after birth—somebody who will commit to the long term, who will understand that, if he is not anonymous, then fathering means loving. You see, I think this person and I—if he is the right person—can negotiate with each other and come up with a broad-stroke arrangement, that is, a description of my obligations and his obligations and rights on both sides. There is no reason we have to base this on any existing contract. We are free to create our own arrangement, if we want—"

"Belle, this is wonderful. Does Joseph know you are talking to me?"

"Oh yes. I told him I was going to talk to you, that I already have talked to you a little, and he said he was going to talk to you, so I think you—and Andrew—are going to hear a lot about this in the near future. This is the beginning of a conversation among us whose title might be, Getting Belle Pregnant and Raising a Child With Belle. How to Do One or Both of Those."

On the way home, I bring up my questions.

"You know, you haven't mentioned another part of it that interests me. I assume that the two of you—whoever you choose to ask—can come to an agreement about the details of how a straight woman and a gay man conceive a child and give birth and raise it. What I am not clear about yet are the other questions. Why does a straight woman want to get pregnant with a gay man? And why would a gay man want to father a child at all, and further, why would he want to father it with a straight woman? There are a lot of other questions I could think of about all this. I don't mean we need to talk about all these things tonight, but I will be interested in hearing what you are thinking. One of the aspects of a heterosexual marriage is that when married heterosexuals conceive a child, the child is going to be theirs, and it will grow up in their house until it goes out on its own. But that's not what's going to happen between you and whoever you ask, unless you decide to live together. One of you—or maybe both of you—is going to be giving up a good bit of the kid's life to the other parent."

We're home. I have a bag of ice on each shoulder. Joseph, standing in the kitchen organizing supper, looks confident, like he can handle anything, and he looks from me to Belle and back, a broad smile. "Hey, were you two in the middle of something? I'll put this in this bowl, and I will get out of here so you can finish."

I put some of the ice in the refrigerator.

"No, Joseph, we weren't in the middle of anything. Come here."

I put the rest of the ice in the sink and turn to him, and I kiss him. He looks at Belle and says, "I'm falling in love with this guy. And with Andrew, too. What is it about you guys that makes your brother come all the way from Houston to be with you right now?" He hugs me.

Joseph kisses Belle. They are about to go out on the roof to check on the charcoal, when I ask Joseph to stay. I watch Belle climb through the window.

"Joseph, can I talk to you for a minute?"

"Sure. What's up?" He looks at me seriously.

"It is hard to get a minute when we're alone, big guy. You want to move in with us."

"Uh-huh. I would like to. I hope that doesn't piss you off."

"No." I laugh. "I think both of us are happy with the idea. We've talked about it a little bit, and we don't want to say, 'No,' but at the same time it's hard to sit down and think about this, with all this going on. Can we just put this off for a while, until the riots are over and things settle down, and it's easier for all of us to think about our lives? I know we're asking you to live with uncertainty, and that will be hard for you—"

"Oh, no. I'm learning to love you two—that's not hard—and I wanted you to know where my mind is. I can live with putting this off for a while."

I put my arm along his shoulder, my hand on the back of his neck. "We're learning to love you too. We didn't want you to think we were ignoring you or were turned off by the idea. The idea is a great one. Why don't you stay with us as much as you'd like for now?"

Belle comes back in and looks from one to the other of us. "Is it OK if I come in?"

"Sure, Belle."

Joseph puts his arms around Belle. "How are you?"

She thinks for a minute. "The charcoal in the grill is burning well. I am well. I am happy we had our conversation. I have told Bo about it. Everything seems to be turning out well." She smiles. "I like being here among my friends."

She glances at me, a certain anxiety in her eyes.

We hear shouting on the street. "Bo! Bo! I'm here! I'm fuckin' here! Come get me, you beautiful man!"

Everybody bursts out laughing, and Belle goes to the window. The rest of us clatter down the stairs. Andrew comes away from his writing for a minute to welcome Billy.

He is just paying off the taxi. He turns to look toward the door. Billy has dark red-blond stiff, coarse hair, a thick mustache and short, trimmed, beard. He's the beautiful man. He's almost as tall as I am, stockier, better built. When we break out through the door into the street, he turns toward us grinning, his arms wide open. "God, I've been looking for a good fight for days! I haven't had a serious fight for at least a week. I hope you're going to provide one for me."

I hug him. Even before I hug him, he pulls back and looks at the bandages on my forehead. Then I kiss his neck and then turn him so he is facing Andrew. They hug and kiss—that always moves me, when I see them do it, on the mouth—and then Andrew does his duty.

"Billy, this is Joseph. He's an actor in Bo's new play, and we're all hangin' together while the riots're going on."

Billy opens his arms for Joseph. "Shit, I want to get to know you, man."

Joseph smiles.

"And Billy—" It's Belle upstairs, in the window. "—come on up here and give me a hug. I'm making you a drink right now."

The apartment is hot, after the relative cool of the street, but we have the roof behind us, and pretty soon we'll move the action outside. Andrew goes back to the bedroom.

Adam in the Morning

Belle kisses Billy and then runs her hands down his shoulders and arms. "Oh! You're a sight for sore eyes! Bourbon, wasn't it?"

He grins—"Bourbon. Please"—and leans down and hugs her again, his arms around her waist, and picks her up. "I want to hear all about you, Belle." Then he looks around our apartment, checking it out. "Oh, Jesus, I'm glad to be here! I want to hear about everything. What is this?" He is looking at the clipping about us on the refrigerator from this morning's Times. "4 POLICEMEN HURT/IN 'VILLAGE' RAID." He takes it down and reads. "I see you guys were interfering with the policemen going about their lawful duties. That's terrible of you!"

"Oh, yes, Billy, and we're going to keep on doing that every night until they find some other lawful duties to perform, somewhere else. Welcome to New York. We've missed you. But to change the subject for a minute. I think the corn is ready. We can put it in the water when Mitzi comes. Are we in a hurry to eat? How do you guys feel? I'd like to wait until Mitzi comes, if you can handle that. Are you too hungry to wait?"

They can wait.

Billy goes into the bedroom. I can hear him talking to Andrew. They laugh. He comes back.

Billy checks out Joseph. "Man, you're something else." He puts out his hand and grips Joseph's shoulder—his deltoid muscles—and kneads them and says, "You're in Bo's play."

"I play Caliban, the monster. It's a comic part—"

"And one of the biggest parts in the play."

"I'm just getting to know Bo and Andrew."

"You're new to the acting company. Where were you before?"

"The New Lafayette, up in Harlem."

"Oh, I know them."

"You've seen their shows?" Joseph is impressed.

"No, ah, a little. I know them. I've seen plays by, ah, Bullins, Ed Bullins."

"In Houston?"

"No, up here, in Harlem, with Bo and Andrew."

"I want to get to know you better."

Billy puts his arm across my shoulder and grips my delts. "How're you, big brother?" Then he slides around in front of me and puts his hands on either side of my head. "Can I see your cuts? Now what is going on with your head?" This is one of the reasons he came to New York from Houston. To check me out and to be sure I am OK.

"Bo," Belle speaks sternly, "sit down at the table so he can see the top of your head."

I do. I enjoy it when Billy looks after me. He searches the top of my head, and then around the sides, using his fingers to separate my hair and get down to my scalp.

Then he kisses my scalp. "OK, big guy, you can get up now. It appears you were telling me the truth. Those are some nasty cuts. But wait, what about your ribs and your back? Do you have any pain? Can I look for bruises? What are these on your face?"

"You're sweet, Billy. Yes, you can look for anything you want. I can't say no to a brother who has come all the way from Houston. But I should say that Andrew and Joseph have already searched me. We've all searched each other. The red things on my face are where cops hit me in the face with their sticks Saturday morning and where they hit me again Saturday night. They're sore, and they're red, but I don't think they broke any bone."

"I really wish I could find someone who wanted to search my body so thoroughly," Belle says. "I might even ask whoever it was to search my body even more thoroughly than that. I wouldn't want anybody to miss any potential life-threatening injury, such as the one I have here on my forehead."

"Life-threatening? On your forehead? Let me see. On your bottom, lady, take the chair."

"Belle, Billy is a football coach, and he has had some training to help him deal with injuries among his players."

"Should I trust him, Joseph?"

"Oh, I think he knows what he's doing, lady. He's got good fingers. Sit back and enjoy."

"I trust him absolutely." She slides onto the chair and, very daintily, allows Billy to run his fingers through her hair. It is only after he has finished searching her scalp that he looks at her forehead. "Did you put this bandage on your forehead, or did someone else do it?"

She speaks meekly. "I did it."

"Bo, do you have gauze and pads and disinfectant?"

"Yes, plenty of all of that."

"Can I take this bandage off and check you out?"

"I really don't think that's necessary, but if you want to."

Adam in the Morning

He does, and then he cleans the wound and redresses it. "There. For a life-threatening wound like this, you appear to be recovering with remarkable speed."

"Oh, Billy." She runs her thumbs through his Levi belt loops, one on either side. I am reminded that these two are the only heterosexuals in the apartment. At thirty-five, she is about six or seven years older than he is.

"I checked out Andrew, Bo. I checked out his scalp, and I asked him to take off his shirt, and I checked out his back and his ribcage. He said you'd done it, and I don't mean to imply that I don't trust you, but it does help if you have an outsider do these things. And besides, I have to take a complete report back to Mom and Dad. I also checked out Joseph. He's OK too. He's fine. He's built better than any of the rest of you, and he's apparently the only one of you guys who knows how to take part in a riot without getting his head bashed in."

Joseph grins.

Andrew comes in from the bedroom. "I want another drink." He puts his arm around Billy's waist. "I don't consider you an outsider, big guy. I think you're one of us."

Billy grins broadly. "One of us. I like that." He thinks about that for a moment while Belle stands up. "Us. But who is that? So far, you've got three gay men, a straight man, and a straight woman for supper. And Andrew says that another person is coming. A young woman named Mitzi. Where does she fit into all this? Are we us?"

"How was the writing?" Belle wants to know.

"I am not even writing yet. I have been pretty desperate to get notes down on paper, and that is all I've been able to do. Just words and phrases that I hope will jog my memory—"

We hear someone pounding on the door downstairs. I go down to let her in. And when I open the door, I find that it's not Mitzi. She's a little taller, and a little heavier. She has dark straight hair. She wears jeans and a t-shirt.

"Bo here?"

"I'm Bo."

"I'm Violet."

Mitzi's sister. "Hey, that's great. Come in. You're welcome here." The first thing a person notices about Violet is that she was struck across her eyelid, which is swollen a good bit. It's the street fighting,

I guess. "You're Mitzi's sister. She told me about you. Is she coming?"

"She told me to meet her here." Violet speaks in a low, soft voice. It may be that she's afraid. She's still standing in the street.

"Would you like to come in?"

"I think I'll wait for Mitzi here, outside, if that's OK."

"Fine." I'm thinking, hard, fast. "Can I wait with you? Is that OK?" I don't want to crowd her, since she is here, alone. I hear someone behind me coming down the stairs. I do the introductions. "This is Joseph, and he moved here a year ago from California. He's been in the Lower East Side a couple of months." When I introduce him, she lets her eyes rest on him for a second, and then she makes a little shy noise that sounds like um. "Billy, my brother, and Belle, our friend, are upstairs." I point. "They're hanging out the window." They wave at us. "And Andrew, my lover, is upstairs in the bedroom, writing. He'll join us later." I get Violet's attention again. "Is it OK if we wait down here with you?"

She shrugs.

"Can we sit down?" It is as if Violet has become the hostess, here on the street. Joseph sits down on the steps. I can hear Belle and Billy coming down.

Belle enters the outdoors as if it were a particularly well-designed sculpture garden in midtown which she has never seen before. She looks around. "Oh," she says, "it's heavenly, isn't it?" She speaks to Violet. "We haven't met. I'm Belle, and I'm here to keep all these men in line. I can't tell you how happy—how relieved—I am to have another woman here to help with the task. I sometimes think I am losing control. Aren't men a handful, dear?"

Violet mumbles something—Belle has overwhelmed her—and turns away. But she is smiling. Belle has made a friend.

We sit down on the stoop and wait for Mitzi.

"Violet," Joseph asks, "Can I get you something to drink? We're all drinking. We have beer, and we also have some grass upstairs. We also have lemonade. Tell me what you'd like, and I'll get it for you."

"We'll start cooking when Mitzi comes." I think she may be hungry. "It shouldn't take more than half an hour."

"Beer?" Violet does not smile. "Can I have a beer?"

This is good. Whatever else is going on, Mitzi trusts us enough to come to supper and to bring her sister, even to send her sister. We may bring her in off the street yet. As for the alcohol, Mitzi and

Violet can get anything they want on the street, including hard drugs, so their drinking is nothing new. The important thing is to get them off the street and out of the sex trade. One thing that's bad for her at a time.

"You can have a beer." Then Joseph's inside and up the stairs.

"So," I say to Violet, "what've you girls been doing today?"

"We hung out." She lifts her chin noticeably. "All of us talked about what happened last night and what we're gonna do about it tonight." She is holding something small in her fingers, passing it back and forth from the fingers of one hand to the fingers of another. Then I see that it is a small silver charm—a peace symbol.

Billy is concerned. "Were you hurt last night?"

"No."

The answer closes discussion on that subject, although it doesn't explain her swollen eyelid.

Joseph comes back with the beer. "What are your plans for tonight?"

"We know what we're going to do."

"What's that?"

"We're going to rip their fuckin' hearts out, for one thing."

Joseph takes a deep breath. "And I am going to be there when you do that. I'll be next to you when you do. I'll be doing that same thing."

"Will you really come?"

"Yes. I'll really come."

"We needed you last night, and you didn't come."

"I'll come too," Billy says. "That's why I came up from Houston."

She doesn't know whether she believes Billy. She says it again, "We needed you last night, but you didn't come."

"Violet, they may not have been fighting next to you last night," Billy says, "but they have been fighting somewhere—"

There is no point in this. She believes what she feels. We can convince her over time that we are on her side. "Would you like to sit down?"

"I'd like something to eat."

"Good. We've got stuff upstairs. Wanna come upstairs?"

So we do. And things get better. We all have things to do to prepare for supper, and she sees us doing normal, usual things. The atmosphere relaxes. The others go out on the roof to tend the charcoal, but Violet and I stay inside. The steaks are ready—we don't usually have steaks around here, but this is special, for Billy—and the water is ready for the corn. The greens are ready for the salad dressing. I get the napkins and the flatwear and a big plate for Andrew to put the steaks on. Violet leans against the arch into the bedroom and watches me.

"You do the women's stuff, and he does the men's stuff."

"Is that the way you see it? I think I do what has to be done, and I think Andrew is the same way. I don't think we divide the chores that way—women's things and men's things. If one of us does a job regularly, I think it's because we've agreed he does that job better than the other one does."

"You're doing the kitchen stuff, the other one is in the bedroom writing something. He's doing the man's job."

"That's just what you're seeing tonight. We both cook. Usually we cook together. We both stay afterward and clean up until the kitchen is clean. Does that make sense?"

"That's what Mitzi said you did."

"You and Mitzi talk about these things?"

"Uh-huh. We talk about falling in love with a man and then settling down somewhere, and he'd go away to work every day and I'd stay home and keep house—"

"—very old fashioned."

"Sometimes I think that too. But what do you know about women? You're a faggot."

"That's OK. I'm a faggot, but that doesn't mean I don't know anything about women. It's 1969, and women's lives have changed in the last twenty years. It's hard not to know this. Everybody knows that women's lives have changed."

"I don't know whether I'd like to stay home and keep house or have a career."

"What does Mitzi say?"

"She wants a career, but she also wants to stay home and look beautiful so when her boyfriend comes home from work, he'll love her." Violet smiles, her first since she came here. "I think she wants to lie on a sofa and wear a lot of eye makeup and smoke cigarettes." She laughs at the picture.

Someone pounds on the door downstairs.

"That's Mitzi. Do you want me to go down and let her in?"

"Thanks, Violet."

146

Violet's open and gentle and funny—and harsh. I wonder what she is like around Mitzi.

Someone has entered the front door and is now clumping up the stairs. The door swings wide open, and there is Mitzi. The first thing I see is her temple. She has a wide—something—just above her temple. A bruise, a blow with something hard that took of a layer off her skin. It is scabbing over now. Behind her, in the shadows of the stairwell, is Violet.

"You guys start without me?"

"Come here."

I take her in my arms and hug her. She struggles against me. "I thought you weren't coming! Thanks for coming!" I'm laughing, hard.

"Hey, leggo! You big faggot!"

"You're beautiful." I let her go.

I drop the corn in the water, and then I give the tray with the steaks to Violet. "Take these outside to Joseph or Belle. I'll be outside in a minute."

They go. I hear them stop in the bedroom and talk to Andrew, who must be having a hard time finding time to write without interruptions. I can hear Belle's sharp voice, and in my mind I can see her long fingers with their red nails gesturing to emphasize the drama of it all. It is good to have her around. I can also hear Joseph's laughter. It's good to have *him* around, too. I hear Mitzi's tenor asserting her rights—"Yeah, I want a beer!"—and Billy saying something. I want Billy and Mitzi to know each other. I hear Joseph calling out, "Oh, Billy, don't go! Stay, please!" But Billy doesn't, because, before I can follow them, Billy comes in. He hugs me and then he kisses me on my cheeks.

"I missed you big guy." He looks closely at my face. "Being in the middle of big riots seems to suit you. You look good." Then he grins. "Aside from the slices in your head and the bandages. I think you swagger."

I laugh.

He sits at the kitchen table. "You know, I wish you'd invite Mom and Dad to New York sometime, and I could come, and you could have all your friends—like now—and let Mom and Dad meet them."

"Would they like that, you think?"

147

"Do you know Mom and Dad, or what? Of course they'd like that. I think they'd like to see you with all your friends. You know they worry about you being lonely—being alone."

"Alone?"

"The only experience they have with gay people is Uncle Duncan and Uncle Albert, neither one of whom really has a life of his own. Duncan and Albert've both always been a part of someone else's, and I think it may also be their age, their generation—that is, Mom's and Dad's and Uncle Duncan's and Uncle Albert's—"

Billy talks about us and our parents. It is about seven o'clock. Our building faces southwest, our street runs northwest, and the sun would be shining directly into our windows if it weren't for the line of buildings across the street. Ten days ago was the summer solstice, which means that we hardly get geared up for fighting after the sun goes down before it is coming back up again. Short nights designed for this kind of rioting.

"They are going to love Violet."

"Don't forget Mitzi."

"Well, I don't know her yet. I've had a glimpse of Violet. They're going to want to take them back to Texas with 'em. They always wanted a daughter, you know. They'd love a gay daughter."

"Straight daughter. Straight daughter. Both Mitzi and Violet are straight. Be careful about that now."

"Right. How does that work?"

"It's not about genitals. It's what a person feels. They feel themselves women attracted to men. So, they're straight. I feel myself a man attracted to men, so I am gay. And, you, big fella, are goddamned lucky to have so many people attracted to you wherever they're coming from."

He gets up and puts his arms around me. "I am very lucky to have a brother like you who loves me. Thanks for letting me come." He puts his face in the corner of my neck. "We were so worried about you, about all of you. We know how the cops can be, and how dangerous it can be to get in a fight with them." He pulls away and looks at me. "You should have seen Mom last night after we heard about the riots. She was pacing up and down in their living room, mad as a hornet, remembering all the times one of their friends had been assaulted by cops on the rampage during the big civil rights demonstrations—the sit-ins and the first Freedom Ride in 1961. She doesn't believe for a minute that they will be restrained in their exercise of power. She told me, 'You go up there and make sure he is all right.' Apparently, I am to tell you that your job is to make sure that I don't get killed in these riots. Now, I can see you have a lot to look out for, so you don't need to look out for me. I can take care of myself. But I am also going to be looking out for you."

That is like Mom. Billy and I are supposed to look after each other. "Should we call her?"

"That'd be good, if you feel you can do it."

"After supper." I give him the salad. "Here, toss this."

And in a few minutes, everything is done, and I pull Andrew away from his desk. We climb through the window onto the roof. We serve ourselves and find chairs to sit on. By now the sun is so low in the sky behind the buildings across Weehawken that there is a slight breeze and things are a little cooler while we eat.

Andrew tells us about his work.

"You guys know I write articles pretty often for the local counter-culture papers in the Village—the East Village Other and the Guardian—and I suspect that those newspapers are going to want accounts of the riots. There are also a couple of papers in Boston. The *Phoenix* and the *Avatar*. Joseph says the papers on the West Coast—*Berkeley Barb* and the *Los Angeles Free Press*—are going to be wanting eye-witness accounts, too. But the bigger thing, the more important thing, is that we ourselves need to know what happened here—what is happening here—so that we will know how we got to where we are. This is now just about the biggest thing in our past. This is like the American Revolution. This is like the French Revolution, where we say, *We will not be governed this way any more.* And people for decades, for hundreds of years, are going to look back on this and say, *What happened, exactly?* Well, it is up to us, the ones who are here, to write it down, to keep records, to save the papers, so that when the future writers and researchers and scholars begin to deal with this, our historians are not dependent only on what *The New York Times* says is happening. You've all seen the *Times* article from this morning. Anyway, folks, keeping records of what is happening so that we can write our own history of this time is one part of our claiming our freedom. We are free to write our own history, and this is where it begins."

"Are you going to be interested in the street kids? I mean, in what happened to us?"

"Maybe more than anybody else."

149

"No shittin'?"

"No shittin'. I want to know everything you remember about what you did in the riots. Will you help me?"

"How can I help you?" She is full of doubt.

"You can help me by telling me what you know. Better still, you can write a story about the riots and what you and Violet and the other street kids did."

"Maybe."

"Mitzi," Belle says, "I could sit down somewhere quiet, and you could tell me about what you and Violet have been doing, and I could help you write it down—or you could help me write it down—so it would be your story of your part in the riots."

Mitzi seems dubious. "You'd help?"

"Oh, yes. And, do you think you'd like to ask Joseph to help too?"

"Yeah, if he would."

Joseph smiles. "I would, Mitzi. And it would be your story of the riots." They talk.

"Can I help you do your work?" Mitzi asks Andrew.

"Yes. You can. What you can help me with right away—this coming week—is help me meet some of the other kids who were fighting. I want to talk to as many of them as I can to make sure I get your part of the story—"

We talk about how we all met and about how long Andrew and I have been together. This is partly for Billy, who doesn't know Joseph and Mitzi and Violet, and partly for Violet. Violet and Mitzi are trying to figure out how we are with one another. Billy, who has known Andrew and Belle for three years, is still working on understanding us. He is fascinated by Mitzi and Violet. I am proud of him when he asks, "Do you have boyfriends?" which is just right.

When Violet answers, she is very demure. "I think so." And she looks down and away. But when Mitzi answers, she is brazen. "Of course I do. And we're going to get married in a few years, too." But neither of them will talk about them.

We talk about the bombing of Cambodia, and Andrew talks about the RYM—the Revolutionary Youth Movement—which he thinks is "cool." Belle brings up the Profile of Cesar Chavez currently running in the current *The New Yorker*. "His experience with the farm workers is like what is going on here."

"In both situations people who were formerly powerless are now seizing power."

"The biggest difference," Joseph says, "is that Cezar Chavez is himself such a charismatic personality. He has been able to create his own situation. He is taking a situation where the people are unorganized and lack focus and drive and building a movement out of them. On the other hand, our riots seem to be a spontaneous uprising of the people. I expect that in the next weeks and months leaders will surface—rise up out of the great mass of gay men in New York—but they will rise up out of a movement that already exists. And I don't expect it will be one person. New York is too big."

Billy asks questions about the riot. "Were you afraid? I'd like to hear everything that happened." Mitzi and Violet tell him the most—Andrew scribbling away at his pad, taking notes—but Joseph and Andrew tell him about the big woman fighting so hard on the first night, and the three of us tell about getting chased by the two cops down Seventh Avenue and then turning around and chasing them up Seventh Avenue, screaming, "Catch them! Fuck them!" a story that Billy likes. I tell stories about Andrew and Joseph fighting with their fists together. Belle tells about missing the first night of fighting because her friends betrayed her and about throwing rocks the second night. We talk about the cops, how stunned they seemed that the faggots fought back, and we talk about the street kids and how brave they were with their kick line. We move all the liquor out on the roof, along with the ice and Belle's Acapulco Gold, and everybody gets sloshed—or high. We are grateful that we have each other and that we are all OK. The sun goes down, and it gets dark.

Billy turns to me. "You haven't mentioned *The Rebel*. Do you think about *The Rebel* during all of this?"

"Why *The Rebel*?" Joseph asks.

"It was one of the books our parents gave Billy and me when we were in high school and college. We'd talk about them at supper. It's about rebellion, a companion to *The Myth of Sisyphus*, which is about suicide. Both of them ask questions about living in a deeply unjust world—the kind of world Camus called *absurd*."

"I read them when I was at Wellesley," Belle says.

"I wondered if you think about it. We used to love that book. I wondered if it is a helpful essay for you now. Does it clarify anything for you?"

"Oh, yeah. He makes it possible to tie together the kinds of crimes he was thinking about—the Nazis and the concentration camps —and the kinds of crimes our generation of Americans has had to deal with. I mean, official, governmental racism, Bull Connor, and, here, official, governmental oppression of gay people. When 'assassins in judges robes' enter prisoners' cells—when it is the *government* that commits the largest and the worst crimes—the only possible response is rebellion."

"Talk more, Bo," Andrew says.

"Camus is looking at crime in our century—he is thinking of the millions killed by government action—which is most often committed by those in authority, by officials, by judges, by political leaders and those who make the law. We are either victims of these crimes, in murder, or, because of the way the system is set up, we are complicit in these crimes—*unless we rebel.* He says, 'in order to exist, man must rebel' (p. 22). He proposes, instead of *I think, therefore I am*, 'I rebel, and therefore we exist' (p. 22)."

"I don't think I understood a third of what was in that book," Billy says, "but what was most powerful about it was the respect our parents had for it, for rebellion."

"Oh, yeah, Billy. They looked around them and were met on all sides by examples of the government committing murder on its citizens."

"He was a beautiful writer," Belle says. "It was in 1960, the night he died, and I read about the accident in the paper, and that night—it was in the winter, in January, 1960—and I was so distressed, so grief-stricken that I walked up Broadway in the snow in the dark, knowing that I had never felt so alone in my whole life."

"Most revolutions result in murder. Murder of the king, of the tsar, the emperor, the president. There's a reason why the guillotine is the sign of the French Revolution and so of all revolutions. Maybe today it is the firing squad. A rebellion has a different goal. It's a refusal to accept the way things are. It is also a way of defining ourselves. *We are this thing*, and therefore we rebel."

"What are we doing here?"

"I don't know. I don't think we know. I don't think the gay man in the street knows yet, and we don't know what will be the effects of our riots."

"I think you're hard on us," Andrew says. "I think most of us have it figured out. The rioting is going to result in some kind of organization being formed, and we're going to work for a city in which the cops don't engage in entrapment and don't use their billy clubs on us and don't bust our bars. We want the rights of straight people."

"Yes, absolutely. The laws have to be enforced equally." I speak slowly, thinking. "The cops don't bust straight bars. But aside from that I don't think even straight people have it so good. Do we really want *only* the rights that straight people have? Do we want to be treated exactly like straight people? We have to address the problems that Andrew is pointing out, but then, next, do we want to just do it all over again? The question we ought to ask is, 'What kind of people are we? and what kind of world do we want afterward?' We are defining these things in our riots."

"Talk more," Belle says.

"Most of our difficulties come from our culture's fear of sex and our culture's strenuous attempts to control it. Is the sex of humans really the business of government or of anybody or any power in our culture? Why can't we all have sex any way we want and with any person we choose within certain broad limits. Beyond these really basic requirements, why can't we move away from where we are toward celebrating sex wherever it's found?"

"I like that," Mitzi says. "Fucking A."

"That's going to shock everybody, Bo."

"It may be shocking, Billy, but now is the time to talk about it. We could have a world in which men and women have sex without shame—the shame of being seen, of having what we do known by some other person, of feeling that sex is embarrassing or extraordinarily private. I am talking about straight people *and* gay people, about everybody. I imagine a world in which we separate *love* from *sex,* in which nothing sexual is the sign of love or of devotion or steadfastness, in which men and women don't put pressure on ourselves around sexual matters, don't weigh sex down with meanings that it doesn't naturally have. I imagine a world in which men and women find the maximum degree of freedom in his or her relationship with others, as Andrew and I do in each other."

Billy laughs. "Most people think that falling in love means losing your freedom."

"You're describing a utopia, Bo," Belle says.

"I don't know that that's so, Belle. Look, Billy. We are in the middle of the biggest gay riots in the history of the world. And what these riots are about is that our culture is determined that we, that gay people, are not going to be free. And the government is using all its power to keep us from being free. That is the *point.* But the larger point is that our culture is constantly telling us—telling *everybody*—that we cannot be free and we cannot express our sex in freedom. And what we are saying, out there on the street, on a particular street in a particular city at a particular time in the history of the world, is this, *We are determined to be free.* So now, for the first time ever, we are in a moment when it is possible to look at the whole structure built up by our culture around sex and to say, *We are going to start all over.* The question now is this, *How are we going to organize our sexuality?* We want to be free to express our sexuality according to our desires and needs. We want to be able to say, *I want to celebrate my body and what it will do.* And if there was ever a moment to do this, to start all over, now is it. Now is the time to propose radical solutions."

Andrew speaks. "Do you think that's possible, Bo? Could we get there from where we've started?"

Billy speaks to Joseph. "You're quiet. Joseph, tell me about yourself."

"It's good listening to you—you brothers—talking and getting back together. I don't have a brother, so that's good to see."

"What do you have?" Billy asks.

"I have my mom, and there's me. She raised me in LA. She still lives there."

"Is she OK?"

"Oh, yeah, she's fine. I'll go see her before the end of the summer. I called her yesterday and again today."

"Tell me about her, Joseph," Belle says.

"She lives in an apartment about the size of this one, and she works for an insurance company. She's a stenographer. She likes movies. And—" He grins broadly. "—she loves me. She loves jazz. When she was younger, she was a Garveyite."

"That's cool," Andrew says. "She sounds like a good mom."

"What's a Garveyite, Joseph?" Mitzi asks.

"Garveyites are black people who follow the ideas of Marcus Garvey. He was a black nationalist at the beginning of this century." Joseph takes a long breath. "Some people say he was the first black liberationist. He said that black people would never be free until they had their own country in Africa."

"I've read about him," Andrew says.

Joseph smiles. "I had a good upbringing."

"Yeah, I think you did."

"And you like each other?"

"Oh yeah. She's an interesting lady. She likes to hear about my life, and I like to hear about her life. She tells me what to read. I tell her what to read. We get along."

"Are you going to invite her to New York?" Belle asks.

"I think so."

"Then I want us all to come to my house for supper when she's here."

"She'd like that. I've told her about all of you, and she thinks you're really interesting."

"Aren't you sweet, Joseph." Belle smiles.

"Tell me what you did before you came to New York," Mitzi says, "—about when you fought the sheriffs in Mississippi."

"Tell us," Billy says.

"Well, in high school I knew about Elijah Muhammad and the Nation of Islam—very, very strict people, absolutists—but I was also a member of CORE—that was the Congress of Racial Equality—when I was in high school and then later at UCLA. CORE was the driving force behind the Freedom Rides. I did the first Freedom Ride in '61. That was pretty hairy. Screaming mobs of white people going berserk, people throwing rocks. You'd get off the bus into the middle of this mob. There was no way to defend ourselves. I got bloodied lots of times. I got arrested, too, and I spent time in jail. Then I got hooked up with SNCC—the Student Non-Violent Coordinating Committee—and ended up dropping out of school so I could stay in the South. I was a volunteer in demonstrations in McComb, Georgia and in Albany, Georgia, in '61 and '62. I became a field secretary for SNCC in Mississippi in late 1962. I did voter registration work all of '63 and '64, which was Freedom Summer. I taught people how to register. I did that mostly in and around Hattiesburg. It's a town in southern Mississippi. I lived with local people, but some of us lived in dormitories in town—you know, houses SNCC rented so twenty or thirty people could stay there. We taught people how to answer the questions on the forms they had to fill out when they registered. I also taught in a Freedom School. Black History, and things like that."

155

Then I say, "I was down there too, in '64."

He grins. "Hey, you were there. Where?"

"I worked in the SNCC office in Jackson in the summer of 1963, and then I did field work in '64. Freedom Summer. I got assigned to Meridian."

"We could have known each other, but I never got to Meridian. I was in Hattiesburg. That's cool that you were down there. You're a veteran too."

The reason we never connected in Mississippi is that we got there and went right to work, digging down into our communities and getting to know the people we had come to help. Usually people in one town in Mississippi didn't get to know people who were in another town. We weren't there to get to know each other. I'm white, and he's black, and it was hard and dangerous in Mississippi to integrate those teams, not because of us, but because of the culture we were in. White Mississippi didn't like to see us all together.

"We have to exchange war stories," I say.

"Joseph?" Andrew says this.

"Yeah?"

"Were you afraid? In Mississippi?"

"Oh, man, yes. I've been with men and women who were arrested and then beaten in jail. Some of them were hurt bad, and they suffered. I was afraid of that. I hadn't ever been hurt before." Joseph stops for a few minutes, and we wait for him to go on. "But then, looking at the whole thing from another perspective, I have to say that I was not afraid. I was there for me and for my people and for all of us, and every day when I woke up, I thought, *This is today, and whatever it brings, it is mine.* I thought, *This is what my life is about.*"

It is hard not to think of the history of the crimes my race has inflicted on his. I want to ask him why he wants to be with us.

Andrew has his chin on his hand, thinking.

"But you haven't told us about the sheriffs," Mitzi says. "Did it hurt?"

"It was 1961, I was in LA. I was eighteen or nineteen. I was in the end of my second year in college, it was in the spring, and I was reading the newspapers about the Freedom Rides in the South. One day I saw a picture of Freedom Riders who had gotten off a bus in Anniston, Alabama. They were in the middle of a mob led by an Alabaa sheriff, these black Freedom Riders with blood all over their faces. I showed it to my mother, and the next day I got on a bus to Birmingham, Alabama, and volunteered to go on the next leg of the Freedom Ride. I faced mobs like that all the way to New Orleans. I got beat up a few times that year, Mitzi, three times by a sheriff. I found I can take a lot of beating. I was afraid, but I found I'm strong."

"Did you fight back?" she asks. "I don't understand. Why didn't you fight back?"

"Well, we believed that the way to defeat people who are being violent and unjust is to show them that they can't defeat you with violence. The idea is to always be able to come back, your head high, able to make your demand again. You defeat them with your ability to suffer."

"Where did you get that from?"

"From a very famous man in India, who defeated the whole British Empire with that idea, and from another man, an American, named Martin Luther King."

"I believe in making them bleed."

"Mitzi, the point is, we won. Finally they stopped trying to make black people drink water at a different fountain, and they stopped trying to make black people use rest rooms set aside for black people. And by demonstrating without fighting back, we got the government to come in on our side and to pass laws that prevented people from trying to stop us from registering to vote. Everything isn't OK, now —you know what America is like—but it is better, and we found out how to make it better, by working together. A lot of people were hurt, and some died, but in the end we won. And it's not over yet."

I say to Joseph, "You rebelled, and you found out something good about yourselves, and you made changes in the world. That's incredibly cool."

"Well, you know, black people in the last twenty or thirty years have been struggling with the problem of how to deal with white people. Some of us think that the way to do that is to separate ourselves from white folks, live separate lives—"

"—the Nation of Islam—" Andrew says.

"Yeah. Pretty much. And then other folks have been thinking that we need to capture the moral imagination of the white majority and make our situation in America better that way."

"Malcolm X and Eldridge Cleaver and Stokely Carmichael and the Black Panthers have all been black nationalists, haven't they? And Amiri Baraka? And Marcus Garvey?"

"Uh-huh, looking after ourselves first, using guns to protect ourselves, and Martin Luther King on the other side. There's been a big discussion in our community on all these fundamental questions. It's a discussion that gay people are going to have go through, I suspect. Separatism may be necessary, for a time."

We are quiet for a while, aware of each other in the dark, thinking of the power of government to oppress the people and of the power of the people to rebel.

"But what happened in the end?" Billy asks. "Did the TPF drive you all off the street? Did you finally have to just leave it to the cops?"

"Oh, no—" Andrew drags out the long OOOO sounds. "—they weren't ever able to drive us off the street. Christopher Street is ours, man. They could clear this hundred yard stretch or that whole street for eighteen minutes, but they couldn't ever clear all the street all the time. It would have taken thousands more cops to do that. Thousands and thousands. They would have had to occupy Christopher Street like an invading army. They would have had to turn these streets into Vietnam, man, and turn this little riot into a vast war in which the cops, complete with tanks and napalm, are the invading army, and we are the Cong, man, blowing up their bridges and setting out landmines. They weren't going to do that, and we realized that, and so we won, and the whole exercise lost its glamour. People started drifting away in the dark. A lot of 'em went home. Some of 'em—all of us—went to the docks to have sex. We knew we could have our street whenever we wanted it."

Billy laughs. "I wish I had gone to the docks with you."

"Would you have had sex?"

"I woulda done what comes naturally, Mitzi."

"What does that mean?"

"It means that when I'm given an opportunity to have sex, I almost always take it."

"We should all have gone to the docks." Belle looks wistful.

"Apparently, the good guys went to the docks. You guys are so much stronger than you think you are," Billy says. "After all this—all the effort on the part of the culture to stamp out gay sex, when the night is done, you all go to the docks and have sex, and you seem unaware of how triumphant you are, what a great victory that is. They can't defeat you. The riot police can come down here with everything they have, but they can't stop men from having sex with men. Imagine how that infuriates politicians." He laughs. "Richard Nixon!" His elbows are resting on the arms of his chair, and he looks at us through his fingers, which form a little roof in front of his face. "The way this is conceptualized, the only outcome possible is your victory. You are so strong."

We have to separate what we are taught about ourselves from what is true about ourselves, and that is a life-time job. We have to listen to what our bodies tell us. What's going on with Billy? Mitzi is not the only one who is fascinated. We spend the first half of our lives learning and the last half of our lives jettisoning all we learned in the first half. I wonder what I am capable of. The world is unstable. Where is Andrew? I reach out, and he takes my hand. He leans over to me and speaks in a low voice, "Joseph would like to spend the night. Is that OK?"

"Sure."

"There's Billy."

"I don't think it's going to matter to Billy."

Billy and I go in and call Mom. This ritual has deep roots—our being somewhere together and knowing that we had to call home to let them know we were OK—and the thought of it is reassuring.

I tell her Billy is here and that he and I and Andrew have had supper with friends. I tell her who is here. I say that we are OK and that we have not been hurt in the riots and that, yes, I will call again tomorrow night. "Don't worry about us, Mom. I love you."

Billy gets on. "Yes, Mom, he's OK. So is Andrew. They have cool friends, Mom. Yeah. I'll make sure he's OK. Don't worry." And finally, "Yes, I love you too."

She's cool about all this. She knows what riots are like, and I note that she doesn't tell either one of us to stay away from the demonstrations. She knows what we have to do. I suppose it is harsh being a parent.

Then Dad gets on and tells us both how proud he is of us. We work some on the dishes. Billy is drying, and while he's got a plate, he nods his head in the direction of the living room. "The poster is new, isn't it? *Marat/Sade*? Did you go? What's that about?"

I grin. "*Marat/Sade* was about sex and repression and violence andrevolution. It's a play for our time, brother. Yes, we saw it."

159

Adam in the Morning

We clean up—finishing about ten, ten-thirty—and we start talking again about the riots. "When are we going up there," Billy asks, "and find out what's happening?"

But tonight, there are no riots. There are hundreds of cops on the street and cop cars with flashing lights, and there are hundreds and hundreds of men and women on the streets, milling about, and there are scores of men and women handing out flyers—we get copies of all of them—and there are people standing on the bases of street light poles haranguing the crowd. There is tension through the whole scene, but the cops are committing no violence, and after walking the length of Christopher Street and showing Billy where different things happened, we begin to break up. Belle leaves us and walks to her apartment over on West 11th Street, three or four blocks north of here. And even though we invite them to spend the night, Mitzi and Violet leave us too and go back to the flock of their friends. So that leaves just Andrew and me and Joseph and Billy. We return to the river, and then we go to the docks for sex. Later, when we walk home, Andrew and I are holding hands, and Joseph and Billy follow us. I glance back at one point, and I see that they are holding hands, too. So.

When we get back, the phone is ringing. It is Heath, the breathless man from the Silver Dollar yesterday at lunch.

"What's up?"

"Did I call you too late?"

"No, we're usually up until midnight or one, at least. This is OK." While I am on the phone, Joseph and Billy and Andrew are getting undressed, walking around the apartment naked or semi-naked, laughing and rough-housing, acting like adolescent boys in a Boy Scout camp. It is hard to concentrate.

"Good. Could you meet with some of us tomorrow, maybe late in the afternoon, around five? It'd be here at my apartment. I think I can get about twenty men here."

I get his address.

We lead busy lives. When we go to bed, Joseph and Billy take the big pull-out sofa in the living room, and Andrew and I take the bed in our bedroom. Joseph calls out from the living room, "Did any of you read Vincent Canby on Judy Garland in today's *Times*?" None of us have.

"What did he say?"

"He called her a 'glamorous Hollywood personality with a built-in destruct mechanism.'"

"I wonder if it's possible that she died at just the right moment."

"What do you mean?"

"I don't see her being the star for the generation of gay men who were fighting the police last night. I think we're different now."

Today, tonight, after it had gotten dark, at some point when there was a lot going on, Joseph took a moment and spoke to me. I was in the kitchen, and the others were somewhere else.

"It's about Belle's proposal. I don't want to be considered. I'm flattered by the idea, but I'm not at a point in my life when I am able to make that kind of commitment." I hugged him. "Do you understand that?"

"Sure. Doing what Belle wants would transform everything in a guy's life. I am not sure I would want to do it."

We hugged again, and he went back to the gang and the conversation, and we didn't talk about that any more.

Things are quiet for a time, and then the noise Andrew and I make is answered by the noise Billy and Joseph make, and this goes on for a long time—at one point Joseph calls out, "Do you guys have a joint?" and we all laugh—until finally the noise we make and the noise they make merge into one another and become quiet, and, one by one, we drift off to sleep. Andrew's last words to me are, "Can we talk tomorrow, just us, sometime in the morning?"

Monday, June 30, 1969

But it isn't so much that he has a particular subject he wants to talk to me about as it is that he feels distracted by the people in our apartment and by what is going on in our lives, and he wants to feel focused again on our thing. Billy wakes up first and starts the coffee, and I hear him and get up, and, as soon as the bathroom is free, I wake up Andrew. We go in together.

"Can we have breakfast together?" are his first words.

We divide up. I will hang out with Andrew, then, at eleven, I will go by the theatre. After that I join Billy and Joseph. I hug Billy. "Are you going to be OK? Is this OK with you?"

"You don't have to look after me. You and Andrew take care of each other, and Joseph and I will enjoy ourselves and look forward to seeing you when you get back. Now go!"

It is another hot, flawless, beautiful day in the city. Andrew and I go up Christopher Street and down West 4th toward 6th Avenue to a café and choose a table on the street. The street is narrow and has trees on both sides, lined with shops and restaurants and cafés, an intimate scene.

"I called the *East Village Other* and the *Guardian*. I tried to reach the *Phoenix* and the *Avatar* in Boston, but couldn't. I tried *RAT*, and *Gay Power* and the other gay rags here. The only ones I could get were the *East Village Other* and the *Guardian*, both of which want me to submit things to them on July 7th, a week from today. So, it's good that I am going to have a place to send my account when I finish it. That's good. I am going to wait for two or three days and think about how best to approach the national magazines. Do you know if Joseph has ever written anything?"

"Uh-uh." I wonder if I know of anybody. "I'll think and see if I come up with anybody."

Adam in the Morning

The Times has another article on us. The headline is "POLICE AGAIN ROUT/'VILLAGE' YOUTHS."

"*The Times* gets it wrong again," Andrew says. "If the police had 'routed' us the first time, and done it properly, they wouldn't have had to 'rout' us the second time. What is happening is that the cops do a half-assed job each time because that's all they can do. They didn't 'rout' us Sunday morning, we left the street when we wanted to, to have sex on the docks. What shit. The real story is that Village residents keep rioting, protesting against mistreatment, and the cops and city hall are not responding, so we are going to keep rioting."

"Well, how are you?"

He puts down his paper. "Frazzled. Pulled in different directions. I'd like to have more time alone with you. And we've had this turmoil in the street—" He laughs. "—which is not to say that everybody else has not been experiencing turmoil in the streets. I think I'm discovering how much I love you." He has his elbows on the table, forearms lying parallel to one another, his shoulders hunched, while he looks at me from the side. "Don't, please, go away."

"I'm not going anywhere, Andrew. You know that. What's all this about?"

He thinks for a moment, shrugs his shoulders, and says, "I don't know. Our community right now—our world—is in crisis, and I feel unsteady. I don't think I've felt this way since you and I met."

He is quiet. Our food comes. Finally he speaks. "When I was an adolescent, thirteen or so, sixth or seventh grade, I began to realize that whatever parenting my mother and father had done up to that point was about at its end. I wasn't going to learn anything more from them that was going to be of much use. From then on I was on my own. I didn't feel ready for that. I didn't really want to be that independent, and I was aware of feeling panicked, afraid sometimes, and it was like regressing and feeling afraid of the dark, even though I thought I had outgrown that. I was cool, though. I was smart in school, so I figured I would go on being smart in school, right on through whatever I chose to do with my life, and I was athletic and good-looking and all those things, so even if I was afraid inside, I was still getting by, and my fear didn't cripple me, you know? Most people have no idea. You're an amazing person. You make it seem possible to do everything that needs to be done. You don't seem to have the deep vein of fear that you are mining all the time that they rest of us have."

Andrew is wrong about me having no fear, but there is no point in me saying, *Oh, no, Andrew, you are wrong about this.* He is paying me a compliment. At the same time, he is trying to describe our relationship, and to do that in a respectful way, and, since I care about our relationship and about him, I don't feel any need to correct him. Conversations like this are always tentative. He will discover, during the time we live together, where and how I feel fear—he already knows that I have my fears, but at this particular moment he can't think of them—and I hope he will discover my fears after he has discovered he doesn't need to believe that I am fearless.

Some people complain of the noise in the city, but I think it has the good effect of providing a kind of cover. The noise on this street—West 4th —is enough to allow Andrew and me to talk in public about private and intimate things without feeling that we can be overheard. Beyond this, what is true is that our intimate words about fear and sex and love, spoken here on the street, become part of the colloquy of the city, link us to everyone else on the street and all this without violating our privacy. It is one of the paradoxes of New York.

"Are you afraid of Joseph?" I ask him.

"I don't know. No. Of course not. I am not afraid of him. I do wonder if what we have—what you and I have—is strong enough to open up and allow him in without losing what we have. I don't want to be the one who has no courage—no faith—you know?"

"Oh, I hope you will tell me—"

"Besides, he is so goddamn sexy!"

"But you have to remember that you are too."

He shrugs. "I know. I get told that. And you tell me, too. And I believe you tell me, too. And I believe you. And now you also know that, in addition to being sexy, I carry a noticeable burden fof fear around with me."

"He told Belle that he is falling in love with us."

"Are you falling in love with him?" Andrew asks me.

"I don't know," I say. "I know I think he is sexy as hell. I haven't seen yet whether that is love. It is certainly lust."

"Is lust enough?"

politics. His politics are certainly right. It's flattering that he thinks our politics are right. I would have thought that, because of his political background, he wouldn't want anything to do with two white guys—aside from a fuck every now and then. But he seems to care about us, in the way you and I care about each other. I am very careful around you. I never want to hurt you. And Joseph seems to care about us in the same way. I like that. Billy likes him, Mitzi likes him—" I'm looking at the traffic on the sidewalk. Men.

"I meant to ask you about that."

"What?"

"Did they have sex last night? Billy and Joseph?"

"I don't know. I think so. It sounded like they were."

"I thought Billy was straight."

"Well, he is. At least he has always acted like he is. But that doesn't mean he can't have sex with Joseph. Joseph seems voracious, vacuuming up every available set of genitals. I don't know what happened."

"Do you think this is funny?"

"Well, it's surprising. And it's wonderful. And, of course, it's funny."

"Are you going to ask Billy about it?"

"I guess. At some point. But I am not going to grill him about it. He—and you also, I should remind you—is free to fuck, or get fucked by, anybody he wants to without having to explain to his big brother about anything he does."

"Right. Let Billy be Billy."

"Those two having sex is not remarkable. They are both sexy men, sexy creatures, and they're going to turn each other on. What is remarkable, I think, is that Billy was open to it, that he allowed it to happen. I think that's wonderful, and I think it's remarkable."

"Explain."

"There is so much that can get in the way of our having sex with someone. What are my buddies going to say, what are my parents going to say, my boss, and the rest of it, what is my whole fucking culture going to say, and apparently what Billy did was say, Fuck that. That's really admirable of him. I think what happens with most people is that the roadblocks to queer sex are so high and so formidable that a straight man never gets a chance to feel desire for another man. Like, a sexy straight man is walking down the dock and seeing all these sexy men writhing and twisting all over the dock, their dicks hanging out, and he won't allow himself to feel anything because the President of the United States says don't."

Andrew laughs.

"I know, but it's not funny. It may not be the President, but people feel these kinds of inhibitions all the time. The Pope, the village priest. Billy is remarkable. Not many straight men would go down to the docks at the end of Christopher Street and come back with a trick. He's very open to what's happening, and he's very much in tune with his own body. That's so great."

We eat for a while, listening to the traffic and aware of the people walking by a few feet away who are carrying on their own conversations.

"Joseph says he is in love with you and me—can you be in love with two people at the same time?—and yet last night he was fucking your brother. He's quite a man. Out of my league."

I propose something. "I think it may be that those years in Mississippi and making his own way in South Central LA have given him more assurance than many of us have."

It's nine-thirty or ten, and a person can sort out the traffic on the sidewalk, some going to breakfast, some going to work, some at work, some on their day off. A person can tell—he can guess—by the way they walk and by the clothes they wear. We have coffee, and I order cheese Danish. Our waiter is a small guy with shoulder-length black hair. He has long earrings. "I think it will be interesting to see how he works this out." This waiter has the ability to caress you with his eyes when he is talking to you. "I think it is possible for a person to engage in several sexual connections at the same time, if he is free about it. It may be that the central thing is how rigidly a person controls himself. If I am open to any possibility that comes along, really open to whatever happens, then it's likely that a lot of things are going to happen. I think that's what happens with Joseph. Maybe." I begin to gather my things. "Get in touch with me in ten or fifteen years, and I'll tell you what I think then."

"Oh, wait. One more thing—"

I relax in my seat again.

"—on Saturday at the Silver Dollar, we were talking about the change that we hope is going to come from these riots. We talked about the ways our culture abuses gay men and women—the SLA, the Mafia, entrapment and the rest of it, the determination by psychologists and psychiatrists that gay people are sick—and you brought up the question of fear, our loss of it since early Saturday morning. I have thought about that since then, about fear and courage and their effects on things that really ought not to be affected by them at all. Why we have to be courageous to get our constitutional rights. In our culture, only the brave and the strong—and the rich too, of course—get their constitutional rights. The constitution doesn't say anything about limiting rights to the brave and the strong and the rich, but that is effectively what we do. What we need to drive toward is a fundamental restructuring of our government, something new in which every particular citizen gets his or her rights—even the weak, and the poor, and those who are full of fear."

Andrew and I stand up. He talks while surveying the street.

"I think we can do that in our culture here in America, if we always have a kind of divided vision—on the immediate need to control out-of-control cops, among other crimes, as well as on the long-term need to change our culture's take on sex, among other failures. I think we can do that. But the question of our civilization is much, much bigger. A culture is near to us and in our control, and a civilization encompasses many cultures and is not in our control. I think what Marcuse was saying was that our civilization cannot be restructured. It is what it is, and it does to us what it does. What we must do, if we are determined to be free, is to liberate ourselves from this civilization. We must refuse to accept its requirements. It's what Marcuse calls a Great Refusal. I think it's what we do already, you and me, and now Joseph and Billy. We mustn't hang our hopes on changing civilization. We must be strong and free ourselves. And we must be steady."

We leave the restaurant—Andrew will go on to Zanes on West 10th, and I will go to the theatre to check in with Sergei and Matt—when Andrew raises a different subject.

"Are you collecting the flyers you get on the street?"

"Oh yeah."

"My history is going to be fairly short, concentrating on what actually happened, say 10,000 words, and my deadline is a week from today—July 7—for the *East Village Other* and the *Guardian*. I'll write something longer, maybe more interpretive, something with a different slant—Mitzi's street kids—for *RAT*, or *Queen's Quarterly*, or *Gay Power*, or *Screw*, if I can ever reach them. One of the other counter-culture rags. Or perhaps one of the papers on the West Coast. Joseph can help me with that. And then I would like to take the same material, rework it into something longer and more thoughtful, and try to sell it to a different class of journal. For example, *The Atlantic* or *The New Yorker*, the big national magazines that might be interested in an analysis of what is happening among gay people in the Village. I want to interview you and Joseph and Mitzi, and other men and women I don't know. So—" He takes my hand. "—I am going to be busy for the next several weeks. Is that OK with you?"

"Tell me what you need." We are in Sheridan Square, passing among the people passing out flyers. I take one from each of them. Aside for the usual anti-war signs, one heading reads, YOU ARE INVITED. We are invited to a meeting, different from the meeting to which we are invited this afternoon. I remind Andrew.

"What do you think is the question I should organize my narrative of the riots around?"

"I'll tell you what I am thinking about these days. I'm thinking that, until now, we haven't been clear about how to recognize manhood—what it is, what are its attributes and qualities. It may be that the most manly men are those with flowers in their hair—"

"And that the least manly are those behind plastic shields."

"Mitzi and her sisters have been in the front lines of the fighting every night. How do you deal with that? The ones who have been the most stereotypically masculine are also the ones who have shown the least courage and the least imagination and the least faith in themselves. Write an essay On Men."

He grins. "You're beautiful." He asks me if I have read the Post this morning about the SDS meeting in Chicago. "Jesus! I want to be a part of the Revolutionary Youth Movement." Then he's off to Zanes until 10:30 or 11 tonight.

It is very hot. I find a phone booth and call home.

"What's happening there?"

I hear Joseph laugh. "Billy and I are hanging out. You have a mighty attractive brother, Bo."

"Do you two want to meet me for lunch? I feel like a decent meal." We make plans.

Matt and Sergei are on the stage in their canvas chairs, Matt talking. "Ariel is the most sympathetic character in the play. She is beautiful, she works magic, and she has the safety of the Neapolitans in her hands. She was put under a spell by Sycorax, Caliban's mother, and placed in a cloven pine for twelve years. Prospero has threatened her with another imprisonment—this time in a cloven oak—if she doesn't obey him. Yet, Ariel still is clear that she wants 'my liberty'—"

"I can't stand this," Sergei breaks in. "He! He! Ariel is he! We have a man playing Ariel. He. Say, He!"

"Sorry—and it is implicit that Ariel and Prospero have been through this exchange before. She—sorry, he—starts moping around on the stage while Prospero is giving her one task after another—I'm very sorry, I can't seem to get that fixed in my mind—"

"I'll get the actor who is playing Ariel down here tomorrow, so you can see him and you can remember that he is a he. HE. Do try to remember that."

"I'm sorry. It's just that in every production I've ever seen, Ariel has seemed so feminine."

"Right. Well, he's not. He's a bloke, as you will see tomorrow morning. You be here. He's got a dick."

Matt is disconcerted. "I'm sorry. I can't remember what I was trying to say." He looks at both of us and shrugs, helplessly.

"You were talking about Ariel and Prospero, and how they have been through this exchange several times before, where he—Ariel—shows that he is unhappy, and Prospero rehearses the whole long tale of how he liberated him from his imprisonment in the cloven pine, only to enslave him again to him, and then you were going to tell us what you thought that meant for our production of the play. It was about Ariel and freedom."

"Thanks Bo. Thanks. Right. What it means is that Ariel has guts. He is not the endlessly malleable creature we usually think of who is enslaved to Prospero. He keeps reminding Prospero, You promised to free me even though each time we can imagine Prospero responding in the same way, by rehearsing how Prospero had freed Ariel from the cloven pine and by threatening to 'rend an oak/And peg [Ariel] in his knotty entrails till/[Ariel] has howled away twelve winters' [1.2.294-296]. Prospero's sadistic—he keeps reminding Ariel of his suffering. He's also tyrannical. He treats Ariel as badly as he treats Caliban. I believe his power over the inhabitants of the island and over the visitors corrupts him. Prospero acts in this play like a man under immense stress—the most notable example is in act four, when, in the middle of enchanting Ferdinand and Miranda, in some passion he suddenly announces, 'Our revels now are ended' [4.1.148]—and I think the stress he is under parallels the labor of Caliban or the labors of Ariel. It is a labor none of them can escape. Once you see the pattern, you see it everywhere. Ferdinand carrying his logs, Caliban, and Trinculo and Stephano laboring under their delusions, the King and Sebastian and Antonio laboring under their delusions, everybody in the play in some way laboring under the lash of some whip, and the progress of the play is specifically to bring that to an end, to liberate these men and this woman on this island from this labor and end their suffering."

"I can see that Ariel and Caliban are enslaved to Prospero, but who—what—enslaves the rest of them?" Sergei asks. "I keep trying to get a grip on what this play is about."

They should be way beyond this. They should, both of them, know the standard mid-twentieth century approaches to the play, and they should be aware of the principal productions of the past fifteen or twenty years. They should be able to move fairly rapidly to what they want to do. They don't seem to understand that these meetings should have a structure, beginning with our first meeting last Friday —standard mid-twentieth century versions of the play, detour past major earlier versions of the play, new approaches to Shakespeare in the last twenty years, major flaws in the standard versions of the play, goals for a contemporary production of the play, specific proposals for a contemporary production of The Tempest. The theatre is a great place, and wonderful things—that is, things that are full of wonder—happen there, but there are ways to create a powerful production and ways that seem to lead inevitably to theatrical failure. The longer this goes on, the more likely our production will be a failure.

"Help me, here. Bo? Do you have ideas on this? What frees them?"

Oh, Jesus. "Matt talked about this. Almost everybody in this play is enslaved to something or someone. Antonio and Sebastian show that it is in some ways being human that has enslaved them. Antonio and Sebastian are slaves to their ambition and greed. This can be helpful with others. Prospero wants revenge. Stephano and Trinculo want alcohol. Sebastian wants to be king. Only Ferdinand and Miranda seem to be free of basic human failings. They are young people of clear feeling and no corrupt thoughts. But they are not free. They are enslaved by their youth, and they must suffer for a time before they grow up and gain their freedom. All the rest seem to need to suffer for a time before they can be brought to understand why they are suffering—because I wanted to kill the king and become king myself, because I overthrew my brother and sent him into exile, because I drank too much and thought I could overthrow Prospero, because I didn't understand myself well enough, because I didn't understand my condition well enough.

"At the end of the play, are they free? Most of them are. There is an inevitability about the action of *The Tempest* that seems to bring it forth. All of these late Romances, as if by the return of planets in their orbits, bring back to the audience what we have lost. A production of one of these plays should be careful not to injure one's sense that, if one were to stand aside and let it happen, all losses would be restored and sorrows ended.

"Gonzalo, in his famous speech near the end, just after Ferdinand and Miranda have been found playing at chess, marvels at all that has happened on this voyage.

> In one voyage
> Did Claribel her husband find at Tunis;
> And Ferdinand, her brother, found a wife
> Where he himself was lost; Prospero his dukedom
> In a poor isle; And all of us ourselves,
> When no man was his own. [5.1.208-213]

Their finding themselves is inextricably bound up in their finding their freedom. It may be that for these people here at the end of The Tempest, they are the same thing. Finding their freedom enables them to find themselves, or finding themselves frees them."

We have had four days of hot cloudless weather. I unbutton my shirt and walk up Washington Place to Sheridan Square, feeling the hot air on my skin. I have agreed to meet Joseph and Billy in Sheridan Square. We will go from there to a restaurant they have chosen for lunch. I look forward to their talking about what has been happening between them since last night on the pier. Have they lost themselves? Found themselves? Are they willing to talk? Capable of talking?

Joseph and Billy are not actually in the park. They are at the other end, at the Northern Dispensary, where Grove Street ends in Christopher Street. They look like two gay men, Joseph leaning back on the tree in that triangle of ground, Billy standing in front of him, his arm straight out, past Joseph's shoulder, his hand on the tree next to Joseph's head. They are deep in conversation.

"Hi, guys."

Billy turns to meet my eyes. What is immediately interesting about them is how much alike they are in affect. Neither seems interested in veiling or hiding his emotions. "Bo. Wonderful. I thought you might have forgotten us."

Joseph is almost smiling, his eyes slightly widened.

"Uh-uh. Sergei could not get us to focus on what is important, so the three of us have spent the last two hours wandering around on a desert island. Sorry I am late." I join them. I hug them both. "So. Where are we going?"

"Great to see you, Bo."

"Yeah. We've missed you."

"I have an idea," Joseph says. "I propose we get sandwiches and eat outside. We can go down on the docks, or we can go somewhere like Washington Square Park and lie in the grass. Or if you would prefer something more civilized, we could go to one of the restaurants along West 4th Street and, if you'd like, eat outdoors."

Billy smiles. "It's up to you. We'd like to do whatever you'd like to do."

They are charming. I move between them and put my arms along their shoulders and pull their heads in toward me. "You're cool dudes. Let's do both." I let them go and lead the way toward West 4th. "Let's have lunch at a restaurant Andrew and I know on West 4th and Perry. Lots of green, leafy trees, narrow street, plenty of interesting and beautiful people walking by, superb cuisine, and then afterward, we can get ice cream, or a pastry and some coffee, and go down on the docks. How's that? Or Washington Square Park."

So we cross Seventh Avenue and head up West 4th Street. They laugh and look at each other and seem to find me funny. I guess they are high.

The restaurant is an old one, Isis, on the corner, and the tables outside are under an awning and separated from the sidewalk by a railing. We're late for lunch, so we get our choice of tables. We choose the corner table, the one most exposed.

"So." I look at both of them. Billy sits next to Joseph, across from me. "How are you guys?"

They laugh, but they don't say anything.

"What have you been doing this morning?"

"We hung out at your apartment, taking a long time getting breakfast—" Joseph turns to Billy.

"—and cleaning up the rest of what was left from last night. We took out the trash. We got everything looking good again."

"That's good. Thanks. You're good."

"We talked a lot. Billy told me about growing up in Houston."

"And Joseph told me about growing up in Los Angeles."

"Are you guys holding out on me?"

"Uh, well—" Billy looks at Joseph.

Joseph looks at me. "Well, look, I hoped you wouldn't be pissed. We talked about it, about whether we thought you'd be pissed, and decided you wouldn't, but then I still feel a little uneasy—I think we both do—but I am not sure I know why. We don't want you to be pissed at us."

"It's lovely to see such big, sexy guys blushing."

They grin. Billy is the first to speak. "It is OK, Bo?"

"Of course it's OK."

"You're not pissed?"

"No, I'm not pissed. Billy, you know I wouldn't be pissed."

"I don't know. I guess I felt I should have talked to you first—"

"You didn't need to do that—"

"Are you sure?"

"Yes, absolutely."

"And then Joseph was your friend, and I thought maybe I should have gotten your permission—"

"Joseph is my friend, and both of you are free to do what you want to do. Neither of you needs my permission for anything—"

The waiter is here. Joseph looks up at him and smiles, "Could you give us a minute?"

We go back to our conversation.

"Are you going to tell Mom and Dad?"

"No, you know me better than that. You can trust me with anything in your life. And as far as Mom and Dad are concerned, you need to deal with them yourself."

"I don't think I'll tell them. At least for a while yet."

"You spend one night with a man, and you go all guilty on me."

"Is that what's happening?"

"Probably. I have no idea, really. But hey, you two, I want to hear about it. I want to hear how it happened. I want to hear how you guys feel about it—aside from feeling guilty—and Andrew is going to be really pissed when he discovers we talked about this when he wasn't here."

"We'll talk about it all over again when he gets off work," Joseph says.

"So what was it, Billy? Talk to me!"

"I think it's that he thinks fags are cool dudes," Joseph says.

"Well, Joseph hit on me down on the pier—he put his arm on my shoulder—and when I turned, there he was, and he kissed me. I've never known such a sexy man. We got it on down there on the pier, right then, before we came back up to your apartment with you and Andrew. It all was natural. Even to sleeping with Joseph later. He's just incredibly sexy. And remember, Joseph was a member of your gang, so that must mean he was one of the two or three coolest men in all New York."

I laugh. "Did you think, 'Most straight men wouldn't do this?'"

"Nooo. I didn't think about any of that. I just thought about what my body was feeling."

"Do you feel differently about yourself, now?"

Joseph is watching and listening intently to all this.

"I don't know. No. I really liked what happened last night—and again this morning—but I'm the same person."

The waiter comes again, and we tell him what we want.

I think something amazing has happened. "Is this something you've been thinking about for a while?"

"I don't think I think much about sex beforehand, but everything in my life—you, Tommy Sante, Andrew, the way our parents raised us, Uncle Duncan, all meant that I am pretty much open to things—" Billy thinks about what he's saying. "Ever since you told me about being turned on by boys, I've paid attention to my own body. And I get turned on sometime. Not as often as with women, but still often enough. And I notice what turns me on, what kind of men."

"Do you mind me asking questions?"

"No."

"What you're describing's different from the way it was for me. I knew I wanted to be with a man a long time before I ever saw a man who was available. I used to see pictures of men in magazines, and men in the movies, and then I used to fantasize about them when I went to bed."

Joseph looks from Billy to me.

Billy asks me, "Have you ever wanted to be with a woman?"

177

I think about that. "I have wanted the experience of being with a woman. Other men have been with women, and I don't want to go through life without having that experience. I talked to Joseph about this a couple of days ago."

"Then that's the way it is for you. For me, you've been a big influence on me, all my life. I think I have always gravitated toward women. I am straight. At a party, with a room crowded with men and women, I tend to pick out the women, but you taught me—or made it OK for me to see—that men were sexy too. That happened years ago, when we were kids. I know that I feel things around men that most men don't feel. I think I am open to feeling the things men are putting out. There have been times when I've visited you that I almost had sex with one of your friends. When you first moved up here—"

There is no traffic light on this corner, and cars stop and sort out who has the right-of-way before proceeding. It is interesting to watch them do this, this small civilized procedure going on constantly just beyond our reach and in the background of our vision.

Our food comes, and for a few minutes, we devote ourselves to it, the sounds of utensils on china.

"I think," Billy says, "you and I have had different experiences. You have lived all your life in a culture that is hostile to homosexuality. I guess that has had a deep effect on how your sexuality is expressed. On the other hand, I have lived all my life in a culture where my native sexuality is the approved sexuality and where the disapproved sexuality is also the sexuality of the man I have most loved all my life. I think that has given me more freedom, maybe, than you have had. I never felt limited to one sexuality in a way that you may have felt limited. Most of the time, in most circumstances, I am probably going to end up in bed with a woman. At the same time I can say, 'But I feel free to have sex with a man, if I want to.' He looks down to his food for a minute, then at me. "I haven't ever done it before. But I think I did it this time because you are here, and you love me, and you love Andrew, and it seemed friendly for me to have sex with a man, too. I feel very open to what is happening in New York. And Joseph is here, and he is very handsome and sexy, and political like us. And remember, Joseph loves you too, and that's a big turn-on."

Joseph, through all this, is paying attention to his food, his shoulders slightly hunched over his plate, listening to us talk. He looks at Billy sitting next to him—he has to put his hands on the tablecloth and to push back slightly from the table to do it—and says, "I thought you liked me because I'm so good at sucking cock."

Billy grins and takes his hand.

"Do you think you are falling in love with me and Andrew?"

Joseph places his hands on the table edge and looks at me. "Yes, I think so."

"I may be falling in love too. I wish Andrew were here to take part in this. Let's not talk about this until he comes home tonight. Is that OK?"

"Sure. Yes, that's right."

Billy has a question. "Are we OK? You and me?"

"Yeah, Billy, we're OK, you and me."

We pay attention to the food for a while.

"I hope you enjoyed it," I say to Billy.

"Ah, yes." He smiles.

"I hope so too, Bo—" Joseph says, "—I really hope so too."

"I think it's great that you two have connected."

Then Billy says, "What are you going to do about Mitzi?"

"I think we are going to keep on doing what we have been doing the last couple of years—be supportive, be here for her if she wants our help and, very carefully, encourage her to think about getting off the street. There is nothing more we can do. We have no control over her."

"I suppose not."

"It is frustrating that he can't do anything else," Joseph says. "It is hard to understand that the whole legal structure of society prevents us from giving her the kind of aid that would be helpful to her. There are no legal social services that Bo and Andrew can obtain for her. She is outside of the culture we live in. It's terrible to have to live with that. It makes you want to burn down City Hall."

"Or," I say, "to get as far as possible outside of that culture myself."

"What does she need, specifically?"

"She's under age. Her mother and her stepfather threw her out of her family home. She has been beaten up plenty of times, and she does—I think all her gang do—drugs all the time, mainly speed and acid. They all drink, even the youngest of them. So the first thing she needs is a place to live. A family environment would be the best thing. Andrew and I can give her that, but we can't force her to come to live with us. Remember, when her parents threw her out, in her mind she no longer owed any adults any respect. She has been told, 'Support yourself.' And she does that, so now none of us—the adults around her—can say to her, 'You have to come in off the street,' or 'You have to do what I tell you to.' She doesn't have to do anything anybody says. I don't think any of us know how deeply wounding it must be to have your parents throw you out on the street. Anyway, she needs a place to live. She needs a family-type environment. She needs medical care, and at a minimum, she needs medical care providers who are respectful of her and knowledgeable about exactly what medical care means in her case. Beyond this minimum, what does she need? Maybe minimal things, maybe very very expensive surgery which isn't even performed in this country—although there's a hospital in Yonkers that we hear rumors about. And, in addition to that, she may need some kind of therapeutic care—a shrink or someone. It goes without saying that she doesn't have any insurance. She needs to get back into school, make up the years she's lost and catch up to her age-group. And in every single encounter with any caregiver, she needs to sense that the other person is respectful of who she is and knowledgeable about who she is and able to help her on her terms. To get all this for her, at least to get it from the city government, where such things usually come from, the city would have to give some legal recognition to transsexuals—some respectful legal recognition that they exist and have the same rights the rest of us have—which is simply not going to happen in Mitzi's life time."

"But Bo," Billy asks, "I think you can get some of those without going to the city, can't you? If she came to live with you and Andrew, she would get some of the things she needs, except medical care maybe—"

"Sure, we could do much of it, and we know people in the Village who could help. Health care is the most difficult, I think, without insurance and with the probability that any health care provider is going to be ignorant and disrespectful. But the main problem is to get her to want to come to live with us. Would you, if you were fifteen and were accustomed to absolute freedom in the city, be willing to give up that freedom and go to live with two fags twice your age?"

Joseph grins. "If it was you two—"

"You're insatiable." We are finishing our meal. "Did you know that around the time we first met Mitzi, she was called Luis? Then she was Tina? She has come a long way. Once when I said something about a girl being trapped in a boy's body, she said she wasn't trapped. She said her body was just fine. She said, 'It's all of you guys that don't think a girl should have a dick.'"

The restaurant is almost empty.

Joseph stands up and goes to check in with his agent.

Perry and West 4th is a pattern of green and gold and shadows. We finish, and when Joseph comes back, we stand up to leave. Joseph is going over to her office on West 13th Street. He says he'll meet us at five at Heath's apartment.

"You know, if you guys take this on," Billy says, "I could help you financially. In any way I could, not just financially. You could count me in, given the fact that I live in Houston. You know, when you get to that point."

I hug him.

Then he says, looking down Perry Street toward the river, "I wonder what it feels like, to feel like a woman."

"Not to feel like a woman, but to feel that you are a woman."

We walk away from the river on Perry, toward Waverly Place. All these streets are small, narrow, parking and trees on both sides, single-family, four or five story brick houses whose façades are usually covered with vines and whose main entrances are directly from the street. These streets indicate a domestic architecture, and the main concerns of those who live here are domestic. They work somewhere else. Mothers, fathers, sisters, brothers, children, babies. It feels very different from Christopher Street, just a few blocks over, which is principally apartments, and where people may live and work in the same neighborhood. Christopher feels more gay.

Joseph leaves us, and Billy and I turn back toward the river.

We go down to the pier at the foot of Perry and work our way out to the end, where we take off our shirts and find a place to sit and, like boys, let out feet dangle over the side. Tom and Huck on the Mississippi.

"So how are you?"

"You're not going to ask me again why I had sex with Joseph last night?"

"No. I think we'll probably be coming back to that again, though, at some point, but right now I want to know about other things. How are you?"

"Can I get right into it right now? Or do I have to have an introduction and then a beginning, and then—"

"Jump in."

"I don't know what I am going to do with my life. I'm twenty-seven, and I'm a coach for the football team at Austin High School in Houston, and I enjoy that, but I think this is not what a man does with his life, so I am beginning to feel unsettled. Besides, Austin is segregated. I was embarrassed to tell your friends last night what I do. I didn't think this through and come to this conclusion. I realized I was beginning to look around. It's like being in a relationship, and you're thinking everything's fine—you're not unhappy—and then one day you discover that you're looking at women."

"Do you have ideas? What would you like to do?"

"No. Most people in my situation say, 'I want to go back to school to get a graduate degree.' I don't want to do that. You were the intellectual in the family. I don't want to have anything to do with more schooling."

"I thought you were the intellectual in our family."

"Not me."

"Is this a crisis?"

"No. I'm signed to a contract for this coming school year, so I have a while before I have to sign a new contract. But I want to start talking about it. With you and with Mom and Dad."

"How are they?"

"Worried about you."

"These riots?"

"Yeah. They've always been uneasy about you living in New York. On top of that, they know the police, and they know something about bigotry, so they see you in danger."

"What about the rest of it?"

"What do you mean?"

"I'm a carpenter with a Master's Degree. I wonder if this is what Mom meant when she said, 'Oh, do something that matters.' I suspect not. I don't feel so settled, either. I feel even less settled since this weekend."

"Tell me."

"I feel like every decision I have ever made now needs to be rethought. As if I wasn't grown up enough to make the decisions I made and now I am. It's as if I say, 'OK, now let's start all over and do it right this time.' It has something to do with these riots, but I haven't figured it out yet."

We swing our feet, and push down with our hands on the lumber at the edge of the pier, and stare into the bright, flashing water, and we contemplate what we are saying.

"We seem to be in the same predicament."

"Yep." I wonder what Mom and Dad are going to say about both their grown sons thinking that they want to start over. "How long are you going to stay?"

"I don't know. I have an open-return ticket. Mainly I came to see that you are OK so Mom wouldn't have to come. Course, I also came because I love you, I love New York, I love your friends, and I would have been pissed if any other person had come up here in my place. After a few days, and about the time I begin to think I am overstaying my welcome, then I'll let you know and I'll go home."

"Look, you see how we live around here. You know you're welcome. Andrew loves you, and now so does Joseph—"

"Tell me about Joseph. Do you guys make a threesome?"

"Not yet. He came home with us early Saturday morning and has been here ever since. He asked if he could spend the night—No, we asked him if he would like to stay—and then he said he was falling in love with us. That was no surprise. There was a lot of sexual energy between us. Andrew and I decided that we'd let him stay with us as long as he wanted, but we didn't want to deal with the question of his moving in with us—it would make us a threesome, instead of a couple—while all this other stuff is going on. We told him—I told him yesterday—that, and he seems willing to let everything stay in flux for a while. I am falling in love with him."

"He's wonderful."

"He's likes you, too."

"Do you know that I never held a man's cock before last night? Never touched one except my own? Never knew what a hard cock felt like? It's an amazing thing. I find I can't get it out of my mind. I look at his, and suddenly mine is big as a house."

"You're turning into a fag." Then, "Wait, I don't mean that. I don't think you're a fag. I don't think that's possible in any case."

He doesn't laugh. "That's the interesting thing. I'm the same person I've always been, but now I'm this too. I know what it is like to have sex with a woman, but I am also discovering what it is like to have a cock in my mouth." Billy grins. "I can't believe I just said that."

"People who can go either way are sometimes called 'bisexual.'"

"Maybe. But I don't think I am equally—evenly—either way. I am a straight man who has had sex with a man and thinks it's wonderful. I wouldn't say I am bisexual." Then he poses a question. "Do you suppose I am a straight man who has fallen, once, for a man? Is there a word for that?"

"You ought to get a copy of Kinsey's *Sexual Behavior in the Human Male*. It doesn't try to apply a word—like 'bisexual'—to particular sexual behaviors. Instead, it just tries to gather as much data as possible about as many people as possible and then to analyze the data. He comes up with things like 'Twenty-five percent of human males has had more than incidental homosexual experience for a period of at least three years.' Kinsey's book was published in 1948, so it is about twenty years old. There's one chapter on homosexuality, and if you want you can skip all the other chapters and just read that one. It'll tell you a lot about what you're doing." I put my arm around Billy's neck and pull him backward with me onto the deck of the pier, and I scrub his scalp with my knuckle. "I've been reading Kinsey for years, and I've never had any difficulty reading about men who had relations with men—and then, apparently, go back to having relations with women—but you're the first one I've ever known. In my experience, it's always been a one-way street. Kinsey's figures are pretty big—I think he says that almost two-fifths of all men has had some overt homosexual experience—so there are a lot of men out there who are lying to everybody except to Kinsey. And yet, here you are."

He sits up again. "Here I am."

"Could you make it just with men?"

He thinks about that for a minute.

I stroke his back.

"With women on the side?"

"Not fair, now."

"No. But then three days ago I wouldn't have said I was capable of getting fucked. Now I know I am. So who the fuck knows. I have heard before, a number of times and from different sources, that, if you get in the right circumstances with the right person, just about everybody will have queer sex. I'm beginning to believe that, now. You know you can't light up a joint without having somebody say,

'Well, you know, Freud says that originally we were all bisexual.'"
Then Billy lies down next to me and poses a question. "Does it work
the other way?"

"What do you mean?"

"We've been talking about a straight man discovering he can have
sex with men. Can a gay man discover he can have sex with women?"

I sit up. "I assume so. I've been thinking about it."

"Planning it?"

"Thinking about it. Thinking about planning it. I have been
thinking about proposing to Belle that we have sex. She wants a kid,
and I think I could help her. She's not thinking of me, I don't think. I
think she was thinking of Joseph, but he doesn't want to, so it may be
if I made the suggestion—" Then I get more pointed. "But to be more
precise. Sure, absolutely, the right person, the right time, the right
place, for the right reasons, most of us would have sex with most of
us. Let me change that. Not most of us but many of us. I think we're
already doing that. We're just not admitting to it." And then I say,
"Mom and Dad have the Kinsey reports. You can borrow them from
them."

He pats my back. "I love you."

I smile. I pat his leg. I lie down next to him. "You like Joseph?"

"Yes."

"You think he's a good man?"

"Yes."

"I do too. He doesn't seem selfish or self-centered."

"Are you checking him out as a boyfriend for me?"

"No. I was wondering if you thought he might be good for
Andrew and me."

"I do. Yes." Then, "Would there be room for me?"

"Always room for you, Billy."

"Would you guys let Joseph—uh, I don't know how to put   this
—"

"What you want to ask is, 'Are you guys going to be
monogamous?' And you want to know what the rules are, because
you want to have sex with Joseph. Isn't that it?"

"Yeah, that's it. Is that terrible of me? What are the rules?"

"No rules. Joseph does what he wants to do, just like Andrew.
And no, it's not terrible of you."

"Does Andrew have sex with other people beside you?"

"All the time."

"All the time! Andrew would have had sex with me if I had asked him?"

"If he wanted to." I'm smiling. This is so new to Billy.

"How do you feel about that? Does that piss you off when he goes off with somebody else?"

I grab Billy around the neck with my arm, and I wrestle with him for a minute. "Nothing Andrew does pisses me off. You know that. I love him. He loves me. When he has sex with some guy, that's just sex, that doesn't threaten us or what we have together. I don't own Andrew, and he doesn't own me. We don't own Joseph, either. I presume he'll continue to have sex with whoever he wants to have sex with."

"Then what does it mean for you to love each other?"

"Well, it doesn't mean any promises. It doesn't mean vows. It means we love each other and we care for each other. It means that our apartment on Weehawken is our home. And it means that we are committed to the well-being of each other. It means we have sex with each other."

"I don't understand."

"You still think love means sexual ownership. Andrew and I rejected that. We want each other to be free. We separated sex from love, and overruled I don't know how many centuries of Western Civilization in doing so."

"Does that work for you?"

"You've been seeing it work for the last three years, little brother."

"I didn't know that's what you were doing."

"All the time, since the beginning."

"Holy shit. I feel like a kid who's just been introduced to the way the grownups do it."

"I suspect this is not the way our parents do things, but I don't know."

"Would you ask them?"

"In our community, here in New York, it's a legitimate question to ask people when you get to know them a little. 'Are you monogamous?' Maybe you could start by telling Mom and Dad about this conversation, and then you could ask them, 'Are you monogamous?' On the other hand, in our community, asking this question is also a covert announcement that you would like to have sex with one of the people you're talking to. So maybe you shouldn't ask Mom and Dad. It's more than just a question. You can tell them what I have said, and then see what happens."

We are lying down side by side, and if there were clouds in the sky, we might be looking at the shapes they make. But the sky is blue, without a cloud, and I close my eyes.

"I don't think this is true of Mom and Dad, but with a lot of straight couples, the thing you are most aware of when you are with them is struggle. I think mainly this has to do with struggle for dominance. The woman over the man or the man over the woman. I don't sense that with you and Andrew. You seem to be very accepting of each other, as if you left the struggle way behind somewhere. Is that the two of you? Or is that what relationships between men are like?"

"I think it is partly the result of putting the two of us together. We may have self-selected so that neither of us has much need for dominance, as if I searched for a man who was like me, and Andrew did the same. Is that boring for the people around us? No conflict?"

He laughs. "No, it's not boring. Actually, it is a relief to come here and not be thrown into the middle of a continuously unfolding family struggle for control. How did you do it? Did you decide, just as you were about to start your first struggle, 'Hey, wait a minute, let's not do this. Let's not ever do this'? And so you reordered your life so you would never struggle with each other? Or did you just pick the right person?"

"Another possibility is that the solution to all the big struggles for dominance may be implicit in the two men, so that before they speak the first words, they have already resolved all issues of dominance. I know men like that."

"Yes, I imagine so. But I don't think you and Andrew are like that. You don't have someone on top."

"Well, wait a minute. Before you get too far away from reality, you have two men here in our relationship, both of whom have been brought up in the standard Western Civ definition of masculinity, which is that we are strong, we are leaders, we fight to protect our own, *Don't Tread On Me*, et cetera et cetera et cetera. Andrew and I have all the standard destructive impulses of our gender to struggle against. But we do love one another. If what you're saying about us is true, maybe the reason lies here. We love each other, and we're very careful about each other's welfare, and I find it's really easy to give in to Andrew when he wants it."

"There, that's it. I don't think many men find it easy to give in to their partners, and what I am asking is this—Is the ease with which you give in to Andrew a consequence of your being gay, and his being gay, or is it a consequence of some very rare virtue of your own, which is matched by an equally rare virtue in Andrew? I guess I'd like to hear you talk about gay people. What are they? We've been talking about men and also about gay people. How are gay men different from all other men?"

"I don't know that I can do that."

"Why not?"

"What makes us gay? I don't think we know how to define a gay person. There isn't enough data, Billy—and you really should read Kinsey. There is the business of wanting to have sex with another man, but that makes you gay as well as me. I think every year Darwinian biology throws up a certain percentage of infants who are going to grow up and be attracted to their own sex, and aside from that they are exactly like all other male children born at that time. I don't think there is a gay person. I think it may also be that we do that to ourselves—it's self-protective. We create a whole character and personality to protect ourselves in a culture that disapproves of people who are attracted to their own sex. I think also that the culture we live in—Western Christian Culture—encourages gay people to think of themselves as a distinctly different kind of people as a protection for straight people, so that straight men can say, I am not a gay man, so I am never going to suck cock. Well, as we know, that's bullshit."

I close my eyes. "Billy?"

He answers.

"I said something wrong a minute ago about Darwinian biology throwing up a certain percentage of children who are going to grow up and be attracted to their own sex."

"What's wrong with that?"

"That implies that there are some children who are attracted to their own sex and some who are attracted to the opposite sex. I don't think it is that clear cut. I think some children grow up to be adults who are attracted to the opposite sex every single time all of their lives, and there are other children who grow up to be adults who are attracted to the opposite sex most of the time. Kinsey has a seven-point scale reflecting this. I suspect it is a lot more complicated than even Kinsey has it. A man could be straight as far as his wife and children are concerned, and could still be attracted to certain body types among males, or to certain sexual arrangements among males, or to any number of other characteristics. And the same things operate in reverse, that is, a man could be gay but still attracted to certain characteristics among females."

"Then why do we say gay and straight?"

"Because we don't know anything more precise than these words, and because it is so very difficult to be precise about what we mean, even if we had the words. Because we're lazy, and we don't want to go to the trouble of being precise about what we mean. Besides, there has never been a time in the history of the world when men or women had an opportunity to come together in the daylight and look around at ourselves and to say, "Who are we?" It's nice and all that Kinsey has asked so many people about themselves, but that's really worthless once we start speaking for ourselves. What the psychiatrists and psychologists have written about us is also totally worthless, because now that we're here, in the daylight, we can look around at ourselves and speak for ourselves. We can tell the truth about ourselves."

After a while Billy talks about Joseph. "How much do you know about him? He's had an amazing life."

"Not a whole lot. The last five or six years I guess."

"His family is from the French West Indies, and they came here— the US—in 1941. His mother was pregnant with Joseph, and at first they went to Miami and then to New Orleans and finally to Los Angeles. I don't think they got to LA until he was two or three years old. His father got a job there doing defense work. I think he was an electrician. Joseph remembers him having two or three jobs at a time the whole time he was growing up. He drove a taxi on the weekends, and he did odd jobs. Then he died when Joseph was about ten years old. His mother raised him. He went to local schools. He graduated from high school in 1959, and then he had a couple of years at UCLA. He was a member of CORE in LA, and he did one of the Freedom Rides with CORE. I think it was one of the first ones. He was in McComb, and then in Albany at the voter registration drives there, and then he went to Mississippi with SNCC, doing voter registration work as a student volunteer or running Freedom Schools. He said he slept on the floor in cabins—shacks—in the backcountry. He was in LA in his last terms at UCLA when the Watts Riots exploded. He said he came here because he felt bad about himself—

that's hard to believe—and he wondered if being with other fags would make it feel better. He's been an actor since 1965, when he graduated from UCLA."

"The thing about Joseph, I think, is that if he moves in with us he won't stay long. He's moving around. Actors move around. I keep thinking that we're white, and he's not going to want to stay long with us."

"He knows you think that."

"Does it bother him that I think that?"

"No, I don't think so. He says that you told him he doesn't have to make any promises, and he's grateful for that. He says you two are very welcoming. He appreciates that."

In a few minutes, Billy speaks again.

"He told me that you haven't made any promises to each other— you and Andrew. Is that so?"

"Yep."

"Wow. No promises. One day at a time."

We lie here on the pier while the sun slides toward the harbor, and even though neither of us is looking at it, I know what the landscape looks like, the river getting wider and wider toward the south. With the sun from that direction, everything in the harbor seems to take on an added prominence, until it is possible to see, unmistakably, the Statue of Liberty on its immense plinth on the western side of the harbor. It is too far away to see detail, but we know exactly what the great Goddess looks like from up close, how imposing and how calm and how welcoming. Up close, there is no irony, which is found only in the neighborhoods of the city.

"Would you like to go to the Statue of Liberty?"

"I've never been. You've never wanted to take me before. Is it a good thing to do?"

"I think so. I haven't been since my high school class trip in 1957. It might be fun."

"Is there going to be more rioting?"

"I don't know. I sense that there will be, but I don't know."

"Why do you think so?"

"The tension in the air. The sense of things not having been concluded. People still want to fight some more. They are still very angry. Nothing has been resolved. We don't know what we're going to do, so we're going to fight."

Adam in the Morning

We lie on the pier a while longer, and then we get up and make our way up into the city on the island, toward the apartment of the man called "Heath," where we are to meet other men like ourselves who are interested in the Revolution.

Heath—the breathless man on the street in front of the Silver Dollar on Saturday—lives on West 10th between Sixth and Fifth in a garden apartment, with a front door that opens off the sidewalk, one step down. Heath answers the door. Beyond him the room is full of men who must have come early, since it is just five o'clock. There is a range of male types from dockworker to men who are pretty obviously wearing makeup, and ages from the late teens up to their sixties, mainly white with a few Hispanic and black persons. There are no street kids.

I introduce myself to Heath, and then I introduce Billy. I see Andrew and Joseph, sitting on the floor. Billy and I go in and sit by them. Nobody pays us any attention.

I whisper to Andrew. "I thought you were working."

"I got off. This is important." He is seriously concentrated and has his notebook at the ready. Joseph reaches over and touches my shoulder.

The room is a large combination living room-kitchen, and after I have been here for a few minutes, I see that it is a bedroom too. An eighteen-inch statue of David by Michelangelo stands on the coffee table next to a stack of art books. Beyond the kitchen is a glass wall leading to a city garden about the size of a standard room-sized oriental rug.

A man is talking to the group. His name is Jack, and he explains how this meeting came about. Jack proposes a way to proceed, which is accepted, but very quickly the group reverses itself and decides to spend an hour or two just listening to what men have to say on the riots or about anything—no agenda and no subject to talk about—and then, if there is enough interest, they might do organizational and business matters. One man says, "I think we are all so scattered, so drenched in feelings about these riots that we need to unload some of that before we consider whether to set up an organization and what kind and how to run meetings and all the rest of it."

Men all around the room raise their hands, and, without waiting to be called on, one starts talking. "We've been told for so long who we are, told by psychiatrists and by priests and by cops and by everyone else in our culture, that I don't think I have a good idea who I am. I'd like to start all over, with some really simple stuff, and build up a definition of who I am. I'd like to hear other men talk. You know what I mean. Before, we never did this, except in psychiatrists' offices. It would be therapeutic, it would be revolutionary, to hear men talk about themselves, about being gay—the different ways to be gay—and what that's meant to them."

The moderator Jack is about to call on someone when another man, a very neat man with parted brown hair, near the door, seizes the meeting. "When we started fighting the cops three nights ago, I began to feel like I was bigger just because I was there when it was happening. We have never stood up to the cops before, and now we were standing up to them, and it was as if we had become stronger all at once. We've suffered the indignity of being called queer and faggot, but now we've made the cops back off and even run away from us. I agree that we ought to talk about ourselves first—only I think we should identify ourselves when we speak—"

A very tall thin blond man whose hair hangs down on his cheeks, sitting at one end of the sofa, speaks. "I believe I have never been asked to do this. My parents, and all the straight people I have known in my life in Indiana, including my brother, didn't want to know how it was to be homosexual." The man speaks with his head tilted back slightly and his eyebrows lifted a little. While he speaks, he looks around the room, letting his eyes rest on one or another man. "And when I arrived in New York eleven years ago, the homosexual men I met here already knew how it was to be gay in America, and they didn't need to hear anything I knew. But that is all right. What I knew was unique to me. I knew both how strong and courageous I was—because I knew what I had survived—and I knew that nobody else had survived exactly what I had survived. I never saw a shrink, because I knew what they did to homosexuals, so I have reached the advanced age of thirty-six without ever having told another soul how I feel about my life. I don't want to talk about myself. What I came to this gathering for is to find out how we can change the conditions of our lives. I want to be able to go to a legally licensed bar and buy a decent drink at a decent price, and I want to be able to pick up a man along the waterfront without fearing that he is a cop in disguise who is going to surprise me just when I tell him that I want to suck him off. I am very, very angry, and I want to work with the other men in this room, if you share these goals too. If not, I will go out and do it on my own. I don't know. I suppose I could learn how to make bombs and how to throw them." And then, because he forgot, he says, "My name is Bertram Ross."

This is only the second time in my life when I have been in a room of gay men, all of us out, discussing our concerns. I am thirty years old. I feel odd, and I think it is because what we are doing here is radically new. The only other time I have been in a room with gay men who are all out—the phrase is young, radical, homosexuals— was back at the end of May when we met to develop a critique of heterosexual supremacy, so I haven't done it enough to be familiar with it. What we are doing right now is way beyond what we were doing at the end of May. Develop a critique. Now we're meeting to discuss what it means, now that we are fighting in the street. Way, way, beyond. Whatever power the old order had that kept us all in line—kept us all closeted—has now been swept away.

"My name is Roger. I came this afternoon because I wanted to know what we're all thinking about now. I mean, like, we could go in the direction of armed rebellion, if we wanted—I think we may already be there—and I'm ready for that. I don't think the enemy is ready for any kind of accommodation with us on anything that matters to us, and I think the only thing they are going to respect is a clenched fist that causes them injury. The more injury the better." Roger is a dark blond man with a kind of shaggy crewcut. He's small —short—stocky and muscular. He's got a thick Brooklyn accent. "I've been fighting along these lines since I was in junior high school, and I don't ever let the other guy get away with insulting me without getting a fist in his face in return. I know how to take care of myself. I'm apprenticed right now, since I was 18, to be a plumber, and everybody I work with knows I am a fag and I don't take no shit. That's the way it's been for me since I was thirteen. Now I have a question for all you guys. Were you serious about fighting on Saturday? Is there going to be any more fighting? Are you going to let this thing die down? Or are you going to make sure that when the cops think of fags, they think of pain and injury and hurt and defeat? What're you thinking of here?"

The power the old order had was essentially the power to withhold respect. If the old order found one of us was queer, it withheld respect. We learned this when we were kids, usually even before we were aware that our difference was a sexual difference. We learned it so young that when we learned we were different sexually,

193

we already knew the costs of being what we were, and so we hid, which was all we could do at eight or nine years old. When we grew older, the withheld-respect deepened into scorn and derision, and sometimes into physical violence. What is happening here in this room—what makes this room different from the room at the end of May, when we met to develop a critique—is that we are saying, "We no longer seek your respect." We don't know yet what the consequence of that change is going to be.

Jack is trying to impose order on the room, but the men are not sitting still for Jack to call on them.

"I think I agree. My name is Charles. I am twenty-four, and I think that the only good things I've done in my whole life have been violent things. The best thing I have ever done in my life was fighting the TPF on Saturday. The system is set up to make us end up hating ourselves, and the times when we end up respecting ourselves are the times when we rebel. I felt great on Saturday, and the only reason I don't feel great now is that I don't know what you fucks are going to do—wimp out or plan a fucking military campaign. I tell you what I want. I want to start feeling good again!"

Suddenly, Andrew is talking. I can feel his body tense up next to me. He sits with his back against the wall, and his arms around his knees, and he starts off speaking quietly, looking first at the David, which is in his line-of-sight.

"My name is Andrew. I live with my lover, Bo, in an apartment on Weehawken. Bo came back to our apartment about three in the morning on Saturday to wake me up so that we could fight in the riot together. I think fighting in the riot is probably—easily—the most important thing I have done in my life. We fought for our ownership of our street—We said, This is our street.—and this is the answer to all those in my life who have said that, because I am queer, I am somehow unworthy or less than a man. I fought along with other gay people on the street early Saturday morning and then again on Saturday night, and we did what men do, we fought for our place and our homes and our safety when we were being invaded by forces who were better armed and better trained but who had nothing important at stake in the battle. The great thing about Saturday is that when it was important to fight, we fought, and we brought the New York cops to a standstill. The thing that has always been true about gay people —that we are afraid—is beginning not to be true any more. We are going to have a different future because of what happened on

Saturday. It may be that this whole country is going to have an entirely different future because of what happened on Saturday—"

As he gains control of what he is doing, he lets his eyes range over the crowd, the ones close to him and the ones farther back. His eyes dart around the room, knitting us all together. There must be twenty-five or thirty men in this room. They occupy all the chairs and all the space on the floor except a little path from the door to the counter where the coffee is and then into the back, where the bathroom must be. The men are quiet. They listen intently—there is a stillness to their listening that suggests concentration. Andrew speaks softly, almost conversationally.

"I think it's important that we have a rough idea what we are fighting against. The churches have their reasons—they say it is the Bible—and the government says we are security risks. Just about everybody, all the power centers, in our culture has some reason for condemning men and women who have sex with their own gender. I think that behind all these different reasons to condemn us is a coordinated attempt to control men and women. I think the power centers in our culture want to control how men in our culture express our being men and how women express their being women. They say, 'If you are a man, it is unacceptable for you to have sex with other men,' just as at other times our culture has said, 'If you are a man, you must go to church, be the head of your family, support your family, raise children, show no emotion, honor your father and your mother.' So when we fight back, when we get out there on Christopher Street and fight against the cops and the TPF, what we are doing is saying, 'There are many ways for a man to be a man.' When we fight the cops, we are engaged in redefining our gender. Men, good men, admirable men, worthy men, may suck cock. When we were in Sheridan Square early Saturday morning in front of the Stonewall, fighting the TPF, we had with us men who are tired of the old narrow, rigid ways of being men, men who are strong but who don't beat up on their partners, men who are open to their emotions, who are finished with the violence that the old ways have brought us, but who are willing to use violence against the system when it's necessary, and who want to suck cock."

A man speaks directly to Andrew. "Andrew, what you see is that we give up the actions that have always characterized men, our need to control and our tendency toward violence, and we replace them with actions that have characterized women—the ability to feel our emotions, caring, submission."

"No," Andrew says. "I see us out there expanding hugely what it means to be men. A man is proud, a man is sensitive, a man is capable of fighting to defend himself and his loved ones, a man can fall in love with another man or with a woman, a man can wear men's clothes or women's clothes, a man can stay home to look after the children while his spouse goes out to earn a living, and he can go out to earn a living while his spouse stays home to look after the children, a man can share the duties of earning a living, a man can have vaginal sex and he can have anal sex, a man can decide to have children or not to have children. Our gender is not limited by artificial barriers. We are capable of an infinite range of things even while we are decent, proud men. We are free."

"It's about time—"

Men around the room talk among themselves.

"I want to be free."

"All the men and women who come after you must be free to define their manhood for themselves. Or their womanhood."

"Andrew's right," an older, soft-spoken man says, "We don't want to exchange living by his rules for their rules or your rules."

"I don't want to define my manhood," Andrew says, "by anybody's rules but my own."

There is an extended exchange among the men on the value of violence to gay men, after which a number of us go out to the street to smoke.

"I thought," Billy says, "that it was just about kicking ass."

"I think," Joseph says, "I feel how critical this moment is—these few days in late June, 1969—when we are placed in the position of having to know why we fight. Nothing in our culture is helping us right now. We have not been used to thinking about the root of anti-gay feeling, because everything in our culture—science, religion, tradition, literature, rational thought—has been used against us, and it is difficult, almost impossible right now, to imagine how these things can be used to help us. Those men in there are right. We have been told we are shits by every source of knowledge and opinion in our culture, and now, suddenly, in a matter of hours, really, we have to redefine what we are, in a way that doesn't do the same kind of violence to our sense of ourselves that we have lived with for the last twenty years, since we were children. What are we? that is, if we are not shits? I don't think we have any idea what we are doing. But I do think we understand how critically important this is. We don't know what it is, but this is the new beginning of our lives."

"Thanks, Joseph." I put my arm around him and draw him to me. He looks at me and smiles. "Thanks."

"I think Andrew got something else, too," I say. "What he said is that we don't need to come up with any answers for everybody. Each man can decide for himself what kind of man he wants to be, and who he is going to fuck, and what clothes he is going to wear."

"Several of the guys in there said they want to be free."

We go back inside.

"OK, guys," says a kid with tousled, dark brown hair, "I guess it's my turn. I'm from here, I'm from the Upper West Side, where I still live, and I've always lived here. I think I've always been out—I mean all the people around me always knew that I was queer, my parents, my teachers, the guys at school—and sometimes it has caused me problems, but most of the time not. My name is Arnold, and I am twenty-one years old. I've been a member of SDS since I was in high school, and all the way through Columbia, and so I'm pretty political, and during college, my last year in college, we had the Student Homophile League. You've heard of that. But now that I've graduated, I don't know what to do, and I am glad this is happening. I'm ready for some serious political activity."

By the time he finishes, a man named Harold raises a point. "Folks, what I would like is for the men, if they'd like, to also address the question, 'What do I want to happen now, after these riots?'"

"I can tell you what I want," Arnold from the Upper West Side says. "I want a really active, really tough queer organization that can take on the power structure in this city. Something that's not afraid to be way out and way daring. My queer political organization is going to have classes for us in community organizing and training in street fighting."

"My name is Edmond, and I live here in the Village, and I was a part of the rioting on both nights. I can tell you right here what I want. I want a decent gay newspaper. I hate the Village Voice. There are enough gay people in New York to support a gay newspaper, and there are certainly enough gay writers in the city—shit, right here in the Village—to support a gay newspaper, and I can tell you what I want it to be. I want it to be sophisticated, knowledgeable, professional, leftist, sexy, and fun to read. I come from Providence, where my parents are among the Portuguese immigrant population up there. I left when I came down here after high school. I went to NYU and then to the Columbia School of Journalism, and I have been out the whole time. Like the last speaker, sometimes that caused me problems and sometimes not, but I don't think I have ever been closeted. I think now is the time when we need to yell the loudest and be the most outrageous, because now is the time when we are most likely to get what we demand."

Walking home, Andrew says, "I took notes on everything that happened back there, and I got the name and number of Edmond, the man who wants a newspaper. We're going to get together tomorrow. I gave him my name and number and told him I am writing an account of the riots. Can I have the meeting tomorrow in our apartment? There may be more than just two of us. You guys go somewhere else?"

We laugh at him, since it is his apartment. Of course.

It is almost dark now, and we walk west on West 10th, spreading out to four abreast when the sidewalk allows it, and tightening up when we pass trees.

"—anyway," Billy continues, "there is a lot of shared ground that came out of the meeting. Even an organization was described broadly, as a kind of community center—did you notice how many people talked about needing to have gay and lesbian dances?—and also as a focus of political activism."

"I think there was agreement too," I say. "Nobody seemed interested in expressing anger at any of other people in the room."

"Did all of you get on the various mailing lists?" Andrew asks. "I hope?"

We all did. Even Billy. "I put your address on their list, with my name, and when I—if I—go home to Houston—"

"You're thinking about not going home, Billy?"

"I don't know what I am thinking about, Andrew. Do you need an answer right now?"

"No. You can do what you want. That is what Bo and I want you to do, what you want."

"And I want you to do what you want, too, Billy," Joseph says. "So, I think now is the time to raise this issue: Since Billy is visiting you two, I think I should go back to my apartment as long as he is paying you a visit, particularly if he is going to be here for long."

"Oh, wait, guys. I know what you're doing," Andrew says, "but it's not necessary. You and Billy can both stay with us, if you want."

I say, "I like having you both at our place on Weekhawken. Billy?"

"I'd like that. Joseph?"

"OK," Joseph says. "It suits me, if it suits everybody else. I don't want to intrude."

"OK, good. You're not. We'll all stay where we are. But on another matter, you know, guys, life is going to be a little more difficult if each of us is free to define for himself what it means to be us."

"Why?" Andrew asks.

"If there aren't any givens," I say, "if we really are free to define ourselves, if there is no one out there who is trying to control us, and if everyone out there is willing to accept us at our own evaluation, then we're going to be constantly analyzing ourselves, asking, 'Is this what I want to do to express myself and my freedom?' It is going to be impossible to live thoughtlessly. It is going to be impossible not to live a considered life. We're going to have to spend a lot more time than we have spent, just thinking about ourselves. And I suppose we're going to make a lot of mistakes."

"I suppose that's the point in the kind of culture we live in," Andrew says. "Some people are unwilling to do much real thinking, so they like it that they are given identities that fairly narrowly confine their choices. Get married, have sex only with women, with only one woman, act butch, fuck, don't suck. We are about to take on the burden of being free."

Billy laughs. "You guys really are free, aren't you?"

"Yes, we really are free," I say. "And I think you are one of us."

"Am I free too?"

"You're free too."

"Holy shit," Billy says. "I thought it was that I want to be free at some point in the future. You say we are free now."

"Yup. Except for the consequences. Billy and Joseph fuck, and Joseph—or Billy—falls in love, and then the other one has to deal with the consequences, whatever they are, of having a 6'2" beautiful, heartbroken man on his hands—or something."

"I think you guys are rushing things a little," Joseph says. "Freedom is a state you achieve after working for it. We are not free. As gay men, we are working toward a condition of freedom, but we are a long way from getting there, as I believe you actually know."

"Yes, I know." I do know, but I also know we can achieve a state of freedom in our minds, without regard to the conditions of our lives.

We drift on, through one of the loveliest neighborhoods in the city, in the night, in summer, in the city, talking about freedom and its consequences.

"I would like," Andrew says, "to express myself and my freedom to own a town house on Gay Street."

We laugh. "Why don't you ask for enough money to pay for such a house," I say. "Then you could quit your waitering job."

"You will notice that I don't ask for a man who is more beautiful than I already have, and I don't ask for one that loves me more, and I don't ask for one who is richer than the one I already have. I only ask for a town house on Gay Street. I would let you all come spend the night."

"The loveliest street in the loveliest neighborhood in the city," Joseph says.

"Uh, Andrew," I say.

"Yes?"

"We all are already spending the night."

A person might say that Billy and I, having had the upbringing that we have had, have always been as free as it is possible to be in our culture. I think that's true, because we have been free where it mattered most—in our minds—and that is the principal gift Mom and Dad have given us. But we have been trapped by many of the same constraints that everybody else has been trapped by—the severe limitations put on men's actions in our culture—and neither of us has addressed that. These constraints our parents have been powerless to lift. A guy must know how free he is, and what limits his freedom, and most of us don't. What is man's work?

Mitzi is on our front steps, in shorts and flipflops, a torn t-shirt, and no makeup. She's got blood in her hair and down her side, and she looks like hell.

"I got knifed, guys." She grimaces. "Can I stay here tonight?"

Knifed. "Of course." She doesn't stand up. She seems to have difficulty breathing. "Can you stand up?"

We gather around. She looks at the ground.

"I think."

She tries, but she wobbles, and then she sits back down. I—and Billy, too—lurch to catch her.

"I guess I can't." Her eyes make a quick tour of our faces.

There doesn't seem to be too much blood. Maybe it's a shallow wound, and it's stopped bleeding. Maybe she'll be OK.

"OK, we'll try it this way. Is it all right if you lean on us?" I move in under her arm and, without waiting for a reply, hold her wrist behind my neck—Billy's doing the same thing on her other side —and we slowly, gently, stand her up.

"Is this OK? Can you do this?"

She can. Joseph and Andrew get the doors, and we make our way up the stairs to our apartment, where we deposit her on the sofa in the living room. Andrew moves around the apartment turning on lights, getting sheets and pillows, and Joseph opens the short sofabed.

"What happened?"

She grimaces, then she takes a breath. "A guy started messing with me. I made him stop. I think I surprised him, because I'm stronger than he expected. But then he came back and started messing with me again, and this time he fumbled on something he wasn't thinkin' he was goin' to find. He grabbed my dick and wouldn't let go. He started beatin' me around the head. He said he was lookin' for a girl, and he said he had half a mind of making me a girl, even against my will. He had a knife in his hand, and I was trying to get away from him, from it, and that was when he cut me down my side —"

"Can I see it?"

"No."

"How'd you get here?"

"I walked. I held my hand to the cut, and I walked."

"When did it stop bleeding?" Andrew asks.

"A long time ago. It hadn't been dark long."

"Where was this?" Andrew asks.

"On West Street. The trucks."

"A gay man?"

"Jesus. I don't know. I thought he was straight. I thought he wanted me."

Billy gets our attention, and we go in the kitchen and talk lower. "Guys, I think Mitzi ought to be seen by a doctor. Even if the cut is not serious, we ought to get it professionally treated. Penicillin shots. Get it dressed properly. Where can we get that?"

Andrew shrugs. "St Vincent's. Not far. West 11th Street."

Joseph sees the point. "I'll go down on the street and up Christopher and find a cab. I'll bring the cab back here to pick up you guys. Is that what you want me to do?"

"Wait, we have to get Mitzi's OK to this." I go back in the living room. "OK, Mitzi. We think you ought to go to the Emergency Room at St Vincent's hospital. Just to have somebody clean and dress your wound—"

"Goddamn it," she's yelling at me. "I thought you'd do something like this. What I want is a place to sleep. I don't want you dragging my ass all over the fuckin' Village. And when I was walking over here, I was thinking, 'They wouldn't do anything like that dumbass thing, now would they?' and here you are, getting ready to drag me —"

"Mitzi, your wound," Andrew says, "your cut, needs to be cleaned up. If it's not, it will get infected, and you can die from an infection like that. Now we don't want to do anything that you don't want to do. We can't make you do anything. We are not going to try to make you do anything. But we can help you, if you will let us. To begin with, it would be good if we could see all your cuts and could clean them with alcohol." Andrew is using his most soothing language. "I can see how you wouldn't want to strip down in front of all four of us big fags, but maybe you would be willing to pick just one of us who could help you find where you were bleeding and could help you clean the cuts."

So that problem is solved.

I raise another. "What about Violet? Won't she be worried about you?"

"Prob'ly. I'll go out to find her tomorrow. Sometimes it takes a long time to find somebody. It don't take much time for somebody you been with all day to disappear."

"OK. We'll think about all that stuff tomorrow. Is that the way we'll do it?"

"Yeah. I think so."

Mitzi picks Joseph to help her, and they go to the bathroom. Billy and Andrew and I go to the kitchen and begin getting something for us to eat—while hearing Joseph's low quiet rumble and Mitzi's harsh objections—and plan the future.

Billy says, "No matter how much he can clean her up in there, she should still be seen by a doctor."

"I don't think anybody disagrees with you, Billy. It is a question of getting her to agree with you. I don't think she wants to be examined by just any doctor. Emergency rooms can be brutal places. We may have to do what we can do tonight, and then tomorrow take her to a place that is welcoming—receptive, respectful—for young women. For now, I think we have to depend on Joseph's being able to recognize how critical her cuts are and being able to tell us whether or not she has to go to an Emergency Room tonight."

We root around in the refrigerator. There're enough leftovers from last night—steak, corn, greens for a salad—for us to repeat last night's meal, all cold. I like cold steak, if it's rare. I get plates and glasses, Billy ice, Andrew the whiskey. We help ourselves.

Two years ago, when Mitzi was Luis, he was stabbed in his side, during a fight on the Lower East Side. He was only thirteen, and the girl who stabbed him was fifteen. We got a call from the hospital. We grabbed our things and jumped a cab and went over. They said that Luis told them Andrew and I were his uncles. We got ready to explain it all when we realized the hospital didn't care. They were going to fix him up—stitch up his stab wounds—and release him, and they didn't care who we were. He had been pulling tricks over on First Avenue when it happened—a fight with another kid over a john. He had just started pulling tricks, and he must have been too eager to get the customer. Some other, bigger, older kid pulled a knife on him. He was apprehensive when he first came out to the waiting room because he didn't know how we'd respond to the hospital's calling us. We were OK, so he relaxed. We brought him back to our place and dispensed the antibiotic the doctor had prescribed and put him to sleep on the sofa bed in the living room. He was still young enough to let us do these things, so we did, without asking many questions. You can still see the scar when she wears shorts with a halter. It's about half way between them, on the right side.

We've gotten other calls during the time we've known her. She's been in emergency twice with stab wounds, and she's been in jail twice—but we didn't hear about those until she got out. She was picked up when the neighborhood she was working was involved in a sweep, and she ended up in jail with other prostitutes and druggies and other violent, anti-social types. The last time, when we got her, she came out beat up. She had been attacked in the holding cell—they put her in with men—and she was beaten up. I should say she was sexually abused by some fully grown men. The word is raped. We persuaded her to go to our doctor to be examined. He gave her pain medication, something for her anus, and antibiotics. She said afterward, "Jail is not a good place for girls like me or for gay boys." She grew up. She went from being thirteen to being fifteen and seems older than that, now. She has learned better how to care for herself. She says, "I don't take no shit from nobody."

The truth is, at fifteen, she has to take shit from a lot of people, because that's the way things are set up. It's the system, is what people say. It's illegal for her to be on the street the way she is, and the cops can sweep her up and charge her with any number of crimes —with loitering, with panhandling, with creating a public nuisance, with prostitution, with vagrancy, with having homosexual sex, with wearing clothes that the arresting officer can say are not appropriate to her gender—and throw her into juvenile detention where she'll be held until the criminal justice system is ready to send her to serious incarceration, and to do this so often that she will accumulate a long list of convictions so that each new sentencing will be of a repeat offender. She will end up spending the rest of her life trapped in the criminal justice system. It's a trap she's in and can almost not get out of, and all of this over gender violations so innocuous that, left alone, they would not damage a fly. It is important to remember that the folks charged with her care—her parents—threw her out on the street when she was thirteen. While murders go unsolved and public funds are embezzled and public officers are bribed—and the Constitution deeply violated by the highest officials in the nation—Mitzi and her brothers and sisters are tracked down in the public street by all the armed might of the city. Our culture never gave Mitzi much to begin with, and then it took away what it gave, and then it hounds her for not having what it's taken away. And in the end, the newspapers call her and Violet and all their brothers and sisters the "dregs of the city."

What distinguishes us—Andrew and me—from Mitzi is mainly class. Andrew and I sleep indoors, we have jobs, and when we commit the crime of having sex with each other, we usually do it indoors and out of sight. But the main thing that unites all of us is that we—Mitzi and Violet and Andrew and I and Joseph and now

Billy—violate the norms of behavior. I think that Mitzi is perhaps a greater transgressor than Andrew and me, but it may be that it is impossible to determine who transgresses the most, and in any case, that is probably a silly thing to try to determine, just as it may be pointless to try to determine who suffers the most from our system as it is. It is certainly true that Mitzi and Violet are punished more severely than we are.

When Joseph and Mitzi come out of the bathroom—Mitzi wrapped in a shirt of mine that comes down to her knees—we get her seated at the table, then the rest of us join her.

"We're eating last night's meal all over again," I tell her. "Would you like some?"

"Yeah." She leans over her plate and stares down.

Joseph asks, "Are you tired?"

She nods.

"And the cuts hurt, too?"

She nods.

"OK, we're going to leave you alone, OK?"

The fight has gone out of her.

After she has eaten, Andrew goes with her into the living room and puts her to bed in the small pullout sofa. We hear him explain to her that Joseph and Billy will sleep in the larger pullout sofa in the living room when they come to bed later. She doesn't object.

I go in to her. Her bed is low, so I sit on the floor, my arms around my knees, close to the bed and facing the head, so I can see her.

"Hi, beautiful."

She takes a long time answering. "Do you really think I am beautiful?"

"Yes. Right now, you look tired. Tomorrow everything will be OK again." That is not so, but I say it anyway. One of those things people say that aren't true.

"Do you think I will be pretty tomorrow?"

"Yes."

She thinks about that for a while. "I don't understand you."

"What do you mean?"

"All this. All of you. Why do you do these things for me?"

"We are all in this together, Mitzi. And you're so much younger than we are, and it looks like sometimes you could use a little help, so we offer. We want to help you."

She doesn't answer for a while. "I don't know. It seems like you and me are really on different sides of this thing. I'm a girl who likes straight men, and you're a gay man who likes gay men."

"Do you believe we want to help you?"

She thinks again. "Uh-huh. Yes. I think so."

"We want to help because we can help—we've got an apartment and a little extra money and sometimes you need a place to spend the night. It would be terrible if you needed it and we had it, and we didn't want to give it to you."

She slips one hand under her head, and looks at the ceiling, but then immediately she moves the hand back to the sheet, next to her hip. It must hurt her to put it under her head. "Would you tell me something?"

"Yes."

"You see, I don't know where I fit in to things."

"Probably into several different places. Most people do. They have homes of different kinds with different people."

"You do?"

"Uh-huh. I have a home here with Andrew, and I have a home with Billy wherever he is—"

"Do ya like that?"

"Uh-huh. I like having different homes. I feel free."

"Yeah. I like that too. Gotta feel free." She pauses. "Where do I have homes?"

"One is with your brothers and sisters—with Violet and the others —that you've been living with for the last couple of years."

"Can I have a home with you and Andrew?"

"Yes."

"Would Andrew let me?"

"Yes. We've already talked about this."

"Can I live with you, if I want?"

"You can live with us, if you want. Yes. That's for sure."

She is quiet for a little bit. Then she says, "But how do we connect? I'm a straight girl, and you're a fag, and what's the connection? I still don't understand that."

While I'm thinking of an answer, she speaks again.

"I'm a kid, and fags don't want kids running around."

"Oh, I bet you just don't know how many fags there are with kids right here in the Village. Besides, you're almost grown up." Then I decide to bite off the big one. "Mitzi, don't you see it? The world—

you know, everybody—doesn't really approve of Andrew and me, and of Joseph. Andrew and I love each other instead of loving women, like they think we should. And they don't approve of you, either, for a similar reason. They want to look at what you carry between your legs and say, That makes you a man, and You have to act like a man, and they're going to say, You can't call yourself a woman. But you're just like Andrew and me. I think you believe that it is up to you to decide these things, not the government and not anybody else."

I wait for a few minutes before I go on.

"I think this is where we connect."

"I don't think I understand all that."

"Let me make it easier. Do you ever feel like a criminal?"

She laughs a small laugh. "Uh-huh."

"So do we. Andrew and me. According to regular people, all of us —you and Violet and Andrew and me and Billy and Joseph—are all outlaws. That's where you belong, sweetie, with us, with the rest of the outlaws. Besides, we connect with you because we love you, and we want to help you grow up and get an education and find the kind of life you'd like to live for yourself."

"What do I have to do?"

"You'd have to do your share of washing the dishes. You have to do your share of the chores, Mitzi—we all have to do those—but aside from that, nothing."

"Nothing?"

"Nothing."

"Is this what Andrew believes, too?"

"Yes. Would you like to hear him say it?"

She is very quiet. Then she says, very softly, "Yes."

"Back in a minute."

So I go into our bedroom, where all three of them are.

"Things OK?" Joseph asks.

"Oh, yes. Everything is fine. Andrew? Can you come talk to Mitzi?"

I leave him sitting on the floor next to Mitzi's bed, answering her questions, and I'm thinking of all the things we have to do tomorrow. Find Violet. Take Mitzi to a doctor. Find out if Mitzi is serious about the changes that may be about to happen in our lives. When I get back to our bedroom, I find Billy and Joseph having sex on our bed. Holy shit. Two teen-aged boys. Leave 'em alone for a minute, and look what they do.

In a little bit, I hear somebody pounding on the door downstairs, and somebody yelling in the street. I go down and find Violet.

"Is Mitzi here?" Before I can answer, she says, "Is she all right?"

"She's all right. Come in." And walking up the stairs, talking over my shoulder to her following me, I tell her the news.

I take her to the living room, where Mitzi is, and I go into our bedroom, where Andrew lies on the bed and Billy and Joseph sit on the floor.

"No," I say, "I told her just briefly what had happened, and then she went into Mitzi. I don't know what's going to happen, but I think they are going to sleep."

"I think," Andrew says, "they are going to come live with us."

"Both of them? Or just one?"

"I don't know. I suppose that will be part of the negotiations."

"Are you OK with just one?"

"Sure. I told her you and I have talked about this for at least a year. I told her I was thrown out by my family too, only I was older."

Things are quiet for a moment. Then Joseph speaks.

"How was that for you, Andrew?"

There's a pause. "It was rough, but it was nothing like what Mitzi's gone through. I was already an adult. I had three years of college, and I was still able to graduate. I was embarrassed by what they had done—they just weren't the progressive, sophisticated family I thought I had. They didn't come to my graduation. It was more my feelings were hurt. But look, I was never on the street like Mitzi. I think I was just really disappointed, once I started understanding my own sexuality, that they were such trogs about it all. And I was surprised, you know, to find myself alone in the world. That wasn't ever really true—I had my friends, and I had professors at Columbia who thought I was hot shit—but I was stunned when my family made it clear that I was not to come back where they lived any more, because I had never thought my parents would abandon me like that. It was just such a surprise. Such a stunning surprise." He pauses. "And, of course, it hurt."

"Andrew went on to get a master's in history at Columbia."

"I had started off well, when my parents were paying the bills, so I was able to talk the bursar into letting me stay. I'm still paying for that. I work hard."

"I think you do," Joseph says.

Adam in the Morning

"Mitzi thinks I do too. She likes that. She doesn't really understand what the rest of you do, but she understands waiting tables."

The room is dimly lit. Our apartment is hot, and the cross-ventilation from the front windows to the back window onto the roof is not enough.

Andrew gets up and roots around in a drawer. He has a sheet in his hand.

"What are you doing?" I ask.

"Thumbtacks. I am looking for thumbtacks." He finds them, and then he lets us know what's on his mind: he tacks up the sheet over the door to give us privacy.

"Billy, I think you and Joseph owe Andrew a full explanation of what happened last night on the pier that led to your flipping from straight to gay." They begin to laugh. "Because, since Andrew and I are considering letting Joseph move in with us, this evidence of Joseph's incredible sexual power is of some considerable interest to us. I suppose the question Andrew and I would most like the answer to is this: Are any of us safe around Joseph?"

Joseph rolls over and puts his face in his hands, laughing.

"Well, Andrew," Billy begins, "Joseph is a powerful figure, I'll agree. But I think I have to take responsibility for my own actions." And then Billy talks about Tommy Sante and growing up my brother, the Men's Co-op, and playing football at Oberlin. He tells about being into women, but "I think I am more open to things than many men. I think some men are just dead to the sexual signals other men are giving out, but I am aware of them sometimes, in the right situations. I think there've been plenty of times in my life when I could have gone down on a guy, but didn't, just because the social pressure is against it, just because it would take too much explaining in a community that wasn't open to it. But here? In your community, it's wonderful to be able to explore what I am capable of. And then Joseph is wonderful. Can't I be like this? Is this so strange? Can't I have sex with anyone I want to, no matter what his gender is, here in New York, in the Village, just off Christopher Street, here in late June, 1969? Isn't this the time and place to explore what freedom means, and what humans are capable of, at their best and most courageous and enlightened?"

We are lying around in our underwear, smoking grass.

209

"Yes, it is. Of course you can," I say. "It's not strange. You're fine. I think people are going to say you can't do this. They're going to want you to choose either gay or straight, and once you have chosen, they're going to want you to stick to your choice—even gay people—"

"—but I can change my mind at any time, can't I?"

"Of course you can," Joseph says, "and then, if you get tired of the way I suck cock—even though I have the reputation for giving the best head on both sides of this continent—you can move on."

"Oh, Joseph, I like you for a lot more things than the way you suck cock—although I think you do that fairly well."

"On the other hand," Andrew says, "it may be that you like what he does—or what he is—and you decide to spend the rest of your life together, or all day today together. It may be that on a daily basis, or minute by minute, you realize that right now you'd rather be with him than with any other person on earth. Life is interesting that way." Andrew lies down and stares at the ceiling. While he talks, he stops from time to time to hold the smoke in his lungs and then allow the smoke to float out of his mouth, between his lips. "It is a way of living that is intensely aware of the moment, an awareness on a moment-by-moment basis of the necessity of choosing. I am a free man, and I am choosing at this moment to be here, with this man. I don't think you can get here without exploring the possibilities of freedom. You have to be able to say, at every moment of your life, I am here because this is better at this moment than every other possibility."

"You're telling me I have to explore my possibilities more?"

"Sure, my chick, be free!"

We are aware of someone walking through the kitchen on the other side of the hanging sheet, and we go silent. I stand up and pull back the sheet a little. It is Violet, dressed for outdoors—that is, with shoes and the cloth shoulder bag she carries everywhere.

"Hi, Violet. Is everything OK? You need something?"

"Oh, yeah. Everything is OK. Mitzi has gone to sleep. You guys are good to let her sleep here tonight."

"You can stay here too, if you'd like." She seems about to run away.

"No, I think I'll go back to our gang, over on First Avenue. I'm glad that Mitzi is OK and that she has somebody to look out for her."

"Does she know you're leaving?"

"Yeah. I told her before she went to sleep."

She turns and walks down the stairs. At the door, she turns to me and smiles. She seemed so sad most of Sunday night, and it is good to see her face light up for a second. "Can I come back tomorrow, to visit her?" Then she is gone, and I close and lock the door after her.

"Violet left." I lie down next to Andrew on the bed. "Billy, do you think it is too late to call Mom and Dad?"

"No. Not too late. Let's do it."

"Let's not tell them about Mitzi. You can tell them about her when you get home. Is that OK?"

"Yes. I think that's right."

So we go on the roof and call them and tell them news of the riots and of the meeting at Heath's and of what we did today, and they seem pleased. Then, they want to know about tomorrow.

"Will there be more rioting tomorrow? Or do you think that is over?"

"Mom, I can't tell. We have an explosive situation here. Angry cops, deeply angry gay folks, and a tightly confined geographical location. But I can say that, if I were going into a street fight, I couldn't imagine a better gang to be going with. Billy and Andrew and Joseph are all very capable men, Mom. We're going to look out for each other, you can count on that." She takes that, I suppose because she has to, and then, when I pass the phone on to Billy, I hear him saying the same things to her. Poor lady.

Back in our bedroom, I get back into bed with Andrew. We are both on our backs. I have my arm out, and he puts his head in my armpit and looks at the ceiling. Billy and Joseph are arranging themselves on the floor.

When they get sorted out, and when a joint gets passed around to everybody, I speak, softly.

"OK, Joseph. What did you find when you looked at her cuts?"

He waits for a few minutes before answering. "The biggest one, down her left side from just under her breast to her hip bone, is more of a scrape than a cut. I don't know how he made that. I don't think any bone was exposed, but I think it must be painful, especially when I tried to clean it up. She has several cuts and bruises on her scalp, and she also has what appear to be honest-to-god stab wounds or cuts in the flesh down her left side, and also on her upper right arm and just at the front, inner, top of her left leg. She was telling the truth. I think the man was trying to castrate her."

We are quiet for a few minutes. Joseph's news is terrible and difficult to absorb.

"I think it was not only that she didn't want to strip in front of men, it was that she didn't want us to see how badly she was cut."

"Poor girl," Andrew says.

"What about the Emergency Room and the doctor?"

"I would like it if we could get her to the ER right now," Joseph says, "but I don't think that's possible. She was exhausted when I finished dressing her wounds. She's sleeping now. I feel we should let her sleep and deal with a doctor tomorrow."

"I agree. Everybody else? Does anyone know a doctor who would be amenable to her issues?"

"I think I have a number to call," Joseph says. "Several numbers. When we wake up tomorrow morning, I'll call and find someone. The theatre is a big community."

Tuesday, July 1, 1969

We are all waked up by Violet, yelling in the street. It's all about her wanting to know if there's anybody up here awake, or getting up today, and whether we thought it'd be a good idea if she came back later in the day. Or maybe she said later in the week, I don't know.

I pull on some clothes and go down and let her in. I don't even want to know what time it is, but then I find it is eight-thirty, so that's not so bad.

I tell her Mitzi isn't awake yet. "Sit down. I'll get you something to eat."

I start with bacon, which wakes up everybody in the apartment, if they had gone back to sleep after Violet's shouting. I get out the eggs and the milk and bread—and the coffee, which I start right off with a full pot. I take this minute of quiet to hang another sheet, this one between the kitchen and the living room, which gives Mitzi some privacy. In a few minutes, the guys start spilling out of our room, dressed decent, and waking up. The guys go in the bathroom one at a time, and when I turn around, I find Violet has slipped behind the sheet to visit Mitzi.

Andrew is the first to speak. "Hi, beautiful." He kisses me. I like to kiss him. I like feeling his beard on my lips.

Violet comes back and asks for help with Mitzi. She'd like to come into the kitchen but walking is difficult.

"Hey, wait, Bo." Billy says. "Joseph and I will take care of that. You go on with what you're doing."

In a minute they have her seated at the kitchen table, and people are getting food. Joseph is in the bedroom—I can hear him—calling doctors for Mitzi.

Andrew and I get coffee and go on the roof. The hot, slightly gritty breeze of the city blows against us. We are both in our jockey shorts—nothing else—and flip-flops, and we arrange our chairs to face the sun, in the south-east.

We talk about the article on the front page of the *Times* about the men cutting down the trees in Kew Gardens in Queens. The headline says, "TREES IN QUEENS PARK CUT DOWN/AS VIGILANTES HARASS HOMOSEXUALS."

"Do you know that happened last week?" Andrew says. "It's taken the Times a while to print a story." Then, "But, hey. I want to talk about Joseph."

"What do you want to say?"

"I want to make some progress on this."

"Do you want it to happen?"

"I do."

"Me too." I have my head tilted back to get the sun, and my eyes closed. "The truth is that Joseph has been able to find a place for himself here without increasing the turmoil, so that answers most of the questions I had. Everything is better with him around."

"He cares for us. We care for him. I am realizing I am caring a lot for him."

"I care for him too. It's also that Joseph's political background is going to be helpful to us. He's where we are, or ahead of us. We don't have to bring him up to speed on anything."

We discuss it, and we agree that we should offer him the chance to move in, if he wants it, with the same rules that Andrew and I have about money and space.

If he does want to move in, he will give up his apartment. At some point down the road, we three will decide whether to make this permanent. The three of us will get a bigger place somewhere in this neighborhood, some place with a room for Mitzi.

Joseph and Billy have taken her to a doctor on West 13th. Later this morning, here, Andrew is going to have his meeting of men interested in a newspaper, and in a little bit, I am going to go to the theatre.

"What about Billy?" Andrew asks.

"I don't know. I wonder if even Billy knows what is happening with him."

"Is he staying?"

"I don't know."

"Do you want him to stay?"

"Sure. I love Billy. I'd love to have him here in New York. But maybe not in our apartment. Or maybe in a larger apartment. And I think our parents would shit, with both of us living in New York." I think I can sort all this out easily enough. Billy is my brother. Whatever Andrew and I do with respect to Joseph, Billy is always going to be a part of our lives. Whatever Billy and Joseph do is between them. I can't worry about this.

"Bo—one more thing about Joseph—"

"Yeah—"

"If we ever feel that he is coming between us, then we need to talk."

"Right. Have you read the article in the *Times* about the Charleston hospital strike? The paper now says the talks failed. The other side reneged—refused to hire back the striking workers. They betrayed the strikers."

"Good God! I had hoped you could bring those two downstairs to their senses, and yet Matt tells me you three are still discussing the point of the play! What is holding you up? I asked Sergei what our production was about, and he seems to have no idea. What are you going to be talking about today?"

"Belle, I am the Technical Director. I build what the Director and the Artistic Designer tell me to build. You know this. If you want to get a comprehensive view of what this production is going to be about—or if you want to gig the Director into making decisions faster —you need to talk to him, not me." She talks to me because I am easier to talk to.

She grunts. "Do they have any idea what they are doing?"

"Actually, they may put together a brilliant production, if we don't all go insane first. Give them a little more time."

"How much more? We're beginning to spend money, and it is already two months before we start collecting any. We can't do much of this."

I tell her about Mitzi.

"Oh, my God! Is she injured badly?"

"I think she'll be all right. We'll know more about that after she has seen the doctor."

"What can I do? I'll go right over."

"She'd like it if you went over to see her, but I think I'd wait until she gets back from the doctor's."

"When will that be?"

"Call this afternoon. It may be that after she sees the doctor, she is not going to want to come back to our place, so check before you go."

Sergei and Matt are downstairs on the stage, in their canvas chairs.

"—try this, then." Sergei walks to the edge of the stage. "The first scene will take place in an entirely darkened room, employing flashing lighting to suggest the 'tempest.' I am thinking of scene one being played out all over the auditorium—at the backs, behind the seats, down here in the middle of the performance space. After that, all the scenes will be played out here, including all the fantasy scenes, I mean 'the revels,' which we can do right in front of the audience, with the imaginative use of lights. There will be a backdrop behind the risers on all four sides that has surreally large ferns and a step pyramid or two. This arrangement will be imaginative, flexible, creative, moving, and relevant to the contemporary New Yorker. Our playgoer is going to be enchanted. I am working on a complete plan of where we will need lights, and all the rest of it, and I will be able to give that to you by the first of next week, Monday." He turns fully toward the stage, his back to us, and folds his arms across his chest. He has triumphed.

"Wow, Sergei," I manage to say. "Suddenly it all falls into place for you. Congratulations."

"Thanks, Bo. Now, Matt, you should begin to think about costumes. Bo, you help us find someone to sew the costumes—or, I suppose, we should check out the possibilities of renting them."

"I'll get names and numbers. We need sketches first, however, to show the seamstresses."

"Right. Now, is there anything I have forgotten? Doesn't this take care of everything we need for right now?"

Matt raises his hand slightly. "Oh, yes, Sergei. This all sounds very exciting, and I am amazed that you have been able to pull it all together so quickly, but could you sketch out for me—maybe Bo would like to hear it too—your overall conception of the play? It would help me when I begin to work on the costumes."

Sergei laughs. "Of course. I am also going to write all this own so that we can put it in *Playbill.* I think it will be useful for our playgoers. Maybe put it on flyers, too, and get some people to hand them out in West 4th Street and Sheridan Square and Washington Square Park. Everywhere. Have you noticed how many people there are on the sidewalks of the Village handing out flyers? You'd think the whole world was in rebellion. Anyway, here is the idea. The tagline of our production is going to be—and we are going to have this everywhere in the Village, so that the connection between our tagline and our play is going to be inescapable—'COME TO OUR ISLAND AND FIND YOUR FREEDOM AND YOURSELF.' Then, under that, in smaller type, some paragraph that says something on the order of—" Sergei has a card in his hand to read from. "— *'No matter who you are, no matter what your place in life, for a fuller, richer, more deeply imagined life, for unimagined freedom, come to our Island, survive current storms, go home again with everything you thought you had lost—and with everyone you thought you would never see again—and in the end, just when you thought it was impossible, FIND YOURSELF.'* How do you like that?" He looks at us and grins. "Something, huh? I imagine us taking the signboards on each side of the main front door of the theatre on Sixth Avenue and, as soon as Monday, putting up as large a poster as the signboard will hold, painted white, with large black letters, COME TO OUR ISLAND AND FIND YOUR FREEDOM AND YOURSELF. Then, in two or three weeks, we can add more text, giving more explanation for the tagline. And more and more, until we fully announce ourselves."

"That's fine, Sergei." Matt says. "Could you give me more of a hint about the play itself? Is it going to be a classic production, where the evil attempt to disrupt the order of the world and are punished? A kind of early sixties anti-colonialist, anti-conquistador kind of thing? Maybe a dreamy, drug-induced vision of ravishing beauty? I'd love to hear your thoughts. It would be wonderfully grounding to hear what you have been thinking."

"It's interesting that you mention a dreamy, drug-induced vision of ravishing beauty, because that is exactly what I think our play should be, a dreamy, drug-induced vision of ravishing beauty. We are going to work very hard on the lighting—I see golds and purples and greens flowing over us as if they were transparent liquids—and the feelings induced by our production are going to range from the anxiety of a bad trip to the euphoria of hallucinogenic drugs described in Castenada's *Don Juan.*" Sergei sits down in his canvas chair.

"Of course you would like to hear what I have been thinking. Get this. 'Freedom' is the dominant theme of the play, and the setting free of Antonio and Sebastian and Trinculo and Stephano—and even Miranda and Ferdinand—is only a pale prologue to the grand climax of the play when Ariel and Caliban are freed by Prospero, and Prospero himself is freed by us. All of Shakespeare's great Romantic Comedies end in marriages, and this one ends in the betrothal of Miranda and Ferdinand—"

There is a clatter of noise at the front of the house, and a young man strides into the auditorium wearing a torn t-shirt and short shorts and flip-flops. He comes down between the risers to the barrier at the edge of the stage, coming toward us like a young prince, fully aware that all our eyes are on him, aware of how beautiful he is. He is perhaps twenty-one, his hair a tangle of light blond curls. He is athletic, he has the arms and shoulders and thighs of a gymnast, and it is clear, from his shorts, that he has a sizeable basket. He looks like —exactly like—the sculptural representations of Alexander. This young man stops just in the shadows at the edge of the stage and waits.

Sergei doesn't seem to notice this kid, concentrated, as he is, on Matt and me and the narrative he is spinning out. "—but it will also end in another commitment, never before seen on the Shakespearean stage. At Act 5, scene 1, line 294, Caliban is told to 'trim' Prospero's cell,' and he exits after line 300, apparently to disappear and never to return, but, surprisingly, he returns to the stage, this time, noticeably out of character—no collar and no leash now!—and as a mortal, to hover in the background while the concluding twenty lines are spoken. Ariel stays on the stage near Prospero until the very end of the play, and then leaves the stage on Prospero's words, 'Fare thee well!' at line 319. At Prospero's line freeing him, Ariel disappears from the stage and then reappears out of character and as a mortal— no wings on this fairy!—in the background of the group of actors near Caliban. In the moments—the two or three seconds—as the play ends, Caliban and Ariel are drawn to each other. It begins to become clear that, like Ferdinand and Miranda, Caliban and Ariel are a couple. They now appear to be fully human, neither fairy-like nor clown-like, which is what the white-skinned European conquistadors have required them to be throughout the play. Now, as the actors gather to leave the stage with the *exeunt omnes*, the last to leave are the actors who formerly played Caliban and Ariel. They are left for a moment alone on the stage and leave hand-in-hand, as a couple, free to express their affection for each other, fully in possession of the island which Prospero's prolonged visit has deprived them of. They are now fully out of character and depart the stage by walking toward the audience and through the audience to reach their exit. This ending gives dramatic embodiment to the liberation of Caliban and Ariel and demonstrates that now there are no slaves on this island. All are free, absolutely free to feel as they will—and specifically to show affection where they will." As he finishes, Sergei looks from Matt to me and then turns around to the exits, where he sees the young blond man for the first time.

"Ah," Sergei, seeing him, speaks. "Come in, and I will introduce you."

The beautiful young man comes to the stage—he grasps the barrier and swings his legs over in one graceful move—and approaches us, smiling.

"Bo, Matt," Sergei says, "this is Ariel. Ariel is in love with Caliban. Do you suppose that is probable? Will our audience buy this very minor addition to the stage business of the play? And do you think, here in the Village, two months after these present riots, our audience will like to see these two holding hands, about to take possession of their island?"

Sergei leans back in his chair, his hands interlaced behind his head, and smiles deeply, staring at the ceiling. "You see, as these days went on, I found it more and more impossible to contemplate mounting a production of *The Tempest,* which is about freedom, and to do it without some gesture toward our own brothers and sisters in the streets around Sheridan Square, who are so heroically seizing their own freedom from those who would keep them enslaved. We could not ignore these momentous events." Then he looks at all three of us, "I do hope you are with me, and that you can do what I am asking of you."

Adam in the Morning

I leap up, applauding. For a second, I am the only one of us applauding, but Matt joins me, a broad grin on his face, and then young Ariel, his arms above his head, fists clenched, punching the air, leaps up over and over again in an ecstasy of pleasure and excitement.

"Do you like it?"

Belle and I leave the theatre and walk to Christopher Street, going home.

"I'd love to stop along here—" She nods toward the restaurants along West 4th. "—and have lunch. I do want to talk to you about all you've told me."

"I don't think I have the time, Belle. I need to get home to Mitzi. You know that Billy and Joseph need us."

"Oh, I know. And you are exactly right. Going to Mitzi is far more important, but that doesn't stop me from wanting to stop all through here—" She looks wistfully at the boutiques and cool little cafés.

We hurry on.

"Are you OK with what Sergei told you this morning?" I ask.

"Oh, Bo. Of course I am. But this is the fourth time both of us have worked with Sergei, and he has done this each time. He sits through endless preliminary meetings—and makes all the rest of you sit through them too—and it becomes clear afterward that he is soaking up what everybody is saying. But he is letting all of you think that he is not paying attention or that he hasn't read the play yet or that he doesn't quite get it yet, and just at the moment when all the rest of you are about to pull your hair out, he comes in, smiles, sits down, and exultantly lays out a brilliant, imaginative, *to-the-point* production of whatever the play is, leaving all the people who have been forced to yammer on for hours in previous meetings dumbfounded that he's pulled it off again. One of the characteristics of his performance is that he puts together a brilliant production, frequently made up of bits and pieces of things his colleagues have said, without ever acknowledging that half of what he proposes is not original with him but was in fact proposed two days or four days ago by someone else, now sitting paralyzed in some canvas chair, speechless as Sergei puts it all together in a new way. He's brilliant, of course, and we can't gainsay that, but he's also a thief. No getting

around it. Now you remember yourself what happens next. He is
going to make everybody do what he wants them to do, no matter
how hesitant we are to go along with him and no matter how good
our reasons are for resisting his proposals, and then in the end, on
opening night, Sergei will get a production like the one he has in his
mind, and at one a.m., when the reviews come in, we'll find that the
Times and the *Post*, and all the others that matter, will have fallen in
love with what Sergei has done. It could, if you let it, drive you
crazy, drive you to say you won't do another play, that you are, right
now, leaving the theatre permanently, and then Sergei pulls the
craziest stunt of all. He'll come up to you—we'll all be at the
opening night party, half drunk, high on whatever we can find—and
he'll say, 'Bo, I want you to know how much of this belongs to you.
We could not have done it without you. You are essential to the
success of this company, and I want you to know that I have told
Belle that I won't take another play with this company unless Bo is
the Technical Director. You are the best I have ever encountered, in a
lifetime of work in the theatre.' Then he'll hug you and kiss you, and
then he'll go off and give the same speech to someone else—to *me!* if
I haven't gone home in a fury—and soon we'll be back in this whole
process all over again. We are all part of the creative process in
Sergei's mind. We have no independent existence. We exist only to
enable him to be able to understand this play. Give up, Bo."

"Oh, Belle, you are light years ahead of me." She totters along the
hot street in her high-heeled espadrilles with the straps around her
ankles, known in the Village as "fuck-me shoes." I don't know how
she manages not to break her legs.

"I wish," Belle says, "that I had your equanimity about these
things. I feel unpleasantly like I've been screwed. It's terrible, just
terrible. I want a drink. Can I have a drink when I get to your house?
I do know it's early. What is it? Not yet 1:30?"

I laugh. "As many as you'd like, Belle. And I got some new grass
this morning, too, and you can have as much of that as you'd like,
too. I think the idea is that we just need someone there at the house
while Mitzi sleeps. The doctor sent her home to rest, Billy says, with
penicillin and instructions on dressing her cuts, and Billy and Joseph
both say that we need to have someone in the house with her while
she sleeps, but that they can't be there. So that leaves us. Besides you
and I need to talk."

We make it down Christopher Street as fast as we can—past the Lucille Lortel theatre and the PATH station and the lovely old rose-brick wall around the churchyard of St Luke's, and finally to Weehawken.

Mitzi is asleep, and our conversations with Billy and Joseph are carried on in whispers.

"The doctor said everything is going to be OK," Billy says. "He took a few stitches on two of her cuts, but otherwise he left them alone. I mean he cleaned all of them, then stitched some of them up, and dressed all of them. Am I making sense?"

I laugh.

"He gave her some pain killer and said it would make her sleepy for twenty-four hours. He also prescribed an antibiotic. I've already given her, her first dose of both of those. Here—"

He hands me bottles of pills.

"—are his prescriptions. And we stopped off at the pharmacy and restocked your supply of bandages and tape and disinfectant. So. He wants her to take it easy and to rest for two days. Don't worry, I am coming back by supper time, and I will bring food for everybody." He turns to Belle. "Would you like to stay for supper? I'll bring enough for you too." He takes her in his arms and says, "You and I need to remember that we're the straight ones around here, don't you think?"

"I don't know. I don't know. Things have gotten so mixed up recently that I don't know whether it's a good thing that you and I are the straight ones in this crowd. On the other hand," she says, trailing her brilliant red fingernail across the part of Billy's chest that shows above his shirt, "I do know I want to spend the afternoon—once I see for myself that Mitzi is OK—prostrate on some surface around this joint, and grass no farther away from me than my hand can reach. So I may be here when you get back. Only don't dawdle. You could join me." She kisses him.

Everybody laughs.

Billy and Joseph turn toward the door, when I speak.

"Hey, wait. What happened to Andrew? Did he have his meeting this morning? Where is he now?"

"Apparently Andrew had his meeting. They set up the meeting for 10:30, here, and Billy and I left around 9:30 with Mitzi. Then we got back about one, and nobody was here. So I guess they had a meeting, but we never saw anybody, and there was no sign of a meeting anywhere." Joseph frowns. "Andrew runs a clean meeting, don't he?"

"OK, he'll call and let me know what's up." Then I bring up another thing. "Joseph, you are coming back, aren't you? At some point, Andrew is going to be here, and the two of us want to talk to you about us—about your moving in here with us. That is, if you think you'd like to have that conversation—"

He leans across the space between us and kisses me. "Anything you say, beautiful. I want to have that conversation. I'll be back with Billy around five or six. In the meantime, I am going to call you in about two hours, just to check in, to see that you and Mitzi are OK. OK?"

Then they're gone.

But I have another idea. I go to the door and call down the stairs. "Go to the Statue of Liberty!"

They laugh, and then they go out the door into the street.

Belle is getting out the ice and also checking out the lunch possibilities in the refrigerator.

"Slim pickins."

"Did you check out Mitzi?"

She looks at me. "Yes. She's asleep. She's peaceful."

"Why don't you settle in here—there's also our bedroom, and the roof—and I will go down on the street and find us something to eat."

There's a deli on Washington, and I load up on sandwiches for the three of us. When I get back I find that Belle is asleep on our bed, and Mitzi still hasn't moved in the living room. I check and find her breathing regular.

I roll a joint and sit in the kitchen. We are going to have to get a bigger place. I wonder if they do actually go to the Statue of Liberty. It is a long way, and they won't have time to go there and get back by, say, six. The statue is inspiring because of what it is, I think, rather than because of what it represents—huge, exaggerated by the height of the plinth, constructed of copper, an immense classical statue of a goddess whose face, it is said, is the face of a man— Apollo the Sun God—in its improbable place in the harbor. When I think of it, I keep coming back to the scale of it all—the scale of the idea, and the scale of the execution, a statue placed in the most imposing of possible sites, connecting the nineteenth century with fourth century B.C. Greece. France, the United States, the long struggles for freedom, Rhodes, Alexander, Apollo, eighteenth century revolutions, nineteenth century American immigration, freedom, liberty, independence.

But it's not a monument to twentieth century liberty, which lately has seemed more often to be fought by poor people, by colonized people everywhere, black people in European-dominated nations, gay people, and women everywhere. In each generation and in each century, the fight for freedom transforms itself, according to the conditions at the time. How are people oppressed? According to the place of their birth? their religion? the color of their skin? their gender? the ways in which they express their sexual desires, by how little money they have? It would be impossible, now, in 1969, to determine how most people are most oppressed, but it does seem true that many people—hundreds of millions of people—are oppressed in their gender and in the ways in which they express their sexual desires. We are oppressed by the culture in which we live and its determination that there are two genders, that gender is determined in only one way, and that there is a narrow range of behaviors appropriate to each gender. Everything else is forbidden. And in that fight for freedom, to be whatever gender you say you are and to express that any way you want, there aren't any "Statues of Liberty." Some day there will be a monument, a fine monument, made of something lasting and valuable, and breathtakingly beautiful, that will connect our struggle for freedom with all the other struggles for freedom in the twentieth century and the nineteenth century, going back through the eighteenth century, back all the way to the first conception of Liberty in the fourth century B.C. And such a monument will move you to tears.

The phone on the wall next to the sink rings, and then rings again.

It is Andrew. "I thought you weren't going to answer."

"I was thinking, and I didn't move to the phone fast enough. What's up?"

"I'm at Zanes for the lunch shift. I had my meeting this morning, and then I came over here. I'm to get together with Edmond. He's the guy who brought all this up yesterday at Heath's. I'm to get together with him again this afternoon. They're going to meet me here and then come back to our house. We'll meet wherever you guys aren't. Maybe on the roof. There'll be three or four of us. That OK?"

"Sure. Joseph and Billy are coming back around five or six, and Belle is here now—"

"How is Mitzi?"

"She's passed out in the living room—that is, she's taken some painkillers, and they have made her sleepy, and she is asleep in the living room."

"What did the doctor say?"

"Some of her cuts required stitching, and he gave her antibiotics and pain medication. He told Billy and Joseph to keep her in bed for two days. She agreed to come back here."

"Maybe I shouldn't bring this crew back there. We already have a full house."

"Look, it's a warm, good evening. We can eat on the roof. Everything will be OK. Come home, bring your guys, I love you."

"You sure?"

"I'm sure."

"Hey, wait a minute. What happened at the theatre this morning? What did Sergei do?"

"You won't believe it—"

"What?"

"He has a dude as Ariel, and he proposes that Ariel and Caliban get it on."

Andrew laughs, and then for a few seconds, he doesn't stop laughing. "Well that won't require acting."

"No, you should see Ariel."

"What's he like?"

"Gorgeous. Different from Joseph, but gorgeous."

"Your director has an eye for these guys, doesn't he?"

"Uh-huh. The point is that, at the end of the play, with everyone having been set free, the ones who had been most enslaved are now most free to express their desires, and they do it—these two men—by holding hands. Look, finish your work, meet up with your guys, then all of you come home. Everything is under control. Uh, well not really under control, but at least happening in a fairly orderly way. Everything is fine."

I hear him laugh.

I putter around the kitchen, laying out our sandwiches, checking the beer in the refrigerator, checking the levels of scotch and bourbon and gin and vodka and the jug of white wine. I think everything is fine. There's enough to get us through tonight—get us through to the stores opening tomorrow, which is the essential thing. We have enough grass, and we have enough papers. Billy and Joseph said they'd bring supper. Sunday night's food—and Monday night's—was provided by Joseph and Belle. And now Tuesday night's is going to be provided by Billy and Joseph. Can't let Joseph pay for anything else for a while. Andrew and I are providing the alcohol and most of the grass. From each according to his ability. Everything is working out.

What's happening here is we are drifting toward a commune. The long-term prospects for our commune are that we will move into a larger place, with space for all the adults, plus some space for Mitzi and Violet. But we could go further in this direction. One of the serious needs in the Village that's becoming obvious is a home for street kids. We could get a large apartment with a bedroom for Andrew and Joseph and me, plus a couple of bedrooms that we could turn into dormitories. We could put maybe four bunk beds in one bedroom, that is, four top-and-bottom combinations, sleeping eight. Then we'd run fund-raisers to pay for it. Cool. We could assign one of the adults the job of finding jobs for the kids—for those that want them—and somebody else the job of teaching the kids how to cook for themselves—teach them enough to help them survive in this city. "If you stay with Andrew and Bo, you have to help." That could be our motto. I wonder if any of them would want to come in.

But in the short run, we have this apartment, and we have Joseph's—assuming he wants to join us—and we ought to hold onto both of them until we find something bigger. We ought to make use of both of them—some of us sleeping here, some over there—until we get used to all of us and figure out just what we're doing and where we're going.

"Goddamn it!" I hear a screech from Mitzi's room. "Have you gone away and left me here alone? I knew I couldn't trust those fags!"

Mitzi.

"Beautiful, here I am." I go in to her. "Billy and Joseph were here until I got here—" She's sitting on the bed, looking up at me. "— and I've been here since about one-thirty. Belle came with me. You've never been left alone. We would not have left you alone."

She starts to cry—heavy, body-wracking sobs. "I thought you had left me." Her face is bunged up, and there are the bandages. "And I thought I was in your apartment—here—by myself."

"No. You haven't been alone. Belle is in the other room."

"No, I'm here." Belle is behind me, in the door to the kitchen. "Hi, Mitzi. Oh, dear, I was so distressed, and so angry, when I heard you had been attacked. Oh, I was just so—so angry!" She moves into the room beside me. "How do you feel, dear? Can we get you something? Won't you lie down again, dear? I think the doctor wants you to rest, if you can bring yourself to do it. That's better, lie down, and I will get you something to drink. What would you like? Lemonade? Water? Bo brought us some sandwiches. Would you like one?" She turns to me. "Tell her what you bought us, Bo." She turns back to Mitzi. "And if you don't like the sandwiches, I can go down and get you what you do like."

"Roast beef, corned beef on rye, and hot pastrami. Potato salad, latkes. Would you like lemonade?"

I leave them in the living room talking, or being together, and get them both sandwiches. I bring in a chair from the kitchen for Belle next to Mitzi's bed.

"We're OK, Bo. I'm going to sit here with Mitzi for a few minutes, and then when she is ready to go back to sleep, I'll come out and be with you. And, would you check the doctor's prescription and tell me when Mitzi can take her next pain pill?"

So that's what we do.

I wonder what running a home for street kids would be like. Hectic. I'd never have any time for myself—or for me and Andrew— but the need is so great that I'd never feel I was doing enough. And once I started doing something like that, it would be impossible to stop doing it. Andrew and I never discussed whether or not we'd take on Mitzi. Both of us just knew that's what we'd do, then we started talking about how to do it and about whether or not Mitzi would allow it, and what would be involved. I wonder if this has crossed his mind. This new administration—Nixon—is like the last one, so deeply involved in making illegal and unconstitutional war on the nations of Southeast Asia that they can't see the needs at home. And they're worse than the last administration because they're so uptight and so controlled and so disapproving and afraid of everyone who is the least little bit free. What Andrew and I—and Joseph, if he wants

—can do is not much, but even as little as it is, it still needs doing. I don't know anyone who has ever run a home for street kids. I wonder if Joseph will still want to join us—will he still be in love with us—if we decide to do this?

I roll a joint and toke. I eat the sandwich. I climb out on the roof. The sky is dark blue and is still without clouds. It is still early. Four o'clock or so. Three-thirty. I sit in a chair—they are the folding aluminum kind with green plastic tapes woven to form seats—and put my feet up. I wonder if there is a book in the library on housing or shelter for street kids. St John's in the Village, over on Waverly Place at West 11th. They have a soup kitchen. I'll go, and maybe I can find someone there who will be able to steer me toward someone who—

"Isn't it glorious?"

It's Belle, climbing through the window. Poor Belle. She is not much older than I am, but she has not lived her life and made her decisions in such a way as to make it easy to climb through windows. I think it is easy to climb through windows, but I am very uncomfortable in hundreds of places in the city. Funny about that.

"How's Mitzi?"

"Asleep again. She appreciates the sheet you put up. She's fine. Where's the grass?"

"Kitchen table. Oh, wait a minute, Belle. I'll get it for you. It's easier for me."

"Thank you."

"Bo, I think she feels humiliated by what has happened."

"I think so too."

"So we have to be very very careful around her not to condescend and not to patronize. That could be very wounding, if she felt it. She must sense our respect."

"Right. Have I been OK?"

"You? Oh, yes. Of course. I was worried about myself. I am not as sensitive to other people's needs as I should be, and I was just reminding myself to watch it, dame. I would just die if I hurt her feelings in any way. I would rather cut off a big toe. Several of them."

"Belle, you're fine. Just sit there for a minute and rest, and I'll get the grass for you."

When I get back, Belle says, "I told her that we will not leave her alone and that you and I are going to sit on the roof while she is sleeping. She seems comfortable with that."

We smoke for a while, facing the sun, our eyes closed.

"She may come here and live with us."

"She told me."

"I hope she does."

"I hope she does, too." She takes a toke off her joint. "If you and Andrew are her parents, I want to be her aunt."

"Sounds good to me, Belle, but we'll have to clear all this with Mitzi, you know that. Right now, I'm keeping it to 'would you like to live here with me and Andrew.' She has had a bad experience with parents, you remember."

"Right. I am going to start with small gifts, and then we can see where we go from there."

"Start with small gestures, sweetie, then go to gifts." I think about this for a while. Belle and I are talking this out at a very low velocity. Long pauses. "I think she might not know what to do with a gift. Remember, she's been living on the street, Belle."

"Right. You will help me with all this, won't you? I want to do the right thing."

It's wonderful, here on the roof in the sun. "Do you mind if I take off my shirt?"

"Please do. How about you? Can I take off my blouse?" I open my eyes, and she looks at me sternly. "I don't have anything on underneath, you know. I don't want to drive you mad."

"I'll try to control myself."

I close my eyes again and wait for the next sally.

"Bo, do you think it would have been a good idea for me to ask Joseph to help me get pregnant?"

"I think it was a wonderful idea. *He's* a wonderful person. Good genes. You needed to talk out the details, I guess. But wonderful."

"Oh, I am so thankful. I was afraid you thought it insane."

"No. I sometimes think I'd like to have children, too."

"Have you? I could ask you, then?"

"I think you could ask any of us."

"Would you? Oh, what a lovely thing for you to say. I never expected that. Would you agree, if I asked?"

"Oh, well, Andrew and I would have to discuss it. It's a big step. But I think Billy would think seriously about it also, if you asked him."

"I had no idea. I have assumed—"

"That we're gay, and so—"

"Something like that."

"But you know Billy has been having sex with Joseph the last couple of nights, don't you?"

"Yes, but they're both so gorgeous—"

"Well, one of them is gay and the other of them is straight. They do what they want, Belle."

"Well, I thought—"

"I think, dear, I know what you thought. But you should remember this. People can do what they want. And I think that, whether they are gay or not, they'll take the question seriously. That doesn't mean they are going to agree to what you're asking. But they will treat the suggestion seriously."

"Bo, you know I don't mean to be a troglodyte. You know I don't mean that."

"I know. Let me be sure I've got this clear. You want some man who will have sex with you and get you pregnant. Is that it? And the question of parenting is separate, right?"

We go quiet for a few moments.

"You're the coolest woman I know, Belle. You're going to be a wonderful mother. You're scattered, and you can be overwhelming, but kids can take that, because the important thing about you is that you are totally loving, and your kid is going to realize that right away. You're going to be very protective and supportive, and he'll know that right off." I take a hit on my joint. "You're steady where it matters."

"You're very kind."

We take in the sun for a while and hear, distantly, the sounds of the city mixed with the sounds of the river.

"I can't decide whether to raise this child by myself or to ask someone to share parenting with me."

"But without marriage."

"Yes. No one has mentioned marriage."

"Right. I think I am not able to help you on this one, Belle."

"Would it be all right if I wanted to do it myself?"

"I don't see why not. Kids grow up all the time in families with only one parent, a mother or a dad. It doesn't even require comment. You only need the other sex for its DNA. It's easier if you can share the duties with someone else, though."

"Would you be willing to share parenting?"

Long pause.

"Belle, you go right to the heart of the thing, don't you? Actually, I'm thinking of maybe starting a small home for homeless kids—"

"What a wonderful idea! A kind of year-round summer camp! No. A commune! Bo!"

"Now, Belle. Take it easy. I don't know. What I'm doing is turning things over in my mind. I think I'm getting to the end of my contribution to the Olympic Theatre, and I'm considering other things. I think I could make a home for street kids be my job. That wouldn't be true if I decided to parent a child."

"What does Andrew say?"

"I've only just begun to think about it, just this morning. What do you think?"

"You'd be helping young people like Mitzi and Violet."

"Yeah. Give them food on a regular basis, a bed every night, some lessons in how to get along in the world. Chores. Some classes. I don't know. My idea is to explore this with people who've done it."

"You have incredible courage. Energy. I can hardly keep my ice trays filled."

"You are going to have a child."

"Yes. I am going to have a child. And I think I would rather have some man help with the parenting, but I am willing to do it alone, if necessary."

"When are you going to decide?"

She shrugs. "Soon. Sometime soon."

Now is my moment. "Talk to me, Belle. Tell me about what this is all about."

"What do you mean?"

"What's driving you? I think there are a lot of reasons for wanting a kid. What are yours?"

"Don't you trust me, Bo, to have the right reasons? I thought you loved me."

"I don't think that's it. It's that we—all of us—have the tendency to let things stay on the surface because it's scary or hard to dig down and really tell the truth about things. Can you talk about wanting a baby?"

She begins to talk, slowly. "It would be easier if I could say something like, 'I want a baby because in some way my life is incomplete,' but my life is complete. I have friends, I have a good job that is intellectually satisfying and stimulating. I have a moderately good relationship with my parents. I get sex when I want it. Usually. It may be that I am aware of being—of having a superfluity of many things. I have some money, I have a good sized apartment. I have time. I have more than I need, if you know what I mean, of just about everything. I think I have more love to give than I have people to give it to." She is embarrassed by what she is telling me. "Does this make me sound like a self-satisfied bitch? I hope not. I'm not self-satisfied. I want to be better than I am. I want to be kinder to people, more thoughtful. Only you, Bo, could drag all this out of me." She smiles—grimaces—and takes a deep sigh. "I want to find a way to take what I don't need and to give it away. To help make someone happy." She has tears in her eyes. "But that's not quite it. I want to be able to sacrifice for someone else. I would love to be able to make a child happy. I've never told anybody all this before. Is this enough, Bo? Is this enough to make it OK for me to ask to bring a baby into the world?"

We enjoy the sun. Why don't people who live in New York spend more time in the sun, like this? We only lie in the sun when we've gone to the beach. There are plenty of places in the city, and time, but we don't do it.

The phone rings. It is Joseph.

"I wanted to know if there is anything you need. I am not planning to get to your house until about six, in about an hour and a half—I'm bringing supper—but if you want anything, I can get it and get over there in about forty-five minutes."

"No, thanks, Joseph. We're OK."

"How's Mitzi?"

"She's asleep. She's waked up a couple of times since you guys left, and we've talked a little, but now she's back asleep. She seems to be doing well."

"OK, that's good. How many are going to be there for supper?"

I tell Joseph that there will be five of us for supper, and maybe three more. I tell him to call just before he buys anything, and I will give him a firmer number.

"Who are the other three?"

"Andrew's three friends who are having a meeting about the paper."

He says he will take care of everything.

Later, Belle and I each go into the apartment to check on Mitzi. When I go in, Mitzi is sort of half awake. She has her arm on her good side across her eyes, which she pulls away, and looks at me. "You still here."

"Yes, I'm still here. I told you I wasn't going to leave."

"Wasn't Belle here?"

"Yes, she's still here. She's out on the roof. Would you like to talk to her?"

"Naw. I just wanted to think about her being here."

"You OK?"

"Yep."

So I leave her, and she goes back to sleep.

I tell Belle.

"I like that."

The phone rings again. I'm thinking it is Joseph again, but it is Heath, the man from the Silver Dollar who had all of us to his house yesterday.

He asks me if I am happy with what happened. He and Roland are inviting people to their house for a meeting next Monday, same time, and he says he has gotten in touch with two other groups who are meeting in the Village. Also, one of the other men is in contact with the Mattachine Action Committee, who are planning a community-wide meeting in about three weeks. They already have a place to have the meeting. I check our phone book for Heath's number. He asks if I will contribute to the cost of a mailing to everybody who attended yesterday.

I roll another joint—I roll several, because we have people coming over—and Belle and I share.

Later, I hear people coming up the stairs—Belle is putting on her blouse—and then men are climbing through the window. Andrew and the man called Edmond—dark, black curly hair—from the meeting yesterday at Heath's and two other men I don't know, small, intense men.

Andrew introduces us. "Guys, this is my lover, Bo, and our friend Belle. Another friend of ours is asleep in the living room because she was knifed yesterday. Her name is Mitzi."

"Is she going to be OK? Maybe we should have our meeting somewhere else."

"We took her to the doctor this morning, and he took care of things and told us to try to keep her in bed for two days, so I think she's going to be OK."

Andrew turns to us. "This is Edmond, and this is Craig and Jeff." We shake hands all around.

"Joseph, who lives here, and my brother Billy, who lives in Houston and came up for the riots, will be coming back later." This is the second meeting these guys have held in this apartment today.

"This is great." Craig walks around on the roof, taking in the breeze and the late afternoon sun. "You are lucky to have a roof to use in the summer."

The phone rings. It is Stephen, the man with blood in his hair the first night of rioting who stood at the foot of the steps to the high stoop and asked if we were all right. He invites me and Andrew to a meeting Thursday night at seven at his apartment. The men will all be SDS members. I tell him I will also bring Joseph, who also has experience in Mississippi and who is our roommate.

As soon as I hang up the phone, it rings again. Joseph, from the grocery. "I'm getting supper. Any special orders? How many people do we have?"

I tell him. I join Belle on the roof again.

Andrew passes around the weed and gets something to drink for the ones who want it.

They settle down, a little way off from us—and Belle and I continue to talk in subdued voices. "If we want," I say to Belle, "we can go in the kitchen or our bedroom."

"Uh-uh. This is fine. Late afternoon sun, breeze, things winding down. Let's stay here."

Andrew and his friends seem to be in the middle of their discussion.

"—is through distribution of a mimeographed sheet, and I don't
see why we can't do better than that. Our population will support a
paid newspaper, twenty-five cents per issue, say."

"That's steep. What about the populations that can't afford
twenty-five cents? That's half the cost of *The New Yorker*—"

They talk about distribution and sales and advertisements. Gay
businesses—the bars, the baths, organizations in the Village and on
Fire Island, clothing stores, cinemas in the Village, restaurants—can
be expected to contribute to the cost of a newspaper by buying ads.
One of them wants to know whether any of this is really true. Perhaps
the cinemas and the others will continue to buy ads in established
papers and not buy ads in a new, local gay rag.

"I think we should do two things," Andrew says. "We should start
right off here at the beginning collecting a staff of politically hip
writers who are not going to need time getting up to speed, and we do
that in two ways: We put an ad in the *RAT*, and we pass out flyers in
Sheridan Square announcing a new newspaper. And at the same time,
I think we ought to collect an editorial board, a group of men and
women who are politically hip who can meet frequently—at least at
the beginning—to set editorial direction. And then I think we also
need a business manager for the beginning."

The man called Craig says, "What are we doing? I mean, are we
going to try to get out a newspaper this weekend? When? Then how
often after that? We need to set a timeframe at the beginning. If we
want to get a paper out by Sunday, say, there's a lot of stuff we
should skip. We have to go right to story assignments. Get one of us,
maybe the business manager, to explore the publishing aspects of all
this, the best place to buy paper, and to find a mimeograph machine
for free, while the rest of us write stories. And I don't think four of
us can put out a paper. There's just too much work. On the other
hand, if we're not going to try to get out our first issue until a month
from now, or longer, we have more time to put together an
organization." He looks around at them. "Do you know what I
mean?"

"Right," Edmond says. "And there are all the questions around
what kind of organization would put out a paper. I go for a not-for-
profit co-op."

They are trying to nail down things that have to be talked about
and decided, but they are just beginning to get a grip on the job

they're taking on. Andrew asks me to get more paper for them from the desk in the bedroom. Edmond is not good looking. His eyes are interestingly round, with heavy eyelashes and eyebrows, and he has a prominent jaw. But he looks sharply intelligent, he is sexy, and he probably gets more guys than men who are more conventionally handsome.

Belle turns to me. "I would like to have some part in all that," she says, nodding to the group talking about the paper.

"What?"

"I used to manage a newspaper when I was in college."

"Belle, you are as bad as me. You already have a full life. Do you have time to take on the job of getting a new newspaper up and running?" She is thinking about it. "Talk to Andrew about it later." It may be that she has already made up her mind.

Edmond is talking. "Why do we need a newspaper?"

Jeff, dark tan, black hair in long wavy curls to his shoulders, grins. "Because we're writers and this big thing has happened, and we want to write about it and show off." They all laugh.

"We have to be on one page about this, Jeff. It's way, way bigger than anything personal. We need a newspaper to reflect the reality of the lives of gay citizens—for gay citizens."

"OK, Edmond," Jeff says. "I was joking, really."

"Well, if we are agreed, we can move to specifics. What about it guys?"

They are in agreement.

"Wait," Andrew says. "I want to say something. What's happening right now is that gay people are changing, minute by minute, day by day. We're becoming different, and our newspaper is going to be the record of that, so that years from now people will be able to flip back through our old issues and can say, 'Look what they were concerned about then.' Or, 'Look what they were doing then.' Or, 'Look what gay people were back then.' This is going to be the chronicle of our time."

Edmond clutches his fists and brings them above his head and pulls them down in a great jerk, "And that, Andrew, is going to be our name! *The Chronicle!* That's brilliant! Andrew, you write up a paragraph telling us why we have chosen *The Chronicle.* Is everybody in agreement on that?"

Adam in the Morning

Chronicle. I like that. There is something serious about that. And
it is certainly not going to be the 'chronicle of wasted time,' although
that is Shakespeare's most beautiful sonnet.

"OK. Good. There are four of us. That is not enough to put out
any kind of paper very soon. I think the next step is to get more
writers."

They get agreement.

"Wait. Is this a co-op? Are we agreed on that?"

They move on.

Belle is sitting back in one of the aluminum chairs, her head
against the brick wall, her eyes closed. It is approaching six o'clock,
and the light is beginning to get a yellow glow. "I think I may get
pregnant without asking any of you for help. I don't want to be in a
position of asking any of you men to give up being gay, even for a
minute, so I can get pregnant."

"Belle, there is no brick wall between gay and straight. Being gay
is not something you can give up, no matter what you do, but it's also
not something that governs every single sex act and thought you
engage in. Things are much more fluid than that. I think your bigger
problem is finding someone to commit to parenting your child with
you. That would cut seriously into the activities of your normal gay
man's life." I take a deep breath. "And into yours too, Belle. For
something like the next fifteen or twenty years."

"I am not sure that gay people should get married and settle down
into long term relationships and have children."

"Look, gay people can do anything they want to do."

"Oh, I know. This is so complicated, isn't it? Maybe the
heterosexual population already has it right. We should all find
someone of the other sex and tie a legal knot with them first, then
screw for the first time, and then when the baby comes, it already has
a Mommy and a Poppy, and all of the questions that pursue
everybody else are already answered. Only I have one question. How
can I become a virgin? Isn't that necessary for marriage? I mean, to
wear white?"

"Belle. Find a guy who is not a virgin, and then neither of you has
to think about it. In a community that doesn't give a shit about
virginity. And I don't understand anyway why you need a man of any
sort. I will give you all you need—and if you don't want to know
whose, I can arrange that for you too. What I don't understand is why

239

you need a man for parenting. You are a wonderful person, and you are an accomplished woman. There is nothing required here that you can't do all by your self."

She tokes her joint and blinks her eyes against the smoke. "You're right, of course, as always. I never do need anyone else. I suppose I thought—" She closes her eyes, and then she looks directly at me. "—that it would be less lonely."

I hear people coming up the stairs, and then they are at the bedroom window onto the roof. It's Billy.

"Hi, guys. We're home." Billy withdraws his head from the window.

"Let's go into the kitchen and see what's for supper."

Belle and I go into where they are in the kitchen, unpacking the food from the grocery store. Joseph. Billy. Wait. Another guy—

"Uh, Bo—" It's Joseph speaking. "—I think you've already met this man." He points to him. "Ariel."

I bust out laughing. "Yes, I have met him. Welcome to our apartment." We hug. "Belle, this is our Ariel, have you two met?"

I see Belle has not been able to take her eyes off him since she walked in. "No, but I'd really, really like to, young man. I know you're playing Ariel, but I wonder if you have another name—" She raises her eyebrows. "—one that you might have been given when you were born?"

"My name is Augustus Glenn. My friends call me Gus. You can call me Ariel, if that's the custom around here." He looks around at all of us, checking us out. "Joseph and Billy said I could come for supper. Is it all right?"

"Of course. How did you guys contact?"

"I was at the theatre, talking to Sergei about my role, and Joseph showed up with Billy. I was introduced to Joseph, and he introduced me to Billy, who is, by the way—" He turns and smiles at Billy. "—a really nice guy."

"I think so too."

"You two have talked about what Sergei wants to do with your roles?"

"Uh-huh."

"And you're OK about that?"

"I'm fine with it," Gus says.

"Right," Joseph says. "I think it's going to be huge. Everybody in New York is going to want to see it." Then he puts his arm around Gus's shoulders and says, "I think it's going to be fun, too. I only wish our big moment happened earlier in the play."

"You two are going to be much talked about." Belle says. "You're going to be famous."

"The most famous lovers in New York," I say.

I go to the window and ask Andrew to start the charcoal grill. We begin to concentrate on food. They bought ground beef and what we need for hamburgers. Beer. And, according to Billy, more pot. Billy makes joints and gets an ashtray. Joseph and Belle start making patties, I give Gus the salad things and send him to the sink to wash lettuce. I make drinks for everybody who wants them. It turns out, the guys out on the roof would like another joint. When I get back into the kitchen, I hear Mitzi.

"Bo! Bo! Goddamn it! Fuck this!"

"Mitzi, I'm here. We're cooking hamburgers. We can make one for you, too. And we have some friends over. You can come out and meet them, if you want. Can I come in?" I am standing by the door into the living room, the opening draped by the sheet I put up this morning.

"Yeah." She starts out tough and hard, and then melts into something more forgiving.

I push the sheet aside, enough for me to get through, and slip into the living room.

She is sitting on the side of the bed.

"How do you feel?"

"I don't know, Bo. I feel shitty. My side hurts a lot, and every time I move it hurts a lot."

"The doctor gave you some pain pills to take. Would you like another pill?"

"I hate the way I feel on those things."

"I know, the pain is awful, but the pain medication is almost as bad."

"I think I'd like to put off taking it for now. I didn't know it would hurt this bad."

"Do you want to come out and meet people?"

She thinks about that for a minute. "I don't know." Then, "Who are they?"

"Us. Andrew and me. Joseph and Billy. Belle. Gus, a friend of Joseph's and mine from the theatre. And Andrew has invited three men over to talk about starting a newspaper. Andrew and the men are on the roof."

"Can I come in the kitchen?"

"Yes. Or if you'd like to stay in bed but you want to see what's going on, we could pull back the sheet so you can see us and we can see you."

"I think I'd like to come in the kitchen, if that's all right."

I offer to help her, so she and I move slowly to the kitchen, past the sheet, and when we get into the kitchen, we find Belle and Joseph and Billy and Gus standing there facing us, staring like they are witnessing somebody just getting up out of her grave.

She sees this. "I'm not dead, guys."

"Mitzi," I say, "we have a new friend here. This is Gus. He is an actor, and he is in the play that Joseph is in, the one I'm working on sets for. He plays Ariel."

Gus comes over. "I'm sorry you got stabbed."

She looks him over. "Are you a fag?"

"Yeah—" He's being careful.

But she's over it now. "Oh, man. Don't ever get stabbed. You have no idea how bad it hurts."

"I know. I don't."

"I don't know which hurts worse, the stab or what they do to you sewing it up."

"Mitzi," I say. "Does it feel better to lie down or would you like to sit down here at the table?"

"Bo, I think I'll just stand up here for a few minutes, and then I guess I'll go back and lie down again. I been lying down all day, and I was beginning to get antsy. Can I have something to drink?"

I get her lemonade.

"You know, Bo," Belle says, matter-of-factly. "If Mitzi is having difficulty with pain, and if she doesn't want to take the pain medication the doctor prescribed, I always think the best remedy for pain is grass." She picks up a joint from the ashtray and holds it aloft in her roach clip.

"Of course. Why didn't we think of that. Mitzi? Grass?"

Gus moves over next to her—they're both leaning against the wall —and begins a conversation. They share a joint.

"If you want help getting back to your bed, I'm your man." He says it very gently.

She's as tall as he is, but he has pronounced musculature, while she is slender, even skinny. They are, maybe, six years apart in age. I think he is twenty-one.

"That must have been tough. Would you be willing to tell me about it?"

"Oh, man, you don't want to hear about that. It was the worst thing ever. I thought I was gonna die."

"It must have been terrible. If you ever decide you'd like to tell me, I'd like to hear." Then he says, "Would you like a chair?"

I am finishing with the salad.

"I love this." It's Billy. He's leaning against the wall, his arms folded across his chest, surveying the scene, which includes all of us. Belle and Joseph stop making patties and look up.

I turn around and put my arms around him. "I love having you here."

"I love your friends, Bo, all you guys."

I kiss him.

He takes a toke on the joint, and then he looks at it, turning it from side to side and looking at it through squinting eyes.

Joseph hugs him. He kisses him. "I love you too."

Gus, watching all this, speaks to Mitzi. "Are they always like this? Or is it the grass?"

"Always. All day long. It's the way they are. Drives me nuts."

Belle says, "Let's go out on the roof."

"I think that's really cool. I mean, he's straight and all." Then Gus says, "Do you want to get back in bed?"

"Yeah. I'm tired."

Gus helps her.

Belle and Joseph go out on the roof.

"This is so fine." Billy is talking about the weed, I think. "But bro, it may be fine here and all, but I have to start thinking about going home." He's leaning against the wall, his head back, his eyes closed. "Do you think you're going to have any more fighting?"

"I don't know. Hard to tell. Maybe not. I can understand if you feel you need to go home. I don't want you to go, but I understand if you feel you have to."

"Well, tomorrow I'll call the airlines and find out what's available."

"OK, and then we'll talk about it again."

"Well, look, if—when you get your play up and have a little free time—why don't you and Andrew and Joseph come down to visit us?"

Billy and my parents have always been supportive of me, but they've been in Houston. I settled in up here, and what I forgot was what it felt like to have Billy with me while I do what I do. Now, when Billy moves to join me in something, like when he's moved in to take a part in helping with Mitzi, everything we do reminds me of our years together. I'm gonna miss that.

Billy laughs and scrubs my scalp. "You gonna miss me?"

"Yes. I'm gonna miss you. I'd like you to stay here."

That seems to stop him, for a minute. As if he hadn't really expected me to say that. "I know. I want to stay. The trouble with me coming up here and visiting you is that it makes me dissatisfied with my life in Houston. I love having my parents around me all the time, and I have a bunch of guys, but the way it all adds up, it seems awful tame compared to you guys up here. Life here is like a Toccata and Fugue."

That Billy. "Mitzi thinks you're wonderful."

"And she's wonderful. I like not knowing where the energy is going to come from. I don't like going back to Houston and feeling that I have to fit myself back inside a tight frame. You know how my life is. I am going to use my final year on my contract to make some big changes in my life. I just may come back up here and get involved in whatever you are involved in."

Andrew comes in, followed by Edmond and the others.

"What's happen'n?"

"I think we're through with our meeting. We're going to meet again in two days. We each have assignments."

"Can you talk?" Belle prompts them.

"Wait," I say. "Have you guys met everybody? Have you met Billy? This is my brother, Billy, from Houston."

There's a lot of "Hi, guy," and Billy shakes hands with all of them.

One of the small, intense ones looks at Billy and says, "Jesus, two of you. Do you have any more like you at home?"

Adam in the Morning

"I think," Edmond says, "we all think that the biggest need right now is to give people information about what's going on right here, and we need to do that soon. So we are going to see what we can pull together by Friday. We are going to try to keep it simple. A few main kinds of information. Let people know who we are. Tell 'em what our name is so they can look for us next week. What's happening politically in the Village—a list of meetings, contact names and numbers, a paragraph about us, what our plans are, a statement of our politics. Then put out something more substantial a week from Friday. Friday will be our publication day." Edmond has a reassuring manner of presenting their agreements.

They start moving toward the door.

Andrew says, "Come on guys. Stay for supper. It's just hamburgers on the roof." He puts his arms around the necks of the two small intense guys, Craig and Jeff. "We can tell everybody what we're going to do for the *Chronicle*."

And they do. They head back out to the roof. Gus comes in from the living room, where he had been seeing about Mitzi.

"How's she?"

"Asleep, I think. I stayed and talked to her for a little bit, and now she's asleep. The grass was good for her." He looks around. "Where's Joseph? And Billy?"

"They're out on the roof with Belle. You go through there, and then climb out the window. You'll see the others."

"Is it OK if I go out there?"

"Yeah. It's OK."

He leaves.

"He seems like a good kid," Andrew says.

"I think he is."

"Are we alone for a minute?"

"I think so."

"Good, let's go in the bedroom."

We lie on the bed. "I've been thinking of something all day today. It comes out of the attack on Mitzi, and her being here." I tell him about my idea for a home for kids—not a very big one, maybe something with about eight beds. "What do you think?"

He puts his hand behind my head and pulls me to him and kisses me. "Oh, yeah man."

"You're willing to explore this?"

"You knew I would be. Right now, because of Edmond and the newspaper, I have my plate full, so you'll have to do the initial investigations, but you can count on me. Right after we get this paper up and running, I am going to be right there with you."

I hug him. "The initial issue that I see is Mitzi. We are committed to her, and we have to see that through. We get her to move in here and we get her settled here, and after that we can talk about other kids."

"Right."

"And we need to tell Joseph what we're thinking."

"Right."

"Thanks, Andrew."

We hug, we kiss, we go out on the roof, where the charcoal is now the right color, get the hamburger patties, and Joseph takes on the grilling.

Later, after the others have left, I'm sitting on the roof, my back up against the brick wall, next to Joseph—Billy and Gus sit on his other side—smoking a joint. Andrew is on his back between my legs, his head in my lap. I stroke his forehead. Joseph speaks, slowly, as if thinking out loud: "I don't think the experience of black people tells much about the experience of gay people. I think black people are more of a people than gay people are, probably because we are born into black families. It is probably true that each gay person has to create himself. I know I created myself as a gay man in a way I didn't have to create myself as a black man. I think that if bigotry recedes— if our culture gets more comfortable with men and women like us— the numbers of us will recede. Fewer and fewer of us will describe ourselves as gay at the same time we are still clear about our being oriented toward other men. That process will take longer for black people. In the meantime, it is important for us to do what we've done this weekend, find a safe spot to operate from, not always to be exposed and in danger. What you and Bo do, here in your apartment, is you give the rest of us a chance to be ourselves for a little bit, before we go back on the street, back to the battle. I appreciate that— what you've done for the rest of us."

"Thanks, Joseph." I reach out and stroke the nape of his neck. "You're fine."

"You said you wanted to start feeling good about yourself—" It's Andrew.

"Ah, yes," Joseph says. "I went through all these things, but I always felt lonely—you know?—like I was the only one on the planet. I was a member of the black community, but I wasn't a member of any community for another part of me that was as important as being black. I felt alone. I didn't want to hide. I wanted to feel OK about myself, in a community of gay people who felt OK about themselves."

"I think I know how that one feels—" Andrew says.

"I came down here. I had tried everything else."

We are quiet for a while and watch the stars. We pass around a joint.

"I've talked to you guys about Mississippi, but I haven't told you much about afterward, and I think maybe I should. Or it may be that I want to. It's about the things happening in the black community during the last five or eight years and how I ended up down here with you."

"That's cool," Andrew says.

"We've made some advances in the last eight years, primarily in civil rights, things that can be treated by laws—" He smiles. "—what Mitzi calls fighting sheriffs. But a question can be raised whether black people are any closer to being—" He pauses, thinking. "—Americans. There are more black people than there are fags, I think, and we've had a lot of brilliant people looking at this issue—I mean the issue of How does a black person live in America?—and you see where we are. You'd think we would have solved this problem by now."

The stars are as big as they ever get. The sky is a deep, dark blue, almost black, and, as is always the case in New York, the closer the sky gets to the horizon—to the buildings on all sides—the less pure is its light and the fewer stars there are. Joseph's voice is low and quiet, and he speaks now very slowly, pausing between his words and sentences. When he laughs, it is low and quiet, a kind of rumble that comes from deep in his chest. It is very satisfying—comforting—listening to him. In the background is the crackle and pop—and the occasional wail of sirens—that rise from New York streets.

"It's not just a question of whether we've got the vote, or whether we all drink at the same water fountain. The criminal justice system is deeply biased against black people, the whole economic system works to keep us indentured—that word should be 'enslaved'—and the system works to keep us isolated from those who are our natural allies. These are characteristics of the system in America that are not going away. They are permanent characteristics of the system that are built into the way it works. Always, since the founding of America, there has been a permanent underclass."

We listen intently.

"I am describing this situation using language that is less emotionally loaded than the published discourse, because I am among friends. I'm doing this because my real point is something we haven't talked about. And that is that almost all the best writers and thinkers who write about our condition of servitude in America also describe the condition of native peoples around the world oppressed by colonialism. Stokely Carmichael, Huey Newton, Eldridge Cleaver, Malcolm X and the others, writers who have developed theories of the relationship between the white and the black races, which they call imperialism and colonialism. All of these writers have been influenced by the Algerian writer Frantz Fanon. Fanon wrote a book, *The Wretched of the Earth*, that analyzes the condition of colonial peoples, principally in Africa and in Arab countries, and, by implication, oppressed peoples everywhere. Just about all these writers have concluded that the strategy for obtaining our freedom is for all oppressed peoples to join together and to use our collective might to throw off the chains that bind us. Just about every radical black leader during this decade has understood that he had to stand with Fidel Castro against the capitalist pressure from the mainland. Black people in the US and Communist Cubans are natural allies. Also Algerians, and blacks in South Africa, and the Chinese, and the Vietnamese, and others. Black people have been learning during this decade that we have millions and millions of allies—hundreds of millions—around the world in our struggle for freedom here in America. We are not alone.

"What Frantz Fanon has to say about natives in African countries or in Arab countries and their relationship to colonialists is also true of gay people and their relationship to straight majorities in Western countries. Read *The Wretched of the Earth*. See what it has to say about us, here in New York. When he comes to deal with the question of gaining our freedom, he describes us. In his opening section,

"Concerning Violence," Fanon says, 'The colonized man finds his freedom in and through violence.' It is important to know and to remember that. The colonized man finds his freedom in and through violence. He says, 'Violence is a cleansing force.' That's important to remember when you're fighting cops in Christopher street. Violence is a cleansing force."

"If fags are to become free," Andrew says, "we will do it by finding allies among other peoples who are not free, and we will find our freedom in violence. I think, when I was reading Fanon, I wasn't thinking about gay people. I didn't know he was talking about us."

"We had not become politicized for you yet."

"No."

"But there's more. If one black man in Harlem looks downtown, and if all he sees is a bunch of white men, it is likely he will stay where he is in Harlem. But if a gay black man in Harlem looks for allies in his struggle for freedom, it is likely that he will look downtown to Christopher Street. This is likely true even if there is a group of gay black men in Harlem looking for allies. Ultimately it is likely true that the natural allies of black people in America are the gay people of America. The writers who have studied this issue for a long time understand that the natural allies of any community of oppressed people are all the other communities of oppressed people. So, as a gay man, and looking for allies, I look for the largest, most vibrant community of gay men on this island. As a black man, and looking for allies, I look for the largest, most vibrant community of oppressed people on this island. So everything I am—" Joseph throws out his arms, the fingers on his hands out and his palms upward, a gesture at once beseeching and trusting and open. "—has led me downtown to you."

No one says anything for a moment.

I put my hand on his shoulder. "Joseph, Andrew and I would like to welcome you here to Weehawken Street. We want to invite you to move in with us."

Joseph smiles. He squeezes my knee. "I'd like that." He kisses me.

Andrew reaches up from his prone position on the roof to take Joseph's hand. "I love you, man."

"I think we're already beginning to learn how a couple of men expand and become three men."

"I understand. It will take a little time."

"Maybe, but not long."

"And—" Andrew says, "—how a black man and two white men can be each other's allies."

"You are a beautiful man, Andrew," Joseph says.

Andrew, I can tell, is pleased that Joseph is content.

"Bo, Andrew, I do have one question, now."

"Sure," Andrew says, "what is it?"

"I know you guys are cool guys, but I wonder how much thought you've given to the fact that I am a Negro."

Things pause.

"As that affects our living with you?"

"Yeah."

"We haven't talked about that at all."

"Well, we've got to talk about that, guys, because there are a lot of people who are not going to be happy seeing two white dudes and a black dude walking down the street together, or in gay bars and restaurants, and all the rest of it. And I mean that, even though we ought to be each other's main allies, still there is stupidity and there is racism and there is homophobia, and both black men and white men are going to be unhappy, both straight and gay, seeing us together. I want to live with you, but I want you to know what you're getting into."

Now it's Billy who speaks. "Oh, Joseph, they know. We know. Nobody's going to be surprised by anything. Bo and I grew up in Houston."

"And I grew up in Brooklyn. I think we have the chance to be something good for each other—I'd like us to be allies—but I want to talk about it until we've talked it into the ground, until we're all comfortable with what we're doing. I don't think we should ever do anything until all three of us are comfortable."

"That's fine," Joseph says, "but I think there's more to it than that. I think Bo has an idea that we ought to think about, talk about."

"What's that, Bo?" Andrew looks at me.

I pass it back to Joseph. "Tell us, Joseph."

"I'm not sure that, at this point in the history of our country, white men and black men *should* be living together. Or can live together. Half the history of my race in the last ten years has been the history of people's attempts to discover what we are, *separate* from your race. And that has been a good effort, and I respect that. I think you're cool, and I think you're sexy, and I want to try it—not just try it but try to make it work—but I think we're more likely to make a go of it if we understand all the different forces that are driving the races—and us—apart right now."

"I like that—" Andrew says. "—going to the heart of things."

"You guys are white, and I'm black, and we're all fags, and what we need to talk about is *What can we give up to be together? What are we unwilling to give up? What are we unable to give up? What do we need from each other? How can we help each other? Can we love each other?* There must be others."

"When I grow up," Gus asks, "can I move in too?"

"Gus," I say, "you can move in any time you want."

We sit under the cool light of the stars for a while, aware of each other. Finally, I speak.

"Where did you two go this afternoon, after Belle and I came back here?"

"You wanted us to go to the Statue of Liberty!"

Billy and Joseph laugh.

"Did you go?"

"No," Billy says. "We discussed that, but I asked Joseph to take me up to Harlem and show me his places up there. So he did."

"I showed him where I lived before I came down here, and I took him to a restaurant in the neighborhood."

"He introduced me to some of his friends. We went to the New Lafayette Theatre. He introduced me to all these actors."

"Tell 'em, Billy."

"He introduced me to a man who used to be his boyfriend, who is a good-looking dude. He's as big as Joseph. And I promised to come back at Christmas for whatever show is on."

After a time, Gus speaks up. "Hey, guys, I'd like to say something."

We laugh at our beautiful, Harvard-educated Ariel. "Speak on."

"I'd just like to say *Thanks* to Joseph for giving us a unified theory of the races and sexualities, which I *think* applies to all the genders, too. Most people don't understand these things well enough to do that. Thanks, big guy."

"Do you know how wonderful you are?" Andrew speaks very seriously to Gus.

251

Gus stammers. "Can I spend the night?" He grins.

I get a joint. We're drifting toward a cool evening, but before we get too deep into it, I get Billy, and we call Mom and Dad.

Wednesday, July 2, 1969

Today is the day Billy has said he will decide when to leave New York and go back to Houston. I understand that he has to go, but I am more aware of my connections to family and antecedents. We are not alone, and I am more aware of valuing him than before.

The sun is already up and here in our apartment with us. I lie here listening. There is the sound of Andrew breathing next to me. I am on my back, my hands under my head, and that is uncomfortable for him, who, in his sleep, can't find a way to connect with me. He lies on his side, facing me, and my arm is in his way. I put out my arm along the pillow above his head, and he slides into the opening. He slips back into deep sleep.

Gus lies on his side, spoon-fashion behind Andrew, his arm over him, still asleep. Beautiful Gus.

Billy and Joseph are on the mattress on the floor next to our bed. I hear them turn over and rearrange the sheet. Billy coughs occasionally. Joseph wraps him up in his arms. I watch them. Joseph kisses Billy on the back of his neck, and Billy shows a trace of a smile.

I hear Mitzi mumbling in her sleep in the living room.

Today I have to go to the theatre to see what Sergei and Matt are doing. I haven't yet learned what carpentry is going to be needed for this production. We haven't solved the question of Prospero's cell—where Prospero is going to pull back the curtain and reveal Miranda and Ferdinand playing chess—and we haven't solved the question of Caliban's cave, in which Prospero imprisons Caliban. How do we show enslavement—what it is—so that we can show freedom when it happens? The things that happen on this island are momentous. How do we show that?

I expect Andrew won't have to work today. He has had to work Sunday, Monday, and Tuesday, and he may have today off. We'll have to arrange something for Mitzi. Get somebody to stay with her. She should stay in bed again today. I listen for a sign from her, but I don't hear anything. Andrew comes closer to me, lying on his stomach, his arm across my diaphragm, his face up close to my lats. We learn, over months and years of living, how to get close. Much of this happens while we are asleep, as Billy and Joseph—their hugs and kisses—unconsciously show. The impulse to intimacy is way, way deeper than the level of conscious thought.

Mother's line was, "Oh, do something that matters, Bo." I wonder if she would include in that "something" my love for Andrew. Her love for my father matters. I know that she would include our sense of responsibility for Mitzi. She is the kind of person who is most comfortable with doing those things that "matter" that somehow cost her. It may be that she would think that I am getting too much back from Andrew for my love for him to be the altruistic sacrifice that she thinks of when she thinks of things that "matter." I don't know. How forgiving is she? I often wonder how easy-going I am. Do I need to sacrifice myself for some good in order to feel OK? I'd like to think that I am a fairly laid-back person, but having the parents I have, it is difficult to tell. I'd like to think that I think it's OK to experience pleasure.

I kiss Andrew's forehead. It is interesting about our faces. Saturday, early morning and at night, we must have gotten hit in the riot—all of us—in ways that didn't really show right at first. It didn't break the skin and bleed, so we didn't know it was there. Then the place where one of us had gotten hit, on our forehead, over our temples, on Mitrzi's eyebrow, that place began to turn red and then, by the second day, by Monday, had begun to scab over, like when I used to skin my knee when I was a kid. The scab is getting darker and darker. It's the mark of a blow we don't remember getting. Andrew has two of these scabs now on his forehead, one of which is about two inches wide, and one inch long, and one of which is about half that size. I have one that starts in my hair and moves down across my forehead to my eyebrow. The mark gets more and more pronounced the more distant we are from the moment the cop hit me.

Adam in the Morning

Being awake, I disentangle myself from him and get out of bed. It is almost eight. The one bad thing about our apartment is that when a man wants to sleep—needs to sleep—there is no way for the rest of us to give him quiet. I start things. Mitzi is stirring, being young and growing and needing her food. Our apartment is like life, we are all connected. I start things, and then I watch the whole apartment wake up.

Coffee first, the odor of which, alone, will wake up everybody. The problem today is going to be persuading Mitzi to stay in bed.

"Bo?"

Mitzi. "Hmm?" Then, "Good morning."

She looks better than yesterday. Less wasted.

"Come here, sit down. I'll get you something to eat."

"Thanks, Bo."

I get her juice. "What do you want?" I tell her the things we have.

"Just coffee. I'm going to be gone in a minute."

"Oh, Mitzi. Please. The doctor said he wanted you to stay in bed for at least two days. You need to stay in bed one more day."

"I need to go, Bo. I need to find Violet, and I need to find my gang."

Then Andrew is in the archway.

"Listen to Bo, Mitzi. You need another day at least for your cut to heal, before you go back out on the street. Stay here. Please let us take care of you."

"Aw, guys, I appreciate what you're doing, but I can't hang out here another day. I got things to do."

Then Gus is standing beside Andrew.

I hear Billy and Joseph. I don't want it to look like we're ganging up on her. They're in the archway too, now.

Joseph speaks. "Will you let me clean your cut and dress it before you do anything?"

Mitzi thinks about Joseph's idea.

"Can I take a bath?" She is talking to me.

"Yes. Sure." I give her coffee. "You change your mind about food?"

"Naw." She stands up and goes into the bathroom.

"When you get finished and get decent," Joseph says, "call me and I'll come in and clean and dress your cut."

She shuts the door, and we hear water running.

Adam in the Morning

"Can I use the phone?"

Billy sits down with the phone book and starts to call the airline.

Mitzi will not commit to us. Whatever is going to happen, it is unlikely that she can change her life enough to move in with us.

We are walking up Christopher Street toward Seventh.

"I love New York," Joseph says.

"I know." Billy looks at the street, checking out the buildings and storefronts on the block. "It glistens, doesn't it. It shines and glistens."

"It's the weather—the beginning of summer, there are no clouds, the sun is kind, there's a gentle breeze." Andrew steps out in front of us and then turns to face us, his arms out, walking backward.

A man walks toward us. Andrew, hearing the man approach, steps to the side and lets him pass. "Excuse me!"

I catch up with him. "Beautiful." I kiss him.

"Big guy, one day you are going to get in trouble doing that on the street."

"I know. Or it may be that the time when I would get in trouble is now past. I felt like taking the risk."

We four walk along toward Seventh. We pass the rose brick wall around St Luke's churchyard, the PATH station, the Lucille Lortel Theatre, and the leather shop, the Silver Dollar, and then come to Seventh Avenue.

"One of the things that is true of New York," Andrew says, "is that, when you get up in the morning and walk down to the corner for the paper, the city feels very old. Old and worn. I don't know what makes it like that. The smells of last night, of many people in a small space. It seems dirty. Yet sometimes it seems entirely new, as if this morning were the first morning in the history of the world."

I walk along, my hand on Andrew's shoulder, feeling his body move. "We are new, aren't we?"

"I get that. All new men. We are just waking up, and we don't know anything. The beginning of the earth, and we have to learn everything. Who we are, what our powers are, how we want to define ourselves." He turns to us and grins. "What our dicks will do."

"Oh, I know," Joseph says, distressed. "It's this thing between my legs, and I don't know what it's for. What is it for, and what it can do. I need help!"

"You need less help than anybody I know," Andrew says. "You're doing fine by yourself. It's called self-discovery."

Looking around, Joseph asks, "Does anybody know where are we going?"

Billy has decided to go back to Houston tomorrow. After he made his phone calls this morning, he told us he was going to have to pick up his tickets from an airline office on lower Fifth Avenue. One of us could have gone for him, or he could have gone himself, but I thought we could all go and have lunch. Gus needed to go to the theatre, so that's where he is. This afternoon, I have to go by the theatre for a meeting.

"Well, Joseph, up ahead is Greenwich Avenue. We're going to the big building directly ahead, which is the Women's House of Detention. We walk around that—go left at Greenwich, and then right on West Tenth—and then head east 'till we get to Fifth."

We saunter along the street. There are four of us, and we take up the whole sidewalk, the way young men do in the summer in the city, except when someone is coming, and then we give them space with elaborate courtesy. "Excuse us!" We smile and laugh.

We are on West 10th, going east, just before we get to Sixth Avenue. "Marlon Brando lived on the little cul-de-sac off to the left when he was studying acting at the New School. And Djuna Barnes still lives in the same little cul-de-sac. She may be there in her apartment right now."

"Who is she?" It's Billy.

"Your past. She wrote a novel about gay life in Paris during the twenties," Joseph says. "It's wonderful. Very dense. T. S. Eliot liked it very much."

"Is Marlon Brando gay?" Billy asks.

"Everybody says he is, or that he is sometimes," Andrew says. "I don't know, but it does seem like he ought to be, he is so beautiful. Was so beautiful, when he was young."

"I'd do him in a minute," Joseph says.

"Man, you'd do anybody in a minute." Andrew punches his arm.

The Jefferson Market Branch of the Public Library is on our right, which used to be the Jefferson Market Courthouse. Very medieval. Towers, arches, wrought iron gates. Nineteenth century medieval. We see the Women's House of Detention from a new angle.

"Before this current House of Detention, there was a jail that matched the library on the same plot of land," Andrew says.

"The current one is ugly."

"One of the loveliest things I've ever seen," I say, "was during the riots Saturday morning, when the prisoners in the Women's House of Detention lit pieces of paper and floated them down to the gangs of men in the street."

"Did they set anything on fire?" Billy says.

"Uh-uh. They'd go out before they reached the ground. They were just little pieces of toilet paper."

"But they were pretty. Benign. A blessing on all of us."

"I wish I'd seen it," Billy says.

"Just goes to show," Joseph says, "that when you are going to be blessed, you have *no idea* where it's going to come from."

"Or what it's going to consist of."

Half the time, when we're walking along the sidewalk, Billy and Joseph are walking arm-in-arm. Joseph has his hand in the crook of Billy's arm, and they're laughing at their own jokes.

"Jesus! What have we done!" Andrew asks me. "We've set loose something that I think we're going to regret."

"I know. Some things are just better not loosed. Teenaged lust."

"Teenaged romance."

"Scary in men over six feet."

"Who haven't been teenagers in eleven years."

We cross Sixth Avenue and walk toward Fifth. The sidewalk is wider, and we walk abreast. I think I could defeat all the cops from the Sixth Precinct. Just me.

"I think you're swaggering again, Bo."

"I think I am. Why do I feel like this?"

"I don't know," Andrew says, "aside from the fact that we've enjoyed the last four or five days."

"Well, there's been the sex," Joseph says, "which has been put to many and various uses."

"But aside from all that, it feels like something wonderful has happened."

"Well, it has," Billy says. "I've been here with you guys, and that's new and different for me."

Adam in the Morning

Joseph speaks. "I'm happy, big guy, that I met you. That's another thing I have to be grateful to your brother for." He puts his arm around Billy's neck and pulls him to him.

"I'm grateful too," Andrew says. "It's good to have a brother."

We're not getting at what I'm thinking about. We are happy with each other, but we're also giddy with ourselves.

We get to Fifth Avenue and find the airline office. Billy gets his ticket, and now we're sitting at a table on the sidewalk outside a restaurant in Cooper Square, Billy and Joseph next to each other, across the table from Andrew and me.

"Did any of you actually see *Life* magazine this past week?" I ask.

"The one with the pictures of the soldiers?" Joseph asks.

"Yeah. I have one back at the apartment. I think it is incredibly moving."

"What I find so amazing about it is that it is *Life* that has published it," Andrew says. "That organ of corporate America."

"How do you read that, Andrew?" I ask.

"I think it means that every so often even organs of corporate America are going to stumble onto the real truth."

"I sat down and looked at it, and then I realized I had to look at every picture. You can't skim it, looking for the headlines or the italicized bits. There is just one picture after another of men who've died in Vietnam, and there's no way you can give more attention to one than another. The optics of the thing force you to be democratic. The effect is—can be—overwhelming. All these beautiful young men. And what each one says is, *See me*. The result is that you have to give each one his due moment of respect."

"This corrupt government that sent them into harm's way," Andrew says.

The subject makes us go silent for a time. In the middle of a very busy urban square, we all study our silverware.

Finally I speak.

"I'm sorry we couldn't provide you with a big fight, Billy."

"Me too," Billy says. "I would have loved drawing blood. But you provided your brother with other things."

"You'll come back, though," Andrew says.

"Will you visit me in Houston?"

Joseph looks around the table. "Is that an invitation to me? Yes, certainly. When you tell me when to come, I'll come." Then, "I've never been to that part of the South."

"It's beautiful." Billy says. "Very southern in a lot of ways. Of course, some things there are still segregated."

"How do you deal with that? Uh—how do I deal with that?"

"Billy and you can deal with that together," I say. "He and I have been dealing with that since we were kids. My first boyfriend was African-American, and we studied how to get around segregation laws."

"I know a lot about getting around the laws in Georgia and Mississippi. I left college and spent most of 1962 and '63 and '64 there."

"I never forget that," Billy says. "I think that must be one of the things that make you what you are."

"Why don't we start a fighting school for gay men in the Village?" Joseph asks. "A school for street fighting and also one for self-defense?"

"Is that where you learned street fighting? In SNCC?"

"Most of the time I was with SNCC, their programs were totally non-violent. I didn't get into anything violent until later—Watts and later."

It would be easier if Billy came here to us—New York is freer than Houston—than if Joseph visited Billy in Houston, but eventually Joseph will want to go to Houston.

"I'll want to come back to see how Mitzi is getting along."

"I think she'd like that. She likes it when we pay attention to her."

Joseph asks, "Do you think she will move in with you guys?"

"Us. Us. You too. I don't know—" Andrew reaches across the table and takes Joseph's hand for a moment. "The longer she waits—the older she is—the less likely she is going to want to move in with us. We offer security and safety, and the older she is the less she is going to need that. Or want that. She's already on the tipping point at fifteen. Maybe we already give her the only help she is going to be able to use. I don't know. We'll see."

"But I see us continuing to do just what we've been doing. We're here for her, and she comes to us when she needs what we have to offer."

262

"Right. You're welcoming," Billy says. Then he grins. "I know that. You are very welcoming." He is sitting next to Joseph and puts his hand on Joseph's thigh.

"Right," Joseph says.

"I am such a kid about all these things. Just discovering how to be." He looks at Joseph. "I keep thinking that I've been a man all my life, and I am only just now discovering what it feels like to sit next to another man and hold his hand."

He isn't of course. Billy is at least as thoughtful about things as I am, and he is just as open as I am to the ways of people. What has happened in the last three or four days is that he is discovering just how many ways there are, how much he didn't know about himself. That puts him in the same boat as all the rest of us.

The restaurant is new, and heavy on style. Andrew has brought us here because he checks out all the new restaurants in the neighborhood. It constitutes a kind of professional gossip among his colleagues at Zanes. They talk among themselves about new restaurants the way other people might talk about the new models of cars. He reads the menu critically and makes recommendations—three appetizers to go with light luncheon specials. When the waiter comes, Andrew takes care of the ordering.

He looks around at us. "Yesterday, something happened at Zane's. It was the lunch shift, and I had the patio tables—there are four of them—on the sidewalk, all filled. One couple—a straight couple—were apparently from out of town, or maybe from uptown. They were dressed as if they had gone to a meeting of some kind. He was wearing a suit, and she was wearing a dress with big jewelry, and I could tell they were not from around here where we are. They were paying more attention to what was happening on the street than to each other. I got them drinks, and then in a few minutes I went back to get their orders. The couple were talking and ignored me. They ordered another round of drinks. They were talking about what was happening on the street. You remember yesterday. There has been a *lot* of activity on the streets of West Village—people handing out flyers and haranguing the crowds from light poles—ever since Saturday, so there was a lot for this couple to talk about. Except that what the man was saying, over and over, was about what the 'faggots' were doing in the street."

Adam in the Morning

We are listening to him, waiting for his words to come out, as if he is describing, second by second, what it looks like to see a car crash coming.

"And I stand there hearing them talk about 'faggots,' until the woman says, 'They're just so shrill. That's what I don't like. They're so shrill.' And the man says, 'They want to be women, all of them.' The other customers stop talking to listen. The man used the word 'faggot' again, and 'queer,' and then I went over to them and explained, in a low voice, that there are many gay people in the Village and even right there in the restaurant, and that it is provocative for the man in the suit to use that kind of language. I tell them it is likely to offend other customers. The man says, 'Are there queers here?' I say, 'Yes. I am one.' The man in the suit is apparently stunned. 'You're a queer?' It's a dramatic moment.

"I didn't think they had looked at me until then, and now they were staring at me, their jaws hanging open. The man said, 'What the fuck—' I thought the man was starting to get up out of his chair. And then I said, 'You should know that half of the kitchen staff are gay. There are three managers here, and two of them are gay. The manager who is on duty *right now* is gay. There are five waiters on duty all the time in this restaurant, and three of us are gay. You should also know that we're not going to serve customers who come into this restaurant, drunk, and insult gay people, who are our customers as well as our staff. Now. I don't want to hear any more language from you that is disrespectful of gay people. Is that clear?'

"I said, very sternly, 'If you feel you have to disrespect gay people, then you will have to go somewhere else to do it,' and the man in the suit said, 'Why you faggot—' and at that point, all the waiters came over to stand behind me, then the manager came out too and came through the line of waiters. He told the couple, 'I am the manager here. It would be best if you left the restaurant, now.'"

"For a minute it looked as if the man was going to fight us, but then he must have realized he was going to have to fight five waiters and the manager, and he might have to fight some of the other customers too, so, with a lot of huffing and puffing, and grumbling, he and the woman left."

"A week ago," I say, "we would have accepted the man's bigotry. Now it is unacceptable, and even more clearly, we tell the man so."

Adam in the Morning

"Do you remember, guys," Joseph says, "the first night, when we were sitting on the high stoop, and Bo said, *What now?* and Mitzi, I think, said she was hoping things would change?"

We remember that.

"And the question was, 'What kind of change?'"

"Sure. I remember that." Andrew says. "What's your question?"

Joseph has his arm over the back of his chair, and his free hand toys with his silverware. "Our strategy is to change one criminal city policy after another, and at the same time see if we can get the folks in all five boroughs to love us. I think our strategy is going to leave us tied in knots."

"Oh, man, Joseph," Andrew says, "the problems we face here in the city—from the SLA withholding licenses from legitimate establishments so that gay people will have no place to go to meet one another and socialize to the laws that criminalize the ways we have sex, the whole long unhappy list of the legal oppressions of gay people—exist on the level of the local neighborhood and the local precinct, all the way up to problems that can only be solved by action of the president and the Congress. Some of the problems we have to attack and solve are not going to be solved in our lifetimes. We will work on them all our lives, and the next generation of gay men will be working on them all *its* lifetime. We won't have all our freedoms even in the next century. But we can't avoid starting here in our own neighborhood and at our own local precinct and finding out how we can force change *here*. And after we have made a start here and now, we can then look at the larger questions, the longer, more difficult problems, the question of what kind of culture we want to have. I'm clear where I stand on all that. I don't want to live in their world. I don't want to be mistaken for a straight person. I don't want to change. I want *them* to change. I don't want to submit my sex to their rules. I think the way Bo and I live is far wiser and more realistic than the way my parents live, who are among the stupidest people I know. *Monogamy, virginity.* Shit! But I don't think we can try to change our culture until we have a safe neighborhood on Christopher Street."

We look across Cooper Square to the Cooper Union, big, red sandstone, built just before the Civil War, which sits in the middle of the square, Third Avenue going down one side and Forth Avenue down the other. At some point in the past, there were trees in the square, and at another point, there was an elevated train down Third Avenue, but now it is empty of all that and populated with students from the Cooper Union and NYU and all the different types drawn to St Mark's Place.

"Abraham Lincoln gave a speech there before he was president. It may have helped him become president."

Billy looks at the square and furrows his brow. "Was he gay?"

"I don't think so. And then right down there, about halfway down this side of the square is where Walt Whitman lived during the Civil War. And yes, he was gay. There is no question about that. Read his poetry. I think of him moving through Cooper Square, looking after wounded and lonely soldiers."

"Great image. Hugging them. Kissing them," Joseph says.

"W.H.Auden lives on St Mark's Place."

"*Now?*" Billy asks.

"Now. In 1969."

"Is he gay?"

"He sucks cock, as I believe he says in his poetry."

"Where?

"A poem called 'The Platonic Blow,' which has circulated in manuscript for years here in New York. I have a copy back in the apartment. It's about a blowjob."

"Wow," Billy says. "You don't find anything like that in Houston, do ya?"

"Are there any world-famous poets in Houston?"

"Maybe not world-famous gay poets in Houston, but plenty of gay people and, actually, plenty of famous people."

Joseph laughs at my brother and me.

"Anyway, The Public Theatre is about a block and a half away, where Joseph Papp and the New York Shakespeare Festival are based when it is winter and they can't use the Delacorte Theatre in Central Park. He did the first production of *Hair*, with the unforgettable lines, 'Sodomy, Fellatio, Cunnilingus, Pederasty—'"

"Oh, Jesus," Joseph says, "say that again, that's so lovely—"

"'Sodomy, Fellatio, Cunnilingus, Pederasty!'"

"You guys," Billy says, "You're just trying to shock me."

"Over here, on this side of Fifth Avenue, there's a bohemian life that's completely different from the bohemian life over in the West

Village, where Christopher Street is. There's gay life all over the city." It's a nice thought, gay life *all over the city.*

"Of course it's going to be a dreamy, drug-induced vision of ravishing beauty. We established that yesterday. It's the Sixties, isn't it? or did I forget something? The music will be electronic, something avant-garde—do either one of you know of a young man named Philip Glass? *just* the thing I'm looking for—and something that our audience here will realize is speaking to them. Perhaps one of his keyboard pieces. I'll take care of getting that. The beauty of the show, everyone will realize, will come directly from the fact that everything that happens on this island, everything the audience sees and hears, is coming from the mind of Prospero. Pay attention. Miranda and Ferdinand will be revealed at chess in the middle of the playing area with the help of lights and the same actors playing 'spirits' who helped earlier with the 'revels.' A moment of dimmer light, some electronic music, a gang of people all of whom are beautiful and naked, carrying palm fronds, and, suddenly we see a prince and the daughter of a duke, in the middle of the jungle, at chess! Now, there are four exits, one at each corner. At both sides of these exits, but placed carefully so as not to obstruct them, are very, very large ferns, suggesting the jungle." Sergei stops pacing around the stage.

"To get an idea of what Prospero looks like with Caliban, we need pictures—portraits if possible, in color—of Renaissance grandees. I have in mind one that I have seen somewhere—it may have been a scene from *Don Carlo*, staged by Visconti at Covent Garden of a Renaissance court strolling through a forest near a palace. The King's court, with a man walking a pair of dogs, mastiffs perhaps, comes upon the Queen's court in the forest—near Saint-Just. The King's man controls the dogs with a collar and a leash. Also, there is a tradition in sixteenth-century art from Venice and elsewhere in which black Africans were used as gondoliers. There are also large, grand-manner portraits of Renaissance figures, both men and women, who have pages at their sides, holding parasols or carrying pieces of armor. Sometimes these pages are Moors and sometimes black Africans, that is, sub-Saharan Africans. In sixteenth century Italian art, there is a tradition of African pages being used in portraiture. There are several in Titian's work. The one I think of right now is one of the grandest works from the Italian Renaissance, *Marchesa Elena Grimaldi,* by Van Dyke, in the National Gallery in Washington. She's coming out of a palace onto a terrace—there are large columns behind her—and she has a small African page following her, holding a parasol over her against the sun. That is the image I want. Prospero, in gorgeous robes—actually the grandest of early seventeenth century costumes of the highest-ranking Italian nobility—calls Caliban to come forth from one of the exits in Act 1, scene 2, line 321 and, when he appears—remember, Caliban wears a collar and almost nothing else—Prospero attaches a leash to his collar. Caliban is costumed in the early seventeenth century English conception of native tribes—a loincloth, barefoot, feathers in his hair. The three of them—Caliban on a leash walking in front of Prospero and Miranda as they speak the next 55 lines—then go a slow progress around the stage. The extreme visual contrast between Prospero and Miranda in their gorgeous constumes, on the one hand, and naked Caliban on the other is what we are going for and is going to establish Prospero's power and Caliban's enslavement. The collar and the leash connect them, and it is the collar and the leash, at the end of the play, that are given up. It is this giving up that frees Caliban. The audience can clearly see what he is being freed from. So, one second, two seconds before the end of the play, Caliban and Ariel reach out toward one another, their hands touch, and in that moment is the climax of the play. It is what everything in the play has driven toward. After it, the play is over. They are allowed a second or so to show what they are in their freedom, before the lights come up and people applaud the company. The transformation that Caliban and Ariel undergo here at the end is more profound than that of any of the other characters, but the way they demonstrate what they are, is the simplest of all moments similar to this in all Shakespeare. They touch hands. I don't think Prospero means that Caliban and Ariel will fall in love—certainly not in the same way that he means that Miranda and Ferdinand are going to fall in love—but by freeing them of his control, by giving up his *idea* of them, he allows them to assume their own idea of themselves, and so he allows them to fall in love. All through the play, the actors playing Caliban and Ariel have remained in character, that is, in the character that Prospero wills. When they return to the stage *out of character,* they are that new thing, totally new and free men, and so are almost unrecognizable, transformed, *transfigured* by their sudden freedom. The first way they express their freedom is to reach out toward one another. And *this* is what is new about our production and what will make it memorable." Sergei looks at both of us. "And, of course, buried deep within our production is the clear answer to Gonzalo's great question, which is at the center of this play." The characters wake up to freedom from Prospero. "I should say that both of you should read Frantz Fanon's, *The Wretched of the Earth.* That's what our play is about."

Around five, I leave the theatre and turn right into Washington Place, which takes me to Christopher Street. This way takes me through Sheridan Square, with its high-decibel political speechifying, many men gathered in small groups, talking and listening to speakers standing on the bases of lamp posts or on the bumpers of cars parked on the south side of Christopher. There is a noticeably high level of energy in the Square. People interrupt the speakers and shout and speak to each other in loud voices.

I walk up to a group of men. "Wassup?"

One turns to me. "It's the *Village Voice.* They had two reporters at the first night's riots, and now the *Voice* has printed their accounts. Their issue is going to be released in a few minutes. Apparently pretty rancid stuff."

In a few minutes, more men have arrived. This feels very familiar. "How do you know what's in it?"

He pulls his attention from the speaker and answers, "We've heard. People have seen it." Then he's back to the speaker again. Talking to me while listening, he says, "We've heard it's terrible."

The Voice doesn't have a good reputation in the Village. They don't cover our events as news and are generally uninterested in the gay community in the West Village. They've refused to take classified ads for gay publications whose titles include the word "gay." They believe the word's obscene, yet they proclaim how progressive they are.

The Voice's offices are in the three-story, red brick building with white trim, arched French windows on the first floor and a steeply slanted roof, on the northeast corner of Seventh and Christopher. Between the *Voice* building and the Stonewall are two brick buildings. The first one, east of the *Voice* building, has an entrance which you reach by stepping down from the street. The second one, which is two doors from the *Voice* building and next door to the Stonewall, has the high stoop that we sat on early Saturday morning. Right now, a group of twenty or so men are gathered around the main door of the *Voice* building. People are shouting.

"Come out and answer us!"

"You're afraid of us!"

"Come out and tell us what you're printing!"

"You don't know anything about gays!"

The crowd is getting larger and larger by the minute. There are, now, a hundred people in front of the building, and I see men running from both ends of Christopher Street. It's time for me to get my gang. There's a pay phone on West 4th, another one in the Village Cigar. The one in Village Cigar is not being used.

Andrew answers.

"Andrew, it's me. I'm here in Sheridan Square." I tell him what's happening.

"When is the *Voice* issue going to be released?"

"Around six—"

"Look, Bo. OK, we've been making supper here. I want to be a part of whatever happens in Sheridan Square, but I'm hungry too, and I fight better on a full stomach. Come home to us, we'll have supper on the table when you get here, we can eat right away, strip for action, and get back up to Sheridan Square about the time the *Voice* is on the street."

So that's the plan. I'm jogging down Christopher, mainly in the middle of the street because it's easier to dodge cars than it is to get around the other people on the sidewalk. Today, this afternoon, just as I was leaving the theatre, I ran into Belle. She brought up her proposal again, and then she asked if Andrew and I could help her. She explicitly asked me if I would be her donor, and if Andrew and I would share parenting with her. So now that has landed on our doorstep. What would make gay men commit to such a thing? Andrew and I must now answer the question that I posed to Belle yesterday. I wonder. What will I say?

I open the door at the head of the stairs and announce, "OK! Let's eat!" I start emptying my pockets, like Mitzi told us Saturday night, feeling as if I am still running. The room seems crowded.

"Hi, beautiful." Andrew puts his arms around my neck and kisses me. "We're all ready for you. Food is ready."

Adam in the Morning

We serve ourselves from the counter and the stove and are to eat in the living room. There are Andrew, Joseph, Billy, and Gus. Where did he come from? Where is Mitzi?

"Hi, Gus. Where is Mitzi? Has anyone heard from her?"

"No. Not all day."

"But if what you say happens tonight—if there is more activity—then I bet we see her tonight," Joseph says.

Joseph is right. We'll see her tonight at the *Voice* building.

"We can find out how she is then."

"And Gus. Welcome."

Gus blushes. I think that's what it is. "I left the theatre when you were downstairs talking to Sergei and Matt, and I ran into Billy and Joseph in West 4th St. They asked me to come for supper. Is that all right?"

He's still shy. "Of course it is. Have they also invited you to the riot?"

He's a beautiful kid.

"Yes. They said it would be OK if I came."

Sweet. We eat. I wonder if there will be a fight tonight.

"I want to give Belle a call and tell her what we know."

"Right. That would be good, but I'll do it," Joseph says. He and Billy go in the bedroom.

"I'll clean up."

"I'll help."

Gus wants me to give him permission.

"Sure, Gus. Cool. You help Andrew and me." We organize the kitchen. Andrew puts things in the cabinet and in the refrigerator while Gus and I put dirty things in the sink. Our apartment is like a well-oiled machine. The number of men here changes—increases, decreases—regularly, but the life of the apartment goes on. Life here accommodates any number, who find their place and take on chores and jobs and expenses and errands as necessary.

"How was it at the theatre today?" Gus asks me.

"Sergei had a grip on things. He didn't leave many stones unturned. I am going to go to the public library tomorrow to see if I can find a picture of a pope walking an Afghan hound or an Italian nobleman with an African page—that's to give us an idea of the kind of effect he wants when Prospero takes Caliban out for a walk on his leash—and I'm going to call around and see who has the biggest ferns for the least amount of money. I don't even know what the largest ferns are." I'm doing the dishes, Gus is bringing them to me and drying what I've done, and Andrew is putting things away. "Andrew, have you had time today to do your own work?"

"Oh, yeah." He's redistributing jars in the refrigerator. "As soon as I got home from lunch, I worked. I had a couple of hours, I think. I was going to work tonight, but I didn't expect there to be a riot tonight."

"You take notes during fighting."

"Oh, yeah. I did Saturday night. I'm always taking notes. I'm going to tonight. I have my notebook." He flashes a small notebook.

"Maybe there won't be any fighting tonight."

Joseph and Billy come back in. "Belle has been taken care of," Joseph says. "Actually, she said that she had already heard and had already gotten out her new sandals, she said to tell you, and taken off her makeup."

"I didn't tell her to do that."

"Somebody did."

"Well, come on, guys," Billy says, impatiently. "We need to get up to Sheridan Square." So, it's all done, our pockets emptied of everything but driver's licenses and keys and one five dollar bill, which is, I think, more than Mitzi recommended. And in a minute we are thundering down the stairs.

A crowd of men surrounds the door of Village Cigar. There are cops around everywhere. A kid at the door shouts, "One at a time, gentlemen! One at a time!"

And, one at a time, men exit the store, the *Voice* in their hands held up close to their faces, reading.

We wait in a crowd. The first ones out scan theirs quickly, curse, and hand off their papers to whoever is standing nearby—or simply drop it on the street—and turn away from the rest of us. So, very quickly everyone in the crowd around the door of the Village Cigar has a copy, and there are copies blowing on the pavement in the wind, getting run over by cars and walked over by pedestrians, trashing the street.

The words we hear from everyone are "fag follies." Fag follies. That's what the *Voice* called the riots. *Fag follies.*

Adam in the Morning

The five of us cross Seventh to the Voice to join the crowd there of five or six hundred men and women. A line of policemen stands between the crowd and the *Village Voice* building. We are in the crowd, facing the front door of the *Voice*. Andrew has his small pad and is writing furiously.

"How are you doing, Billy?"

He puts his arm behind my neck and pulls me to him. "You guys just fight your riot. Don't you worry, I got ya."

I kiss him, and he lets me go.

"Fag follies! I can't believe that."

There is an article in the Voice by a man named Howard Smith and another by a man named Lucian Truscott IV.

Truscott does use "fag follies," and he also uses "dyke," "forces of faggotry," "fags," "queers," and he uses them over and over. He doesn't have any respect for us. It's garden variety bigotry.

Gus, standing by me, doesn't agree with the crowd's assessment. "I don't think the articles are as bad as people are saying. There is some bad stuff, but not a whole lot, and Truscott seems to have figured out what was happening, don't you think?"

"Yeah. Truscott has figured out that this is the start of something new and big. He ends his piece with the clause, 'the liberation is under way.'"

"It's just that he takes detours to prove he doesn't like queers *too* much."

"He quotes Allen Ginsberg toward the end of the article on how beautiful the guys are." I look for the quote in my copy. "Here it is. Ginsberg came down on Sunday to tour the battle site. He went into the Stonewall. After he came out, he's talking about the men inside. Here is the quote. 'The guys there were so beautiful—they've lost that wounded look that fags all had ten years ago.'"

"Yeah, and Truscott didn't need to use that quotation. Allen Ginsberg is a much bigger name, a more important person than Truscott is, and Truscott must have known what he was doing when he quoted him. 'The guys were so beautiful,' carries much more weight coming from someone like Ginsberg than Truscott's 'forces of faggotry.' Even the headline says, 'Gay Power Comes to Sheridan Square.' That's direct enough, and gets the truth about the riots in the headline. This is better than anything the *Times* has published."

"Gus, the bad thing about Truscott's article is its tone, which wavers between straight respectful reporting and snide condescension, a sort of mocking insult. It's a lot more complicated than the crowd would have it, but it doesn't matter, because we're back into riot mode, and the details about the article probably are now irrelevant."

There isn't any automobile traffic coming down Christopher Street from Sixth. There's too much foot traffic, and the crowd around us fills up all of Christopher. The whole area around Sheridan Square is crowded. The cops are unsure of themselves. Some of them are running up toward Greenwich Avenue, and some of them toward Seventh. They shout back and forth. Somebody is giving orders, but it's hard to tell who, or what the orders are. They seem to be giving orders to each other.

"Is this the way it was Saturday morning?"

"Well, Billy, something like. This is the area. But the crowd feels different. On Saturday, it seemed like most of the people were from the Village. Tonight, it feels like a lot of these people are from outside the Village—"

"How can you tell?"

"The way they're dressed. All of 'em are scruffy, but the Village scruffy is different from the scruffy from everywhere else in the city. They seem harder in some way than Village people."

The crowd around the *Voice* is shouting at the closed door. One male voice shouts out a sentence, then another shouts out another sentence.

"Come out and talk to us!"

"Write something about us!"

"Write something *serious* about the riots."

I speak to Andrew. "This is the reason you need to put out your newspaper."

"You see me writing it all down. These two articles are the reason we need our own press. Neither of the two reporters for the *Voice* did more than write down the things gay people in the street were shouting. But neither of them actually interviewed any gay person involved in the rioting."

"Smith's article was all from the point of view of the police, and Truscott was a little better, but it's still noticeable that he didn't get close to any gay person."

And more voices in the street.

"Don't be afraid of men in women's clothes!"

"Ask us what caused these riots!"

"Ask us what's happening on the street!"

Here are riots on the doorstep of the *Voice,* and they've made no attempt to cover the cause. What would make two or three thousand men take the kind of physical abuse from the police that they've taken for the last four or five days? Why is it that all the gay bars in the city are illegal, get raided all the time, and are owned by the Mafia? Why is that? Why is it that the Stonewall was one of the few places for men to dance together in all of New York? Why is there a law against having sex the way we do?

I speak to Andrew. "Are you going to be able to get out a paper on Friday?"

"Yes. It'll be eight pages long, double-sided, double-columns, single-spaced. We've got access to a mimeograph machine, free. And we need money for paper. I'm counting on you for a contribution, and I'm counting on a *big* contribution from Belle."

Joseph is listening. "Hey, you haven't asked me for a contribution. The idea, I guess, is that this is seed money? You'll be able to sell enough of these papers to buy more? How much do you need?"

Andrew tells him.

"I'll give you half of that."

"That's really generous, man. You sure you can afford that?"

"Andrew?" It's Gus. "I want to make a contribution too. I'll give you the other half."

"Oh, Gus. That's too much. You've just started work. You need your money. We'll be able to get money."

"But you need it now, and you've got other important things to do than run around looking for money. And I'm really lucky. I've got a good job just when it's important that I have some money. I'll give it to you tomorrow. I know why you're doing what you're doing." Then he grins. "Besides, you invited me to supper *twice,* and I want you guys to like me."

"We do. We do," Andrew says. Gus stands in front of Andrew, who takes hold of his traps and massages them. Andrew turns to me and raises his eyebrows. "So, between Joseph and Gus, we have enough money for the first edition of our paper."

Adam in the Morning

The crowd on Christopher between Seventh and Waverly Place is very thick. There seem to be more cops, and I'm wondering when the TPF are going to arrive. The police usually get the TPF in before things get too far out of hand.

There are plenty of the street kids all around us. I look for Mitzi. There are also the groups of men that I think are from elsewhere. One of the differences is that the gangs from the Village seem younger than these who are now arriving from elsewhere. The Village guys are less practiced. These guys sound like they're from the other boroughs, and none of them act gay. They're just tough young guys, and they've come for a fight. Other than that, it's hard to tell who they are. They've been reading about the unrest down here, and now they've come down to find out about it.

"These guys are not us," Joseph says. "The feel here is different. These guys are bent on destruction."

Now the cops are going through the crowd and breaking it up, making sure everybody knows they're here and they're in charge.

"Move it on, now, move it on!" They're swinging their clubs, and some of the men who don't move fast enough are hit across the shoulders or on the butt. We can hear howls, but not screams, yet.

"Is this what it was like Saturday?" Billy asks.

"This is still early."

I would like to make the *Voice* answer us somehow. They called our riots "fag follies," and never talked to any fag involved in them, except Allen Ginsberg—and he wasn't in the riots. I've heard straight men use "fag" and "faggot" all my life, and been indifferent to it. Now, since this weekend, I've become hypersensitive. I want the *Voice* to pay for it every time they use the word. "I want to burn down their building."

"Whoa!" Andrew says. "Is this Bo speaking? Mr Equanimity?"

"I'm tired of it, and I want to make them suffer for what they've done. They were indifferent to their power to hurt people. They casually called our riots 'fag follies' and didn't give a shit about the effects of any of that. That man Truscott wanted to hold us up to derision. He didn't bother to try to find out the cause of these riots, and he made only a minimal effort to determine what the riots mean."

There's a man on my left who shouts out, "Burn it down!"

And somebody else, "Burn it down!"

"Burn the whole motherfucker to the ground!"

Adam in the Morning

The cry is being taken up by men all around us.

"OK, OK, that's enough now. Break it up." The cops come through the crowd, swinging their clubs more seriously, reaching out, searching the crowd for an object, finding someone weaker, and then going for blood, leaving men in the crowd with serious bloody heads. Men are getting tense. The object of their hatred tonight seems to be switching from the *Voice* to the cops.

The trash can across from the *Voice* breaks out in flames. The cops are jumpy, unsure of what the crowd is going to do next. They try to impose their will on the men around them, not just swinging their club randomly, as before, but targeting men they think are leaders.

A cop strikes the man next to me. His head is bloody, but instead of running away, he turns to grab the cop. He has the cop in a clinch, but one of the cop's arms is still free, and he beats the man's head. Then Billy—Billy!—slides through the crowd, comes up behind the cop, and wrestles the club from him. He comes down hard on the cop's head, drops the club—someone kicks it, and it rolls to the side of the street until someone kicks it into a storm drain—and disappears. The crowd is very thick around here.

Hey, Billy! That guy. Where did he go? Is he OK?

"Holy shit. Look at that!" Joseph says. "You've got a tough brother, Bo."

"I jus' love a butch man," Andrew says. "My boyfriend is one, and his bro is another. It's just so fine to see."

This from the toughest man who lives at our address.

"I'm concerned about you, Gus. I don't want you to get hurt. You stick with me."

"What!" Gus is offended. "I can handle myself. I been in street fights with cops since I was a kid."

"Sorry. Don't mean to offend you. Where're you from?"

"Baltimore. All the neighborhoods in Baltimore are tough. I got a scholarship to Harvard. Just because I went to Harvard and am playing Ariel doesn't mean I can't bus' some serious ass on the street. I can take care of myself. It's important that we each carry our own weight."

The bloody cop has gone back to his colleagues, who are berserk, now. There are fights all around us. And fires. Trash cans all around Sheridan Square are on fire—dramatic, now at twilight. The fights—

the ones I can see around me—are sometimes between a street kid and a cop, the kid taunting the cop and throwing something. They throw beer cans and soda cans, and sometimes they throw rocks and paving stones and trash cans. I look for Mitzi.

"Guys, everybody look out for Mitzi."

"I'm looking for Billy too."

"I think both of them can take care of themselves, actually," Joseph says.

We hear whistles. It's the TPF, coming down Christopher from Greenwich, pushing the crowd in front of them. Gus has made a collection of cans—you do this by going through trash cans—and is now throwing them above the heads of the crowd at the cops on the sidewalk. They spin on an axis going over.

"Gus has the right idea. Let's throw some rocks." Andrew gets rocks from the park in the middle of the square, and throws them. They pierce the air with the purposefulness of a thrown football. Everybody else is doing this too. Aerial warfare.

The TPF is getting closer. They are the same as Saturday night— black uniforms, and helmets, plastic shields, unearthly blue glow to the shields, accompanied by the curious sound their boots make on the pavement, *shu-shu-shu-shu-shu*. In front of them is a mass of Village people, mainly street kids, backing up slowly toward us, keeping a distance between them and the cops. Great scene—the rocks and the cans hurtling overhead, the TPF coming toward us in their plastic shields, the mass of citizens backing up toward us.

I see Mitzi, her arm extended straight above her head, looking back to see if she is being followed. The goddess. This is good that she's feeling well enough to be out, bad that she's out in her condition.

"OK, guys, we have to join Mitzi. Let's get up close."

"As close as we can." Andrew leads the way into the mass of surging people.

We plunge into the crowd. I'm holding on to Andrew's arm. I have my other hand on Gus's shoulder, and Joseph grips my shoulder from behind.

I hear a familiar voice.

"Hi, guys. Thought you'd never come."

Billy, in the front, just behind Mitzi.

"Billy, *this* is what it was like on Saturday."

He laughs.

"You got away from the cop OK?"

"Oh yeah. He never knew what happened to me. You OK?"

"Yes. We saw Mitzi and decided to move in close to her."

"Does she know we are here?" Gus asks.

"I don't think so. Shall I tell her?"

"No, Billy, let Joseph do it."

Joseph moves past us. Gus follows him. I see Joseph speak to her and then he returns to us. We are in the small triangular space of Sheridan Square. The Stonewall Inn, behind us, is the only two-story building. In this small space, surrounded by six and eight-story buildings the noise echoes and reverberates. People shout, and it is difficult to tell what they are saying.

"She feels OK. I don't know what that means. She thanks us for coming, but she wants us to stay away from her. I told her we wouldn't be very far away." Joseph turns to Billy. "How are you? You know the real fighting is about to begin."

"I figured that."

"Be careful around those guys. They are trained to bust heads."

"Right." Then Billy grins. "I've never kissed a *man*, and then gone off to fight a fight. This is a first for me."

They kiss.

"Andrew. Kiss me," Billy says.

Andrew grins and does it.

"Somebody kiss me," Gus says.

"Ah, man. Let me. Let me." It's Joseph. He does, and then all the rest of us do too. Gus is pleased as we gather 'round to kiss him.

I can see Mitzi. Her attention is focused on the TPF shuffling toward her. The street kids are taunting the cops.

The TPF keep coming, their fronts and sides covered by their shields. We can hear someone shouting mysterious military-like commands at the TPF, and it is difficult to tell whether they are responding or not. They keep coming at the same rate.

The gang of street kids, on the other hand, represent profound chaos. Their line is not ordered, they don't back up at an orderly rate, they seem unconcentrated. Except for a few, like Mitzi, who are staring down the TPF as if glares are a legitimate weapon of the Revolution, most of them are glancing at the TPF, then to the right at the crowds on the sidewalk and then to the left at the crowds there. It is a furious search for weakness in the enemy line.

Finally, one of the kids shouts out, "Girls! Take your places!"

They do. They get in line, arms across each other's shoulders, and —this is all done to the accompaniment of the *shu-shu-shu-shu* of the TPF—and their leader shouts, "Girls, on my mark, three, two, one, kick!"

So they kick, ragged, wildly energetic, defiant, proud.

We are the Stonewall girls,
We wear our hair in curls.
We wear no underwear:
We show our pubic hair.

Joseph speaks sternly, "Come on guys. Get in line. We can do this too."

"Oh, no," Gus says.

We get in line, and then we hear Joseph say, "On go. Three, two, one, *go!*"

And off we go, kicking first and then, improbably, singing.

We are the Stonewall girls,
We wear our hair in curls.

Joseph is trying to keep us in time with the kids at the front, but it's difficult. We're twice as old as they are, twice as heavy, half as limber. We're all laughing.

"Are you guys like this often?" Gus asks.

We're laughing, and nobody answers Gus.

Billy says, "Jesus guys, I didn't know this is what I had to be able to do!"

Then he yells out—shrieks out—and he has blood all down his face. All three of us turn around—there's a cop behind him, and I can take in in a moment that the cop is alone. Joseph rises up to an unbelievable height, his arms stretched out above his head. He comes down on the cop, and I go for the cop's arm nearest me. He's trying to use his stick to keep us off him, and he gets in a whack or two at both of us before Joseph envelops him in his arms and prevents him from moving.

"Take his stick!"

I get it and throw it away toward the storm drain.

I tell Joseph to disappear. He does, and I see Billy go with him. Andrew and I and Gus go in the other direction. Just as we do, I am aware behind us of two or three other cops coming through the crowd looking for the one we've just disarmed. The line of street kids has dissolved and is running in every direction. And all through the thick mass of people in front of the TPF, cops—alone or in pairs—are trying to start fights. I regret breaking ours up before we hurt him good.

"Did you see where Mitzi went?"

"Yes," Gus says. "She went west on Grove Street. I can go over there and see if I can find her."

"Thanks. What do you think, Andrew? Should Gus go find her?"

"Yes, if you don't mind, Gus. I'd just feel better if one of us were with her. The doctor said stay in bed for two days. Do you mind?"

"No. I can probably find her. I bet, aside from running away from the cops, she's not doing a whole lot of running around. I agree with you. One of us ought to be with her."

"On the other hand, she seemed to be doing OK a minute ago."

"OK, Gus, go and look for her. And if you don't find her, come back here to—" I look around the square. "—to the high stoop next to the Stonewall. The north side of the square. They can't close that down. We'll look for you there. OK?"

He goes. He admires her, too.

"We should have set up a place to come back to if we get separated, for everybody. Joseph and Billy."

"Bo, don't worry. We're not going to lose anybody. Billy and Joseph left together. They are going to take care of each other."

"I think about Billy's being a visitor to New York, and I worry that he can't handle—can't protect himself here."

Andrew puts his arm around my neck. He laughs. "It is an open question whether any of us can protect ourselves here, beautiful. The police and the TPF appear to have it as a stated goal to make us unsafe here."

The TPF have marched on to the intersection of Christopher and Seventh, and they wait there, in formation, for their next move. We stand on the sidewalk on Grove, behind them now, watching them pawing the ground like horses.

"Some people," Andrew says, "think that the government of the city—Mayor Lindsay and the Governor Rockefeller—wants to drive us out of the city completely. They certainly want to drive Mitzi and her friends out of the city. And for the rest of us, with no bars, nowhere to go to dance, no park to use, *no civil rights*, no safety on the public street, and unable to tell anyone that we are gay, subject to these random assaults from the police *and* all the violent homophobes in the city, it seems like they don't want us around here."

"You know, I think you're right. Should we move somewhere?"

He gives it a long pause.

"No. I think we've got our roots here. We've got our lease. I think there's nothing to do but stay and fight it out." He grins.

"OK. Let's go bus' some ass."

We turn back toward the fighting. We are in an area of hand-to-hand fighting. Mainly it's the cops trying to hurt Village residents, using their clubs.

"What do we do? Stand here and let them find us? Or go looking for them?"

"Let's look."

Andrew points toward West 4th. "Over there." And then he's off, me right behind him. I hear his bellow again. "This. Is. Our. Street!"

There is a little group of cops on West 4th, on the sidewalk. They are surveying the crowd, looking at us coming toward them.

Andrew is moving through the crowd as if he is in waist-deep water and trying to run. Two of the cops locate the source of the bellowing and move toward him, swinging their clubs.

Then I am struck, hard, from behind. I feel my blood down my face and in my mouth. I stagger and throw out my hands to catch myself. I try to keep from falling, and I regain my footing. I turn and see two cops behind me.

I step back, trying to get out of their range. I am struck from behind, on my shoulder. There are more than two. I swing my fists at the two in front of me and connect with one. He goes down, and his club clatters on the pavement. I am struck again on my shoulder. I feel someone's arm around me, holding me up. I get another blow on my head. Shit.

Someone else is fighting with me. The cops who are after me are being attacked by—I don't know. I make clubs with my fists, and I swing hard. One of them gets my right rib cage before I come down hard on his head, then, in a lateral swing, I get his partner on the side of his skull. Somebody else gets my head again. I am beginning to lose it. I can't see through my blood in my eyes. I spin around. Suddenly I have a cop's club in my hand—it is the God of All Revenge that placed it there—and the cop in front of me turns and runs. I swing the club hard at the ribcage of a cop. He crumples to the pavement.

Then I hear, "Disappear, Bo! Disappear! This way!"

I turn, and there is something that might be Andrew, but it is hard to tell, he is so bloody.

"This way!"

I follow him, and the crowd envelops us. Someone holds me up. Two men hold me up. Someone else has Andrew.

We cross West 4th and go south. We are in an alley, and they allow us to sit on the pavement. We are all breathing heavy.

One of the men holding me asks, "Are you OK?"

"I think." I ask for Andrew.

"He's OK."

"Can he talk?"

"Yeah, Bo, I can talk. I'm OK. That was fucking close, wasn't it?" Then, "Thanks guys. You found us just in time."

They laugh, then they sit down on the pavement too, and we all breathe heavy, exhilarated that we escaped the cops, that we are alive, and that we are still gay.

It's fully dark now. The TPF are still in formation at Seventh Avenue. And the local cops, who don't have armor, are patrolling the street in squads of two and four, using their nightsticks whenever they have a chance. On the other side of Sheridan Square, under the arched windows of the Voice, a gang of men and women are carrying signs. GAY PEOPLE/DEMAND RESPECT/FROM THE VOICE and THE VOICE INSULTS GAY PEOPLE. And, most frequently, THE VOICE IS BIGOTED. There are also a couple which are difficult to categorize. They could be signs for these riots, and they could be anti-war signs: STOP THE VIOLENCE. We cross the street. Near the doors, a man standing by himself holds a sign, POWER TO THE PEOPLE. A man on our left is lighting a Molotov cocktail. Several others are preparing Molotov cocktails to throw. I think that isn't going to work, but they are going to enjoy themselves before they figure that out.

Andrew and I cross Seventh Avenue to Village Cigar. From here, I can see a long way toward the river, maybe two long cross-town blocks, to Hudson Street. I can see fires burning in the trash cans the length of Christopher Street. Bonfires at regular intervals all the way to Hudson Street, and beyond. The length of Christopher—as far as I can see—is crowded with people, and there is no room for cars.

Whatever the cops are trying to do, they are failing to drive us off the street. The fires, the crowds in the street, the mob around the *Voice* trying to set it on fire. This scene is barely under control, and may not be under control. Why are they not trying harder, bringing in more riot police, more local police? It is as if they just want this to be an intimate little scene of violence and brutality. The crowd seems bitter. There is more of the desperation of the first two riots. And the fury.

Andrew looks me over. "Jesus! You're bloody."

"You too, big guy."

"You all right?"

"I think." I hurt so much in so many places that I don't really know if I am all right. We can talk about all that, later.

Then I see him pull at his t-shirt, ripping the bottom off. He looks at me. "Help me."

I see what he's after. I pull off the bottom five or six inches of his t-shirt. "OK. Let me clean up your face." I try. I use my spit. He looks a little better. "Without more water, that's as good as I can do."

He tries the same thing. "I think you're better, a little."

"Andrew?"

He stops and looks at me. "Yes?"

"Remember what Joseph said last night."

"What's that?"

"*Violence is a cleansing force.*"

Andrew looks deeply into my eyes. "Yes. A cleansing force. That's right. Thanks."

We hear noise that doesn't sound like holiday gaiety. Breaking glass.

"Let's check it out, Andrew."

We run into Christopher Street. People are trashing stores—restaurants, shops—shattering the glass windows and taking out what they can carry away. They've already broken into three or four and are running west on Christopher, apparently picking shops at random. We thought that all the people in this crowd don't live here in the Village. They are probably not all gay, either. Some of these are really gay shops, and I don't think a gay crowd would trash them like these guys are doing. *These guys are not us.*

"Look," Andrew says, "the cops aren't doing anything."

"Like the trashing of Kew Gardens."

"Yeah." When the cops didn't stop the 'vigilantes' from cutting down the trees in Kew Gardens a week or two ago, where gay men went to cruise.

"What should we do?"

On the other side of the storefront—fifteen feet away from us— are Billy and Joseph. I check 'em out. They look like—they seem to be in the same shape as—they did when they disappeared half an hour ago. The blood on Billy's head has dried, and there doesn't seem to be more of it. And Joseph. He's OK and does not seem injured.They come to us, and I put out my arms, and they let me hold them. They're really solid guys. Great to hold.

We kiss.

"I love you," Billy says. He looks me over carefully. "What happened to you?"

"Jesus. I'm going to miss you." I can feel it already. "Andrew and I tangled with some cops."

"Are you OK?"

"Oh, yeah. I'll live."

"You're really bloody. Both of you."

"Yeah, it was rough there for a minute or two."

His eyes are moving fast from spot to spot all over us. "I'll check you out later."

"I'm going to miss you."

"I'll be back. I'm going to come back lots of times."

"And all of us up here—" Joseph smiles. "—will come down to see you."

"Now, what about this looting?"

"Let's go down Christopher and try to stop it," Andrew says.

"Well, wait. I told Gus to meet us at the high stoop next to the Stonewall when he found Mitzi."

Adam in the Morning

So we split up. Andrew and Joseph are going down Christopher, and Billy and I are going back to the high stoop.

The difference between Billy and me, it turns out, is a valuable difference. Being straight, he's had a different rearing than I have had —and a different relationship to our culture—and so he has had a different life. This has been a good thing. It has made us try harder to know one another, and it made us learn how to do that. We always assumed it was different for the other one, so we asked questions. Most people assume everyone is like them, so they don't ask questions to enable them to find out what the other person is really like. Billy never assumes he already knows what he needs to know about me. So I'm grateful. We can really talk to each other. Life is good with my straight brother. I think the lessons I learned from my brother have made my relationship with Andrew better and are going to make my relationship with Joseph better too.

We go over to the high stoop, but there are no Gus and no Mitzi.

"Now, tell me."

"About what?"

"Your head. Andrew's head. It looks like the two of you ran into Patton's tanks. What happened?"

"So you can tell Mom?"

"So I can decide for myself what to tell Mom and what not to tell her, big guy."

So I do, everything. He asks me if I have a headache and about my eyesight and if I have trouble walking. He asks me to walk in a straight line. He seems satisfied that I'm OK.

"Would you like a cigar?" Billy asks. I think he means this as a kind of congratulations. *Congratulations, patient, you appear to be still alive! Would you like a cigar?*

I laugh. "Sure."

So we go back to the Village Cigar, and he goes in, and in a few minutes he comes back out with a handful of cigars. I don't know what *swagger* is, but a guy can get a sense of it when he is holding a cigar. Unavoidable. We stand in front of the store, watching the activity around us. The trashing of the stores on Christopher Street suggests that these riots are coming to an end and that the emotional thrust of the riot is dying. Directly ahead of us is a crowd around the *Voice*, apparently still trying to burn it down. The TPF have marched up to Greenwich and back since we were on that side of Seventh.

286

Adam in the Morning

Now they stand in parade formation just where Christopher Street comes into Seventh Avenue. There are huge crowds everywhere, blocking traffic in Seventh and in Christopher, but no real activity. I think the police have learned that these crowds are peaceable, and if the police avoid stirring them up with brutal actions, they can get through the night without mob revolt.

"How many of these did you get?"

"Two for us, and two for Andrew and Joseph, and two for Gus and Mitzi."

"Do you think she'll want one?"

"I don't know, but I wouldn't want to be the guy who has one and doesn't give her one, if she thinks she's entitled."

"Billy." I put my arm around his shoulder and grip him.

"I have an idea," Billy says. "I think I'm going to ask you, when you guys rent an apartment for the three of you, to rent an extra room. For me. Then I'll have enough space when I come up here on weekends, and I won't feel that I am crowding you so much."

I'm selfish enough to let him do this because I want him around. "That's cool. I think Joseph's going to move in soon—I mean, bring his stuff over from his apartment—and we'll need to see how big an apartment we need." Actually, I don't think Billy has any idea what an apartment that size would cost in New York, and it is almost certain that, even with all four of us contributing—Billy, Joseph, Andrew and me—we can't afford it.

We walk back through the crowds across Seventh Avenue and up Christopher to the high stoop next to the Stonewall. Billy and I climb to the top and sit down.

"I'm really sorry I wasn't there when you and Andrew tangled with the cops. You know you look like hell. Are you OK, really?" His eyes search my face.

"I'm OK, Billy. I'm going to live. And I think I got a few cops good." I have a chance now to see more of the blow on Billy's head. It's forward, not in his hair.

"Hey, Billy, I think your wound is going to leave you a good scar. Right on your forehead, just outside your hairline. Very noticeable, very romantic. Sexy. It'll get you plenty of women. They'll want to know how you got it."

"If I were to want women."

"Joseph has really affected you, hasn't he?"

"Maybe. I don't know."

"Will you stay in touch about this thing?"

"Yeah. I can say now, though, that this little quick visit to you has done a real number on me, Bo. Left me feeling right disoriented."

"Are you all right?"

"Uh-huh. But I hate to leave Joseph. Oh, man, I hate to leave that man. It's odd. He makes it possible not to be a man. If you know what I mean."

"I think I do. It may be that when you get home again, back to the crowd you've always hung out with, this will seem less traumatic, more of an interlude. You'll have your feet on the ground again."

"Maybe." He is not convinced. He searches the crowd.

"Well, you can come back up here this summer, or maybe we can go down to see you this summer—you know, before school starts in September."

"You'd come too?"

"I think. It'd be hard to get away, but I'd like to see you again, and I know I want to talk to you and Mom and Dad."

"About what?"

"Oh, you've heard me this week. What am I going to do with my life."

Billy smiles. "Oh, that." He furrows his brow. "What are you thinking of?"

"Running for office."

"Office?"

"Political office."

"Jesus!"

"I want to start talking about the power issues behind the oppression of queers. What would C. Wright Mills say? I think he'd say they're hidden. The real power is not out there where you can see it. The real power is not out there on the street where we can throw rocks at it. What is the best way, the most effective way, to get at the power that drives the oppression of gay people in New York? I bet it's running for office. It's in politics." I turn to Billy. I hit him a smart blow on his shoulder. *Vote for Bo Ravich.*"

Billy absorbs what I am saying.

"I am also thinking of having a kid with Belle or opening a shelter for street kids. I don't know. The real power may be among those who read books, so to reach them, maybe I have to learn to write a book. Suddenly everything is up in the air. But I've got a goal, you know? Now I've got something I'm working toward, and I've never had that before."

I see Gus and Mitzi coming across Sheridan Square. There's such a crowd between us—filling all of Sheridan Square—that they can only move slowly. And there is Belle. She sees us.

There's a guy standing at the foot of the steps. His long straight glossy black hair is held back by a leather band around the crown of his head, Indian style. He looks up at me and says, "Bo Ravich?"

"Yes." Then I worry. "Anything wrong?"

He smiles. "No, no. Sorry. Nothing's wrong." Then he says, "Are you OK?"

"Me? Oh, sure. I'm told I look worse than I am."

"You look like hell."

I laugh.

"I keep seeing you at these things, and you've been on my list to call. We are trying to get a group of us together to talk about what's been happening since Saturday. Would you be willing to meet with us —other men and women pretty much like yourself—to discuss what's been happening and where we think we ought to go now?"

"Oh, sure. We met at the apartment of a man named Heath on Monday afternoon, and we're to meet at another man's apartment tomorrow evening at seven. His name is Stephen something. My lover usually works in the afternoon, so he may not be able to come, but I can usually come."

This man is sweaty, and his t-shirt has sweat stains in his arm pits and down the front. His face and the skin on his arms glisten with his sweat. Very sexy.

"I think we all know that people are meeting around in people's apartments. We're hoping to get together in about a week at one of the churches. Get a larger group than have been meeting in people's apartments. I have a notebook here, and I have been asking everybody to put their names and addresses in the notebook so I can get in touch with you next week."

He passes me the notebook, and I write our names—Andrew's and mine and Joseph's—and address and phone number.

"I assume you're inviting everybody that lives at our address."

"Right. Here's how it will work. We've got some guys who are going to type up this list. We are going to mimeograph it and mail it out to everybody on the list. Then, when we find a church to meet in, we'll do a mailing with all the meeting information."

"Great. What's your name?"

He has little sheets of paper, about the size of a wallet photograph. His name is Ben Blackstone, and he lives down near us, on West 10th.

"How did you know me?" It may have been some bar.

The man laughs. "Man, everybody knows Bo Ravich."

I laugh. Sweet guy.

"In addition to contacting as many people as we can by phone and mail, we're going to put ads in as many of the local papers as we can, as we can afford. We hope to pull together a group of serious, committed, politically sophisticated, activist queers to discuss our future in New York. And most of us think that the first thing we need to do is to address the bigotry of the *Village Voice*." He is totally serious. "Are you with us?"

"Oh, yeah, man. I'm with you, only what I think we ought to address first is the SLA and its power to keep us out of legitimate, licensed bars."

"Yeah. That too. That's exactly what we need to be talking about."

Gus and Mitzi arrive. I stand up and introduce everybody. "Mitzi, are you all right?"

"Take it easy, Bo—"

Ben backs off. I call to him. "Send us your mailing!" Then I call to him again. "We also need to look at the source of the power that drives the oppression of gay people!"

He grins and sticks up his thumb at me. I grin.

Then, to Mitzi, "Come sit down."

She does. Gus stands over her, fairly obviously a protector. That's good. I look, and I see that she doesn't have any blood stains on her side, so her wounds have not opened up.

"Tell me everything."

She looks up at me. "Jesus, Bo. You look like hell. Are you gonna live? What were you doin'? Did you try to take on the whole city TPF all by yourself? Next time, wait for me, and I'll help ya. OK? Are you gonna live?"

"I think. Billy and Andrew say I am. Now tell me about you."

"Well, I think we did pretty good. We never let the cops drive us off the street, and that makes three nights when there were all these riot cops down here, and they were never able to drive us off the street. I got in some good licks at some of them." She looks up at Gus. "Didn't I, Gus?"

"She did. She bloodied two of them. And she kicked one in the nuts."

Billy and I whoop with laughter. "You are great!"

Just then Belle appears out of the crowd in front of us.

"Oh, dears! I am so relieved to see you all here and not severely injured!" Then she looks us over suspiciously. "You *aren't* injured, are you? Damaged?"

"We're fine, Belle. I think we're all fine."

"Andrew and Joseph too?"

"Andrew and Joseph too, we think."

"What's all that blood all over you? You'll never be able to wear that shirt again. You know you can't get blood stains out. Are you OK? Has Andrew called an ambulance? Oh, dear. I knew this would happen. I am going to be so distraught if something happens to you, Bo. I'm going to be so angry, you have been one of the really, truly good things in my life, and I just cannot, *cannot* get through without you—"

"Hey, wait up, Belle. I'm OK. I'm going to live. Both Andrew and Billy say I am."

She looks at me suspiciously. "You sure?"

"Yes."

"He's going to live, Belle, I promise," Billy says.

"Well, if you promise, then I can tell you I fought my way through this crowd to invite you all to my house for dinner on Friday night and for whatever else we want to do to celebrate, and to tell you, Billy, that I am desolate that you are going back to Houston tomorrow morning. Come here, and give me a hug."

Billy climbs down from the steps. "I'll do better than a hug, lady!"

He kisses her—an open-mouthed, tongue-in-back-of-her-throat kiss—then, with both of his arms around her shoulders, he pulls back and looks at her admiringly. "You are such a great lady!"

Watching all this, Mitzi says, "Why don't those two get it on? I mean, both of them are straight, aren't they?"

291

"And you are the sweetest Texan I know! I loved seeing you! I want you to come back again real soon!" She pauses. "I may even write you a letter."

They kiss again, and then she turns to us. "I'll call about Friday night. I want all of you. Bo and Andrew and Joseph and Gus and Mitzi and Violet, OK?"

Everybody grins and says OK, and Mitzi is pleased.

Then Belle is off.

"Oh, this hurts, guys. I wish I had not decided to go back tomorrow."

The company of TPF cops is marching back up Christopher toward Sixth Avenue. I bet they are going back to their home precinct. They are not under attack, so they march at a regular pace rather than their usual *shu-shu-shu-shu*. Much better, and they are quickly gone.

"Would you like to come back to our place and spend the night tonight?"

"Naw, Bo, I gotta get back to Violet as soon as I can. I only came over here 'cause Gus told me it would hurt your feelings if I didn't. I don't mean no disrespect, but I gotta get back to my people. I'll see you around town."

Then she does something that surprises me no end. She kisses me on my cheek. "Thanks, big guy, you're real sweet."

"Will you stay in touch?" I am feeling sad about all this. Then I say, "Do you need money?"

She stands up on the step two or three down from where I am sitting and turns to me and says she'll stay in touch and that she doesn't need money. "Thanks, again." Then, "See ya." She turns around and goes down the steps and into the crowd and in a minute I lose track of her.

I watch her for a long time, long after I can see her. Her slender, powerful courage. *Stay in touch.*

I turn to Gus. "Are you OK? Were you hurt any?"

"No, Bo. I'm fine. I was not hurt at all, although several times, with Mitzi, I thought I was going to die."

A few minutes later Andrew and Joseph find us. They look us over carefully. "How are you?"

"I haven't died. What about you?"

"Oh yeah," Andrew says, "we made them put out all the fires and put back the stuff they were stealing, and consequently, we saved Manhattan—as well as most of the rest of the civilized world—from burning up entirely!"

We laugh. "Sit down you two. And tell us the truth. And Billy has cigars for everybody."

Everybody laughs.

We rearrange ourselves on the steps. Joseph and I are on the top steps, and Billy and Andrew sit on the next step down, between our legs. Gus finds a place for himself between Andrew's legs. He leans back, his head against Andrew's chest. The cigars are passed out.

Andrew says, "We stopped them trashing a couple of stores. Maybe three. That's the truth." He sighs. "Have you seen Mitzi? I looked for her but didn't see her."

"She's fine. Gus was with her, and they came over here. She's gone back to Violet now."

"I couldn't get her out of my mind."

"I'll tell you about her, Andrew," Gus says. "She's an awesome fighter."

Andrew grins. "I know. She's awesome, isn't she?" He turns to the rest of us. "So, guys, what's going to happen now?"

"I think you're supposed to invite us all back to your place for breakfast, Bo, aren't you?" Joseph says. "Isn't that what happens after riots in New York?"

"Of course. *Mi casa, su casa.* We have eggs and bacon, grits, toast, butter, jelly, and beer and liquor and pot. I don't know why I'm telling you guys. You know what we have at home. We also have two double beds for whoever would like a bed, plus a single bed. But I guess I was thinking of something more long-term. What has happened here on Christopher Street since Saturday? Can we talk about that? What has just happened?"

"Jesus, Bo," Andrew says. "We trashed the place. Look. Broken glass everywhere. That's what we've done."

"Well, the police did most of that. But aside from that," Joseph says, "I think we did something good for ourselves. We learned what we are capable of, maybe. Maybe we can look back on the memory of us sitting here on these steps and say, 'that was when it started.' What do you think? Did the future start here, tonight, in these riots?"

"Oh, yeah. Don't you guys think? The future started right here, now—what is it?—end of June, beginning of July, 1969. Years from now, we're going to look back on this and say, 'That was when it started.'"

We talk about the riots. "Why does everything feel so different now?"

"I know the answer to that one," Andrew says. He holds his cigar, his elbow resting on his knee and squints against the smoke. "Now we know we can fight back."

Yes. Everything flows from that one, doesn't it.

I ask Joseph how they are different from Watts.

"Oh, man. Completely different. Completely different. These fag riots are completely different. There has never been a fag riot before, so it is different in that way. And there has never been a family of fags before. A community. Now there is. We have us. What we've done is we've taken away from them the right to tell us what we are. Who we are. Course Watts was much bigger."

Andrew laughs. "Well the future is going to be fun, then, because I've never known a bunch of gay men who could agree on anything, much less something as momentous as the stuff you're talking about."

"We don't seem to have any difficulty getting along," Joseph says. "Or did I miss something?"

"You didn't miss anything, Joseph," I say to him. "Well, look, guys. You may have heard that Belle wants to have a baby, which requires some help from a man, and she's asked Andrew and me, and so Andrew and I need to talk, but I'd also like to hear what the rest of you think. You're our gang, and I want to know what you think about gay men doing this. Are you our family? Do gay men have families? We have a lot to talk about."

"When does she need to know?" Andrew asks. He rests his head against my abdomen.

"She didn't put any deadline on it. I said we'd give her our answer in the next day or two, but it will surely take longer than that."

"What are you going to say?" Billy is twisted around, looking up at me.

"I don't know. It would change our lives. So would having Mitzi move in, and so would setting up a shelter for street kids."

"So would setting up a gay newspaper."

"Right."

"I'm not sure I want my life changed," Andrew says.

"Are you going to tell them," Billy asks, "or are you leaving it to me to tell them that you are thinking of running for political office?"

"No, Billy, I would much prefer you tell them, so why don't you?"

"Is that true?" Andrew starts laughing.

"Yeah. It's true. I have been thinking the last two or three days about feeling at the end of the road at The Olympic Theatre, and I have been thinking about finding some new way to make a living, and of course here we are right in the middle of the first gay riots ever, so everything that I have come up with has had to do with us, with us being gay, and what can I do with my life that can make our lives better. I think I also told you, Billy, that I was thinking of writing a book, but of course first I have to find out how you do that. I want to research the question, 'What is the source of the power that drives anti-gay bigotry?' 'How can we make things better?' And what I thought we could do is just throw these questions out there—there're others, too—and we could all talk about them. It may be that Andrew is the right one to run for office, and I'll write a book. That may be the right use of our abilities. Or some other configuration. Anyway, we could help each other understand these questions and help us figure out what to do. And one of the questions is, 'Should Andrew and Bo help Belle have a baby and should we take on parenting that baby?'"

"Are you sure," Joseph asks, "you want to be having this conversation with all of us here?"

Gus says, "Maybe I should go get a beer."

"Well," Billy clears his throat, "as the prospective uncle of this kid, if there is to be one, I think I should be here, although I don't think I'll actually *vote*, just throw in my two cents worth every now and then—" He checks us all out. "Of course, if I'm going to stay, my guy, the big one back there—" He nods over his shoulder to Joseph. "—needs to be able to stay too, and I suspect he'll want Gus, the young one with blond hair and blue eyes and the good body who is sitting between Andrew's legs, to stay also. So why doesn't everybody just keep his seat?"

295

"Thanks, Billy, for sorting all that out. Well, guys, we can go back to our apartment and get something to eat and talk about all these things there. That is, about how we think about ourselves and who we are and what our world is going to look like, and about what we're going to do about the rest of our lives."

"—*the rest of our lives!*" Andrew says. "Jesus! Next week, next month. *This summer. This fucking fall.* That's enough. We've just been through the Big Bang! We are in the very first nanosecond of life! We can't be making any decisions about the rest of our lives. We are in *turmoil,* guys. No promises. No vows."

"Right," I say. "I stand corrected. This summer."

"Do you think there are going to be more riots?" Billy asks.

"No," Andrew says. "This is over. Can't you feel it? It's time to move on to the next battle. This has been fine, hasn't it?"

"It's been fine," I say.

And then the others chime in.

"Fine."

"Fine."

"Fine," Gus says. *"It's been fine."*

"Besides, guys, we need to take time this summer to look at the question Andrew raised," Joseph says.

"What's that? I've forgotten."

"The obvious one, the most basic one of all."

"And what's that?"

"Why this one. Andrew asked it this morning on the sidewalk, going to get Billy's tickets." Andrew is enjoying this. *"What are we? What is a gay man? What is he for?"*

Everyone laughs.

"I'm serious, guys. That's the most important question of all. And we don't know the answer to it, either."

We're quiet for a little bit.

"You know, guys," Joseph says, "I'm thinking of all the people not here, who would like to have been here."

"Yeah, that's right. When we get back to the apartment," Andrew says, "we ought to drink a toast to them. *To everybody who couldn't make it. And to all those who survived the time before the riots.*"

"Great," I say. "Remember our brothers and our sisters here and everywhere, now and since the beginning." We hug each other's shoulders.

296

Adam in the Morning

We are quiet for a while, watching the crowd disperse, thinking about our brothers and sisters who are not here.

"I want to hear more from Gus about his life in the tough neighborhoods in Baltimore." Joseph stretches his arms above his head. "I want to hear what all you guys know." His low rumble is a pleasure. "We have our whole lives to talk. We have to listen to ourselves and to each other, and I find I can't do that while all those other things are rattling around in my head. I need silence to hear you, so here I am, listening. I think fags have the opportunity to live free and to know what the word means. We don't have to be colonial subjects. Come with us, Gus, and tell us about Baltimore."

"And," Billy says, "I want to see you all strip down and let me see where you have been hurt, and let me see your cuts and bruises, and let me make sure that your cuts are properly cleaned and dressed, and see if any of you should go to the doctor immediately. OK?"

"Yeah, Billy," Joseph says, and then he puts his arm around Billy's neck and pulls him to him. "I'm going to look forward to seeing you in Houston." He kisses him.

"Remember, guys, *Violence is a cleansing force.*"

"Ah, yeah. *Violence is a cleansing force.*"

Other men stop off at the high stoop and talk with us about what's happening and our plans and their plans. They are sweaty and dirty, and many of them are bloody also. People are tired, and they're glad that tonight has ended earlier than the other nights. Some men are going to the docks, and others are going to the trucks. Some of us are going home. Everybody is feeling good. The TPF is gone, and even though the local cops are still here in force, our side is gradually drifting away. It is the beginning of high summer, it's cool, and a breeze comes all the way from the East River to the Hudson, across our island. The square is strangely beautiful, the discarded paper, the paving stones and tin cans littering the pavement, street lights reflecting off the broken glass. It's a dreamy, drug-induced vision of ravishing beauty. We have, up to now, been an idea in the mind of straight people. Now we find ourselves and our freedom.

I stand up. "Come on guys." I look at all of them, Andrew and Joseph and Billy and Gus. Us. They stand, and Gus leads us down the steps to the square. "Come with me. Le's go home and *feed my innocent people.*"

Adam in the Morning

December 31, 2007—December 20, 2009
Somerville, Massachusetts